M000036235

On The Edge of Love

Mama's Brood, Book 1

SHAY RUCKER

Copyright © 2015 by Shay Rucker
All print rights reserved.
ISBN:978-0-9974733-0-8

On The Edge of Love is a work of fiction. All characters and events are products of the author's imagination or are used factiously and are not to be construed as real. Any resemblance to actual events or persons, living or dead, is entirely coincidental.

Cover Artist: Mario Lampic

ISBN: 978-0-9974733-0-8

Printed in the United States of America.

WARNING
This book contains sexually explicit scenes and adult language and may be considered offensive to some readers.

Dedication

To Ma and Da for all the support and encouragement over the decades. Hopefully I've created a story both of you can enjoy.

Acknowledgment

A special thanks to Lady D, Barbara Staten, and Marsha McNairy for being the first to read Zeus and Sabrina's story and provide invaluable feedback. To all my soul-sista friends, who have shared joys, losses, adventures, and successes, I love you guys! To my very large, intelligent, and yes, certifiably crazy family, I'm blessed to call you kin.

To my editors, Larke Butler and Kathleen Calhoun, you're amazing. Thank you for doing what you do so well.

And a final thanks to Mario Lampic for creating a wonderful cover design for the paperback.

Contents

Chapter One 1

Chapter Two 25

Chapter Three 49

Chapter Four 85

Chapter Five 93

Chapter Six 107

Chapter Seven 117

Chapter Eight 131

Chapter Nine 149

Chapter Ten 159

Chapter Eleven 177

Chapter Twelve 189

Chapter Thirteen 205

Chapter Fourteen 225

Chapter Fifteen 239

Chapter Sixteen 253

Chapter Seventeen 277

Chapter Eighteen 289

Chapter Nineteen 299

Epilogue 311

CHAPTER ONE

He stood over her unconscious body with the soulless blade they'd given him fisted in his hand. The blade twitched rhythmically against his thigh as he scanned the empty building; then he reluctantly looked back at her. They'd left him here with her and the weapon, and he couldn't understand why. He knew they didn't trust him. They didn't even want him carrying his own blades, said he was too prone to using them...and he was. Couldn't help himself. Fighting his compulsion was like trying to fight gravity, and he didn't know how to fight gravity. What he knew was the satisfaction that followed the hunt, the kill. Obviously the bruised and bleeding woman on the ground didn't have the same skill set.

Squatting down, Zeus moved the tip of the blade toward her throat and peeled away the pendant fused to her skin by dried blood. The pendant was an oval moonstone encircled by a twining of gold and another metal that looked to be titanium. It was secured against her neck by a thin red leather cord that resembled the slash from a wire garrote. He'd never used a garrote before, had only used his blades to cut from one ear to the other. Those cuts had left his large hands soaked in blood, had left the eyes of those he'd killed looking at him desperately, then accusingly, then lifelessly. He shrugged off the memories and refocused

1

on the unconscious woman beside him. They shouldn't have left her with him. The more he watched her, the more a strange, hot need, almost as strong as his need for his blades, compelled him to do things, but just with her.

He looked away and scanned the space again. The nearly vacant ground floor of the two-story warehouse was dark, but the full moon's light filtered through the windows at the top of the building, allowing him to see without the assistance of night-vision goggles. The moon's watchful light made the business of stealth and death more visible, but luckily stealth and death weren't about business for him. He smiled. They were a lifestyle. He tapped the blade against the woman's collarbone.

It was a bad idea to leave her alone with him.

He flipped the blade, sliding its hilt along her throat to the scented space between her breasts. Bending closer, he inhaled deeply. She smelled earth green and spicy, like cedar. Unusual smell for a woman from the city. She had nice breasts too. Large and round, they were just the right size to fit comfortably in his hands. He peeled back the bloodstained black tank top she wore to see the shiny gray bra that almost matched the color of his eyes. His dick got hard, reminding him that he hadn't had a woman in damn near two weeks.

They never should have left her with him. His blood was running hot, and the compulsion urging the use of his blade, urging him to take her, was powerful...overwhelming. He was never good at fighting his compulsions. Now they were pressing in against him at the same time. Maybe, he thought. Just maybe the others would understand his need to penetrate something.

The blade danced in his hand. He twirled it, gripped it, tossed it up, and balanced it, hilt first, then blade tip on his palm.

In the moments of trying to distract himself, he took in the woman's chocolate-brown skin. Moonlight got to touch it, didn't seem reasonable that he shouldn't. Her hair was a wild mane of shoulder-length twists or coils or whatever the hell they were called. She'd colored it, some strands red, some brown, some her natural black. He liked the colors against her skin. *I am going to penetrate her in so many ways.* Her body would feel good, strong but soft, yielding and resisting. Perfect for penetration.

He stilled, taking in the woman's full lips. The bottom one was split, the blood there crusting. Her eyes, though closed, were long lashed and tilted up at the ends. The right one was already bruised. It would likely swell shut.

The compulsion was getting unbearable. He could barely breathe from it pressing on him so hard. When he felt the breeze at his back, smelled the dust from the warehouse floor kick up, he knew he'd gotten distracted, let them get too close. He struck at them fast and hard. Warm wetness refreshed his skin. He stayed low, disemboweling one. In a flash from the other direction he cut through a thigh, releasing a gush of femoral blood. He heard shots, stood, and severed an artery in the arm. Another in the neck. He and the borrowed blade danced until the death song faded into still silence.

His clothes were saturated with blood, but his body hummed with pleasure. One compulsion had been satisfied. He glanced down at the woman's body, knowing a fast, hard fuck to round out the evening would be the closest he ever got to pure perfection.

He tried to adjust himself in his jeans, but he was too hard, too big. He unbuttoned the pants and unzipped them just to relieve some of the constriction, and the woman opened her eyes.

Those beautiful brown eyes could melt a cold soul, maybe even mine, he thought as he smiled at her hungrily.

She screamed loud enough to bring down the bloody rafters.

He gritted his teeth in frustration as he re-zipped and buttoned his pants. He hated when they screamed. Fucking women. Didn't make sense they would leave her with him.

Footsteps rushed in from all directions. He knew from the red dancing lasers that he was in the sights of at least three other killers. No, six, all six were moving in on him at a quick clip. The blade stayed flaccid against the outside of his right thigh. He had to repeat the chant in his head so it would stay that way. The chant worked best after the compulsion had been satisfied. I'm not supposed to kill these six people, Zeus recited in his head. They were here with him. They were here for the still-screaming woman.

He rolled his eyes, hoping one of the six could shut her the fuck up; she was quickly losing her appeal. If she wasn't careful, he'd lose interest and she'd miss the best fucking orgasms life had to offer.

"Hey, hey, hey." One of the men knelt next to the woman, his voice pathetically soft. "It's going to be okay, Sabrina. It's going to be okay. We're here to help." The man...Coen, that was his name. Coen. He took the woman in his arms and cradled her, rocking. The woman quieted.

The blade twitched against Zeus's thigh. It didn't like Coen touching the woman. Even if he had been successful at shutting her up, blade didn't like seeing the woman in another man's arms. He hadn't fucked her yet. Once he had, he didn't care who touched her, but he hadn't had her yet.

The blade danced through his fingers.

"Well, shit, son. Couldn't you at least have left one man alive?" the man behind him asked.

Zeus turned. He counted four bloody bodies on the ground around him. He looked at the man who had spoken. Big Country. He had to remember their names. Couldn't mess up and kill one by mistake.

He held up the blade in his right hand. Blood dripped to the ground from his elbow. "Blade's not weighted right. Next time I'll be using one of my own."

"Hopefully there won't be a next time with this crazy fuck," muttered the black-eyed Bolivian, Juarez. Zeus disliked Juarez. He didn't like the others, but he didn't dislike them. He disliked Juarez. He launched the blade with measured force. It pierced Juarez's gun where it held the ammunition clip. Fucker dropped the weapon like it was a snake. Zeus smiled.

"If it had been weighted right, the blade would have gone through your hand," he said to Juarez. But that was a lie. Zeus would have put it through Juarez's hand if he'd wanted to. He turned to the man named Vincent, the leader of the operation. Everybody called him Price. "Using defective blades makes for unsafe work conditions."

The other man snorted. "You're lucky we gave you a weapon at all."

Zeus grunted at the idea that he'd been lucky. He'd learned from experience that if he used his bare hands, his enemies wouldn't be any less dead. And people tended to trust one's sanity even less when one killed with one's bare hands. Cizan, the absentee group member, had shared that bit of wisdom with him. Using your hands meant you had to be more vicious to compensate for the lack of a blade, and then people started attaching labels: psychotic, unstable, sociopath. Whatever.

"Next time I use my own blades," he told Price.

He looked down at the woman still in Coen's arms. She was watching him silently, maybe a little wary. Damned contrary of her to be wary of him after he'd saved her life.

"What are you going to do with her?" he asked Price.

If Price didn't have a plan, Zeus was going to keep her for a little while. Indulge.

The woman flicked her gaze to Price before settling it back on Zeus. He tilted his head as they took each other's measure. His dick thickened again, reminding him its need hadn't been satisfied yet.

"Who are you? Not cops," the woman said.

He liked her voice. It was low, husky. Didn't reflect the fear he'd briefly seen in her gaze. He imagined that voice moaning, crying out as he buried himself deep inside her. It was getting damned hard to repress his need. A growl rose in his throat as he stepped toward her. The woman's eyes widened, and she pressed back into Coen. The sound he made shifted from arousal to warning.

"Price, handle him, or I'm gonna put one between his eyes," Coen said, finger on the trigger of his gun, gaze never straying from Zeus. Smart man.

"Everyone relax," Price ordered. "Kragen's men are dead, and we've got the woman. Let's clear the building and regroup at Mama's House. Zeus, you, Coen, and Bride will ride with me and Ms. Samora. Big Country, Lynx, Juarez, strip any info you can and follow us home."

Big Country nodded.

"Ms. Samora, Sabrina, you okay to stand?" Price asked, extending his hand toward her. Zeus didn't react when she reached out, trusting Price. "I know you're scared, confused, but I promise we're here to help you. This is asking a lot, I know, but can you look at the dead men who kidnapped you, tell us if you recognize any of them?"

"Can't you just tell me what's going on?" she asked. She was attempting to avoid looking at the men on the ground. "This shit is not real," she whispered.

"They're dead. That's real. Touch 'em if you don't believe it," Zeus suggested. Hell, he could comfort too.

"Do you recognize any of them?" Price asked again.

"Keep him the hell away from me," she said, looking at Zeus as if he were the one who had kidnapped and beaten her. Zeus smiled, and she stepped closer to Price. He would have told her that Price couldn't keep her from him, but everything he did and said seemed to antagonize her. He'd let her believe Price could protect her, but he couldn't wait to see her reaction when she discovered that nothing and no one could stop him if he decided to reach out and touch.

"These two broke into my apartment," she said, indicating the gut-wound guy, then the slashed-throat guy. "Never seen him," she said pointing to the femoral-artery guy. "And... *Jesus Christ*." Her hand rose to cover her mouth. "Jesus Christ, that's Barry, he works —"

"Worked," Zeus corrected.

"Front desk security at my office building."

"Big Country, scrub it down. Come on, Sabrina. We're going to get you to a safe place and talk about what's going on."

"Jesus Christ," she mumbled again as Coen led her out of the warehouse.

Bride, who was more resistant to conversing than Zeus, shouldered her semiautomatic and trailed Coen and the woman, Price taking point.

Zeus took one last look at his work. Big Country walked over, stopping at his side and sharing in the moment. Big Country. Brown-haired, green-eyed Louisiana guy was as tall as Zeus but wider, solid, like he'd been fighting gators since he was old enough to walk.

"Why leave her with me?" he asked.

"Juarez said you'd kill her before they did. Coen said you'd keep her safe. Price needed to know you were stable enough to work with the Brood."

"I'm not."

"I know."

"*Puto* bastard," Juarez muttered as he went to set explosives.

"You guys got history?" Big Country asked as they watched Juarez walk away.

"No. But I have a feeling his future will be painted in blood."

"I'll make sure Price lets you have your weapons in the future."

Zeus grunted and walked away. He had blades hidden all over his body; he didn't need Big Hick to do shit on his behalf.

Outside the warehouse he took a deep breath. The air was cool, crisp, slightly weighted with moisture. He caught Sabrina's scent, his eyes lighting on the custom-made black SUV. She was inside, hidden behind the darkly tinted windows that reflected moonlight and wispy clouds. Even though he couldn't see her, he knew she was watching him. His mouth hitched up slightly on one side as he walked to the vehicle, imagining he held her gaze. Opening the back door, he climbed in and slipped in the third row of seats, directly behind her. Bride sat in the passenger seat in front of her and Price sat opposite Bride, in the driver's seat. Coen sat beside Sabrina in the second row, and Zeus sat at their backs. Foolish to leave themselves so vulnerable.

The woman must have felt the same way, because she kept glancing nervously over her shoulder. He didn't move, simply sat there and stared at her. He closed his eyes when the SUV rolled forward and inhaled her scent, letting it fill him. Soon he would wear her essence as if it was his own. He would get so close to her that it would bind to him more completely than the blood drying against his skin. The compulsion to have her would drive him until he fulfilled its need. There was no resisting the compulsions.

He breathed in deep again, fingers coaxing his blade to dance in the darkness of the SUV's interior. Images of the brown-skinned woman's breasts merged against images of his most beloved weapon. Theirs would be a powerful union.

THE OLD WAREHOUSE exploded when they were about four hundred meters away. Sabrina jumped, her heartbeat accelerating when she looked back at the destruction. The bloody man behind her was superimposed upon the reddish-orange flames of the burning building. He appeared demonic as he sat there watching her with those metallic-gray eyes. The intensity of them made her skin crawl. She didn't like being the focus of his attention, yet from the moment she'd fought herself free from unconsciousness, she'd known she had it.

Facing forward, she turned to look out the passenger-side window. It was too dark to see much because the moon had slipped behind a shield of clouds. She knew she was in some kind of industrial area, close to a port maybe. She'd smelled water when she walked out of the warehouse. They were close to either the bay or the ocean, most likely the bay, though, which hopefully meant she wasn't too far from home.

Speeding toward she didn't know where, she couldn't help but wonder what would happen to her once they got there. Her mind flashed to the four dead bodies, remembered the man who had killed them aroused and dripping blood on her, his eyes promising she would be next. She doubted there would have been a quick death for her. He would've fucked her first, maybe fucked her during. Who knew the level of his derangement? She grimaced. She didn't need to know. She needed to get the hell away from these people, hide, hole up, and figure out how and why she had been attacked and kidnapped. The dead guys weren't Ernesto's men; that much she knew.

Both the kidnappers and the people who had rescued her had addressed her as Sabrina Samora, her actual name, not one of the aliases she had used most of her adult life. Not until she'd run away from Ernesto in Florida and moved to New Orleans to be close to her sister Sam had she begun to use her birth name again. Ironically, it was the one name she'd gone by that Ernesto never knew. She sighed. At least she didn't have to worry about that problem.

"You okay, Sabrina?" the man across from her asked. She nodded once, quickly lowering her eyes.

He'd held her, protected her in those first moments of confusion and fear. He was the only one to show her comfort, and she appreciated it. She'd guessed he was the defender-of-the-innocent type, but she knew by the way he'd spoken to the one who would do her irreparable damage that he could be as threatening as the rest of this group.

"Where are you taking me?" she asked because they sure as shit weren't taking her back to her studio apartment in Oakland. She could see a freeway coming up, the golden lights of a bridge on the dark horizon, but not the Bay Bridge. They passed a sign indicating that an on-ramp for the Richmond–San Rafael Bridge was to the right. She knew then that she was somewhere in Richmond or Point Richmond, heading farther away from her home, not toward it.

"We're taking you to a place where it's safe to talk freely," the driver said.

"Seems safe enough to talk in here," she said, keeping her voice hesitant.

"Seems that way."

Those were the last words spoken for the next hour or so.

The vehicle maneuvered seamlessly from road to freeway, highway to small-town main streets. They climbed up a twisting, two-lane highway sheltered by trees, which turned into a dense forest that blocked the moon. It was dark where they were, stretches of uninterrupted black except for the SUV's headlights. The street lamps seemed spaced as mile markers instead of illumination devices meant to keep the darkness at bay. They were more like stingy oases of light engulfed by a desert of dark. At this early-morning hour they hadn't passed another car for miles. She'd lost her bearings again once they had passed the Point Reyes area. The national park was the farthest she'd ever been in Marin County.

Shit. At this distance it was going to be hard to escape from them and get someplace safe and familiar. It's okay, she reassured herself. She had done hard in the past; she'd do it again if it meant saving her ass.

They slowed and turned left onto a dirt road she never would have seen had she been driving. *This guy, Price, must have some kind of inhuman night vision.*

The ride turned bumpy, the incline steep. The forest and vegetation crept ever closer as the road became smaller. There would be no passing if another car came from the opposite direction. One of them would simply have to drive in reverse until they reached a point where they could pull off to the side. Luckily they hadn't met a descending vehicle.

They took a right on what felt like a gravel path, and the truck slowed more. Ahead, Sabrina could see a large shack of a building, above which a neon blue sign proclaimed it to be MAMA'S HOUSE.

Two other vehicles were parked in front of the building, and as she looked about, she saw another gravel trail toward the back right of the building. She supposed it was the road that led down the mountain.

The driver, Price, parked on the outside right of the other two vehicles and shut off the engine.

Sabrina froze when she felt fingers gently pull on one of the twisted locs at the back of her head, followed by a knuckle gliding down the back of her neck. The caress was brief, as if the man behind her had restrained himself the whole ride and could no longer resist the temptation to touch now that they had come to the end of their journey.

"Coen, keep her close," Price ordered as he opened the door. "We don't know who's inside or what business they're about."

The woman they called Bride was typing into her phone, and Coen was checking his weapons, all oblivious to the threat posed by the sociopath fondling her from behind.

Sabrina leaned forward, feeling her hair slip free from his fingers, breathing easier when the break in contact didn't provoke him into grabbing a handful of her hair and dragging her by the head into the backseat.

She reached for the door handle and eased it open. Coen's hand settled on her knee, stalling her exit.

"The others are about five minutes behind us," Bride said from the front.

Sabrina watched as Price walked up the porch stairs and went inside the building, exiting a minute later to wave them in.

"All right, Sabrina. When we get inside, I want you to stay close, okay? Don't try and go off anywhere alone."

She resisted the urge to look behind her. No way in hell was she going off alone with *him* around.

"Okay," she whispered, moving out of the car carefully, not because she naturally moved so deliberately but because she was hurt and instinct cautioned that she didn't make any sudden moves when being watched by a predator.

Coen followed her out of the vehicle, and the man drenched in blood was not far behind. Coen reached out as if to place a comforting hand on her shoulder. She took two steps back when the big man behind him frowned, reaching toward the small of his back.

"Hey, hey, I know you're scared." Coen tried to soothe her, unaware. "But we'll keep you safe, Sabrina. I promise."

She looked over his shoulder. The big man's hand relaxed at his side again, gaze boring into hers until she looked at Coen and allowed him to steer her, without touch, toward Mama's House.

"Doesn't look scared to me." The deep voice countered in the darkness behind them. "Anyone else wonder about that?"

Of course he couldn't just be run-of-the-mill crazy; he had to be the kind of crazy that was too perceptive, watched too closely. Probably killed more effectively because of his uncanny insight about others. It didn't seem to lead him to be more humane. Likely it led him to be more efficient at using, controlling, and killing.

I have to be careful, she thought as she entered the dimly lit establishment. She didn't want him, didn't want any of them thinking she was anything other than the terrified victim they had found on a warehouse floor.

"Well, if it ain't Mama's Brood...plus one." A voice rang out from behind the bar. Sabrina leaned forward to see around Coen. The owner of the voice was a fiftyish man with long straight black and gray hair. He was about Coen's height – five feet nine, five feet ten – and was whipcord lean in his worn blue jeans and indigo T-shirt.

"Chief," Bride muttered to the older man as she sat at the bar and waved a finger toward a bottle of whiskey.

"Aw, Princess, I keep telling you I'm too old for you. You can't come in here playing pretty and think I'm going to leave my woman and give you the world."

Bride rolled her eyes and downed the double shot he poured, motioning for another.

Sabrina walked over and leaned against the bar beside Bride, opting to stand instead of sit. Coen stepped up on the other side of her and reached out to shake the bartender's hand. Up close she saw the man behind the bar was Native American. He had the bearing of a leader, so it stood to reason that he could be a chief, but she had a feeling Bride was just being derogatory.

"Still got the mad dog playing tame?" the bartender asked, looking over Sabrina's shoulder.

She snorted. She couldn't help it. The idea that the man standing behind her could be tamed, even in play, was ridiculous. Maybe Zeus could be put down like a mad dog, but she had a feeling he'd be hell on hell just like he'd been hell on earth.

"He killed four men before we could get to him," Coen informed the bartender.

"Well, that does account for the amount of blood soaked into him," the bartender said, tossing a key to the big man.

Sabrina turned to see him walk toward the back of the bar and exit through a riveted steel door. She sighed.

"You're next," Chief said, sliding a glass of clear liquid across the bar to her.

"I'm sorry," she said, pushing back the glass. "I don't drink."

"Me neither. It's water. And I meant you're next in line for the bathroom."

"Thank you."

She lifted the glass to her mouth and gulped the cool water, careful of her split lip.

"So you've found yourself in a bad situation."

"I don't understand what's happening," she mumbled, head down, both hands wrapped around the cold glass.

"That's why you're here, Sabrina. So we can all understand what Kragen wants with you."

"Who's Kragen?"

Bride hissed with what sounded like irritation.

Chief frowned at her. "She deserves to know the name of the man hunting her down. The more information she has, the more she can help us and herself."

Bride rolled her eyes, shrugged, and knocked back another shot.

"She drinks enough to make up for the both of us." The bartender smiled at Sabrina, holding out his hand. "I'm Terry."

"Sabrina," she said, introducing herself formally.

The front door of the bar opened, and Terry saluted the three figures that entered.

"Firewater would be good 'bout now, ol' man," Big Country said.

"One day you're going to get enough of courting those fire spirits, boy."

"Since that day hasn't come yet, make it a double."

Sabrina heard the three advance as Terry reached beneath the bar and pulled out a mason jar with clear liquid inside. He unscrewed the lid and poured two single shots so carefully the alcohol could've been acid.

Juarez beat Big Country to the first glass and inhaled the shot. And paid for it. His eyes teared, and he fell to the floor, grabbing at his throat as if invisible fingers were choking him to death. It was at least two minutes before he was able to fight himself free of what she presumed to be the fire spirits' wrath and sit up, inhaling and exhaling one deep full breath. Everyone stood around and watched – Sabrina mainly out of surprise, the others in humor.

"Where's Mama?" Big Country asked as he stepped over Juarez and took the second shot of firewater, downing it smoothly before shaking his head in disgust at Juarez.

"Diablo," came Juarez's hoarse whisper as he used a bar stool to stand.

"She's in the dungeon with Price," Terry answered.

"Why y'all hanging around up here?"

"Getting acquainted."

Juarez stood next to Sabrina, glaring down at her as if his display of anger would reclaim some of his pride. "You don't seem worth kidnapping."

Asshole, she thought, but she wouldn't say it, not if she wanted to continue to appear the frightened rabbit ready to bolt to the nearest hiding hole. Instead she bit the inside of her lip so hard tears filled her eyes, blurring her vision. "I don't know why anyone would want to kidnap me. He's right; I'm nobody," she said, warm tears spilling down her cheeks.

"Don't go taking anything Juarez says as something worth listening to," Big Country said.

She forced more tears out as she held her hands over her face.

She heard Bride stand, making a sound of disgust as she walked away. "Stupid ass," she muttered. Sabrina thought the other woman was speaking of her until she heard Juarez say, "Hey, I'm just calling it how I see it."

She heard the metal door open and close, and for at least five heartbeats no sound distracted her from the raspy voice of Bobby Blue Bland singing in the background. As she cupped her face in her palms, she could feel the swelling around her right eye. Shit. She hoped it didn't swell itself shut. Aside from the aesthetic detractor, it would hinder her ability to see when she decided to run away.

Unnerved by the lack of banter and the silence, she looked up and saw all the men were facing the back door. Expecting to see Bride, she turned and saw that Bride had exited the room. The one person Sabrina never wanted to encounter again was standing there. The fact that the blood was gone, that his hard muscled chest was bare, scarred, that his powerful legs were in a pair of loose-fitting blue jeans and his manly feet were bare, didn't make her want to see him more. Especially not when he had a knife in his hand bigger than the one he'd left the room with.

"She's crying," the big man, Zeus, said.

Sabrina wiped the tears off her face, then wiped her hands on her jeans to try and erase any evidence of her tears. The way he said it, eyes burning, face and voice emotionless, made her fear that tears might trigger his homicidal tendencies.

"Juarez was just being an asshole," Big Country said.

She pressed closer to the bar when the blade streaked by, embedding in Juarez's shoulder.

"Son of a *bitch*," Juarez shouted, both in anger and in pain.

Zeus had another knife in his hand and walked toward Juarez unhurried, loose. Images of the gritty warehouse floor strewn with bloody bodies flashed through her mind. Juarez was going to fall to the big man's blade like those warehouse men. Terry and the others tried to talk to Zeus rationally, Coen and Big Country reaching for their guns when words didn't seem to penetrate.

Acting on guilt-inspired instinct, Sabrina threw herself at Zeus, hugging him to her, hoping she didn't get cut up or shot in the back for her efforts.

Zeus stopped, and she wrapped her arms tighter around his back, resting her head on his massive chest. His heart beat strong and steady, none of the rapid hammering that came from strong emotion. His skin was warm, feverish even, but he'd just showered, she remembered. He smelled clean, not the rancid smell of someone who walked so closely with death. Nothing about his scent would alert the senses that some inhuman entity dwelled within him. But she knew. Every cell of her body had objected to even acknowledging his existence; yet here she was molding her body against his to save someone else. Self-sacrifice was, until this moment, foreign to her. Guilt was not.

Having interpreted her actions as only a sick individual would, Zeus's hand gripped her ass and pressed her against a rapidly growing erection. Shocked, she looked up, and he was watching her, his mouth tilted up on one side. Jesus, was this him happy? She struggled to free herself from his hold.

"Be still," he ordered, and she froze, his voice having a Medusa-like effect.

Fast and agile, he turned her around to face the others. Two weapons were pointed toward them. Lynx helped to support Juarez, while Terry grinned behind the bar.

She didn't see what was so funny, but apparently a necessary skill of bartending was being able to maintain a jovial attitude. She wasn't feeling jovial. She had been beaten, kidnapped, had possibly escaped rape and murder at the hands of the very man she was shielding, and for her efforts she may get shot by the ones who had claimed to want to protect her. Whatever she had done to piss off the spirits of good fortune must have been some kind of bad for them to abandon her so completely.

"Zeus, put the knife down and let Sabrina go," Coen said. His voice was hard, demanding obedience. Unfortunately crazy people didn't respond well to the rational demands of others.

The big man pulled her tighter against him. The finality of that one action made her want to cry. If two men with guns trained on him didn't convince Zeus to let her go, it felt like nothing would: not her rejection, not her eventual escape attempt, not anything. If she succeeded at eluding the Brood, the man responsible for her kidnapping, even Ernesto, who she was sure was still searching for her, she had a bad feeling it would be near impossible to hide from Zeus. He would be the genie and she the bottle he always returned to, or the demon ever bound to the one it possessed. She had fought so hard to make a semi-normal life for herself, and this big fuck was threatening all of it.

She would *not* cry.

He was big, he was crazy, but she was a survivor. She would fight, even if the outcome resulted in her losing.

Sabrina tilted her head back and looked Zeus straight in the eye. "I'm not yours."

One side of his mouth tilted in what she was coming to identify as humor. On him it held none of the lightness of the emotion, more a dark caricature, a primitive display on par with a beast baring its teeth at an opponent.

"Until I'm done with you, you are. You ran to me, makes you mine."

In what fucking backward world was that true? She'd run to him to prevent mayhem. She already felt bad enough that her little playacting had resulted in Juarez taking a blade; she didn't want it to be the reason for his death, for any of their deaths.

"She ran to me for protection," he said, looking back toward Coen and the others. "Anyone touches her, hurts her, makes her cry...well."

Coen looked over to Big Country, apparently coming to some agreement, because at the same time they lowered their guns.

Terry whistled. "You've gone and done it, sister. Sure you don't drink?"

"Rum, overproof, Haitian if you have it," she ordered, not fully believing even an alcoholic haze would diminish the fact that she may have just been claimed by a sociopath.

Zeus guided her to the bar stool farthest from the others and walked back to the grouping of men. He reached out and freed his black-hilted blade from Juarez's chest. "This is also mine. I was nice enough to let you touch it, but like the woman, I'll keep it."

"I'm going to kill you, you fucking – "

Zeus punched Juarez where he'd been wounded, eliciting another shout of pain, then hit him square in the face, knocking the smaller man unconscious. Only Lynx's supporting arm stopped him from falling to the wooden floor in an undignified heap.

"Welcome to the Brood," Terry said, sliding two filled shot glasses her way.

To hell with that, she thought, tossing back the rum. Yes, she'd wanted to be a part of a family since losing her mother and sister, but this one was definitely not it. She was getting the hell out of Dodge as soon as humanly possible. She looked at Zeus, who had knelt to wipe his blade on Juarez's pant leg. Sooner if she was able.

"What's happened?" Price asked from the opening of the metal door at the back of the room. His voice sounded weary as he passed a hand backward, then forward over his closely cropped head.

Eyes wide with feigned innocence, Big Country and Coen pointed blaming fingers at Zeus. They seemed happy not to be the ones at fault, which let her know they probably got into their own fair share of trouble.

"He threw his blade at Juarez again. He didn't miss this time," Coen said.

"Had my own blade," Zeus said rising. "And I didn't miss the last time."

"You were supposed to leave your blades in your room, Zeus."

"I tried, but they stick to me like skin." He responded with that strange Zeus smile. It quickly faded. Undiluted crazy. "You may not see it, but I'll always have a blade on me, even if I have to pull one out of the crack of my ass to get it."

"Lord, let's hope I never have to see that," Coen muttered.

"You know first aid?" Price asked Sabrina, apparently fed up with conversing with Zeus.

There was no reason to lie. If they knew her name was Sabrina Samora, they probably knew everything about her since she'd resurrected herself in New Orleans. "Yeah, I was an EMT in another life."

"Big Country, bring Juarez down to the clean room. She can get cleaned up and take care of Juarez after."

"Uh-uh," Zeus said.

"Uh-uh what?"

"She won't be patching him up. Can't touch him."

Price pinched the bridge of his nose and closed his eyes. "Why can't she touch him?"

"Because then I'd have to kill him, and for some reason you all seem to want him alive."

"I'll patch him up, Boss," Lynx offered. "Shouldn't be long. I'll meet up with everyone in the living room when I'm done."

Sabrina could see Price was fighting to hold on to his patience. She didn't imagine it was a character trait that came naturally to him. Price gave everyone in the room a hard look and nodded. "Mama's living room in fifteen minutes. Coen, take her to the bathroom so she can attend to herself."

Price frowned when the rest of the men looked at Zeus, fingers seeking the safeties on their weapons.

She hopped off the bar stool. "Maybe Coen and Zeus can watch the door while I shower and change. Having the two of them would really make me feel a lot safer."

"Really?" Price looked at her as if the events of the night had cracked her egg clean through.

No, not really, she wanted to scream. "Yes," she said, glancing at Zeus, who watched her, eyes and face expressionless.

Price shrugged and left in the direction he had come.

"I'll lock up the bar and meet you all downstairs," Terry said, hitting a switch that made the dim lights in the front window of the bar go dark.

Big Country and Lynx lifted Juarez and headed toward the metal door. "You know, you might want to refine your wooing skills, Hoss," Big Country said to Zeus. "In my experience the ladies tend to run from violent men carrying weapons."

"You would know," Lynx said, shifting Juarez's dead-weight.

"Big Country's experience only extends to prostitutes, so he's in no position to give advice on ladies," Coen said.

"Ladies of the night." Big Country grinned back at them.

The two men maneuvered Juarez through the door, and Coen waved Sabrina forward, trailing behind them. Sabrina walked, then paused, looking back to see Zeus directly behind her. She frowned at him to mask her agitation.

"Don't run on me," he warned. "Not unless you want to know what it feels like to get caught."

She barely maintained her composure as she followed Coen through the metal door and down a stairwell engulfed in a red haze of darkness. It felt like she was walking into hell with the devil at her back.

At the bottom of the stairwell they reached a hard, glossy floor, possibly polished concrete or limestone. The walls of the hallway were a dove-gray color, and every five feet black flame-shaped sconces radiated red light. After about forty feet they came upon another hallway that ran perpendicular to the one they'd walked down. Big Country and his group went right and disappeared through the first door they came upon. Coen veered left and stopped at the door there.

"This is the bathroom, and that's the cleanup room," he said, pointing to the door the others had gone through. "In another life Lynx was a surgeon, so Juarez will be fine," he assured Sabrina. "We have sleeping rooms, a kitchen, a weapons room, and a few other interesting areas. Down there" – he pointed farther down the hall to the left, where it dead-ended at another sturdy-looking metal door – "is Mama's front room. That's where we'll all debrief."

Sabrina now understood the roughly constructed bar above was simply a portal linking the mundane world with this surreal labyrinthine netherworld of killer-protectors.

Coen opened the door to the bathroom. "Feel free to use whatever's available."

As she crossed the threshold, a soft, golden light illuminated a bathroom suite swanky enough to be featured in *Architectural Digest*. She suspected it took a lot of money to make a place like this, especially inside a mountain. Who exactly were her rescuers? Did she really want to know the answer to that question?

"Ten minutes, Sabrina," Coen said. He glanced behind him. "For both our sake's, bolt the door behind you."

Zeus leaned around the slight barrier of Coen and looked first inside the bathroom and then at her. She knew, by the lowering of his lids and the slight flaring of his nostrils, that he was imagining her wet and naked, door bolted with him inside with her. She didn't want to contemplate what he would do thereafter.

Forcefully she pushed the door shut when Zeus growled and took a step forward. It was as if Coen were nothing more than a ghostly apparition for him to step through. Once she'd gotten the door closed, she slid the bolt – an honest-to-goodness bolt – into place and expelled a gush of air from her lungs. If she stayed around him too long, she knew the man was going to drive *her* insane. Which was probably his intention.

She sagged against the door, allowing her body to calm from the hyperarousal of imminent danger, and looked around the bathroom. This one room was almost as big as her studio and way more luxurious. It was like a spa room at one of those resorts she could never afford to go to. The walls were avocado green, the floors were limestone, and the cream claw-foot tub was huge, as well as the circular, glass-encased shower that had large showerheads that could spew water from front, back, and above. There was a sauna area and... What the hell did a bunch of testosterone-fed muscle need with all this luxury? She imagined they'd be more comfortable with a bucket of cold water and scouring pads.

She pushed away from the door and headed for the changing area sectioned off by a planked wall of Brazilian wood. Inside there was a bench made with the same wood, upon which a pair of black loose yoga pants and a spaghetti-strapped T-shirt were folded next to a pair of black flip-flops. There was a built-in closet, where four soft, thick white robes hung on one side and on the other was a four-shelved cabinet that held cream-colored towels of various sizes.

Sabrina quickly undressed, dropping her bloody clothes in the large, white linen-lined wicker hamper, which already held Zeus's bloody clothes and used towels. Grabbing both a large and small towel of her own, she streaked her naked ass over to the shower as if a treasure of gold waited for her inside. She turned the faucet and discovered the feel of the hot water was better than gold. This was heaven.

She took her time cleaning her body and face, the water falling from above reminding her of those summer storms in Louisiana that drenched you in three minutes and then moved on. She wanted to dance and laugh out loud she felt so refreshed. It was as if her soul had, just for a few minutes, escaped the shields she'd reinforced around it.

There was a loud banging on the door, and she jumped.

Her time was up. A brief moment of heaven before having to trudge back through hell.

She dried herself, taking special care to dry the moonstone pendant hanging from her neck, and tiptoed to the counter that held an assortment of male and female grooming items. She lotioned her body and pulled out a brand-new toothbrush still covered in thin plastic from a small glass container filled with new toothbrushes. As she brushed her teeth, she took a second to look at the bruising on her face. Though it looked raw as hell, her eye shouldn't swell shut. She shrugged. She would heal. She might have a few more scars to show for it, but her body always healed.

Dressed in the yoga pants and formfitting T-shirt, she unbolted the door and opened it. Zeus stood there, more overwhelming than the actual Greek god ever could have been.

He reached out and ran his thumb over her exposed collarbone. She shuddered, not willing to explore if it was in fear, revulsion, or something else.

"Missed a drop," he said.

She was sure she hadn't. "Where's Coen?"

"Right here," a voice said from the side. "He didn't want me to see you, just in case you weren't fully dressed."

"How...um, chivalrous." It sounded crazy saying it, but what she had seen of Zeus so far, it was probably as close to the behavior as he was ever going to get.

"I really want to fuck you," he said, stepping forward and gripping her around the back of her neck. Her eyes grew big as she reached up to press back against Zeus's chest. She tried to scream, but it came out as a strangled squawk.

A click reverberated through the hallway, the sound of a safety coming off.

Zeus's eyes, his grasp, didn't release her, but he stopped manhandling her. He tilted his head, taking in every detail of her face. His thumb caressed her jaw.

He took a deep breath and sighed loudly as if greatly put-upon. "You're right; you're right, too soon."

23

And Coen withdrew the gun.

Sabrina stepped away from Zeus, trembling from panic and then with rage. She hated the feeling of powerlessness, hated feeling trapped, hated admitting that on more than one level, this *thing* that called himself a man affected her. She was confused, and she wanted to cry. Real tears this time. She never cried real tears anymore. Doing the only thing she knew would make her feel better, she punched Zeus dead in the mouth.

It hurt her hand, but she instantly felt better, especially when she saw blood trickle from his busted lip.

Let's see him try and force a kiss on her now.

"Move," she ordered as his tongue darted out and licked away the blood. He did that caricature of a smile and took two steps back. Coen, careful not to touch her, directed her in front of him and pointed her toward the door at the end of the hall.

"I really want her," Zeus said in a low tone as if conversing with the shadows of the hallway. "Can't be normal to want something so much."

"As if he has any clue about what's normal," she muttered.

"And you do?" His voice was flat. "I watched *The Cosby Show*. I recognize normal when I see it, and you ain't it."

"Are you serious?" she yelled, turning. Coen blocked her from attacking the crazy man. "Is he fucking serious?"

"Come on. Don't let him drag you down into his madness."

She closed her eyes and took a deep breath, trying to calm the agitation. "I need another drink." Her voice sounded tremulous, even to her own ears.

"Bottle's waiting for you on the other side of the door."

Coen looked up at a camera attached to the corner of the ceiling, and a soft buzz sounded. He reached around her and pushed the door open. "Go on in. Me and Zeus will be inside in a minute."

She nodded and walked into the space the others had called the living room without looking back.

CHAPTER TWO

Zeus watched her until the door closed, then turned his gaze upon the other man.

"Stop freaking her out with your psycho bullshit, Zeus. We need her rational. We need to understand what Kragen's motives are for kidnapping her, figure out how she fits into his trip to the Bay Area. You're making that job harder."

Zeus looked up at the camera, wondering who had eyes on them. Wondered if Sabrina was watching him. He liked the idea. Liked imagining her watching him, enjoying the opportunity to take him in at a distance, feeling safe in letting her eyes leisurely linger on all the places she yearned to touch.

"Zeus."

He looked down at the man in front of him. Coen was a pest. Almost as bad as an unhappy old nun with his constant nagging.

"I don't give a shit about how hard things get for you," Zeus clarified.

"Yeah, I expect you don't, but think about this: that woman you want so bad? Kragen hurt her. If he gets a chance, he'll probably hurt her again, kill her even. Are you going to let your lack of control terrify her into silence, or are you going to work with us to keep what you claim as yours safe?"

"She's not like your spineless women, Coen. Not some terrified victim you need to lend a shoulder to cry on."

"Well, I think you're both right," Terry said as he walked down the hall toward them. "You're definitely freaking her out, big guy, but this situation doesn't seem to be putting her under too much duress."

"What, because she's not falling down in a puddle of tears? She's in shock, Terry. You more than all of us know how it affects people," Coen said.

"Sorry, but I don't see shock. There's some fear, yes, but upstairs I saw her think clearly and rationally enough to diffuse a situation that could have quickly turned deadly. She looks us in the eye. Even him. She's engaging, given the circumstances. She's confident enough to ask for what she wants and lets you know what she doesn't want. And she's a liar. You feel a need to protect because she's trying to act like a terrified victim. But it slips. It's not consistent or seamless. She pretends to be passive, but she's not good at it."

Listening to him, Zeus remembered something about Terry having been a specialist in criminal and victim behaviors. The man had verbalized what Zeus instinctively knew. Like him, the woman was a survivor. He was intelligent enough to know that for as long as he wanted to fuck her, he was obligated to keep her alive. After their business was done, Coen could play the dark knight all he wanted.

Tired of standing around interacting with the two men, Zeus banged against the steel door a few inches away from Coen's head, smiling inside when the other man flinched.

The door buzzed, indicating the lock had been disengaged.

Zeus pushed passed Coen and entered Mama's living room. The space he immediately walked into was living room*ish*, he guessed. Nothing like the one in his cabin.

There were a tan couch and love seat, two rocking chairs, and two plump recliners. The large red, tan, and brown patterned rug, probably Persian because that was the only rug he knew the name of, was enclosed by the seating. There were two small tables, one between the couch and love seat and another between the rocking chairs. There were vases, candles, and sconces – the names of which he'd learned about by watching some cable home decorating network. If he were to guess, he'd say the room would be described as *inviting, warm,* or *homey.* He'd describe it as a waste of fucking energy. He snorted, finding his wit humorous.

"He surely is one mad bastard," Big Country said as he and Lynx entered the room behind him.

Zeus went to sit on the floor next to Sabrina's legs, less than two inches of space separating them. On the other side of her, also seated on the love seat, was Almaya, the woman the others called Mama. The two women, drinking what smelled to be peppermint tea, could have been mother and daughter, aunt and niece. Similar noses, an upward tilt of the eyes, same brown skin tone. He looked down at the skin covering his hands and arms. His ancestry was a mystery to anyone who saw him. His skin was the palest golden bronze, his eyes were gray, his hair was a darker gold than his skin, and his facial features could have been found in people across many cultures. Wide, high cheekbones, hard angular jaw, strong nose. The nuns he had been left with said a half-French, half-Algerian woman had birthed him at St. Catherine's Hôpital Pour Les Indigents in Marseilles thirty-eight years ago. He and his mother had moved to the convent area of the hospital when he was two days old. Eleven days later the woman named Zahira Sauvageau, born March 18, 1959, had abandoned the son she'd named Zeus – no last name. The only parental information he had on his birth certificate related to his father was his nationality. Greek. With the closure of the convent when he was nine, the nuns, still uncertain if he was a child of God or of the devil, brought the orphaned Zeus to their sister orphanage in America. Five years later, at the age of fourteen, he'd taken his leave from the place.

Zeus continued to watch the two women, noting details. Sabrina wore her natural hair in a plethora of two-strand twists, while Almaya had dark locs sprinkled with gray, which fell to the small of her back. Almaya was short, no more than five-two, while Sabrina was taller, more muscled, built like a sprinter. He could feel the heat radiating off her. It was the only thing that lay in the space separating them and made some of the tension that always built when he was supposed to sit and interact with others dissipate.

Terry and Coen sat down, Terry joining Bride and Price already seated on the couch, while Coen, being the old woman he was, sat in one of the rocking chairs. Big Country and Lynx sat in the two recliners. Big Country was almost horizontal in his chair, eyes half-closed and arms folded across his chest.

"How's Juarez?" Almaya asked Lynx.

"He'll be out for a little bit, but he's fine. Won't be our sharpshooter for a while though."

She turned to look down at Zeus. "Should I be concerned about you?" He wasn't sure what she was asking, so he sure as shit wasn't going to respond. She leaned back in the love seat and sighed. "I know Juarez has a bit of a temper, but you must be less reactive, Zeus. I know you're capable."

"Don't really think I am," he said, placing the cleaned blade pulled from Juarez's shoulder on the floor beside him. He retrieved a sharpening stone, cloth, and oil from his pocket and attended to the knife's care.

"He's filled with remorse, Mama. He just ain't one to show it," Big Country said.

It was a weirdness that everyone in this group referred to the older woman as Mama. As if she were their real mother, they her children.

One of the few things he knew about his mother was that her name was Zahira, not Almaya.

"You remember our deal, don't you, Zeus?" she asked.

"Yeah, I remember."

She sighed when he didn't say anything else.

"He'll do the job you gave him, Almaya. He won't betray that," Terry said.

If that's what they need to believe, he thought as he slid the blade over the stone at an angle.

"Can part of this deal you've got with him include him not attacking his own team members?" Lynx asked.

"Nope," Zeus said.

"No disrespect, Mama, but can you please explain to me why he's here one last time?" Lynx. Again.

"Because, with Cizan in Guatemala, I needed someone that could match his skills."

"Basically replacing one psycho for another," Coen muttered.

Zeus paused. No, he wouldn't throw the blade at Coen. He'd have to go through the cleaning and sharpening process all over again.

"Lynx, did you find any information at the warehouse that could help us discover why Kragen had Sabrina kidnapped?" Almaya asked.

"Outside of the one man Sabrina identified, there was no identifying information on the bodies, in the truck, or in the warehouse. I took pics and prints so we could run them through Gambit when we're done talking."

"Thank you, Lynx," Almaya said.

Terry looked at the older woman for a moment as if trying to communicate with her silently. Zeus didn't know much about them, but he knew when two people were fucking each other. From what he'd seen over the last few days, he guessed they had been for a long time. Years. He shuddered at the unnaturalness of long-term relationships.

"Sabrina, can you tell us about your day leading up to your abduction?" Terry asked. "Did you notice anything out of the ordinary in the morning before you went to work? On the way? Once you were there? After you left?"

"It was a normal day until they broke into my apartment. I got up, got dressed, got caffeine at the café – "

"Do you go to the same place every morning?"

She nodded. "On the weekends sometimes twice. Can't beat the addiction."

"Know what you mean. Mine is porn," Big Country said.

"Luckily I *don't* know what you mean," she said in disgust.

Zeus frowned. What was wrong with porn?

"I'm helping my supervisor with the graphics layout for a project she's completing," Sabrina continued.

"What is it you do at your job?" Terry asked.

"Nothing worth kidnapping and beating me over. I'm an administrative assistant for a small nonprofit art gallery."

"Bet the pay sucks." Lynx snorted.

"It allows me to live my life," she said defensively.

Zeus shot Lynx a warning look.

"Why does a nonprofit gallery need security?" Terry continued.

"We don't really. There are three floors of offices in the building. The gallery occupies half of the third floor. On the other side of the hall are a suite of law offices. They practice environmental law for the most part. On the second floor is an architectural firm and a nonprofit. First floor is a notary, a pediatrician's office, a dentist's office, and a florist shop. I think security is there to mostly monitor access to the building. They aren't like real security; they don't carry guns or do rounds or anything. There's usually just one or two people working on the morning and evening shifts."

"Was the guy you identified in the warehouse working yesterday morning?" Terry asked.

"He was there for the morning shift. He opened the door for me."

"Was that unusual?"

"Not really. Aaron liked to play like he ran the building. He liked to flirt sometimes, but it usually came off as kind of corny. He was a little interpersonally challenged. His conversations always seemed forced, unnatural, but not just with me. It was like he was practicing homework some life coach or therapist had given him. For the most part, though, he seemed harmless."

"Until he and his friends break into your house, beat you, and kidnap you," Zeus added.

"Tell us about when you left work," Terry said.

"I ride my bike to work. I live by the lake and work in the uptown area, so I was home around fifteen minutes after leaving the job. My studio apartment is located in the back on the first floor of a four-unit building. After I got settled, I went to the kitchen and ate my leftover Chinese food. After I ate, I was putting my dishes in the sink when there was a knock on my back door. My back door leads from the kitchen to the communal patio garden in the backyard. I thought it was my friend Randy who usually stops by in the evening."

Zeus made a mental note: Do bodily harm to Randy if I need to make a point about who Sabrina currently belongs to.

"I opened the door and *blam*, a fist to the face. I remember fighting, but it was two of them. The last thing I remember before I went unconscious was hoping Randy was okay." She looked down at Zeus. "Then I woke up with this big beast standing there about to rape me."

Zeus went back to sharpening his blade when they all looked at him. Disbelief, disgust, anger. He usually wouldn't care about their reactions, but he didn't rape women and felt the need to clarify for Sabrina's sake. Plus, there was no way in hell the woman was going to consider letting him fuck her if she thought he was a rapist.

"I wasn't about to rape you. Was adjusting myself. I got hard looking at you and the way I was positioned in my jeans was getting uncomfortable, so I reached in and – "

"Really don't need to hear anymore," she said.

"As long as you know I wasn't about to rape you. I don't rape."

"Well, that's something."

"But we'll have sex before I – "

"Jesus, Zeus," Coen said. "Can you be sane for one minute? You don't tell a woman you're going to – "

"But I am."

"You were unconscious for the entire trip from Oakland to Point Richmond?" Almaya interrupted.

"You can feel the lump on the back of my head if you need proof."

Zeus paused again. He didn't like that they were aggravating her with all their questions. He put the stone and cloth on the floor, his grip tightening on the hilt of his blade.

"Keep it together, Zeus. No one's harming Sabrina. We're all just having a conversation," Terry said calmly.

Zeus didn't give a shit about what Terry said. He felt the slight press of Sabrina's leg against his arm and shoulder. Not an accident, she did it on purpose. A lover's caress. A promise of something more when the time was right. He picked up his tools and resumed sliding the edge of the blade against stone.

"You used to be a paramedic in New Orleans?" Lynx asked.

Zeus felt Sabrina tense against him. "How do you know where I lived?"

Almaya pointed toward the other area of the living room. The sunken lower level had an oval table at its center, a surveillance center on one wall, a computer area on another, and a decompression area toward the back. The decompression area was Zeus's favorite place here...after the weapons and training rooms.

"We did a brief background check on you using Gambit, our computer system. It gave us some basic information, but nothing that readily links you in any way with Kragen and his organization."

"I already told you I don't know – nor have I had anything to do with – this Kragen."

"Which makes this even more terrifying for you, I'm sure. It's bad enough to be hunted, and it's even more devastating when it's for reasons of which you're unaware," Almay said. "The Brood needs to discover why, because, trust me, you are not the endgame. Kragen's affiliations are global. He ordered a handful of his staff to the Bay Area less than a week ago. Yesterday evening, Big Country shone the light on a communication from one of Kragen's team, informing him his gift had been delivered to warehouse seventy-seven in an industrial area near the Port of Richmond. Kragen is scheduled to retrieve you at six this morning."

"Lucky for you, we were able to mobilize a team to scoop you before he got there," Price said.

"Unlucky for us, Zeus was a part of that team and killed your captors instead of subduing them so we could learn what they knew," Coen said.

Zeus looked at the overly-fucking-sensitive man he should start calling Cry Me a River instead of Coen. "Haven't learned the art of subduing. Don't plan to. If someone comes at me intending death, I give myself two options, kill or die. I always choose the first and thank the spirit of the blade that keeps me alive at the end."

"Sounds reasonable," Bride muttered. First words she had said since he'd entered the room.

"That argument doesn't have much to do with reason," Price countered.

"Long as we know the rules he operates by," Big Country chimed in.

Zeus shrugged. "They change. One time this street kid put a gun to my head and I told him to shoot me because I was feeling curious to see what the next life would look like."

When no one responded, Zeus went back to sharpening his blade.

"And you thought he would be a good addition to the team, Mama?" Price asked.

"I'm really starting to miss Cizan," Coen said under his breath.

———— ❖ ————

"WHY DID YOU leave New Orleans, Sabrina? Why change to a career so different than the one you'd been in?" Terry asked.

Sabrina took a moment before responding to him. The man might have seemed friendly enough, but these questions about her, their need to know felt like a threat. She didn't talk much about her past because it usually involved lying. With this group she knew instinctively that staying as close to the truth as possible would be her best defense.

"I needed a change. I wasn't happy in New Orleans, and as a paramedic there I was... I've probably seen as much death and violence as anyone in this room. A little after moving to New Orleans, depression set in, I gained weight, and I...I wasn't happy."

"So you move to Oakland, a city that has a near nonexistent murder rate?" Lynx said sarcastically. "Like healthy eating, I take it the statistics haven't made their way down South."

She shrugged. "I heard good things about California. All sun and surf, laid-back lifestyle. I didn't want the glitz of LA. San Francisco was where I headed, but it was too expensive...and cold. The diversity of people and places in Oakland ended up being just what I needed. I got re-certified as an EMT here, but when I really thought about it, I didn't want to go back to that work. I came here for change. I like photography, so when I saw the job listing for the gallery, it felt...right. I like my life in Oakland."

"You don't have any family there?" Mama asked.

"I don't have family anywhere. I was put in the foster care system when I was a kid."

"What happened to your birth parents?"

"Overdose. My dad too early to even have a memory of him."

"No foster parents you were close to?"

She snorted. "I've been living on my own, supporting myself, since I was fourteen. Emancipated at sixteen."

"No siblings?"

"Had an older half sister who died, but she left me alone long before her death. So no." Her sister Samantha's suicide in New Orleans almost three years ago was what had led to her decision to move to California.

"I'm sorry."

Sabrina frowned at the older woman, wondering exactly which part of her story had elicited the apology. It didn't matter, really. She'd heard a thousand sorries in her life. Most of them wouldn't have been necessary if someone had thought to stop bad things from happening instead of offering useless sympathy after.

The other woman was probably well intentioned, but Sabrina didn't need another person's good intentions, especially when it helped them justify interfering in her life. She'd had enough of that bullshit. She knew all she really needed to know. Someone, someone new, was after her; she could handle it. Though not impossible, it was damn unlikely that Ernesto and his people had anything to do with a big-money organization like the one Kragen seemed to be a part of.

"I appreciate that you rescued me, possibly saved my life, but I can take care of myself from here on out. All I need you to do is drop me back in Oakland."

"How exactly do you plan on taking care of yourself?" Terry asked.

She didn't like having to explain herself. This was her life, and for the first time in a long time, she was living it however she chose.

"I'll lay low for a while. If push comes to shove and I feel like I'm in danger, I'll call the police."

She didn't appreciate the laughter that met her statement. Even Zeus grunted in derision. It wasn't like she'd actually call the police, anyway. She was just saying what she thought she needed to, to get them to let her go.

"How about, until you come up with a better plan than ours, we watch over you?" Terry said.

"What's your plan?"

"Keep you here safe until we find out why Kragen's in the Bay Area, find out what he wants with you – "

"Kill him," Zeus interjected.

"And yes, Zeus, eventually eliminate the threat he represents."

"Kill him. Simply stated."

It wasn't so simple. She only had their word that this Kragen was behind her kidnapping, and though she felt the crime should be punished, she wasn't ready to have his death on her conscious. "I have a life and a job that comes with a lot of responsibilities. I appreciate your desire to help, but I won't hide out until you solve your mystery."

"You don't seem to appreciate the level of danger you've found yourself in," Price said.

She had some idea. She'd just woken up beaten in a warehouse about fifteen miles from her home.

"Kragen is not a nice man," Mama explained. "He rapes; he kills; he tortures; he exploits. And when he doesn't feel the need to do these things personally, he has enough money and power to have others do them for him. His organization has ties to legitimate companies and government contracts the world over. The Oakland PD will not be able to protect you."

"But you will?"

"I will," Zeus corrected.

"We will." Mama frowned at Zeus.

Sabrina gritted her teeth and closed her eyes, rubbing her temple. It wasn't just her bodily injuries or the stress of having somebody after her. It was them. This Brood. Their personalities, their tensions, their constant energy were causing her senses to overload. She had a low tolerance for social interactions. Every nerve she had was hyperalert from attempting to maneuver safely through the undercurrents swirling around her. She wanted to sleep and blot them all out but was unwilling to leave herself vulnerable again.

She opened her eyes as Zeus reached behind him and secured the scalpel-sharp blade near the small of his back.

"Who are you all, anyway? Not police. Not FBI. Possibly ex-military."

"*We,*" Terry said, spreading his arms magnanimously, "are the good guys."

She snorted. The others laughed outright at the absurdity of the declaration. The only one of them who could possibly pass for good was Coen. In her opinion, not even Mama or Terry pulled it off. Despite their ease and concern, there was something hard about them. They both seemed a bit too complex to fit the simple description of "good guys."

"Though I didn't birth them," Mama said, "these are my brood. My later-in-life adopted children, if you will. Each of them is special to me. Each has special skills, special sensibilities. None of them are good in the standard meaning of the word, but they have been committed to helping me in my endeavors."

"Which are?"

"Maybe it's not the best idea to tell the stranger who Kragen wants bad enough to have snatched from her home a lot about who we are, Mama," Price cautioned.

The older woman shrugged, watching Sabrina with praying-mantis stillness. "I'll take a chance on her. She doesn't strike me as one ready to share secrets."

"Did you forget Kragen has a pretty sadistic way of handling people who don't want to share their secrets?" Lynx asked.

Mama waved the concerns of both men away. "Stopping soulless men and women from destroying the lives, innocence, and souls of others is what we're about," she told Sabrina. "Sometimes, like now, we act independently, choosing to go after people and organizations others either turn a blind eye to or truly don't know about. Sometimes we contract out to others for our various services."

"Like contracting with the government?"

"Well, that question's a little dicey," Terry said.

"A lot of times governments employ the people who need killing," Zeus said, reaching for her leg and draping it over his shoulder as if it were his pet python. He reached under the pant leg and stroked her bare skin. She'd noticed he needed to keep his hands busy. It must be a testament to how tired she was that she didn't object. The repetitive motion actually eased the tension in her body instead of causing her revulsion.

"Bluntly stated, but Zeus is correct," Terry said. "Sometimes people have prices. Governments harbor people all too willing to be bought."

Sabrina let her head fall back on the love seat and closed her eyes. She wouldn't sleep, just rest, listen, ask. She didn't have the energy or the mental capacity to answer any more of their questions without accidentally saying something she shouldn't say.

"So what happens next?" she asked.

"You rest, dear girl. We'll watch over you," Mama said.

"I take care of myself," she muttered. "I always take care of..." She sighed, overcome by a crescendo of darkness.

"WEIRD THING OUT at the warehouse, Mama. It might have nothing to do with nothing, but we thought it best to check in around it," Lynx said.

"What did you find?"

Lynx was silent for a moment. "Fresh wounds, bruising, multiple contusions on the head and throat areas of the kidnappers. At least two of those men took a hell of a beating. Didn't think it was your style to beat 'em first and slice them up after, Zeus."

Zeus paused in his downstroke on Sabrina's leg. "I just cut." He shrugged. "Nothing more."

"Ante up, Lynx. I told you he didn't do it." Big Country rubbed his fingers together, anticipating his winnings.

"It was her," Price said. "It had to be. More than likely the third or fourth man knocked her unconscious from behind. Something about that woman just doesn't sit right. I don't trust her."

"*You* not trust, Price?" Coen said. "So surprising."

"Sounds like she had it rough growing up, makes sense she would know how to defend herself when attacked," Big Country drawled.

"I don't see her beating the shit out of two grown men like that," Coen argued. "I held her when she was on that warehouse floor. She was shaking with fear; there was no fight in her."

"I don't like it," Price said.

"You don't like much," Coen stated.

Zeus looked up to see Bride watching him stroke Sabrina's leg. She looked perplexed. He winked at her. She sneered at him.

"So what does it mean to you that she turned the tables on her attackers?" Big Country asked.

"It means we may want to watch our backs around her," Price said. "Doesn't anyone else find it peculiar that after the last few strikes against the Consortium, there's a stranger in our midst, a supposed victim of Kragen, who has the ability to do what no one in his organization has been able to do since our first attack – put a face to their unknown enemy. A big coincidence our last mission involved exposing their role in the exploitation and abuse of the women in Hallow's House, and we just *happen* to intercept information that, coincidently, leads us to a woman taken for Kragen."

"Maybe we acted too hastily bringing her here, but we couldn't have just left her there," Coen said.

"You don't seem so confident in her innocence anymore. Wonder what she'd think about it?" Zeus said.

Coen had the good sense to avert his gaze.

"Should we really be having this conversation with her right here? She could be detailing everything we say," Lynx said.

"She's asleep," Zeus confirmed.

"No harm, Zeus," Price said, "but I'm not quite ready to trust the judgment of a man who isn't always an active part of this reality. Who just happens to think he's strengthened by some spirit-possessed blades."

Zeus didn't take offense. He didn't care about Price's opinion or his ability to perceive reality. He'd said what he knew. Sabrina was asleep. Shifting, he pressed his back more fully against the base of the love seat and brought both knees close to his chest, placing his feet flat on the ground. He liked the feel of Sabrina's leg pressed flush against his shoulder and chest, her foot dangling limply near his navel. Slowly he removed the flip-flop and massaged her leg from knee to toe.

"Should he be doing that?" Lynx asked Big Country.

"You gonna make him stop?"

"Hell," Lynx said, burrowing deeper into the recliner, "it's not my leg."

"Zeus, you really shouldn't handle her body without her permission," Almaya said. "But she is indeed asleep and will likely stay that way for the next five or six hours depending on how her body metabolizes the sedative I put in her drink."

Price leaned forward, placing his elbows against his knees. "So what are we going to do?"

"We know she's clean," Big Country said. "No tracking or electronic devices attached to or in her. Checked her at the warehouse, and she didn't trigger the system when she entered the bar. Kragen's group has no extra eyes or ears on her. In that sense she's truly lost to him right about now."

"We know, for whatever reason, Kragen wants her," Terry said. "Either she's working for and with him, or she truly needs to be protected from his plan for her. And, guys, have no misunderstanding, he will be in a cold rage over this. Unlike the attacks on the Consortium, the women are damned personal for him. *She* is personal to him."

"Can you dig deeper into Sabrina's history?" Almaya asked.

"Can a bat shit acid?"

"I hope that means yes," Coen said to Price, who nodded wearily. The man who'd led the warehouse run looked close to burned out, tired to his soul.

Is that what working with the Brood does to well-meaning men, Zeus wondered.

"What about Kragen?" Big Country asked.

"Lynx, you, and Bride?" Mama requested.

"Consider it done."

"Sniff him out; put a tail on him; call him our bitch," Bride mumbled.

She was weird. Not like a normal woman. If the need to have Sabrina hadn't been dominating his attention, he would have made Bride his new project. Her strangeness spoke to him.

"Should we move Sabrina to a different location?" Coen asked.

"I'll take her," Zeus volunteered. "We'll hole up, work some things out till Almaya says it's safe to return."

Almaya hushed the objections that erupted around the room.

"Thank you for the offer, Zeus, but we'll keep her here. Between you, Terry, and me, I'm sure she'll be well looked after."

As gracious as she was, and as much as he respected her courage, he didn't like being told no. That's why he didn't usually ask for anything. Almaya had approached him about a month ago, after he'd just ended a hunt. She hadn't been afraid of him when he'd been wild-eyed and soaked in blood. She'd talked to him easy, not like she knew him but like he knew her, trusted her. Her courage and his curiosity were the only things that had kept him from killing her. No sane person should've approached him when he was on a hunt and expected to live. Yet here they both were.

"What about me and Coen?" Price asked.

"Until we have some direction, you can hang out here. But I do have a small errand for you," she said with a slight smile that held a hint of guilt.

"Yeah?" Price asked, looking wary, reluctant.

"Simple drop-off. Juarez will want to return to his family to heal. You will take him there."

Coen groaned, and Zeus wondered if Juarez's family was as irritating as Juarez was.

"He's going to be in a hell of a bad mood when he's conscious again," Price said.

"I can dispose of him," Zeus offered. "It'll be quick. He bitches, I cut out his tongue. Solves the problem of his overworked mouth permanently." There was something about this group that made him feel generous.

"We'll drop him off, Mama."

Zeus shrugged. He didn't want to be separated from Sabrina anyway, but with her asleep, she wouldn't have even known he'd been gone.

"It'll be interesting to learn how Kragen reacts to the message Juarez left in the glove compartment of the kidnapper's truck," Lynx said.

"What message?" Price asked, tensing.

All eyes except Big Country's, which closed in disgust as he shook his head, turned to Lynx. "Like Juarez, seems you need to learn the art of shutting the fuck up, brother."

"Using the digital printer in Big Country's van, Juarez printed one of the pictures I took of Sabrina when we first arrived at the site. He put it in the glove compartment of the truck after writing 'Look what I found' on the back," Lynx said, looking uncomfortable.

Zeus pressed his cheek against Sabrina's knee. "Bet you all wish I had sunk my blade a little deeper. I can still drop him home if you like."

"What the hell were you both thinking?" Almaya demanded.

Old Mama doesn't sound so benevolent anymore, Zeus thought as she snapped at Big Country and Lynx.

"Just for the record, I was finishing up in the warehouse. I didn't find out until after," Big Country said, holding up his hands in surrender.

"Taunting Kragen is not a smart idea," Terry said.

"That's only if Kragen is the one to pull the photo," Mama said. "It's just as likely that the police, the fire department, some random civilian could find the message. They'll figure out there's an unidentified woman linked to the warehouse, and they will also be looking for her."

"Naw," Big Country said. "Lynx drove the truck to a place in the hills up from the area. Kragen has a tracking device on it. His people will more than likely be the ones to find the photo. The warehouse isn't tied to Kragen in any obvious way, so there shouldn't be a link to him, the truck, or the bodies inside the warehouse."

"So what, we wait as Kragen heads back home, locks down all his less than legal activities, and waits until it's safe to go after Sabrina again?" Price asked.

"He won't hole up. It's a matter of pride and ego," Terry said contemplatively. "Remember, she's personal to him. This will be an opportunity for him to display his superiority. He'll accept the challenge. He'll come for her just like he came to the Bay Area to get her in the first place."

"Just so you all know, I told Juarez not to leave the photo," Lynx said.

A pillow flew, hitting Lynx dead on in the face.

Mama's satellite phone rang, and Terry reached beside him to answer it. "Yeah?"

There was a pause as Terry listened; then he rose, waving them toward the decompression area. Almaya preceded him to the lower level, reaching for the television remote.

"Thanks, London. Keep us updated on the police's investigation," Terry said before disconnecting.

Zeus watched the others trail behind Almaya like well-trained puppies. He heard the television turn on, heard the channel being changed to a news report in progress.

As the others huddled around, blocking the sight of the television screen, Zeus looked up and over his shoulder. Finally he had Sabrina to himself. Unlike at the warehouse, this time he didn't mind being left with her. He wanted it, wanted it bad, wanted walls and doors with bolts and a... No, he didn't even need a bed.

"Eyewitness Randy Leon reports that he made a phone call to 911 when he heard a violent confrontation happening in his neighbor's apartment. Mr. Leon was unable to identify the assailants but was able to identify a dark-colored truck fleeing the scene. If you are just joining us, a missing persons report has been issued for Sabrina Samora, who is believed to have been violently assaulted and abducted from her home. Her assailants are as yet unknown, but the police have issued an all-points bulletin for an extended-cab, dark-colored pickup truck, with the first three digits on the license plate of 5DT..."

"And whose idea was it to leave the photo in the glove compartment again?" Terry asked.

Zeus moved Sabrina's leg from over his shoulder and crawled backward onto the love seat. He shifted her body onto his lap. The press of her ass against his groin... He grunted as his dick hardened from the soft cradling press ready to do its part on both their behalves. He tucked her head into the crook of his neck, aware of the nuances of her scent. On the surface, the floral of Almaya's lavender-rose bath gel and the citrus-bergamot lotion, but underneath, the spicy earth scent, uniquely hers, made him want to bury his face in her deepest recesses.

"What the hell," Price said, returning. Zeus sighed and pulled his hand from beneath Sabrina's top, where he'd begun to stoke his thumb over her abdomen.

"She was cold."

"That's bullshit."

"Yeah," he said, tugging on, then releasing, a twisted loc to watch it spring back into place.

"Zeus, please carry Sabrina to the blue room," Almaya requested as she returned to the front room. He stood with Sabrina in his arms, feeling a deep sense of satisfaction he usually only experienced when using his blades. Almaya was seeing the value of letting him have the woman. Between Kragen on her tail and the cops, maybe Almaya believed this would be Sabrina's only opportunity for pleasure before she was free of them. He frowned. Something was off about that, her being free of him, leaving him.

"Zeus, *why* are you growling? I thought you'd rather take her to the room than allow one of the others to do it."

"I'll take her," he said, ignoring the others as he walked toward the decompression area, where a door, indistinguishable from the wall, led to the second sublevel of Mama's house. The blue room was a good place for Sabrina to sleep because it shared an adjoining door with the brown room, the room he was using. Both of the connecting doors had to be unlocked to pass through, but he doubted Almaya would lock Sabrina's door now that she wanted them to have sex. He smiled inside. Despite having to deal with the Brood, taking this assignment was turning out to be one of the best decisions he'd made in a while.

Almaya followed him out of the room and down the stairwell that led to the sleeping quarters. He glanced over his shoulder and frowned, wondering why she was trailing behind them.

"You know, despite the fact that Cizan recommended you, I offered you a place in the Brood because you belong here. I know it might not seem as if you do, but I have a sixth sense about these things."

"You couldn't have kids? That's why you created this facade of a family, isn't it?"

She laughed. Most people didn't usually respond that way to his questions.

"No, nothing stopped me from having kids. I learned early the ugly side of youthful vulnerability, and I choose to fight for the ones who haven't yet learned to fight for themselves. The Brood helps me do this. There are a lot of children, of people who need to be fought for. As I moved about the world doing my work, I found that once you take someone into your heart, claim them as an essential part of you, it doesn't matter if you're connected by blood or not; you're connected, and you do all you can to see to their safety and happiness."

"I have no idea what you're talking about."

She laughed again. "You will."

He guessed this was her attempt at playing the mama the rest of the Brood identified with.

Almaya stepped around him and opened the door to the blue room. Like the other rooms designated by color, the blue room was decorated in various shades of blue. He walked to the queen-size bed and placed Sabrina on it, shifting her so he could pull the covers around her. He sat on the bed and unbuttoned his jeans before Almaya stopped him.

"Thank you for your help. I'll make sure she's all tucked in before I lock the doors."

He frowned over at the connecting door. "She's not going to like waking up alone."

"I'm sure she'll cope."

Zeus walked back out into the hallway. He stood in front of the door long after Almaya had closed it in his face. He turned and walked the few steps to his door. It was chilly inside the room. He walked directly to the California-king-size bed without turning on the lights. Stripping, he lay on top of the covers, hand reaching down to fist his hardening erection. He imagined Sabrina naked in his bed, her legs straddling him as she sank down, sheathing him over and over again as she fucked him without mercy. His hips surged up to meet each downward stroke. They fucked, hard and primal, his grunts, her pleading. He came hard as she screamed out. His body relaxing as he imagined her falling forward, a nipple prodding his lips until they opened and he sucked it in, flipping her onto her back and hammering into her until he came a second time.

As he closed his eyes, feeling only partially satisfied after coming, Zeus resolved that he was going to have to get her away from the others if he was going to make the fantasy real. He needed that hard fuck with her in real life. He slipped into the shadow realm between sleep and wakefulness, the closest thing he ever got to true sleep. He had so many things to teach her about satisfying him. So many places in her body he could stick the one blade he was born with.

———◆◈◆———

LESS THAN TWO hours before dawn, Almaya settled in the bed beside Terry, relaxing as he pulled her into his arms.

"You know, this whole situation has the makings of some very messy business."

"I know," she said.

"You know she's hiding something."

"I do know."

"Yet you're allowing her to remain with us."

"I know it goes against good sense to keep her, Terry, but something tells me she's supposed to be here."

"And him? What happens when he's no longer able to keep his urges in check? You know it's inevitable, Almaya."

"I know."

He turned out the light and settled her beneath him, lightly kissing her neck, her cheeks, her mouth. "Almaya, Almaya, Almaya, the all-knowing one. Let me share some things I know."

CHAPTER THREE

Maxim William Kragen III left his suite at the St. Regis in San Francisco's SoMA district determined that the day would be better than the one before it. He hadn't slept in over twenty-four hours. He'd left New York with the sweetest anticipation and arrived at SFO only to be enshrouded by dense fog and the more demoralizing knowledge that the one he had come thousands of miles to retrieve had escaped his men – his dead men, per reports about the bodies found in the burned-down warehouse – and was missing. A police investigation was underway, and news reports about the bloody abduction of Sabrina Samora were being broadcast over every local news station at what seemed like two-minute intervals.

Slipping into the backseat of the charcoal-gray town car, he sat in silence, looking out on a city that, though not frozen over as New York was in April, looked more dismal due to the obscuring fog that had yet to burn off.

As the car slid down the streets of a city filling with eager tourists willing to face the wet chill and the homeless nestled in tarp cocoons on entryways of still-closed businesses, Maxim undid the only fastened button on his suit jacket and relaxed against the heated leather seat. His personal assistant, Reed Miller, sat next to him. After years of employment, his assistant was well trained in the needs of his employer, one of them being to remain quiet until Maxim addressed him.

Despite all the chaos surrounding this situation, it would be a good day. Before it was done, he would be in possession of an elusive and long-sought-after prize. Sabrina. A woman he had not stood face-to-face with in over seven years. He hadn't known her last name when they'd been together in New York; she was simply Sabrina. He'd come to know many things about her: her bravery, her spirit, her tolerance for pain, and the generosity of her flesh. He had lacked the maturity and sophistication he presently demonstrated when dealing with his most intimate liaisons. He'd unwisely overlooked things in the past, believed her when she told him her name, been so certain of her loyalty when she'd promised so many times that she wanted only him, that she would never leave him, that she would love him to her last breath.

But she'd lied.

"Where is the truck, Reed?"

His assistant flipped open his tablet cover and tapped the surface several times before passing the device over to him.

"It hasn't moved for several hours. It's located in a remote area that has no immediate access to public transportation. If she's not there, it's unlikely she hitched a ride and was picked up. With all the news broadcasts and missing person reports, some authority, be it the hospital or the police, would have been informed. She may be sleeping or unconscious in the truck, Mr. Kragen. Either way, we will have more information soon."

If this hadn't been a private matter, an easily resolvable matter since he knew who she was, where she lived, where she worked, he would have used some of the Consortium's ample resources to manage the situation. But between him, Reed, and his bodyguard-driver Eddie, they would have the matter of Sabrina Samora resolved.

"Has the cliff house been prepared?"

"Yes, sir. Everything will be ready for your use as soon as you arrive."

"And it's fully equipped?"

"Yes, sir."

Maxim focused on the red flashing dot on the screen. The truck was approximately twenty-five minutes away, and given the early Saturday-morning hour, he didn't expect to be slowed by traffic.

"You know, I had thought by not going to London, I'd be able to avoid all this fog."

"It'll be behind us the moment we're out of the city, sir."

"That's as it should be. One needs clarity of vision when embarking upon a destined path."

"Yes, sir."

"Sabrina was harmed. Why?"

"I'm...uncertain, sir. Except for the security guard, Basir provided the manpower. Had he known of our connection to Sabrina's retrieval, maybe he would have ensured her safety. My contact warned the men to handle her with extreme care."

"Yet they did not," he said, recalling the reports of blood and destruction inside her apartment. Because he was highly intelligent, there would be no way the authorities could link the inept men with Maxim, as none expect Reed knew of Maxim's involvement. Not even Basir.

"No, sir. Unfortunately it doesn't seem they did, and that means the police are searching for your lady as diligently as we are."

"Surely not quite as diligently or as efficiently as we," he said, humored by the absurdity of any police force succeeding where he had not. The town car slipped free of the clutching mist, and into sunshine and blue skies as they made their way across the Bay Bridge. If one were to guess, solely based on the current weather in San Francisco, one could believe the world was perpetually cloaked in chilling fog. It was a blessing to discover a warm, welcoming world awaited in the distance.

Despite all he had achieved over the years, his life had seemed gray and cold since Sabrina's departure, leaving him with the weight of his weaknesses. But he had gotten stronger, become the man she could once again respect, no longer one to be controlled but one who controlled much. Since her departure he had stepped into his power and, in doing so, gave himself the means for bringing her light back into his life.

"Do you suppose she beat the odds and killed all four men? There were four bodies found in the warehouse," Reed said.

"The Sabrina I remember was kind, soft, easily led."

"Even the most timid can fight if they're afraid for their life."

"She wouldn't."

"If you're certain, sir."

"I am, Reed."

And it was the truth. Sabrina had never struggled against him. She'd easily accepted his will, then his love. Yes, she'd run eventually, but she'd endured, she'd acquiesced, she'd even reveled in the attentions he'd given her, but Reed wouldn't know that. It had been before his time.

"If those men were not already dead, I would kill them *very* painfully," he calmly promised.

"They would deserve it, sir. It was a simple retrieval, and they turned the matter into a complicated mess."

Maxim nodded, sensing rather than seeing his assistant's anger. He'd always liked Reed's ability to candidly evaluate a situation. The younger man was lean, with compact musculature. He'd always had a hungry wolf look about him despite the expensive, sharp cut of every outfit he owned. Reed had the pale winter skin of his Black Irish heritage. Black, short-clipped hair, near-black eyes.

It had been years since Maxim had watched Reed, then a seventeen-year-old boy, kill Matt Orley, Maxim's then bodyguard, for attempting to retrieve the cell phone and wallet the young Reed had stolen from Maxim's pocket only moments before. Instead of having the semi-indigent boy killed, Maxim had educated and employed Reed. Rather than living in a dump of a house with his mother and three younger brothers, Reed currently lived in a penthouse in Manhattan and had bought a three-level home in Brooklyn for his family, whom he continued to support, just no longer by street thievery.

They rapidly made their way toward the blinking red dot. Unexpressed anticipation coursed through Maxim the closer they came. He returned the tablet to Reed. The thing was making him more on edge, and he needed to be relaxed when Sabrina was reunited with him. She was injured. Probably afraid. Again. Because of him.

He was not a man conditioned or willing to express love or caring emotions easily, but he never lied to himself, and he knew Sabrina would always own a piece of his soul. She had been the first and only woman he had lain himself bare for. She'd accepted him, cherished him. Then one day she was simply gone. No one before or since had come close to satisfying the need she'd inspired. Maxim had found her again, and soon she would return to his side. He would never let her go. He knew his mind, his heart more clearly. He wouldn't bend to the prejudice, fear, and shame of his parents. He knew their interference had something to do with her decision to abandon him, but they would never admit it.

"Your father don't like me, Max. I can tell by the way he looks at me like I'm not worth seeing."

"My father looks down on everyone, even me, even my mother. Ignore him, Sabrina. That's how he and I have managed most of my life. Ignoring each other."

He remembered her sad, uncertain smile. Remembered pressing his lips against her softer, fuller ones. Remembered the unyielding force of his desire igniting each time he touched her, the way she screamed his name as he took her again and again, always begging him for more, always holding him as he trembled from the force of his release.

All he'd had for years were his memories of her, of them, but soon, due to his diligence and dedication, they would create new memories. Better memories, because he was stronger, stronger than his father's threats and stronger than his mother's histrionic tears or her bemoaning the shame she would carry due to his relationship with Sabrina. Maxim knew he'd become the man Sabrina needed him to be.

"Are we close, Eddie?" Maxim asked his driver.

"Little more than a mile, sir."

They were in an area no more than five miles away from the warehouse site. They were close. *She* was close.

"Right there," Eddie called out a few minutes later. Directly ahead of them, on the dirt area along the right side of the road, was the truck the dead men had used. Eddie pulled the car to a stop five feet away. Reed exited the car and came around to open the door for Maxim. Eddie was already approaching the truck, his right hand reaching behind him, moving toward the gun Maxim knew rested there.

"Easy, Eddie. I don't want her frightened any more than she already is."

He knew he was putting Eddie in a precarious position. It was his duty to see to Maxim's safety over all others. But that was before. Sabrina had come back to him. All care had to be taken to protect her. There would be family, friends, and enemies alike who would be all too happy to permanently erase her from his life. He would not allow it to happen. Not again.

As Eddie continued to approach the truck, Reed cautioned Maxim to stay behind the open door of the bulletproof car.

"Perhaps you should wait inside until Eddie gives the all clear, sir."

"I'll remain here. She won't know who Eddie is. If she looks out and sees me, she'll know she's no longer in danger."

"Yes, sir."

Eddie knelt on the ground and checked the undercarriage of the truck. When he stood, the only face reflecting against the black-tinted windows of the truck was his own. Reaching for the door, Eddie pulled the handle, weapon drawn. Eddie leaned inside, searching the front and rear seats.

He ducked back out of the truck. "It's empty."

Maxim's heart stuttered over the despair he felt as he strode forward. He opened the rear door as Reed walked to the front of the passenger side. There was blood within. Not large amounts, but it was there, and despite the reports about the state of her apartment, for the first time he felt fear for Sabrina's safety. She could be hurt and dying. Dead. To lose her permanently after all this time... It was too much to think about.

"Sir," Reed called to him.

Maxim stepped around the back door. Measured steps, controlled. He blinked and felt the anger and frustration as he pulled alongside Reed.

"You've found something?"

"Yes, sir," Reed said, holding out a five-by-seven photo. It took Maxim a moment to realize he was looking at a photo of Sabrina. A bruised and bloody Sabrina lying unconscious on what he suspected was the floor of the warehouse he was supposed to have retrieved her from. It seemed impossible, but even beaten, her beauty was more compelling than he remembered.

But she could be dead based on the formless way her body was splayed out over the floor. She could also be alive and hiding in the surrounding rock formations, bushes, or trees.

"Let's spread out and search the area, Reed," he said as he shrugged out of his suit jacket.

Reed stopped him. "Turn it over, sir."

Maxim frowned at him and turned the photo over. Four black words, written with bold penmanship, mocked him. *Look what I found.*

In less than a millisecond, rage flared, consumed him, turned the steel in his blood molten, and cooled, making his will harder. He folded the photo and placed it in the interior pocket of his jacket, against his heart.

He walked back to the town car and slid inside.

Over the years he had become adept at helping people understand why it was an unwise idea to cross him. But people were people, and so the lessons would have to keep coming apparently.

"Call New York, Reed. Have my men brought over. Let's find out if whoever took Sabrina knew all they'd be sacrificing when they made this unfortunate decision."

Reed pulled out his phone, hit a button, and brought it to his ear. Maxim sank back into the leathered interior of the car.

"Derek, Mr. Kragen wants the team here in..." Reed looked to Maxim. "Now."

"The length of time you need to gather, equip, and get to the jet, then subtract three hours. Yes, Derek, it does mean have your asses on the plane within the hour. Yeah. See you soon." Reed disconnected.

"What do you want me to do with the truck, sir?" Eddie called out.

The truck his Sabrina had bled in, suffered in. The only intact evidence linking Sabrina's abductors to the men from the warehouse. "Take it up high and drive it over a cliff. And Eddie, I need that truck to burn."

"Yes, sir."

Reed slipped back into the car, this time in the driver's seat as Eddie retrieved a canister and flare from the trunk of the town car, then returned to the truck, somehow securing the items toward the back of the undercarriage, near the tank. Eddie quickly drove the truck up the hill, Reed trailing a safe distance behind him. When Eddie stopped the truck, Reed drove up farther, passing him, and made a U-turn. Maxim watched as Eddie sped down the hill, braked, and swerved, jumping out of the car as it went over and into the deserted ravine. The explosion was sublime.

Once he was back in the driver's seat of the town car, Eddie drove down the hill toward the main road that would lead them back to the freeway. Noticing how overcast the sky had become, Maxim realized how much of its vitality the day had lost.

"What happens from here, sir?" Reed asked.

They would return to the St. Regis, where he'd go back to his suite alone and meditate on the photo in his pocket until his team arrived.

Then they would make plans to extract Sabrina and rain vengeance upon the person or persons who'd dared to take her.

———◆◈◆———

SHE FELT SO good.

This is what peace feels like, she reminded herself. The few times she had experienced it, she'd had to name it. It is real, she thought as she snuggled deep. It was warm, and it was quiet, and it was as compelling as a rainforest coming alive with the first rays of morning's light. It made her believe everything could be right with her, with the world. This feeling was so rare she wanted to hold on to it. Wanted to pretend her sister wasn't dead, her infant niece had been born alive seven years ago and was a thriving child, that her mother was clean and dancing in the kitchen of their old apartment with a cigarette hanging out the side of her mouth like she did when Sabrina and her sister, Sam, were girls.

Tears welled behind her closed eyelids. Her mother was dead, her sister was dead, her niece had never taken her first breath, and she was alone. She exhaled as the feeling of peace slipped away. It was a weak emotion that always retreated too soon, too fragile to stand against bitter memories and a lifetime of soul-numbing experiences.

She shifted, pressing her cheek against the cushion of warmth beneath her, letting her legs splay open. She wasn't able to hold on to peace, but she would hold on to this warmth just a little longer.

A band of steel hardness settled across her lower back, locking her body against the cushion beneath her.

"Don't worry; not letting you go." The words rumbled through her, pushing her completely from the nebula of semisleep to alarmed wakefulness.

She lifted her head and opened her eyes to eerie gray ones. "Zeus." Oh, hell. He was the last person she wanted to wake up in bed with.

Flattening her hands against the muscles of his chest, she straightened her arms until their upper bodies were no longer touching.

He frowned up at her. "Lay back down."

"Why are you lying beneath me, Zeus?"

He shrugged, closing those molten gray eyes. "I wanted to be in you. I'm in your bed because it's where I need to be to get what I want. Plus, you're the one that crawled on top of me in the middle of the night."

Her behavior while asleep wasn't the issue; his being in bed with her was. "It's so simple, huh? You have a need, and you just do whatever you want to satisfy it."

"Yep."

She lowered her upper body and rested her chin against his chest, the warmth of him more compelling than her concern over having him beneath her. "Sometimes other people have needs too. You can't just disregard that."

"Yes, I really can. Not responsible for what other people need or don't need. That's their job. I take care of me. That's my job."

Well, she couldn't really fault his reasoning. She'd lived most of her life thinking the same way. When she'd left Ernesto's abuse and run to her sister in Louisiana, Sabrina had begun to shift, to realize life was better with someone you loved in it, but then Sam committed suicide and Sabrina had vowed she'd never allow another person to hurt her just by loving them.

Life, in the form of her neighbor Randy, had made a mockery of that vow once she'd moved to Oakland. Randy had determined she would come to love him, and despite his habitually sorry choice in boyfriends, eventually, she had. Then she'd found a job where she actually liked the people she worked with, and she'd accepted that she couldn't disregard others as she'd learned to do growing up. Zeus obviously hadn't learned those same lessons.

"Where am I?" she asked, settling her head back on his shoulder and closing her eyes, too lazy and uninterested to look through the shadows and make out the details of the room they were in. Warmth had the potential to be a destructive addiction, she determined. It made you not care for much more than basking in it. Even when it radiated from an overtly unstable man.

"We're on the residential level of Mama's House. Second level down. About nine bedrooms down here."

"This place is huge. Is this your room?"

"Ours."

"Yeah, right."

"Yours. There's a connecting door. My room's on the other side."

"Huh." She breathed out, drifting off again. He was so damned warm. The peace that had scuttled out of reach before crept back like an abused animal that didn't know if it should trust her again.

Zeus's hand moved along her spine, fingers stroking the expanse of her back and shoulders. *This* was perfection. She had gone a lifetime without ever having experienced anything like it. Not just warmth. Not just peace. Her bones were evaporating under his touch. Her muscles were like liquid, her legs still stretched out along the outsides of his thighs, absorbing his strength and heat.

His hands slipped down, kneading the flesh of her ass, causing heat to pool between her thighs. The hardness of his erection strained against her core.

"Up," she murmured.

"Humh?"

"Hands back up."

He groaned, a rumbling vibration beneath her.

"You sound like some boy being told he has to walk his baby sister to ballet class and carry her tutu. It's sad."

"It is sad. Do you know how much I want to be inside you?"

She rolled her eyes beneath her closed lids.

"Just try to restrain yourself."

"Restraint is all you've seen from me."

She snorted. "Obviously we have different definitions of the word."

"You people just don't know how controlled I've been." He growled, pushing his hips up against her, his penis rubbing a spot near her navel that made her inner walls swell and throb. Her fingers sank into his shoulder muscles as she fought to control the sharp arousal that was causing the peace to forsake her for these more intense sensations.

"I'm not having sex with you," she stated, a partial admonishment to herself.

He relaxed beneath her, sighing deeply. She liked the feel of being lifted and lowered as he inhaled and exhaled.

"Go back to sleep," he ordered. "I'm tired of talking to you."

Against all good sense, she did.

Sabrina woke to sound. A persistent knock, a shower running. She lifted her head. The room was deep in shadow, the only light coming from the half-open bathroom door to her left and a small night-light near the bedroom door. There were no windows in this room, but of course there wouldn't be with the room being buried in the earth.

She sat up, relieved to see she was still wearing clothes. She moved her hips experimentally. Her body confirmed she hadn't been violated while she slept. She wasn't disappointed. But, that sex-starved part of her mind whispered, he would've given you release. When was the last time a man gave you sexual pleasure? It's amazing, she thought, sitting up and leaning back against the headboard, knees drawn to her chest. Zeus really did have some restraint. All the insanity he'd oozed had made her believe he wasn't capable of it.

She didn't trust anyone else with her well-being. Hell, she barely trusted herself when it came to men, but Zeus hadn't harmed her. He'd actually done the near impossible and aroused her. When he'd pressed into... She flung back the comforter and sheet and launched herself from the bed as if it was responsible for her crazy thoughts, her body's arousal.

She opened the door to Mama balancing a tray as she prepared to knock again.

"I hope you're not vegetarian," she said, her face tense.

"No, the amount of meat I consume doesn't allow me to call myself a vegetarian."

"Oh, thank God," Mama exclaimed, shoulders sagging in relief. "Not that there's anything wrong with vegetarianism, but with this brood, I wouldn't put it past them to carve me up and roast me alive if I tried to make a meal that didn't include at least two kinds of meat."

"Here, let me take that," Sabrina said, reaching for the tray that held two plates, each filled with scrambled eggs, a chopped avocado-tomato mix, bacon, a thick slice of ham, wheat toast, and two bowls of steaming grits with a whole layer of melted butter floating on top. Silverware, napkins, salt, and pepper sat next to small glasses of orange juice.

Wow. The aroma and sheer volume of food made Sabrina's stomach grumble indelicately.

"You, uh, you wouldn't happen to have seen Zeus?" Mama asked as the tray changed hands. Sabrina nodded toward the bathroom door.

"He's in the shower."

Sabrina walked over to the table near the bed's headboard and placed the tray on it, marveling at how strong and well-balanced the other woman must be to have carried the tray down to them. She picked up a slice of bacon and bit into it. Perfect, she thought as she closed her eyes, savoring. She hadn't bought bacon in months. She opened her eyes and turned to see Mama still in the doorway. The other woman's face had lost the kindness of moments before. She looked hard and threatening.

Sabrina frowned, reminded that just because Almaya had brought together a group of killers and called them her Brood didn't mean Sabrina should drop her guard around these people, around Mama. No, not Mama. Almaya, she thought, remembering what Zeus called her. She needed to use the other woman's name to keep emotional distance. It was too easy for a motherless woman to seek nurturing in older females who showed a kindness. She'd done it before. Never ended well. She couldn't even blame such foolishness on the ignorance of youth if she did it again.

"Did he hurt you?" Almaya asked, eyes never leaving the open door to the bathroom. The water to the shower shut off. Almaya was angry.

Oh. Realization dawned. She thought Zeus had... "Oh no. He didn't do anything wrong."

"He did something wrong." Almaya pointed to the open door connecting her room to Zeus's. "I locked the door when I left. He knew he was supposed to stay on his side of it."

Zeus strolled out of the bathroom wearing only a pair of white boxers. He stopped in front of Sabrina, took the rest of her bacon out of her hand, and popped it into his mouth, smirking at Almaya.

"You *wanted* me to stay on my side of the connecting door. Didn't say I would."

"You have a shower in your own room, Zeus."

"I like hers better."

"They are the same." Mama's words were staccato. She walked across the room toward them. Her stride would have been menacing if she wasn't so small. Almaya picked up a piece of bacon from the plate Sabrina had designated as hers and bit into it as if the bacon were the antidote to her frustration with Zeus.

Sabrina picked up the other plate, the untouched plate with all its bacon intact, and walked to the foot of the bed. She was starving, and she didn't feel like sharing. She didn't care if it was selfish. She hadn't eaten in...

"Hey, what time is it?" she asked, then shoved a forkful of eggs in her mouth.

"It's about eleven thirty," Almaya said, sitting on the side of the bed. "I was going to let you sleep longer but didn't want you to starve. I know you haven't eaten since yesterday afternoon."

Almaya reached for another piece of bacon on the plate Sabrina had left for Zeus. He growled, actually growled, before he snatched the plate out of reach. Almaya made an impatient sound in her throat and turned toward Sabrina.

"I want you to make yourself at home here, Sabrina. After you've finished eating, have Zeus bring you back to the front room and I'll show you around. Some places you won't have access to, but the majority of my home is yours to use freely."

Sabrina nodded, and Almaya stood, sending Zeus a warning look before she left the room.

Zeus brought the tray to the foot of the bed and placed it between them as he sat down. "You shouldn't trust her," he said, picking up his glass of orange juice.

"You seem to."

"I tolerate her. Is that what trust looks like?"

"No, I think it requires more than tolerance."

"If you say so."

"For example, I tolerated Aaron, the security guard at work, but I never trusted him. As it turns out, my instincts were correct. I tolerated him, but I definitely did not trust him."

Zeus folded the thick slice of ham and consumed the large chunk of meat in two bites.

"Hungry?"

"You might want to be careful about what you eat and drink around Almaya. She drugged your drink last night to make you sleep."

Sabrina froze midbite while Zeus continued to eat. "Excuse me?"

His gray gaze darted toward her and away as he spread butter and jelly over his toast. "They don't trust you either."

"They don't... What the fuck? I didn't ask them to trust me."

"They don't."

"I didn't ask them for anything except that they take me back home."

"They won't."

Her stomach turned, resentment and dread souring the little food she had just eaten. She wanted to push the food away, rejecting the two-faced cow who had just smiled in her face as if they were trusted friends. "She could have just locked me up in one of the rooms or a cell. I'm sure there's a cell or a dungeon somewhere in this underground asylum. Hell, I could have had a concussion...or been allergic. Did she even consider that before she pumped some drug through my system?"

Zeus shrugged.

How could he be so calm about this? Yesterday he had been willing to kill a man for making her tear up; now he sat there stuffing his face like some muscle-headed bovine.

"What do you know about them anyway?" she snapped.

"They pay well."

"How big is the organization?"

"Don't know. I'm not fully a part of the team, just filling in for Cizan."

"Should we even be eating this food?"

"You should if you're hungry."

"Aren't you worried about being drugged?"

"No. Last night they took the path of least resistance with you. Makes sense. If I hadn't told you, you wouldn't have ever known. No harm, no foul. Why are you so mad?"

Un-fucking-believable.

"You know when I told you it wasn't okay to overlook other people's needs because you wanted to fulfill a need of your own? Well, it's not right for them either. By taking me, drugging me, keeping me here, they've amazingly proven to be less trustworthy than you."

She tried to ignore the fact that again she'd almost succumbed to the idea of belonging, of connection. Betrayal and disappointment attached themselves to those idiotic ideals, and Zeus, of all people, had had to remind her of it.

"Sometimes, like with a kid, you have to do things they don't like because it's in their best interest," Zeus said.

"Are you saying I don't have the sense of a child?"

"Not if you're going to bitch about it. It's just what the nuns used to preach to us when they were trying to guide us toward good."

"Yeah, and how'd that go over with you?"

"Didn't."

"Exactly," she said.

She needed to leave Mama's House and make her way to her own home, or hide out close to it until it was safe to go back. She knew how to take care of herself, and her history of hiding from Ernesto would help her remain on guard if this Kragen or anyone else came after her. She had fought to create this life for herself, and she would fight twice as hard to keep it. Mama's House, these people, the peace she had awoken to was a lie. She just had to remember that.

She continued to eat because she would need her strength to get through this.

"Where do you live, Zeus?"

He shrugged, remaining silent. She stayed quiet as they ate, watching him relax the longer silence reigned. She passed him her last two slices of bacon and her toast. She'd eaten most of her ham but placed the remainder on his empty plate as he watched her with still-hungry eyes. He ate the last of her food without saying thank you; not that she truly expected him to.

"Like me better than before?" he asked when she stood and took the tray to the table by the bedroom door.

"I don't know. I don't think so."

"But you shared your food with me."

"And you didn't even say thank you."

"Thank you."

"You're welcome."

He lay on the bed. "Now can we have sex?"

"You're out of your mind," she said, plopping down on the side of the bed. "For real. I don't think I've ever met anyone as single-minded as you."

"You probably never will. That's just how it is. You have sex with me, the compulsion goes away, and we won't need to do it ever again, won't even have to talk to each other ever again. That's the best part."

"You know, I'm sure this is your best attempt at seduction, but even with all this suave finesse, I am not going to have sex with you."

He grunted. "You will."

She shook her head, falling back on the bed as well. The crown of Zeus's head lay near her abdomen. Maybe it was her imagination, but she could feel heat radiating from his head, warming her side. She might not like him, trust him, or appreciate his obsession with having sex with her, but she had to admit, if only to herself, that her body did like having his near.

"I should head upstairs, explore this new home I've been relegated to," she mumbled.

"You have to make your bed first."

"Excuse me?" she exclaimed, turning onto her side, legs tucking in as she curled up, propping her head on her hand, her body forming a half circle above his head. "I'm not making the bed. I didn't even sleep in it. I slept on you."

"It's your bed. I made mine."

That might have been well and true, but she didn't even make her own bed on a regular basis. It was an activity better left for the weekend... or when Randy came over to watch videos. "Let's compromise. We'll make it together. It'll go faster that way."

"I'll help you only if you help me take the edge off," he said, tilting his golden head back at an angle to look up at her. His mercurial gray eyes glinted.

"There's no edge, Zeus. We're both lying on a comfortable bed, full from a good meal, relaxed, and having the closest thing to a normal interaction we've had since we met."

"To hell with that. I'm on edge. You help me, and neither of us has to deal with a situation we want to avoid. You don't help me, you make the bed by yourself."

He turned on his side, angling his body parallel to hers as he reached his big paw of a hand out to rest on her hip. He stroked and massaged the area of semiexposed flesh, making everything from her breasts to her clit throb and vibrate with intense, unrelenting need.

"Don't be afraid, Sabrina," he said as he stroked just above her womb. "I'll make it feel good."

He *would* make it feel good, that horny part of her agreed. She gritted her teeth, fighting lust, and glared at him. "First of all, I'm not afraid of you, I – "

"I know. You're not afraid of anything, are you?"

"No," she whispered, losing the strength of her conviction. Jesus. The heat his hands created inside her was too much. It was because she hadn't had good sex for an eternity, she told herself. The bad part that controlled the need between her legs responded quick and certain. *You know he will make it good. So good.* Her vagina clenched as images of him inside her played out in her mind.

Zeus sat up on the bed and patted his lap, smiling at her with burning anticipation. She felt her heart blink before resuming its heavy pace. He had the gray-eyed grin of a shark gliding toward an unsuspecting seal from the fathoms below. "Come on, brave girl. Climb aboard."

Abandoning all good sense, she crawled over and straddled his thighs, conscious of avoiding the bulge straining against his boxers. Once she settled her weight, he gripped her ass and wedged her center tight against the hardness she'd been attempting to avoid.

Her heart was beating so fast she couldn't catch her breath. This intoxicating insanity was dangerous, she knew, but its allure was too great, the feeling it brought too necessary, a pyromaniac with an inferno blazing all around her, and she was too mesmerized with the feel of him to leap to safety.

"Zeus..."

"Just a kiss. One little kiss to persuade me to make the bed. Afterward we'll take the dishes upstairs and everything will be neat and tidy all over again. That's what you want, isn't it? Life neat and tidy, no messy complications?"

Was that what she wanted? She didn't know. She couldn't think beyond the throbbing between her legs.

"I want — "

"I know what you want. I'll give it to you."

She draped her arms over his shoulders, felt one of his hands snake up her back, pressing her toward him until her breasts flattened against his chest. She tightened her hold, his lips hovering only a breath away from hers.

"I just want to taste you," he murmured. His gaze fixated on her lips. "Just one taste."

She leaned forward and pressed her lips against his. Lightly, barely. They breathed each other in with rapid breaths. His lips rubbed against hers in an almost nonexistent caress, yet her hips surged against him, her vagina clenching and unclenching spastically as if to compel him into its hot passage.

He licked her lips, suckled them lightly, then with more force. Growing need reflected in his urgency, fueling her own. He growled, fisted his hand at the back of her head, his grip on her hair enough to cause tension that wasn't yet pain. He tilted her head back and devoured her mouth as if it was his long-awaited dessert. She moaned under the onslaught, her hips instinctively grinding against the one thing she knew could ease the tension building in her body.

He emitted an animalistic, urgent sound. His fingers slipped inside the waistband of her pants, finding her liquid center heated by the fever he was creating. She bucked, crying out, fingers gripping his shoulders, as he pushed two fingers inside her, filling her, stretching her. His lips never stopped devouring. His thumb found her clit and pressed, rubbed unrelentingly as his fingers pumped deep, over and over, until her whole body erupted in rapturous convulsions that caused her raw screams to fill the room. Lord, he'd made her come completely undone in minutes. Laid bare and trembling from the swift force of it. This was madness. It was better than peace. She couldn't remember feeling so satisfied, sated.

"Come back, Sabrina," Zeus said. "We're not nearly done."

Her mind registered that the waistband of her panties was circling her thighs just beneath the curve of her butt. Zeus's hand gripped his exposed penis as he shifted her with the other. She could feel the wide head slip against her, then press into her entrance.

She lunged to the side of the bed and fell on her hip. She scrambled back and pulled up the elastic waistband as she went. She leaped over the foot of the bed and crouched, looking up at Zeus, whose jaw ticked furiously.

"The edge is not off." His voice was hard. "You made it worse. Fix it."

She looked at his exposed penis. The thing was huge, rising up from dark bronze curls like a dusky gold obelisk. He was definitely hung like a god, but she would not be sacrificing her middle passage to him. She was only a mortal woman after all.

"I'm sorry, but I am never ever putting that thing in me. Ever."

"You will. You'll like it. All the females do. I'll make you scream out again, louder and longer than before."

Yeah, she thought, but will it be with pain or pleasure?

"You are a man with a hard-on. You'd say anything to get inside me," she reasoned.

"Of course I would," he grated out. "Just tell me what you want to hear. *You're killing me.*"

"I'm sorry," she panted, "but my lady parts aren't well used. I'm sure there are women who would be eager to ride you hard into the sunset, so I suggest you find one."

"Only you; that's how it works. Come here and straddle me. You can decide how much you want to take in."

69

She looked from his face to his erection. Maybe, that part of her that hadn't stopped throbbing whispered, maybe I can squeeze him in, take as much or as little as I want. She would hold the control.

She stood and walked back around to the side of the bed until she was facing him. She stood between his spread knees as he propped himself up on his elbows.

"What are you waiting for?" he asked. More like snarled. A bead of milky fluid trickled down the head of the crown.

"Do you have a condom?"

"Not here, but I'm clean."

Well, that solves that, she thought. She leaned over and reached for the waistband of his boxers, slowly working them back up his hips, over his penis.

"With a condom maybe, but definitely not without it. I'm not on birth control, and the last thing I want to do is get pregnant."

He stood and walked over to the connecting door, glaring down at her as he passed her.

"Where are you going?"

"To do what you were supposed to do. Take the edge off. Again."

"What about helping me with the bed?"

"You'll just have to do the same as me. Take care of it yourself."

He slammed the door on her. She then heard his door lock on the other side.

"Huh." She frowned, gazing at the bed with covers more off than on. She looked back at the connecting door. If she wasn't mistaken, she guessed she'd just witnessed a psychopath having a hissy fit.

She smothered a laugh behind her hands, sure that if he heard her, he would come back in and fuck her senseless.

She imagined him in the other room masturbating to images of her riding him; she imagined his hands squeezing her breast as he suckled one nipple and then the other; she imagined... Her body heated and tingled again. It really had been too long if her body was craving someone like

70

Zeus. Self-imposed celibacy made the most inappropriate people seem desirable. She sighed and made the bed. When she was done, she slipped out of the bedroom and headed down the hall in hopes of finding stairs to the next level before Zeus had a chance to come back for her.

Upstairs, Terry and Mama were sitting across from each other at the conference table and Big Country was seated in a chair with his back to her as he used the computer. Sabrina had opened the door that, once closed, wasn't really a door but a wall panel. These people are so *I Spy* it makes me want to laugh, she thought, moving to stand behind the chair at the head of the table.

"Surprised to see you without your self-appointed escort," Terry said in greeting. "Did you sleep okay?"

"As well as anyone who's drugged is expected to sleep, I guess," she said, folding her arms across the top of the chair and leaning against it.

Big Country whistled.

"Zeus." Almaya spat out the name accusingly.

"He just wanted to teach me a lesson about trusting strangers. I guess I needed the refresher." Sabrina mentally congratulated herself for sounding impassive.

"You're right not to trust us to do anything but keep you safe," Almaya said.

"I woke up with Zeus in my bed, Almaya."

The other woman's eyebrow rose, a subtle sign that she'd registered the change in how Sabrina addressed her.

"Well, sweetheart, you're about as safe as any of us can be with Zeus in residence," Big Country called over his shoulder.

"The men who originally took me may have beaten me up, but they didn't drug me and pretend some kind of dubious protection. It's crazy that the killer in my bed is the most honest among you. I'm sure you'll understand if I don't see you all as saviors protecting me from some unknown bad man."

Almaya reached for a folder on Terry's side of the table. "Do you know this man?"

Sabrina leaned over and pulled the folder to her. Inside was a photo of a nice-looking, expensively dressed white guy. Something about him seemed familiar, but she didn't remember him. She'd had contact with a lot of people in her life before coming to Oakland. She'd chosen to forget many of them. Based on the arrogance and disdain on the man's face, she knew he had to belong to society's elite. She didn't hang out in those circles.

"I don't remember ever seeing or meeting him before," she said honestly.

"That's Kragen. The man who had you kidnapped."

Sabrina picked up the picture again. The guy was younger than she'd first imagined he would be, maybe in his early to midforties, well-manicured black hair, piercing blue eyes. Handsome but in a cold untouchable way. She tossed the picture back on the table. "I have no idea why this man would want to abduct me and only have your word that he did. I don't mean to be ungrateful, but I've decided I want to go home while you settle your business with this guy. I have to be back to work on Monday."

Big Country's gave a derisive snort.

"I say something amusing?" she asked.

"Even if we let you go, you wouldn't be returning to work on Monday. And you'd probably be dead within the week."

Terry grabbed the remote and turned on the television. "We DVR'd this last night. Just about every local news station was running the story."

The bottom dropped out of Sabrina's stomach as she watched the news report on her abduction. The good part was Randy was not dead, hadn't even been injured. The bad part was he'd heard what had happened and had called the police. She would have been grateful if his vigilance hadn't resulted in exposing her to a world she had fought to stay hidden from.

"Every station is running this?"

"Local stations, mostly," Terry said.

Okay, maybe this won't be covered nationally, she thought. She was only a black woman of little importance. If not for the blood and destruction in her place, as well as Randy's bent toward the dramatic, this probably wouldn't have even registered beyond a police report. Maybe after today the local reporters would be on to bigger game. Maybe her face wouldn't be seen on television stations in Florida. Maybe Ernesto Diaz had become deaf and blind. He was already slightly dumb. Maybe he had stopped looking for her long ago, abandoned the drug trade, and returned to Cuba in defeated shame. Shit. That was a hell of a lot of maybes, and the way her luck was running, *maybe* she'd better prepare for the worst.

"I need to get back home."

"I believe you're a resourceful person, but that's not a good idea. The man after you has more resources, and he has already used them to get to you. You go home and he will take you, and you will never return to your home or your life again," Terry said.

"All we're asking is that you give us a little time," Almaya added. "Yes, we want to keep you safe, but we also want to take down Kragen permanently. Whether that's through exposure and jail, or death. His actions should earn him multiple death sentences. Death would be my preference."

"So this is personal for you?"

"In as much as justice is personal," Almaya said, pushing another folder toward Sabrina.

She didn't outwardly flinch when she opened it and saw the bodies. Mostly black and brown women. Bruised. Ligature marks around wrists, throats, ankles. No stabbing, no gunshot wounds she could see.

"Of course the physical similarities are evident in each victim, though they come from different socioeconomic backgrounds, different cultures – African, Afro-Caribbean, African American, all living in the US.

73

Some of the women have kids, some don't. Some have been married for years, and some are single. Some have large families, and some have no known relatives at all. We are aware of at least ten victims in the US, but Kragen travels internationally. The only common denominators are that all these women were raped and beaten, and they all resemble you, Sabrina. If I'm reluctant to let you leave my house, it's because I don't want you to end up another dead body in a photo."

"If he's done all this, why isn't he in jail?" Sabrina asked the question, but it was rhetorical. She knew the answer.

"Resources," Terry said.

"Translation: a heritage of money and power," Big Country said from his station. "With someone like this ol' boy, you have to come with a case already made before you can even get close enough to breathe hot air on the back of his neck. Even then, a conviction is a long shot."

"We've got a man inside the Consortium; the group of men and women bound by money, power, and this shared desire to prey on anyone considered a lesser being. Our inside guy was investigating a man Kragen is close to and became curious about Kragen," Terry said. "Relatively speaking, Kragen's not a big fish within the organization but the son of the big fish. If our operative wasn't such a cat, no one would have made the link. It's taken us almost eight months to get the little we have. Kragen is a bad man, Sabrina."

"And he's got you in his sights," Almaya said, collecting the photos and placing them back inside a manila folder. "You're right. It is wrong to keep you here against your will, even if it's for your own protection. It's still imprisonment. It was also wrong to drug you. I apologize."

"Why did he do that to them?" Sabrina asked. She had seen plenty of violence, death, but this was different. This had the putrid rot of something evil. Ernesto's cruelties didn't compare.

"There is no reason I could give that would justify what he's done. The why doesn't matter to me. All I care about is that he did it."

"You're sure it was him."

"I am."

Sabrina sat at the table. It was true; if this man was after her, she couldn't just go home and live life as normal. She had a gun and knew how to use it well, but she couldn't realistically return and pretend everything would work itself out. She would be checking over her shoulder every other minute, not trusting anyone – new faces or old – because she knew people could be paid off, and sometimes it didn't even have to be for a large amount of money. Sometimes all it took was a new car, a television, a fix. Sometimes just the assurance that the person wouldn't kill your family, and *voila*, sold out.

"As much as I hate to say this, if you want to leave, I won't stop you," Almaya said. "I will make sure you arrive at your place safely, maybe have – "

"Two reasons that's not going to happen," Zeus said behind her. She turned to see him leaning against the sill of the door-wall panel that led to the lower level. The man moved about as soundlessly as smoke. "One, she's mine. No one takes what's mine anywhere but me."

"And two?" Terry asked.

Zeus looked at Sabrina. She could see the obsessive desire lurking in his gaze. He was irritated with her; she knew this because the blade in his hand was doing acrobatics at an alarming speed. It was amazing his hand wasn't a bloody mess.

He wasn't going to part from her until his need had been satisfied. After that he would probably escort her to Kragen without hesitation or remorse.

"Two, he hasn't fucked me yet. That's what you were going to say, isn't it, Zeus?"

"Absolutely."

"You're an idiot."

"If you say so," he said, walking over to the table. He stopped and squatted, elbows on knees, close to her chair. "Don't be mad because I tell the truth. You know what I want. Give it to me and it's done."

"The man is like a broken record," Big Country muttered.

"I'm showing you all an indulgence. I usually don't have to repeat myself."

Sabrina turned, facing him head-on. She placed her hands on each side of his face and leaned toward him, pulling his face so close their noses nearly touched. "You keep bothering me about having sex with you, and I will take one of your blades and stab you in the throat."

He smiled that eerie smile as he leaned closer, pressing his lips to hers in a simple kiss that shouldn't have had her body fighting her for more. He pulled back, and she barely stopped herself from following. He knew she wanted him. "I'll let you have your way with my knives if you let me have my way with your body," he said coolly as if sitting at a negotiation table.

She sat back and removed her hands from his face. He was going to drive her as crazy as he was. He was literally going to make her lose her mind, and she needed her mind. She blinked and took a deep breath before facing Almaya. Zeus stood and hovered at her back like gold-colored demon wings.

"This guy Kragen wants me, right?"

"Yes."

"So why not give him what he wants."

Big Country rose and ambled toward the table, sitting down beside Terry. "He wants you, Sabrina." Big Country said the words as if she had gone simple.

"I know. That's all I've heard since I regained consciousness. If he wants me, take me home and he'll come for me."

"I don't understand. You'll let him beat, rape, and kill you, but you won't let me fuck you? Doesn't make sense," Zeus said, frowning down at her.

"He won't get me unless you all screw up. Don't screw up." She turned back to Almaya. "You want justice, and I can help you get it. When he comes back for me, as you all keep saying he will, you'll be there waiting. You take your justice, and I take my life back."

"No," Zeus said.

She didn't pay him any mind. She watched Almaya look from Terry to Big Country. She could almost hear the other woman's internal dialogue playing odds, weighing pros and cons, thinking logistics, factoring in contingency plans. Almaya's gaze became focused again, and she smiled at Sabrina with regret. "I'm going to side with Zeus on this. I appreciate the offer, but we pulled you out of that warehouse to keep you out of Kragen's hands. I can't willingly place you there again."

"You people don't seem to understand. I am going home. You can let me do it alone, or you can take advantage of an opportunity."

"How long will it take to bring the others back?" Terry asked Almaya.

"We can have Bride and Lynx back within the next couple of hours. Coen and Price, no later than midnight if they do a turn around," Big Country answered.

Almaya wasn't happy, but she nodded. "Call them back home, then."

"Tomorrow is Sunday. We can have Sabrina back in her apartment this evening with full surveillance," Terry said.

"What about the police?" Big Country asked.

"She goes to the police station. You'll tell them everything that happened up to the point of waking in the warehouse. From there you escaped when the kidnappers went outside still thinking you were unconscious. You passed out in the brush along the road, and when you regained consciousness, you made your way to the main road. A Good Samaritan came along and picked you up, and took you to OPD," Terry said.

"We keep Bride and the boys on her night and day," Almaya said, eyes brightening as she smiled at Terry. "When Kragen tries to have her snatched, we take down his men and turn them over to the police."

"In your report to the police, Sabrina, you say that when you were first kidnapped and pretending to be unconscious, you heard them talk about their boss coming for you. A man named Kragen." Terry added. "Maybe then we can leak information about the other women. Women who look like you kidnapped and turning up dead. We can help them draw the same conclusions our man on the inside arrived at."

"No," Zeus said again. They all waited to see what specifically he objected to, but he remained silent.

Sabrina narrowed her eyes as she looked up at him. "Yes," she said, ready to fight for Terry and Almaya's plan. It was reasonable, and she could make the story sound believable. But the logic of the plan isn't what Zeus has a problem with, she thought as she watched him. Zeus wasn't complicated. He wanted her, and he didn't want her being hurt; otherwise that would interfere with his ability to have her.

Changing tactics, she pushed aside her anger and softened her demeanor. "This won't work unless you play your part, Zeus."

"I won't."

Stubborn idiot.

"What part do you want him to play, Sabrina?" Terry asked, following the lead Zeus refused to take.

"My personal bodyguard? My savior? My boyfriend? Only Randy will know the last one is a lie. Zeus would stay with me in my studio, protect me from the inside. As crazy as it sounds, I believe he'll keep me safe from this Kragen or anyone else he might send."

Zeus stroked his jaw. "I get to stay with you?"

"At least until this whole thing is resolved."

His lips turned up in a kind of smug smirk-grin thing. He resembled both a devil and a god. Lord, what had she just committed herself to.

"Sounds like an excellent plan," Zeus stated.

Sabrina rolled her eyes. Of course it did. Now she'd just have to be on constant guard in her own home.

BASIR SAT ACROSS from Maxim, sipping Turkish coffee. The stuff resembles brown silt, Maxim thought as he watched the older man settle the demitasse cup on its saucer. It had been over two years since he'd seen Basir in person. Only eight years older than Maxim, Basir, even with the strands of gray in his hair, looked much younger than his age. He was vain and prideful, so he kept his body taut and slender, his hair well-groomed, his beard and mustache cropped short and meticulous. It all added to the illusion of agelessness. Basir liked to give the impression, to both enemies and allies, that he had been and would be around forever.

A member of the Consortium for over a decade and a half, Basir had managed the group's activities in the Bay from his estate on the outskirts of Union City, California. He was a traditional man, if one did not look beneath his claims of honoring family and faith. He regularly used his spiritually enlightened persona to manipulate his subordinates and those too ignorant to know better. Years before, Maxim had heard one of Basir's staff state that Basir was a "bad prophet," not because he was corrupt or violent, but because he drank alcohol and behaved in ways with women not condoned by their religious teachings. Of course the man who had spoken against Basir had died violently not long after uttering those words. The dead man's insight had reinforced Maxim's long-standing irreverence toward people who proclaimed themselves the mouthpiece of God. Once a man of influence in his native land of Algeria, Basir commanded the same respect, if not more, from the people within his South Bay community, as well as across many other religious faiths.

"Thank you for seeing me on such short notice," Maxim said. "I didn't want to show any disrespect by arriving to your area unannounced. As you may know, I was scheduled to attend the conference in London, but more urgent matters have called me here."

"Can I be of assistance?" Basir asked. Maxim had the distinct impression assistance was the last thing Basir wanted to offer him.

"Thank you for your graciousness, but this is a situation I must handle myself."

Basir nodded as if he understood. "It is good you attend to your responsibilities. It lets those around you know you are a man of worth."

Maxim bowed his head once in thanks. "I will be here on personal business for the next few days. While I am here, I may even organize a benefit in San Francisco."

"This is good," Basir said, hesitated, then asked, "Is it to be a Consortium-sponsored event?"

Maxim contrived a chuckle. "No. I don't have the luxury of indulging in such entertainments this trip, but I'm sure the men gathering in London are enjoying the privileges of membership as we speak."

"Yes," Basir agreed, contemplating Maxim with the cold-eyed regard of a snake in waiting.

Maxim returned the look with self-assurance. He couldn't be intimidated by a mere look. The idea that he could was absurd. Basir obviously didn't understand what it meant to be raised a Kragen.

"It's a mystery that you would not be at your father's side for this conference. There are many concerning matters he must face with the recent attacks on our holdings. I'm certain he is disappointed you are not there. A good son should stand by his father."

Maxim's father had never regarded him as a good son. Maxim certainly hadn't regarded him as a good father. That Basir considered it his duty to scold Maxim was interesting. Was it Basir's delusions of spiritual omnipotence that led him to believe they shared that kind of relationship?

"What I have found in this life is that a man must be his own man first. If not, he is destined to play the role of someone's boy forever," Maxim said, sinking deeper into the wing-backed chair, crossing his legs as he took a sip of the herbal tea that had been given to him. "How is Erani by the way? I thought to stop by and say hello to him while I'm in the Bay Area. Is he still in San Francisco?"

The reason Maxim didn't miss the slight tightening around Basir's eyes was because he had been watching for it. A direct hit, landed squarely at the heart of the other man's pride. One day Maxim would pay heed to Reed's advice and become less vindictive, but at moments like this it was nearly impossible. He was sure Reed would agree.

Basir motioned for the servant standing by the door. The man wore a top and pants of a fawn, linen-like material, with a head wrap to match. The wispy material moved fluidly around his body as he carried a tray of aperitifs toward them.

"So what business really brings the heir apparent of the Kragen empire to beautiful California?" Basir asked.

"My own." There was nothing gained by allowing the other man to believe he had the power or the right to question Maxim's actions.

Basir smiled slightly. "Ah. Your own." He stood. "Well, I wish you success in all you do here and thank you for paying your respects. Please let me know if I can offer assistance in any way. Lamentably I have another appointment scheduled."

Maxim stood, bowing slightly. "Thank you for your hospitality and for making the time to see me. If someone could escort me to a restroom, I will then be on my way."

Basir motioned for the servant, and Maxim followed him from the room and down two halls that led deeper into the home's interior. When they rounded a corner, Maxim stopped. "Can you please wait a moment? There is one bit of business I forgot to impart to your employer."

The servant nodded and stood against the wall to wait as Maxim walked back the way he had come. Nearing Basir's office, he heard voices – one Basir's and the other he wasn't able to identify. His father and a few other members of the Consortium were suspicious of Basir's failure to attend the meeting in London. Especially since one of the three establishments exposed had been within Basir's territory. There was a leak in the organization, and it wasn't beyond the realm of possibility that Basir would betray the Consortium if he believed his reasons just.

"...to have him monitored?"

"Yes, that is the order. It's not that I don't trust my young friend... just that I want to know what it is he does here..."

Maxim didn't wait to listen to the rest of the conversation. He walked back down the hall until he came upon the servant who didn't appear to have moved an inch from his post.

Maxim smiled at the attendant. "I was too late. I think his other appointment has arrived. I guess I'll have my assistant leave him a message this evening."

The servant proved to be less than interested. He led Maxim to the restroom and waved him inside.

Once outside, Maxim walked to the town car. Reed and Eddie leaned against it, talking low until they saw Maxim. Eddie walked around the front of the car, taking his position in the driver's seat as Reed held the door to the backseat open for Maxim. When they were all settled inside and driving down the horseshoe-shaped carport toward the main road, Reed turned to him. "Everything go okay?"

"It went as expected. That is, until I heard Basir give an order to have me followed."

"Sounds expected to me," Eddie said. "From what I hear, the Algerian is perpetually paranoid."

Maxim smiled. "Perpetually paranoid?"

"From what I hear." The driver shrugged.

Maxim wanted to laugh, the first time he'd had the urge since finding the empty truck and no Sabrina. His driver's humor was as dry as a desert stuck in summer.

"The teams made it to the Bay. I put them up at a house in San Mateo. We're headed there," Reed informed him.

"Good." He would have his prize back in no time. "Reed, we need to think about scheduling a benefit while we're in the Bay Area."

"A benefit?"

"Yes, I'm thinking maybe for missing persons or runaways." In honor of Sabrina. "It could negate some of the negative press linked to the Consortium with the recent raids."

"If nothing else, it could help distance the Kragen name from those corrupt members depraved enough to partake in criminal activities."

They shared a moment of laughter.

"In my abbreviated time in Basir's presence I realized how little cash-and-carry information I have on some of the members of the Consortium." Maxim tapped the window as he reflected. "In Basir's own words, 'the heir apparent to the Kragen empire' should know, beyond their awareness, the people he is working with. I want full financial, family, social, religious, and charitable contributions on all the higher-ups. And you can feel free to include any other information you deem pertinent to my understanding."

"Yes, sir."

"Also, find out why Basir is not at the conference in London." He faced forward. "Eddie, before we go meet the team, let's take a trip to the Mission District. I haven't seen my old friend Erani in many years."

Eddie cocked an eyebrow as he peered at Maxim from the rearview mirror, nodding.

"I'm surprised Basir didn't sanction some kind of honor killing against Erani once he came out as gay," Reed said.

"Never underestimate the power of a woman," Maxim said. "Basir's wife is extremely fond of her youngest son, and as powerful as Basir is, there are some battles that are impossible to win. What's happening with the photo?"

"It's clean. No prints, no DNA. Digital camera and digital printer. Beyond that, we just have the image taken."

"Reed," Maxim said as they drove over the Dumbarton Bridge. "I need you to provide me with a distraction until Sabrina arrives. You know what I'm looking for."

"Yes, sir," Reed said as he tapped on his tablet's surface, bringing up the database that identified locations of women in the Bay Area who resembled Sabrina. Maxim didn't presume to understand how Reed had discovered and organized the same information the world over, however, he greatly appreciated Reeds ingenuity and paid him well for it.

He'd made the right decision to come to California and retrieve Sabrina himself, Maxim thought. The weather in Union City was tropical despite the fact that it was the middle of winter. His woman had chosen well to move to the Bay Area. The apartment she lived in was just above common squalor, but the oceanfront house they would soon call home would suit her personality to perfection.

He grew hard as he thought of Sabrina and all the ways he would have her display her gratitude.

CHAPTER FOUR

She had good tits. Not perfect. They hung slightly lower than what he was used to dealing with, and showed a few faint stretch marks when she didn't have her bra on, but they were full, firm. Definitely not perfect, but they would be just right for him. He relived the memory of the weight of them in his palm, the puckered, raisin-colored nipple peaked in greedy arousal, the just-right shape and size for his lips to suck, for his teeth to graze, bite.

He watched her through the thin shower curtain, perched on the edge of the bed with a hard-on powerful enough to puncture six inches of steel plating. He growled low in his throat, a desperately feral sound to his own ears. She was killing him. Never mind that it was his idea to sit on her badly made bed and watch through the open bathroom door as she showered.

He was looking out for her. It *was* his new role. He didn't give a damn about the idiots upstairs who argued that he didn't need to protect her while she was in Almaya's house, that this new duty didn't commence until they left the mountain.

The job began once he accepted it. That's what he made them understand before he followed her back down to her temporary bedroom.

He watched her silhouette as she rubbed her hands over those made-for-him breasts, over her flat stomach, down to the juncture between her thighs. It wasn't until his chest burned that he remembered he had to breathe to stay alive. He gulped air then; he wouldn't miss a moment of this. He gripped his erection, massaged it. He'd jacked off more in the last few hours than he had in the last four years. He promised his dick here and now, once he got her to her apartment, it would be worshiped by the wetness of her core, her mouth. That was the only thing it deserved after displaying such extreme patience and restraint.

Sabrina chose that moment to bend over and lather soap onto her legs. He imagined himself behind her, hammering into her, one hand gripping her hip, controlling her position, and the other buried into her hair as he pulled her head back, the faucet above spurting water down over her face and head.

A strange sound he didn't even want to contemplate escaped his mouth. It wasn't a whimper because he hadn't emitted such a weak sound since he was a six-year-old, beaten to near unconscious by some older neighborhood boys. This was more of a plea, a groan of defeat. He picked up his fisted pace.

He watched Sabrina work her hands back and forth against her pussy, deeper, slower...

"Fuck this," he ground out, pulling his T-shirt over his head as he rose from the bed, fully prepared to work her over until every bit of tension was released within the heat of his cum.

Sabrina stood erect, stilled like a deer in the headlights, then whipped the shower curtain back as she peeked her head out to glare at him. His fingers danced. No blade. Her brown skin was radiant from the steam and heat and water. He needed to glide his hands over every inch of her skin as he fucked her.

"Don't even think about leaving that bed. If you do, I swear to God I'll convince Mama...I mean, Almaya, that it would be best to have someone else be my bodyguard."

He didn't care. He took a step.

"I swear I will."

His world was turning red. Too many needs, too strong, thought disintegrating into –

"Zeus," Sabrina called to him through the haze. "Do you have the black blade on you?"

It took him a moment to comprehend what she was asking him. He frowned. What kind of ridiculous question was that?

"Always have it," he said, knowing the sound of his voice wouldn't register as human to civilized ears. When the need hit strong, it was hard to remember he was a man, not a half-starved boy surviving whatever way he could, not a thing that had been made mostly animal.

"Tuck yourself back in, button up your jeans, and pull out your blade. I like the black one the best."

"Why do you want it out?"

"I want you to teach me how to use a blade like you do." She turned off the shower and reached for the towel. The same one he had used. He liked that she would be rubbing his scent into her skin. "You make using a knife look artistic. Like a dance. Plus, it'll help take the edge off, right? Control the compulsion?"

"Yes."

He zipped and buttoned his pants over his erection, and sat back on the bed, pulling the black blade from the sheath at the small of his back. He wasn't sure if she thought he was an idiot to be patronized and placated, or if she genuinely wanted him to teach her how to work a blade. Ultimately, he thought, twirling the blade in his hand, it doesn't matter. If she wanted to believe that she could manipulate him into behaving, he didn't mind letting her. Sooner or later she'd see not even God himself could make him move in a direction he wasn't willing to move in.

If she genuinely wanted to learn how to kill with a blade, he would train her. He was the best person to do it. He would teach her, she would learn, and in the end he would have her. The way she was fucking with his libido, it would definitely have to be more than once.

Sabrina stepped out of the bathtub with the sage-green towel wrapped around her. She walked to an area of the bathroom outside of the range of his vision, but he could hear her dressing.

"We have to get you your own blades," he called out. He could get her a Bowie or a push dagger, maybe a boot blade. Something that was a good size and weight for her. She liked his black dagger well enough. Maybe he'd get her one of her own. His heart did double-time. He had never contemplated getting a woman a blade before. It was like picking out the perfect diamond, the perfect wedding ring, but people got married all the time, got divorced just as often, so rings had lost their significance.

A good blade, though – he stroked the flat of his dagger – a good blade made your blood sing, like some enchanted treasure from a Grimm fairy tale. A good blade bonded with its owner, metal gleaming even brighter from the melding of human and metallic spirits.

He twirled the dagger through his fingers back and forth.

Pressure weighed on him. No buying a blade from a retailer. Maybe not even Dominic's, his go-to man when he didn't have time to forge his own, would do. Ultimately he'd have to create Sabrina some blades. The compulsion wouldn't allow him to give her anything less than her soul's reflection. He was sweating. It was a big deal making a blade for a woman, wasn't it? Yes, because he didn't do shit for women if he didn't have to, unless it involved sex. But even that was mostly for him. She'd better appreciate this shit. He was thinking of giving her gifts and she hadn't even had the grace to fuck him first. Trifling woman.

She stepped out of the bathroom, her moonstone pendant catching the light, appearing to wink at him seductively. She wore a wrecked pair of faded and frayed jeans, a pair of scraggly tennis shoes, and a short-sleeved, black Betty Boop T-shirt. On her, Bride's clothes were tight. Sabrina was at least two sizes larger.

"I have to get home soon. I can't breathe," she said, pulling at the inside seams of the jeans, then the waistband. "I swear I'm going on a diet when I get back home. Damn bacon."

"You stupid?"

At least the question stopped her from pulling on the clothing, trying to make space when there was none to be had.

"No. I am not stupid."

He stood up. "You made a stupid comment so I had to ask. Can't have stupid people messing around with my knives."

"So what? It's stupid for me to want to lose a few pounds?"

"Your body's fine. Don't go fucking it up."

She shifted into a wide-legged stance, her brows drawing together as her hands came to rest on her hips. She looked like she was ready to go to battle. He stilled the blade's motion, gripping the woven leather hilt. She tilted her head, looking at him like he was something that didn't make sense. Then she smiled, rattling his brain as effectively as a two-by-four to the temple.

"Why, Zeus...whatever your last name is. I do believe you just paid me a compliment."

"I don't have a last name, and I don't *do* compliments."

"Doesn't matter," she said, grabbing his hand and pulling him behind her as she left the room. "I'm going to pretend you just did."

They made their way up to the first level, Sabrina leading as if she'd stayed there for months instead of hours. And most of those hours she'd spent sleeping. She adapted to new places quickly. That was good because he moved around a lot. It would be hard living with someone who couldn't do the same. Not that he was going to be with her longer than the time it took to grab Kragen and cut his throat. If he had to move, it was best if she could do so on the fly and without complaint. The without-complaint part was critical.

"We gotta make a stop before I take you home," he said as they moved from the second level to the first.

She turned around and cocked her eyebrow at him instead of asking a question. He liked that.

"I need to take you to get some temporary blades to practice with. Don't have time to make you one."

"You're really going to teach me?"

"Said I would."

"Yeah, you also said you would help me make my bed."

He shrugged. "You didn't do what you needed to do to make that happen."

"Whatever."

"And who taught you how to make a bed, anyway? The sisters would have had you kneeling on rice for days if you had tried to pass that mess off as a made bed at the orphanage."

She tried to release his hand as they walked up the stairs, nearing the back door of the bar. He didn't know if he'd made her mad by criticizing her domestic inadequacies or if she didn't want the others to see them holding hands. He didn't think she realized how often she initiated touching him. Even in her sleep, she'd crawled on top of him as if she had a right to do so. He wouldn't let her release his hand. She sighed loudly.

"I don't care," he said, letting her know her sighs didn't have any sway over him.

When they entered the bar, the others cut short whatever disagreement they were having and looked from Sabrina to Zeus. Almaya scooted out of the booth she'd been sharing with Coen and Price, while Bride and Lynx sat at the bar with Terry and Big Country.

Almaya stood, waving at the two of them. "See, I told you. She and Zeus have become close."

"I wouldn't say close," Sabrina said even as she pressed against his side to hide their joined hands. "But we get along okay."

"Based on that, you're willing to condemn her to living with Zeus for some unknown length of time?" Coen asked Almaya.

"It was her idea," Almaya said.

Coen and Price looked at Sabrina, seeking confirmation. Zeus tightened his grip, just in case she got any ideas about swapping him out for Coen now that he was back.

"It was my idea," Sabrina said. "I trust Zeus to protect me."

Price scrubbed his hands back and forth over his face, leaning back to let his head fall on the top of the booth's poorly cushioned back. "Okay. All right. After hours of having to listen to Juarez's bullshit – "

"Then facing the women of his family, who clearly blamed us for his fucking stab wound." Coen glared at Zeus.

"I am too tired to argue good sense. If you all decide Zeus will stay with Sabrina, he stays." Price stood up. "I'm going downstairs to sleep for the next ten hours. I suggest no one disturb me."

"I still think she needs someone a little more levelheaded close by," Coen said after Price left the bar. "Someone else she can interact with face-to-face, as a go-between."

"Bride will do," Zeus said, volunteering the other woman.

Bride turned and looked at Zeus with cool contemplation before turning back around to face the bar.

"She should be the easiest to pass off," Sabrina said. "An old friend from out of town I called to support me through this difficult time or some shit. Randy sublets one of his two bedrooms to international university students on a regular basis. It's not rented, so Bride could stay there. It'd be easier than having one of the guys stay there. I wouldn't want to be put in the position of having to hurt one of them if they became offended when Randy made a pass. And he will. Randy likes muscle-bound pretty men. Not that I know your preferences. Randy's a good catch if you overlook his – "

"Bride can play backup," Coen said.

Sabrina shrugged.

Was that disappointment Zeus saw on her face? Had Coen just let her down in some way? Why did he feel like smiling and punching the man at the same time? Curious.

When the remaining details were worked through, Sabrina changed back into her bloody clothes and Zeus covered them by wrapping her in the trench coat he had hanging in his room. Within the hour, Big Country, Bride, and Lynx had packed into Big Country's surveillance van and made their way down the hill, Bride to join Zeus and Sabrina later at Sabrina's apartment.

Back on the main road Big Country turned left and drove about a mile to the garage where the Brood housed their cars when in residence. After securing Sabrina in the passenger seat, Zeus threw his duffel bag into the trunk of his steel-gray Challenger, hopped into the driver's seat, and steered his ride in the direction of the East Bay.

All was working out very fucking well, Zeus thought. Soon he'd be deeper into Sabrina's world, her life; then he'd be making his way into her bed and into her body. This was working out very fucking well, indeed.

CHAPTER FIVE

Sabrina opened her eyes to Zeus's profile and the landscape outside his window whizzing past. She had fallen asleep again when sleep was normally a commodity too hard for her to come by. It must have been a residual effect of the drug and the trauma her body had been dealt. What other reason could there have been for her having fallen asleep in Zeus's presence for a second time?

Observing him, under the guise of sleep, she wondered what it would be like if he wasn't a brutal killer who danced on the edge of madness. What if he was just a man, her man, driving her home after a weekend adventure? What if she wasn't who she was but one of those women who were able to find a relationship that didn't make her feel trapped? One that didn't hurt or cause her to feel ashamed?

Nope, the sad thing was, even with the way violence and indifference made Zeus's face mostly hard and unyielding, tempered his eyes into cold steel, shaped his interactions with others into inappropriate if not deranged experiences, she could see herself with someone like him. She'd always found herself with some similar variation. Since the age where she was finally old enough to choose who she wanted to be with, she'd never chosen well, never chosen anyone a woman right in the head would choose. Hell, a normal Zeus would be totally out of her league.

Sabrina slid her gaze over his body again, liking the way his jeans hugged those tree-trunk thighs and tight ass. Take away the crazy, three-quarters of the possessiveness, enhance his communication skills, and decrease his love for sticking people with sharp objects, and she wouldn't hesitate to have sex with him. She was barely hesitating as it was.

Once he was safely out of her life, she would pull up all his physical attributes, even keeping his golden skin when she preferred darker tones, give him an English accent like Idris Elba – whom both she and Randy were obsessed with – and she would have the perfect fantasy to get through the cold and lonely nights. She hated to admit it, but even with the sections of scarred skin covering his body, Zeus was the closest thing to a perfect physical specimen of man she'd ever had the pleasure of actually touching. Ernesto had been only slightly taller than she was, but he hadn't possessed any of Zeus's godlike presence. He'd been sleek and sexy, made up of hard wiry muscle and cold cruelty, but he could speak the sweetest, most believable words a young woman could ever hope to hear. When she had been younger and in need of safety and affection, Ernesto had provided it. For a while he had been a fantasy come true, until he became her worst nightmare.

The years had made her smarter. She might desire Zeus, she might even have sex with him, but when they had taken care of Kragen, he would be gone and she would have additional defensive skills to deal with Ernesto if he ever found her.

"You're looking at me again."

She jumped, blinked, forced her gaze from his lower body and back to his striking gray eyes.

"You were imagining having sex with me, weren't you?"

"No."

"Yes, you were. You don't have to be ashamed. I think about fucking you every time I look at you. Every time I smell you."

A sign flashed past, the reflective lettering snagging her attention. Sabrina sat up as they exited the freeway at San Pablo Dam Road.

"This is not the way to Oakland. Where are you taking me?" she asked, trying to stay calm. She had a bad feeling this wouldn't end well for her. She looked at the vehicles around them, and Big Country's van was nowhere to be seen.

"Detour. You need weapons to practice with. Maybe get you a boot knife and a dagger like mine. Something small and hard to recognize, like a punch blade maybe, and something to wear at your back and thigh." His response was more like an external expression of his internal dialogue than a conversation with her.

"You're kind of serious about this training thing," she said, turning so her back, instead of her shoulder and temple, was flush up against the seat. They were heading up San Pablo Dam Road toward the reservoir, away from the downtown area.

"Before I leave, you'll know how to cut to kill, how to incapacitate so you can run if you need to. No shame in running if you can't win."

She crossed her arms over her chest, a chill running through her. It was getting hard to imagine him not around. When he was near, he kept the cold away.

"I can't see you running from a fight," she said.

"And you won't. I'm not some woman too ignorant to know the difference between the tip and the hilt of a blade."

She knew the goddamn difference but hesitated to tell him so for fear of how he would react. She no longer had the rest of the Brood to step in if Zeus lost it, so she had to suppress the attitude just in case the big bastard didn't respond to her words well.

"So, that your first lesson of blade defense?" she asked. Despite her best efforts, she could still hear a hint of sarcasm.

"No, my first lesson is hold on to your fucking blade. Second, don't get stabbed with it. That could get you dead. And if you live...that will just leave you shamed and embarrassed. Hold on to your blade."

She was tempted to remind him he hadn't held on to his blade when he threw it into Juarez's shoulder, but she knew he would spout some bullshit about being bigger and more skilled than her or doing it because he knew his opponent wouldn't be able to come after him. Anyway, she knew how to defend herself, and his arrogance was rubbing her wrong. *Look at it this way: he's going to teach you how to protect yourself better.* In this world a woman had to know how to protect herself if she didn't want to wind up being someone's victim...or dead.

They made their way to a house on the outskirts of El Sobrante that looked like something that could be found in a destitute town in the backwoods – a large farmhouse with a wraparound porch. The closer they got the more clearly she could see how dilapidated the wood on the porch was, some planks curving up slightly instead of lying flat.

The yard was big but cluttered with broken toys – a rusty rocking horse with only flecks of red paint surviving the wear and tear of youth and exposure to the elements, an old swing set. A tire hung from a big tree whose leaves had already abandoned it for the weed-and-dirt-patched earth broken in many places by its thick, curved roots. There were smatterings of brown-yellow grass closer to the house, which suggested there was a time in the distant past when the yard had been lush and well cared for. Not like today. Luckily there was only one broken-down car parked in the yard. Not enough to mistake the place for an impound lot.

The house had probably been a bright yellow once, but currently it was a pale lifeless color dulled by time, dirt, and lack of care. She'd bet if someone gave it one good pressure wash, the water would strip not only dirt and layers of paint but would expose what was more than likely termite-infested wood beneath. All that said, she had lived in worse places and really didn't have room to judge. It wasn't all bad, anyway. The windows were clean, and the wispy curtains inside were a pristine cream lace. Actually, the incongruence made the place look even more derelict.

"Somebody lives here?" she asked as they got out of the car and walked closer to the porch.

Zeus's footing was sure; he didn't stumble over weeds, debris, or indentations in the earth like she did. "Dominic and his ex-wife K.C."

"So, what? Neither of them wanted to leave the house due to its sentimental value?"

Zeus looked at the house, then back at her, his expression blank.

"Okay, I'm being bitchy, but really, what's the story?"

He didn't answer, simply grabbed her arm and pulled her toward the side of the house, supporting her as they traversed more uneven ground. As they rounded the back of the house, she saw a second building. Zeus released her upper arm and walked ahead, banging on a large metal door three times when he reached the building.

The double metal doors were pulled open, and the man who stood in the opening was...huge. What. The. Hell.

"Zeus," the man she assumed was Dominic said with a welcoming smile. "Unexpected surprise, but it's good to see you, man."

A small woman leaned around him. She barely reached his chest, but she wasn't delicate in the least. She had thick wavy black hair pulled back in a green scrunchie, a lean, muscular frame with all its womanly curves, and large intelligent eyes. Sabrina would guess the woman was Pacific Islander, maybe Samoan or Fijian.

"Hey man, hey K.C.," Zeus said in greeting. "Dominic, I need some blades for my woman."

Both Dominic and K.C. balked at the comment. Sabrina had to admit that it even took her off guard.

Zeus shook his head. "She's temporary. But I'm gonna let her keep the blades."

His callous words didn't seem to decrease the interest in the couple's eyes as they looked at her.

"Uh...come in," Dominic said, taking a step back. "Come in."

As she entered the building, Sabrina was struck by intense heat, followed by the realization that this was a blacksmith's workshop. Unlike everything she had perceived about the place since pulling up the drive, the inside of the building was all well-kept order. On one wall an assortment of every bladed weapon you could imagine was displayed – axes, scythes, blades, swords, throwing stars... this had to be Zeus's version of heaven.

Dominic held out his hand to her in greeting, and she took it until he quickly let it fall back to his side. She turned in time to see Zeus shaking his head. Apparently his no-touching order extended beyond the people within Mama's House. She had no doubt that every person in the Brood was a killer skilled in offensive and defensive combat. With his size and apparent knowledge of blades she just knew Dominic could protect himself. Why they all just let Zeus have his way was a mystery to her.

Dominic was about seven feet, built like he was a mix of long-haired Viking bred with a polar bear. Where Zeus might look like a Greek god, Dominic looked like he might be a descendant of Thor. Arms and forearms were thick enough to pop your head from your neck if he squeezed you in a choke hold. With his sheer size and obvious knowledge of blades, one would think he would be less indulgent of Zeus's demands.

She couldn't stand by and allow Zeus to get away with dictating other people's behavior. She took a step forward, reached for Dominic's hand, and shook it. "Hello, Dominic. I'm Sabrina. Nice to meet you."

His gaze locked on to their joined hands and darted toward Zeus before he turned a bemused eye back to her. "I haven't crossed you, right? You're not trying to get me killed, huh?"

Sabrina glared at Zeus. "No, Mr. Dominic, I'm not trying to get you killed. I just want to show Zeus that he can't go around attempting to control other people, that it's not okay to be as rude as he wants." She turned back to Dominic. "There's no good that can come from letting him believe he doesn't have to abide within the rules of acceptable behavior. He already walks around acting like a god. People who allow him to have his way only encourage this behavior."

Dominic relaxed as humor replaced worry. He shook her hand before folding his arms across his massive chest. "You really went and got yourself a woman, eh, Zeus?"

"I'm not his woman."

"I'll be keeping her awhile either way," Zeus countered.

Sabrina shifted her gaze toward Dominic's ex-wife. "I'm not his woman," she repeated, hoping K.C. would show more understanding.

The other woman looked at her with an amusement as she stepped closer to Dominic and curved her arm around his waist. "Never in all the years that we've known Zeus has he ever brought a woman to meet us," K.C. said, her voice the stuff of leather and smoke.

"It's not as significant as you think. Zeus and I just met yesterday. He helped me out of a dangerous situation and feels obligated to teach me how to protect myself. He's just getting me some knives," she ended lamely.

The way K.C.'s arm went lax at her ex-husband's side, the way her eyes widened, the way Dominic's jaw fell open as if Sabrina had just spit a gold brick out her ass, made her wonder just how badly she had failed.

"What?" she asked, turning to look at Zeus.

He shrugged.

K.C., the first of the ex-husband–ex-wife duo to reanimate, stepped forward and hugged Sabrina like she was a long-lost relative. Ok, this was downright awkward. Sabrina felt like a hulking Amazon when held against the other woman.

"Hey, sister. I'm K.C., Dominic's sometimes wife and all-times partner in crime." She reached up and lightly touched the swelling and bruising on Sabrina's face. "I'm relieved this wasn't Zeus. For a minute I thought I'd have to send my brothers after him."

"Decision would have made you an only child," Zeus said.

"That's why I'm relieved." She smiled. "You get the guy?"

"It'll get done."

"Make it hurt," K.C. said.

She looked so sweet. But the tattoo sleeves on both arms and across her chest should have warned Sabrina that that wasn't the case. "Welcome to Heart of Steel, Sabrina. This is where we do the heavy lifting for our online business. Zeus is our silent-in-damn-near-every-way partner, while Dominic does the metalwork and I handle everything else."

"Which translates to, you run the business," Sabrina said.

"I *like* her, Zeus," K.C. said as she locked her arm through Sabrina's and guided her back toward the entrance. "Come on. Let me show you around the house while they talk bloodletting tools and techniques."

Sabrina strained her neck looking back at Zeus in a silent plea for help. She didn't want to go in the creepy house where some Leatherface mutation was sure to be lying in wait. Zeus – *the bastard* – nodded his consent. He'd kept her an arm's length away from the Brood, the very people who had saved her from Kragen's men, but he'd willingly let her be dragged into some dry-rotted doom of a house without blinking.

Sabrina faced forward, and with every step she took she knew it wasn't a fear of some fictional movie character that made panic take root and grow. It was the fear of offending or, even worse, of hurting K.C. by saying or doing something that betrayed her dislike of the other woman's home. She might not care about a lot of things, but she hated hurting people who were nothing but nice to her.

"So, of course, I'm about to get into your business," K.C. said to Sabrina before lobbing her first volley. "You may not know this, but Zeus is not the 'come to the rescue' sort, which makes me wonder what made him want to help you. How did you guys meet?"

"In a knife fight."

K.C. nodded and smiled. "Must have been love at first sight for him, then."

"Not even close."

"You're right. For Zeus it was probably something like bloodlust at first sight."

That definitely sounded more accurate.

"You've known each other a long time?" Sabrina asked. If K.C. could push up into her business, she most certainly had the right to do the same. Plus, the more they talked the slower they walked. Hopefully Zeus would call her back before she and K.C. reached the house's back porch.

"I met Zeus not long after I started dating Dominic, about seven years ago. I have four older brothers, all only slightly smaller than Dom and way meaner, so I don't flinch at much, but when I met Zeus...he scared the living shit out of me."

"He does have a way about him."

"I think it took him like a year to even speak to me. He would just... look. And he'd have some blade in his hand, twirling it about, watching me as if I was a moving target. Sometimes I thought he was imagining me strapped to a spinning wheel as he tossed blades at me while he was blindfolded."

"He probably was."

"I felt sick on the stomach whenever he came around, so Dom told him he was making me nervous. The next thing I know, me and Dom are watching a movie one night, and Zeus shows up out of the blue with a tub of popcorn. He hands it to me, sits down between me and Dom, and says, 'make him happy; you're safe. You leave; all bets are off.' After that, everything was less tense. I knew Dom was the man I wanted to spend the rest of my life with."

"Zeus said you were divorced."

"We are."

She wanted to ask why they divorced when they were still obviously together but was more curious about the role Zeus played in their lives. "Were you afraid Zeus would hurt you when you divorced?"

"It was a concern. He's mad unpredictable, but by that time I figured we had enough of a connection he wouldn't do anything. Plus, I wasn't in a place to care what Zeus was going to do. During that time I was so angry and confused I didn't care about very many things." She smiled conspiratorially and said, "I told Zeus to stay out of grown folks business and let Dom and I get through what we needed to go through to get back right again."

Sabrina wanted to know how two people who seemed to love each other got to the point of ending a marriage yet stayed in a committed relationship, but K.C. bounded up the three steps and opened the screen door. Sabrina only got a glimpse of the room as she trudged up the stairs. She remembered Samantha coaching her for years to be nice, to smile, to not make people angry. The first time the county tried to set up fost-adopt parents for them, Sabrina was about five and Sam seven. Sabrina had learned being difficult and defiant went a long way in destroying placements and eventually getting them sent back to their mother. She hoped to hell the control she'd developed at her sister's urging all those years ago would help her fake an appropriately pleasant response to K.C.'s home.

Sabrina plastered what she hoped was a convincing smile on her face as she stepped into a small room. The pretend smile faded away as she took in an office that was more stylish and functional than the one Sabrina worked in at her job.

"Out there," K.C. said, pointing to the Dominic's workshop, "that's Dom's home away from home, but this is my home within a home. This is where the rubber meets the road, baby."

"Wow," Sabrina said, looking around. "I thought it was going to be a dump in here."

K.C.'s expression turned bemused. "I believe you and Zeus have more in common than I first thought."

"We really don't. You have to admit, from the outside this place looks a little dilapidated."

"From the outside it looks a lot dilapidated. The exterior will be the final part of the renovations. If you had been here when we first moved, it would have been your worst nightmare."

She showed Sabrina around the house, and for the second time in as many days, Sabrina found herself in a place that had the feeling of comfort and care. K.C.'s style ran more toward the tropical forest browns and greens and wide spaces of her Pacific Islander heritage, yet both she and Almaya had succeeded in making the places they lived home.

"Come on. Let's get back out there before Zeus comes looking for you."

As they passed through the kitchen, K.C. pulled four bottles of water from the fridge, handing two to Sabrina. Inside the workshop, Zeus and Dom hovered over a lineup of blades on what appeared to be a thick limestone tabletop.

Zeus waved her over, and she gave him a bottle of water as he placed his hand against the small of her back, guiding her to the center of the table.

"This one or this one?" he asked, pointing at two blades that looked similar, but one looked more like Zeus's black dagger she liked so much, so she pointed to that one.

"Told him you would choose that one," Zeus said as Dom pushed a leather sheathing case toward them. Zeus handed it to her.

"Ok, choose between this one and this one," Dom directed her, pushing two more blades forward. These blades were double-edged and with some serration, but one, the one with prettier designs engraved into the flat of the blade, appeared to be more feminine. The other was the same blade without the ornamentation. She chose the basic one because she believed Zeus would think she'd choose the blade with the design.

When she chose, Dom cursed and Zeus smiled, which essentially was a slight muscle pull at the corner of one side of his mouth.

"She's contrary," Zeus told Dom. "She wouldn't want me to be right two times. I can read her." He picked up the adorned blade and handed it to her, Dom handing her the sheath at the same time.

"That's not the blade I chose," she said.

"No, but it's the one you like. Take it."

He placed the pretty, slender blade in her hand, and it irritated her, but she was woman enough to admit he was right. She did like this blade more.

"Okay, Sabrina, last one. You have to help me redeem my reputation here," Dom said, pointing to the last two blades.

These two were both considerably bigger than the previous choices, at half the length of her arm. Again the blades had a certain similarity, as if they belonged to the same blade family. One side of the blade was edged and the other side was flat, curving down into a wicked point as it approached the tip. The hilts were what really distinguished the two. One had an ornate red dragon design that was so beautifully crafted the only use she could imagine was mounting it on the wall for others to marvel over. She couldn't see getting blood on such a beautiful creation. She drew her finger over the intricate work.

"All hand done by me," Dom said, his chest puffing out. A long-haired blond rooster in their midst. She couldn't fault him for having pride in his craftsmanship, though.

"I can't believe you would sell something so valuable."

"For Zeus, anything."

"Well, luckily you won't have to part with it for my sake. I choose this one," she said, pointing to the other blade.

"Well, hell," Dom said, deflated.

"Sorry," she said. "Did I choose a blade you didn't design?"

"No, that one's mine too. Everything in here is mine – my creations, my forging, my designs. Hell." He pulled a worn brown wallet from his back pocket and peeled out three hundred dollar bills, handing them to Zeus while slanting a hangdog look over at K.C.

"How did you know I would pick that one?" Sabrina asked Zeus. She'd barely even glanced at the other blade, but she knew instantly it was the one she wanted. It wasn't as intricate as the dragon-carved blade, but she loved the vibrancy of stones that ran opposite each other down the hilt. The first pair were hematite; the ones below, in the middle, were a smoky quartz; and the ones below, closest to the blade, were iridescent moonstones, inlayed in what looked like a weaving of steel string. The moonstone made her think of the pendant hanging from her neck. Even though it was hidden, she never took it off. It was the last gift her sister gave her.

Zeus tilted his head, gazing down at her as if she were the greatest curiosity that ever existed. She resisted the impulse to reach out and stroke her thumb over the area between the corner of his eye and his temple.

"Most people don't look me in the eye. You don't ever flinch away from them." He shrugged and pocketed the money. "Figured you liked the color of my eyes, so I chose the closest thing I could to them without cutting my eyes out of their sockets and attaching them to that blade. When you hold it, you'll remember the part of me you like so much. Besides my dick."

"Holy shit, babe. I almost think this is worth our hard-earned money you just lost," K.C. said.

Sabrina could only stare at Zeus in response, too stunned to even blink, too unsettled by the fact that he was partially right. She did love his eyes. She had seen them change to each of the colors represented on the blade and more, but she hadn't recognized the link.

She stepped back, as if the motion could stop him from reading her.

"You're an idiot," she said. "I chose this one because...well, because I didn't want to see us mess up the other one during our practice."

"You're lying."

"Whatever, asshole."

"You guys want to stay for dinner? I'm making steak," K.C. interrupted.

"No," Zeus growled, eyes like flint.

"Sorry, K.C.," Sabrina said, happy to focus her gaze on the other woman. "We have to head back to Oakland. Zeus is taking me to the police station to report my kidnapping."

"*You're* the abducted chick," K.C. nearly shouted. "We saw the news story last night, Dominic. Not that they're saying it outright, but I think a lot of people believe you're already dead."

"I probably would be if I hadn't escaped, if Zeus hadn't found me, helped me."

"Been here too long," Zeus said, grabbing her arm and pulling her toward the exit. "I'll call before I head back out of town to let you know when I'll pick up the rest of my order," he said to Dominic.

"Gotcha. Sabrina, though you lost me three hundred in less than five minutes, it was a pleasure."

"We could have used the money for the front porch repairs," K.C. snapped, backhanding Dominic on the arm.

"Sorry."

"Sorry my ass," K.C. said as she waved good-bye to Sabrina. "Call me so we can get together for lunch sometime."

Sabrina waved back as Zeus dragged her toward his Charger.

CHAPTER SIX

She'd gone quiet again.

He glanced at her for maybe the ninth time since leaving Dominic's place. She'd been awake the whole drive, silently looking out the window and ignoring him. Usually he preferred silence, but he also craved the sound of her voice. He didn't like being denied something he wanted, but he wasn't going to coax her into talking. He probably wouldn't want to hear what she had to say, anyway. The only thing she'd said since leaving El Sobrante was "I appreciate the knives." They were about two miles from the Oakland Police Station, and he was feeling twitchy. It was a bad thing for him to feel this way before going into a police station. Cops got real uncomfortable with twitchy people. He tapped his thumb against the steering wheel.

Was she afraid, mad at him?

As a rule, he wouldn't ask. He knew a man should never ask a woman how she felt unless he wanted to go down a long, twisted road that led nowhere but was a pain in the ass to travel. He'd expected her to ask about K.C., Dominic, or the business. He'd been prepared to answer her questions only because he wanted her to feel more comfortable around him. When a woman felt comfortable, she was more likely to lay back and spread her legs with a smile. Show a woman people could like you, that you had lots of money and generosity, and they were ready to overlook all your sins and give you whatever you wanted. Usually. At the moment Sabrina wasn't giving him shit. It was as if he'd stopped existing in her world.

She shifted, adjusting her body to fully face the passenger door window, giving him more of her back. He parked near the Seventh Street police station and turned off the engine, though neither of them made an attempt to leave the car.

A few patrol cars pulled out of the lot as he and Sabrina sat there. People walked down the street, pressing to get wherever they were going while the hard-faced loved ones of the imprisoned left the police station displaying a mixture of emotions: anger, humor, fear, hopeless acceptance.

He turned to Sabrina and watched her finger trace a pattern over the window. His hands clenched and unclenched on the steering wheel. He didn't know what he was supposed to do. Didn't even know if she would want him to do anything.

"Stop growling," she mumbled.

It took a moment to realize she was talking to him, and another to realize his confusion and frustration had been translated into sound.

He stopped growling. "You ready for this?"

"We're not going to be able to wear our weapons inside the police station," she replied.

He snorted. He always kept a weapon on him. Whether anyone found them or not...

"I'll keep you safe."

"It's not that. I just really don't like police stations."

"Not much to like about them."

Her burst of laughter made his body relax a little more.

"Once, when I was a kid, my mother got arrested for stealing from a corner store in our old neighborhood. The police took me in the cop car with my mother so I could wait for CPS at the station. As bad as our neighborhood was, I remember thinking the station felt bad; it felt sick and insidious, like evil. At one point we're in the station and my mother leans over to me and says, 'I don't want you to ever come back here, Bree. Don't ever get taken to jail. Bad spirits live here, and they'll kill you for sure if you ever get locked up.' She was high, so I half listened to her. I always did when she was using. She died the day after she was released."

Zeus shifted, staring straight ahead. What was he supposed to say? Sorry? Tell her bad spirits didn't exist and kill people in jail? He didn't know that. And why would her mother lie? He swallowed and rubbed his hand over his face.

"Relax, big man. I'm not going to break down and lose it on you."

"Good. That's good. Don't know how I would've handled that."

She smiled at him, and his blood hummed. "Would you have stabbed me to shut me up?"

"Would that work?"

"I wouldn't suggest it."

"Only as a last resort, then," he said and followed through on his urge to reach out and run his thumb over rogue strands of her hair.

"I'm a mess, huh?"

"You look better than you did a few hours ago. You're only swollen and bruised. You're clean; you smell good, not bloody...."

"Okay, no more overwhelming me with your compliments," she said, rolling her eyes. She didn't pull away from his hand, which only made sense. His touch should have the power to pull her free from her sad memories because she was his for the moment.

"You ready?"

"I hate police stations," she said as she took off her moonstone necklace and placed it in the glove compartment before reaching for the door handle and exiting the car.

As they moved toward the station's glass doors, he pulled her into the crook of his arm, steadying her when she stumbled over the hem of the trench coat. They were taken to the Criminal Investigations Division without incident. Zeus asked for the detective working on Sabrina Samora's case; then they waited on cold, functional chairs. Zeus didn't hate police stations like Sabrina did. When he was young and inexperienced he'd had the privilege of bedding down in a few, both in France and in the States, but neither the police nor the houses they resided in held any fear for him. Cops were people with guns, authority, and handcuffs. He cared as much for them as he did for any other person, which wasn't much at all.

A black man, maybe six feet tall, in a gray suit, approached them. His shoes were expensive, not worn. His clothes and facial hair gave him the appearance of a competent professional. Sabrina's back straightened when she saw him coming.

"Bad spirit?" Zeus asked. He had to know if he was going to help her be safe.

She laughed out loud and relaxed against his side.

He'd made that happen. The feeling he got from taking her worry away and making her laugh was dangerous. That kind of pleasure could lead to a whole new compulsion, and he didn't need to be compelled by feelings for a female. He had his blades, the hunt, that was all he needed.

"I don't know how bad the detective's spirit is," Sabrina responded, "but his outside is good-looking enough."

Zeus examined the man again. There didn't seem to be anything special about him. Dark brown skin, closely shaven head, slim build... brown eyes that warmed with interest as they landed on Sabrina. Zeus's brow dipped into a frown. He definitely didn't like the manicured cop, bad spirit or not.

Standing, Zeus angled his body in front of Sabrina so she was only partially visible to the other man. He saw the detective's eyebrow rise. A man, being a man, would recognize when a claim had been made, and until Zeus determined she wasn't, Sabrina was his to claim.

Sabrina tried to see around him as the detective approached. "A dead man can't work your case," he muttered, loud enough for her to hear, clear enough for her to understand.

"It's just a simple observation; stop tripping," she said, standing up. "You can't kill a man because I think he's cute. Do you know how insane that sounds?"

He shrugged. Like he cared about how a thing sounded. "Either of you make a move to get to know each other better and you'll see just how crazy."

She rolled her eyes, but she didn't move away from him.

The cop held out his hand to Sabrina in greeting, and Zeus reached out and shook the detective's hand instead. The contact was brief, but Zeus put enough pressure on the man's hand, readjusting sinew just enough to drive his point home.

The cop turned back to Sabrina, all cool and professional. "Ms. Samora?"

Sabrina nodded.

"Good to see you're alive. I'm Detective Cassidy, the lead on your case." He looked Zeus up and down as if recording each detail directly into the computer's criminal database. "And you are?"

Zeus simply looked at the other man, listing all the ways he could fuck him up.

"This is Zeus. He picked me up from the side of the road after I escaped," Sabrina said, holding on to Zeus's hand with both of hers, her eyes tearing.

She was a better actress than he'd thought, which succeeded in stirring his wariness of her again.

"Will you both follow me please?"

They trailed behind until the detective waved Zeus ahead into a small interview room. Another man stopped in the hall beside Detective Cassidy. This cop was white and slightly out of shape, based on his rounded gut. His brown hair was disheveled, like he worried a lot and his hair paid the price, and his pale blue eyes already held speculation about Zeus and Sabrina.

"You think he's cute too?" Zeus muttered to Sabrina.

"Shut. Up," she said, gaze darting away from Detective Cassidy.

Zeus reached for Sabrina, but the white detective placed a hand at the small of her back, speaking low as he gently guided her down the hall.

"Detective Sedgwick is going to take Ms. Samora's statement. Forensic evidence is also going to need to be processed, so she'll likely be here for some time. While they're away, you mind if we talk a little bit?" Detective Cassidy asked. "You two seem awfully familiar for having only known each other a short time. I'm curious about the events that led you to come into contact with her."

Zeus vacillated between wanting to cut the cop and wanting to go after Sabrina, but he focused, remembering what they were there for.

"Zeus... What's your last name?" Detective Cassidy asked.

"Just Zeus. Like the god."

"And Mr. Zeus – "

"Just Zeus."

"Zeus, can you remember where you were when you discovered Ms. Samora?"

He gave a location a couple of miles from the warehouse.

"What business did you have on that stretch of road at that time?"

"My own."

The other man paused from his writing and gave Zeus a level look. He deduced the cop didn't like his answer. He smiled to himself, thinking this was the first time he'd used the word deduced in a sentence. This Sherlock Holmes bullshit interview was making him deduce things. "That's some funny shit."

He realized he'd spoken aloud when the detective methodically placed his pen on the table and sat back in his chair. "What's funny, Zeus?"

He shrugged. "I'm *deducing* things. I think in my next life I might try to be a detective."

"So what do you do in this life?"

"I'm an entrepreneur. Got a business making and selling blades."

The detective wrote the information down and bombarded him with other questions about his life, which he didn't expound on, questions about Sabrina, about Zeus's decision to pick her up and what they'd talked about during the drive. After over an hour, Zeus's interest in the interview waned. He stood up and walked the periphery of the room, eyeing the camera in the corner. "Room has video recording everything we say. Why are you taking so many notes?"

"Old habit," the detective said, scribbling on the notepad.

Zeus continued his stroll, stopping at the center of the wide mirror everyone knew was two-sided. He took in his reflection. He wasn't so bad. Sabrina should find him more appealing than the detective, but she'd never called him cute. Maybe she didn't like his fair skin, that his race was indistinguishable. He knew she didn't like how he spoke to people, but hell, he thought, facing the detective, that was as likely to change as the blood in his veins.

NOT LONG AFTER being separated from Zeus, Sabrina was relieved of her bloody clothing, photos were taken, her body prodded and manipulated as she complacently allowed them to treat her like evidence. She had never felt more like a victim than in those moments, not even when she'd lived in the midst of Ernesto's violence. There was something about exposing your vulnerability to others, allowing them to see and document how much you had suffered, that was so much worse than enduring it alone.

It was the process of reciting the story she had gone over again and again with the Brood and Mama that fortified her.

"No longer than five more minutes, Ms. Samora. I promise," Detective Sedgwick said.

At this point she had been at the station for hours. In the interview with the detective, he attempted to put her at ease, make her feel safe. He listened attentively and clarified her responses, never becoming combative or judgmental, and she appreciated that.

"So this guy, Kragen. You sure you don't know who they were referring to?"

She shook her head. "The only reason the name stuck with me was because of the way they referred to him. It sounded like the men who took me were simply following his orders."

"The crime scene unit has completed their investigation at your apartment, so there's no reason you can't go back home. You might want to get a service to do the cleaning first, though. The back part of your place is a mess," the detective said.

"I don't have money for a cleanup service, Detective. I'll clean it about as well," she said as they stood.

He walked beside her, escorting her back to the lobby. "Ms. Samora, I don't want to cause you more worry or alarm, but I have to suggest you find a safer place to stay until we get on top of this. As it stands, we don't know who's behind your abduction, and you going back home may provide them with another chance to make an attempt."

"It's okay. The guy who helped me, Zeus, said he's done bodyguard work before. He promised to look out for me while he's in town."

"That's awful Good Samaritan of him," Detective Sedgewick muttered.

Detective Cassidy, who had come in and out of her interview, joined them in the hallway. He thanked her for her patience and let her know that he and Detective Sedgwick would be in touch with her. In the lobby, Zeus paced, fingers moving rhythmically at his side. She stopped beside Zeus, feeling an overwhelming sense of relief at seeing him there. They had survived the experience without being jailed.

Detective Cassidy handed her two cards. "Give us a call if you remember anything, if you need anything."

Zeus took the card from Sabrina's fingers and put it in his back pocket. "I'll be the one calling if they make another move."

He reached for the small of her back and guided Sabrina to the exit as she was saying thank you.

"That was rude," she said.

The look he threw her clearly said that he didn't give a fuck. "I needed to get out of there before my bad spirits started misbehaving," he said, holding the car door open as she seated herself. Once he was back in the driver's seat, he leaned over and kissed her, then turned the ignition, revving the engine. Sabrina reached inside of the glove compartment and extracted the necklace her sister had given her, securing it around her neck again. It was the only thing she had left of her sister, and she wasn't about to let it be placed in evidence for who knew how long.

A glittery, green-apple-colored '69 Impala with oversize wheels and spinners cruised past with NWA spitting "Fuck the Police" loudly enough for people three blocks down to hear the refrain clearly. Zeus turned toward the police station as if waiting to see if any cops would give chase. When he looked back at Sabrina, she grinned.

"I hella love Oakland," she said, relaxing back into her seat as he pulled into the ongoing traffic, happy to have returned to her adopted hometown. "Turn left when you get to Broadway."

———————

CASSIDY WATCHED THE man and woman leave the station. Cal Sedgewick, his partner of three years, popped a piece of nicotine gum in his mouth, a sure sign he was feeling unsettled. Twenty years on the job and the only indicator of extreme nerves on Cal was when that tan square of gum made its way into the other man's mouth.

"That guy's not right. Something's off about him, Cassidy. Something that off – and he can't be found in the system – I'm thinking special ops maybe. And did you see the size of that fucking guy?" Cal waved his hand above his head. "Like he was cut from a two-hundred-year-old tree."

"He's just a man, Cal, despite his name."

"That's what you say," Cal said, fingering the gold cross beneath his shirt.

Except for his religious beliefs, Cal was the most pragmatic man you would ever want to meet. It had to be his Roman Catholic upbringing that led him to see angels and demons at every turn. If he was a good Baptist, like Cassidy, he wouldn't be so prone to spiritual hysteria.

"Let's just work from the premise that Zeus is a man. We didn't get a hit on him, but we can run the prints he left on the table. He seemed unnaturally attached to her," Cassidy said. "That kind of connection doesn't come from a few hours of contact."

"Let's include the name Kragen and 'big money' in our search," Cal said. "It just might be that this Zeus is the Kragen behind the kidnapping."

"So we find out all we can on Zeus, search for men named Kragen who have money – someone with enough cash to bankroll a kidnapping – and find out more about the lovely Ms. Sabrina Samora."

CHAPTER SEVEN

Her kitchen was a damned mess.

"Shit."

The dump of adrenaline into her bloodstream made her want to fight and run away at the same time. Zeus's arm reached around her from behind, and he pulled her up against him, muting the panic that clawed its way through her.

"Bree, you okay?" Randy asked, still standing on the path outside. She'd called him on the ride to her apartment both because Randy had a spare key to her place and because it was past time she let him know she was alive.

Sabrina waved Randy forward. "I'm good. It all just caught me off guard."

"I'm just glad you made it back safe. The impressive muscle you've returned with only makes it more pleasurable to have you home," he said, looking at Zeus with cool appreciation.

"Um hum," Sabrina uttered. If Zeus had appeared here without her, Randy would have gladly peeled her name off the mailbox and replaced it with Zeus's.

"I'm serious. I haven't been able to sleep since I called the cops – "

"It's only been a night."

"A night, a day, and almost another night. Waiting, pacing, worrying. Praying you came back safe. Not to wish another person harm, but I kept thinking, 'Why couldn't it have been the new guy in number four?'"

The "new guy" had lived in the building almost as long as Sabrina, but Randy didn't like him, so he was destined to remain the new guy until he moved out.

Sabrina bent down, collecting fractured bits of her Mardi Gras mug from the floor. She was surprised when Zeus assisted her and Randy in picking up fractured plates, glass fragments, and other broken and destroyed items, placing them in the thirteen-gallon metal garbage can.

Her small wooden table and two white-washed wooden chairs with wicker backs were broken beyond repair. They hadn't been expensive, but they had given her kitchen a homey, Southern feel. Dried blood – her blood – was smeared along so many surfaces of the kitchen it would be hard to feel comfortable eating in there.

Zeus hauled the broken pieces of wood to the small Dumpster on the side of the building while she ran enough water to fill the sink. She poured liquid detergent and bleach into the water and wiped down walls, countertops, and cabinets. In some places she was reduced to spraying straight bleach in a last-ditch effort to try and remove the stain of her blood.

"This is grim fucking work," Randy muttered as he swept the floor. As the eldest of five kids, in a household where both his parents had worked labor-intensive jobs, Randy knew how to clean and organize a home better than Martha Stewart. His tall, lean body corded with dense muscle, coupled with his urban style and dry wit, could deceive others into believing he wasn't a domestic slut, but she knew the truth.

Sabrina walked up behind him and leaned in, resting her head against his upper arm. "Thank you. On all fronts."

He leaned his head to the side and rested it upon hers. "I'm just sorry I wasn't here to help you."

She was glad he hadn't been. Randy, a mixed-martial arts fighter in his spare time, had three sisters, so he was naturally protective of women. She had no doubt her kidnappers would have fired on him first and never uttered a question or comment after.

"So..." Randy began. Zeus entered the kitchen and frowned at them before collecting more broken wood. Without speaking, he left to deposit the load in the Dumpster. "Tell me about tall, golden, and handsome."

"Well, he's not normal, not sane, and not housebroken," she offered.

"I bet he can fuck like nobody's business," Randy said in a low, contemplative way that let her know he'd already fantasized about the possibility. Sabrina thought back to the two of them in the bedroom at Mama's House. Yeah, she had no doubt he could.

"You demented angel," Randy said, grabbing her shoulders and holding her at arm's length. "You slept with him, didn't you?"

It was a sad commentary about her life that Randy's tone was more hopeful than accusatory. Since they'd become friends, he'd been obsessed with getting her laid. As if sex could heal all her life problems, when usually it was the thing that made them worse.

"No, Randy. The man is definitely not my lover."

"Yet. The man is not your lover yet. You know I'm the firstborn grandson of Ma Gibbs, so my predictions are not to be ignored."

She rolled her eyes. Being the firstborn grandson of Ma Gibbs, a Mississippi roots woman living in West Oakland for the last thirty years, was Randy's claim to clairvoyant fame.

"Maybe I've been going about this love thing the wrong way. Maybe all I have to do is get knocked over the head to meet the man of my dreams."

"More like nightmares, and I wouldn't recommend it," she said as she turned to see Zeus walk the garden path toward the door. His phone was pressed against his ear as he snarled something, then hung up.

"Who was that?"

"Terry wants to know where the situation stands with Bride."

Sabrina smiled apologetically at Randy, who narrowed his eyes and took a step back, pushing his plastic-framed glasses up the bridge of his nose. Between Zeus by the back door and her blocking the doorway that led from the kitchen to the hallway, he was trapped. "Why do I have a feeling this *won't* be good. And remember, I helped rescue you."

She walked toward him, wrapping her arms around his shoulders as she pulled him into a tight hug.

"It's that bad?" he asked.

"Yes," Zeus said at the same time she said, "You've handled worse."

"Could it at least end with him naked and me posing as your body double?"

"I guess."

"No," Zeus said.

Randy pulled away from her, his brown skin taut over his forehead as he leveled her with his stop-bullshitting-with-me look. "So what's my punishment for being your friend going to be this time?"

"First of all," she said, walking back over to the sink to drain the water, "I resent the implication that my friendship has caused you pain."

"It'll feel like a punishment," Zeus told Randy.

And when the hell did he become so chatty, she wondered as she sent him a stern look. "Think of it as a project, an extension of your desire to see me safe."

"And you'll get paid," Zeus added. "Well."

"So break it down," Randy said, looking reluctant but interested.

"As I told you, Zeus is here to protect me – "

"And do other things to her," Zeus said, rubbing a hand over his jaw as he ogled her breasts.

"Not going to happen."

He snorted and turned back to Randy. "Another member of the team will need to stay close."

"I kind of let it slip you have an extra room you rent out. You'll get a new temporary roommate, and I get the extra protection I need to end this as soon as possible."

"So. Your idea is to pull me deeper into danger by having me house some bodyguard for as long as it takes to capture some crazy guy bent on kidnapping you?"

"Yes, please."

"Is the person as rough-edged as this one?" he asked, waving a calloused hand toward Zeus.

"Maybe worse," she mumbled.

"Probably alcoholic. Hard-core killer, though, won't flinch if death comes knocking," Zeus added. Sabrina knew Zeus thought he was being helpful, but he really wasn't.

"You want me to allow a killer in *my home?*" Randy asked.

"Randy, since I've known you, you've had one cranked-out Russian student, one bipolar French guy, and one dude from Portugal who claimed to be a medium and spiritual savior who stiffed you on three month's rent. A killer for hire would be a step up from a lot of your renters."

"But they were all sexy as fuck."

"Bride is sexy," she said, not adding that the other woman was probably sexy to a Goth, BDSM crowd.

"She's like silent death," Zeus said. Because of course that would be what he thought was important.

"Not very social, but that's the part where you can work your magic," Sabrina said.

"Can drink anyone under the table."

She really wished Zeus would stop trying to help.

After two minutes of looking at them with wary eyes, Randy gave a short nod. "Okay, when does my new project arrive?"

"Within the hour," Zeus said as he sent a text message on his phone.

"Thank you, Randy. I owe you."

"Well, if this Bride guy is as sexy as you say he is, maybe it'll be worth it."

She frowned. "He? He's a she. Bride's a woman."

"Tranny?"

"Straight woman."

"Of course. Because that's just the kind of luck I seem to attract since bringing you into my life." He turned to Zeus. "You know she was only half-civilized when she moved in here. It took a lot of patience, medicinal marijuana, and abuse to my ego to create the two-thirds civilized creature standing before you."

"You're both odd," Zeus said, slipping past Sabrina and exiting the kitchen to make his way down the hall toward the front room.

"*You* are odd," Sabrina said to Randy once they were alone.

"No, you're odd."

"We need to get a TV in here," Zeus called out from the front room.

"I *have* a TV," she yelled back.

"No, you have a picture box," he muttered.

Randy looked at her in that superior I-told-you-so way. Every time movie night was at her apartment, he hassled her. She didn't even like watching television. The only reason she kept it was so she could watch DVDs.

"See, that attitude just stopped me from telling you something that would have had you quivering with pleasure," she informed Randy.

"Holy fuck. She doesn't even have cable," was the next statement from the other room.

She held a finger up at Randy. "Don't say *anything*."

"There won't be anything to say if you tell me your important information." He said it offhandedly, but she knew she had his interest.

She walked over and looked through her empty fridge.

"I gotta go shopping."

"That's not an important fact, Bree."

She closed the refrigerator door. "I'll go get burritos tonight and go shopping tomorrow."

"But here's the spoiler: if you buy the food, you have to cook the food. Not let it spoil or get freezer burn and then throw it away."

It was kind of a sad routine. It was even sadder that it had happened often enough to be appropriately labeled a routine.

"You do some communal cooking twice this week, and I'll buy the necessaries. Plus, I'll give you a hint about the secret. It has something to do with candy."

"I'm off sugar for at least the next two months."

"I didn't say sugar; I said candy."

"Sugarless candy is an evilness I don't have time for."

She rolled her eyes and let her head fall back in complete surrender. Why had she despaired over never seeing him again?

She frowned, squinting at her ceiling. There were dark speckles on her cream-colored kitchen ceiling. Damn. She'd have to get the stepladder and clean the ceiling too. Bringing her head forward, she looked Randy square in the eye and assumed her don't-push-me attitude. "Cook or remain ignorant. You have three seconds."

"Blackmail is illegal."

"Is that your final answer?"

"Cook."

"Smart man. Two words. Eye candy. There will be a lot of it around here soon. Almost-as-sexy-as-Zeus kind of eye candy, in all sorts of tantalizing tonalities."

Her words could have been a near impossible math equation, he contemplated them so hard. She knew he was jumping up and down and squealing like an excited pig on the inside.

"For me?"

"For you to look at."

"Flirt with?"

"As if you could stop yourself."

Zeus stomped into the kitchen, his jaw clenched in anger. He waved Randy in the direction of the door. "Leave," he ordered before grabbing Sabrina's hand and dragging her toward the same back door Randy was moving through.

"What is your problem?" she asked as she tried to pry herself free.

"Need to buy a television and get Big Country to come and install one of his special boxes so I can watch an actual station."

"A few days without television won't hurt you."

"Yeah, but I will end up hurting someone else. Is that how you want me to spend my time here?"

"You okay with one of those big electronic stores?" she asked.

He shrugged.

"Call me when you return with the groceries, Bree, and I'll come down and cook dinner." Randy had the devil in his eyes as he walked up the stairs that led to the second floor of the building.

Zeus's nostrils flared, and his jaw clenched down so hard she was sure his molars were turning to dust in his mouth. "We're not going grocery shopping."

"We are if you want to eat."

He grumbled something and walked away.

"Okay, I'll let you have him," Randy said from above. "His disturbance is a bit much. Even for me."

From the backyard Sabrina could hear Zeus on the street gunning his engine. It sounded like the hooves of a hundred Pegasuses thundering across the heavens.

"He's going to get me evicted from the neighborhood," she muttered.

"Probably," Randy called down from his perch halfway up the side stairs to his apartment. "Call me when you get back."

She hoped Randy was evicted right along with her. For consorting. They'd be homeless together, and that was better than being homeless alone.

On The Edge of Love

Walking toward the front of the building, Sabrina acknowledged she was going to have to manage Zeus better if this was going to work. Just keep him appeased, she thought. How hard can it be?

Opening the car door to Zeus's Charger, Sabrina slid into the passenger seat, prepared to ignore him as much as she could to keep her sanity.

"So... you think I'm sexy?"

"Stop being delusional," she said, but she did. She really, unhealthily, honestly did.

"Coward. Heard you tell Randy I was. Sexy?"

The curious sound in his voice made her smile. "Yes, unfortunately you are."

"Sexy?"

"Yes, Zeus. Sexy."

"You think sexy is better than cute?"

She couldn't believe he was still bothered by the fact that she'd called Detective Cassidy cute. And she wasn't a coward. "The only men I let into my body have to be sexy to *me*. Cute just isn't enough."

Let him obsess about that.

He sat motionless for almost a minute before reaching down and adjusting himself in his jeans.

"All right. I'll take you shopping"

As they drove along the freeway, she noticed he drove more erratically, speeding up and slowing down for no reason. Eventually he came to a stoplight and grunted.

"What?"

"Just wondering why a guy you claim not to know is working so hard to get you back."

Her heart rate increased. "What?"

"Two cars were parked near your building. One was OPD; they stayed when we left, but the other is following us." Zeus grabbed his cell phone, pressed two buttons, and hit Speaker.

"What's up?" Big Country said.

"I'm a mutant," Zeus said.

"As if that were ever in question." Big Country muttered something away from the receiver; then someone chuckled in the background.

"I've grown a tail. And cops are parked outside of Sabrina's place. Sweep it when you bring that magic box. And get Bride up to the Randy boy upstairs soon. May need protecting."

Randy would need protecting, because everything she cared about was in danger.

"It'll be taken care of. We might come close to neutering you, we'll be cutting tails so quickly."

Zeus hit the End button while Big Country laughed at his own lame joke.

<hr/>

EVEN THOUGH HE could feel Sabrina's agitation, Zeus took his time looking for what he wanted, partly because he didn't want a crap TV and partly because he wanted to put a face to the two guys tailing them.

"Why don't you just choose one already? We've been looking at TVs for the last forty minutes." She was putting him on edge.

He pointed to the forty-eight-inch flat screen. The clerk, who'd continuously glanced at Sabrina's battered face, nodded and walked away, as if he knew a fight was coming and didn't want to be close enough to be caught up in it.

Zeus navigated them toward the middle of the store and picked up a video game console and a handful of games. As they went to the checkout, Zeus got visual details of one man wearing faded jeans, a dark-blue tie, pale-green shirt, and dark-blue vest. He was a tall, thin white guy with white-blond hair who obviously didn't have a lot of experience staying hidden. His partner was better. If Zeus had only been using his training he wouldn't have picked him up, but Zeus knew himself to be an instinctual predator. He'd stalked and spotted the bulky black guy.

There is a hardened killer, Zeus thought as he tried to steer Sabrina out of the other man's range of vision. Sabrina must have had some kind of instinctual awareness because she tensed at his side when she looked in the direction of Kragen's killer.

"Think we can skip the grocery store?" he asked as the line meandered.

"Yeah. Do you eat Mexican food?"

"Pass through Mexico all the time," he said, pushing the cart forward. She threw him a perplexed look, then shook her head.

The clerk had the television waiting for them at the checkout station. Zeus paid. Sabrina mumbled something about men who refused to grow up as the cashier set the games and console in the cart with the television. As they walked to the car, Zeus determined Kragen's men weren't interested in taking Sabrina or confronting him. They were simply there to keep eyes on things. Report her moves to Kragen.

"Where do you live?" she asked when they were leaving Emeryville and headed back to Oakland.

"Lots of places. Got a place not far from here, maybe take you there sometime. If you don't like it, I got a place in France, a place in Guatemala, and a houseboat on the bayou down in Louisiana." Women were impressed with men who had property. If she was impressed, she'd be more enthusiastic about having sex with him. When she remained silent, he was forced to ask, "Which one do you want to see?"

She gave him one of those assessing glances. Like he was crazy or something.

"Uhh. I don't believe I'll be seeing any of them. But thanks for the invitation."

He rubbed his palms over his head. It was bullshit having to work so hard to get laid. "Most women find out I own a home and they're trying to move in within the week. You find out I've got lots of homes and you don't even want to visit. What's wrong with you?"

"I'm okay with where I live."

Her apartment was more suitable for raising chickens, it was so cooped up.

"Okay, I can get a place in Oakland," he said. He could make the sacrifice. He'd just have to make sure he found a spot where there was only limited contact with people.

"Why would you want to buy a house in Oakland?"

"So you can stay in it. When I come to town, I'll be at home instead of a guest at your place."

The way she worried her lip with her thumb, he believed she was considering it. Then she shrugged. "My place is good for me. Randy's there. My stuff, meager as it may be to your cultured sensibilities, is there. It's my home."

Goddamn it! He resisted strangling the steering wheel and instead imagined a blade dancing in front of him, just beyond the windshield. That helped him refrain from saying or doing anything antisocial. He would buy a place in Oakland, she would live in it, and whenever he came through town he would stop there and he would fuck her for as long as he liked; then he would move on. It was perfect...unless the sex was bad. Then the whole deal was scrapped.

Huhn. They needed to have sex soon to be sure.

"Zeus, did you ever think you were meant to do something different with your life?"

"No."

"You always knew you'd grow up to kill people?"

"No, but that's not what I am meant to do. I kill to survive or because I get paid to go into dangerous situations. Killing is what I need to do to get the job done, and I get paid damn good money for it. What I am *meant* to do is wield the blade. I've known since I picked up my first knife at three and nearly cut my hand off with it." He held out his hand so she could see the still-visible scar.

"For normal people that would have been a sign to stay away from knives," she said. "Don't you ever wonder what a regular kind of life would be like?"

"Do you?"

She turned to look out the window. "Before all this Kragen madness, my life was the closest thing to regular it's ever been. In the past all I needed was shelter and someone who said they cared for me. I had that with my last ex. But I also managed to allow in all the shit from my childhood I never wanted to exist again. Violence, shady people you couldn't trust always coming around, people using and selling drugs, irrational jealousy. Did I say violence?" she asked, looking over at him with a sardonic smile.

"Is he dead?"

"My ex-boyfriend?"

He nodded.

"To me he is."

"You were together in New Orleans?"

"Thank God, no. He was before New Orleans."

"What's his name?" he tried to ask the question carelessly, as if he were asking for the time.

She laughed. Her real laugh. The one that made his insides vibrate. "Do I look stupid enough to answer that question?"

He held up his hands and shrugged in an if-the-shoe-fits way.

"That's so wrong," she said before giving him directions to the Mexican restaurant.

CHAPTER EIGHT

The Pacific Coast home was made for nature lovers. Which, in all honesty, Maxim was not. The front of the house held the large living room, with windows that brought the surrounding trees and vegetation up to the very door. The floor-to-ceiling windows and French doors at the rear of the room led to a balcony that overlooked the ocean from at least thirty feet above. When he was here, he was forced to bear witness to Earth's exhibitionist nature.

The setting sun, a dying orb that no longer held the energy to fight off the mist rolling inland with ghostly vengeance, hung low on the horizon. Tumultuous waves crashed against the mountain of stone beneath the home, sounding as if a battle for was dominance was taking place.

Despite the setting, this house was his haven. As open as it was to the world, it had hidden depths, places where shadows swallowed screams and tears, where blood never stained reality, where humanity was merely a notion. Yet, despite the temptations inherent in the unseen places of his home, *he* never became a monster driven by them. Just the opposite really. He made it his mission to treat all his guests with the utmost care and regard.

Footsteps approached from behind. He glanced over his shoulder to see Reed step up beside him, handing his cell phone to Maxim as he also took in the ocean's violence.

"There's news," Reed said.

Lifting the phone to his ear, Maxim felt a flush spread over his skin so intensely it bordered on sexual. He pulled the belt of his robe tighter around his waist as he cradled the phone between his ear and shoulder.

"Do you have her?" he asked, because really it was all that mattered. The woman waiting for him below could be nothing more than what she was, a release, a distraction. His life would only have its balance when Sabrina was nestled safely in his arms.

The delay in response let him know he was not going to get the reply he desired. Again. "Speak."

"She's got protection," Eddie said. "We can get her, but it may cause more noise than we want. She's got this big fucking guy leading her around like a rag doll. Won't let her out of his sight. And whoever he is, wherever she found him, he has the smell of a professional."

"Do you think he's the one who left the photo?"

"I wouldn't bet on it. He doesn't seem the type to taunt. Looks humorless. I'll upload a few pics, and maybe Reed will be able to identify him."

"Do you think he can be paid off?"

There was a pause. "All things are possible," Eddie said. "But anyone who approaches better be ready to battle. If you want me to, Boss, I'm ready."

Maxim tempered his rage. This man, this bodyguard had the unfortunate idea he could keep Sabrina away from him? Maxim would not allow *any* man to interfere with what lay between he and Sabrina.

"No negotiation, Eddie. Get rid of him."

"Will do, Boss."

There was another pregnant pause.

"What?" Maxim snapped.

A frustrated hiss of breath met his question. "This chick is hot – and I don't mean looks. She's got cops squatting out in front of her house, and they ain't slackers. They seem to accept the big guy's place at the woman's side. Could be he's her man, and we just didn't – "

"He's not her man."

"Course not. But I'm just saying, the way he touches her don't fall in the realm of what's professional. The cops haven't questioned him or approached him since they got here. Makes me think they've already checked him out, accepted his place in the woman's life, professional or not."

The woman's name is Sabrina, he wanted to correct. His. His only pure thing in this world, who was to be respected and worshipped as avidly as any goddess. Yet some ham-fisted thug thought he could interfere with what they had created. She was his. Meant solely for him. Now that he'd found her, Maxim would dedicate every moment to letting Sabrina know she was his as much as he was hers. He would let the world know.

"Has a police report been filed?" he asked Reed.

"More than likely. Our guy at OPD is off today. I put a call in to him. He'll be on shift first thing in the morning and give us what he knows as soon as possible."

"Eddie," Maxim said, feeling impatient. He needed to go downstairs soon. "Continue to watch, observe, and when the opportunity is right, take her. You get a bonus if you go through the guard to do so." He inhaled and counted backward from twenty. It was his burden to contain the emotions that sprang up when he imagined another man touching Sabrina, stroking her, fucking her.

It wasn't rational, was probably even more foolish, but *he* wanted to do it, be the one to torture the bodyguard, make him realize and repent his mistake on broken knees as he begged Maxim to take his life.

The image tempered Maxim's anger. "Eddie, new deal. I'll give your men a bonus if they have to put him down and a bonus times three if they are able to subdue him and save him for me to take care of. I want you to do what you need to do to keep the police busy."

"Bonus times three?" Eddie asked.

"Times three."

"We'll get it taken care of, Boss."

"I have faith you will," Maxim said before disconnecting.

"You plan to bring the bodyguard here," Reed noted. "I must ask – "

"I know it's an impulsive decision, but he touched her. That can't go without punishment. He needs to learn a lesson before dying. Never touch my woman and think you can survive."

"You do realize – "

"I do."

Reed nodded and slipped the cell phone Maxim returned to him back into his pocket. Walking across the sparsely furnished living room, Reed sat at the sturdy cherrywood table in the dining room. Maxim walked up as Reed laid his tablet on the table. Reed pulled up the photos Eddie had sent over.

"That's the guard?"

"Yes, sir."

Not one to be impressed with another man's physical presentation, Maxim could appreciate qualities in this one. Of indeterminate racial origin, the male in the picture had cold metal-gray eyes and an inflexible jawline. He was large, taller than Eddie, but where Eddie's muscles were bulky, this man's were thick and tight. He had a menacing, predatory look about him. If circumstances had been different, Maxim wouldn't have hesitated in hiring Sabrina's guardian for his special team, just for the intimidation factor alone. Circumstances being what they were, however, demanded the man's death.

The next photo to dominate the screen made his heart fumble around in his chest. It was Sabrina, badly bruised, beautiful, and nestled in the false safety of the big man's arm.

Maxim walked away from the table. He would not put his fist through Reed's beloved tablet. He would put it in the woman waiting for him in his basement bedroom. From experience he knew she would scream with release and pleasure.

Stepping through the hidden passageway that led down the stairs, he unknotted the belt of his gray silk robe and let it slide off his body as he made his way down the hall to the bedroom. He was already hard with anticipation when he unbolted the door and opened it to find the woman bolted to the wall, conscious and in sore need of his attentions if her body, trembling with desire, was any indication. She was not nearly as bruised as Sabrina had been in the photo, but if she was to be Sabrina's temporary stand-in, he would have to make do. The substitutes loved his rough treatment. Always, they enjoyed the violence and the pain, liked the way it increased the intensity of their fucking.

He walked to her and unchained her from the wall before walking to the bed and laying her upon it, face forward.

"Please don't hurt me again. I'll do whatever you want," she whispered.

Maxim's fingers skimmed the mocha-brown skin from the back of her ankles, up her calves and thighs, and rested as they cupped the mound of her rounded ass. He stroked and kneaded until he could feel her trembles of desire increase. He loved how she allowed him to worship her body. His dick compelled him to take her from behind. He climbed onto the bed and straddled her, the tip of his dick pressing slightly against the seam of her ass. She trembled more violently and sobbed.

"Soon," he promised, finding he liked her in this position.

Reed had done well.

SABRINA AND RANDY watched in dazed disbelief as Zeus and Bride ate with silent determination. They fed with the kind of rapt focus of people who'd been starved most of their lives, yet she had witnessed Zeus eat the very large meal Mama had provided this morning.

Randy, who shared the futon with her while Zeus and Bride sat on the floor in front of the table they were eating on, leaned over and whispered, "Bree, I'm not sure it's safe to reach for my food. Will you pass it to me?"

Sabrina knew Randy wasn't a coward, nor was he one to run from a fight. She frowned at him and shook her head. She was only halfway certain Zeus wouldn't bite her hand off, but with Bride she was far less so. Zeus growled when Randy reached for his still-untouched beer.

Hell no, she thought, folding her hands on her thighs. She definitely wasn't hazarding a limb for Mexican food she could go right down the street for, even if her small living room table was full of food. Zeus had told her to order everything *she* liked, and with the way he had eaten earlier, she hadn't limited herself. There were only four of them, but she'd ordered four super steak burritos, two super carnitas burritos, each the thickness and nearly the length of her forearm. She'd asked for two orders of chicken quesadillas, two enchilada orders, a large serving of pico de gallo, two orders of homemade tortillas, and just in case, chips and guacamole.

Zeus and Bride had already consumed a third of the food, and she and Randy were too intimidated to nibble on the broken piece of tortilla chip that had fallen near their feet.

Damn, Sabrina thought as she watched Bride. How could someone so tiny eat so much?

"I'm getting hungry," Randy whispered to her.

She nodded toward the food, indicating he should be brave. Eat.

He shook his head. "You first."

This was ridiculous. It wasn't like they were trying to steal food from a starving pack of wolves.

Yet it was.

What was the safest way to get food from a starving wolf?

A bitch has to make nice with the alpha, she thought.

Sabrina slid from the futon and crawled until she sat on her knees at Zeus's right. Bride was on his left. Sabrina looked over at Randy, and he nodded at her encouragingly. She leaned into Zeus's upper arm and rested her temple close to his shoulder. Zeus froze for an instant, watching her out of the corner of his eye.

"Hey, Zeus. What does a girl have to do to eat a meal at her own table?"

He didn't hesitate as he placed a salsa-dipped chip in his mouth and mumbled, "Kiss me."

Her stomach growled. She rose on her knees and kissed him on the cheek.

He snorted and pick up another steak burrito, peeling back the foil. Was he really not going to allow them to share in their dinner? "Okay. I promise to give you a proper kiss good night when our company leaves."

Zeus looked over at Bride, who shrugged with indifference.

"What do you want?" he asked as he picked up a plate and loaded it with the items she indicated until Bride held her fork perilously close to his Adam's apple.

"Touch the quesadilla and I will hurt you both."

Randy chose that moment to fill his plate, smartly avoiding said quesadilla. When his plate was filled with food, and after he'd dug in, he turned to Sabrina. "And exactly how long do I have to have the emo chick cooped up in my place?" he asked, brave now that he was sitting out of Bride's reach with a plateful of food settled on his lap.

She shrugged. Hopefully they'd have them out sooner than later.

Zeus held a piece of burrito close to Sabrina's mouth, and she bit. She moaned as the cholesterol-laden goodness filled her mouth. She tried to steer Zeus to the enchilada next, but she was forced to grab her plate when he ignored her to feed himself.

"Well..." Randy said after a while. "Isn't this cozy?"

What it was was tight. Zeus alone seemed to take up half the space in her living room. Add three other bodies and it was almost too cramped to breathe.

"We haven't had a party like this since you moved in, Bree. I think you were past due."

Bride looked at Zeus and pointed a forkful of quesadilla at Randy before eating it.

Zeus nodded at her. "Duct tape works," he muttered, low.

Randy raised an eyebrow at Sabrina as if to say, *What the hell's wrong with your boy?*

"Duct tape works for what, Zeus?" Sabrina asked.

"He talks too much," Zeus clarified. "That's my solution."

Sabrina looked from Zeus to Bride. "You two are guests in our homes."

"And I don't talk too much, bitches," Randy said. "I conversate. Learn the skill."

"I'd rather use my eyeballs as pincushions," Bride mumbled around a mouthful of food.

"Don't worry," Randy said to Sabrina. "By the time she leaves here she'll be saying 'please' and 'thank you' and speaking in full, grammatically correct sentences."

Sabrina silently wished her friend luck because Bride seemed to have more disdain for human interaction than Zeus. But if anyone could wear down a person's defenses, it was Randy. He had a way of breaking through walls, sandblasting them with the force of his unwavering attention until he created a space big enough for him to crawl inside and eventually pull you out. Grateful for him choosing to be in her life, she leaned over and kissed his food-puffed cheek.

He tsk-tsked. "Don't thank me just yet. That one is going to be a piece of work. I make no guarantees; I can only work the strongest magic in my bag and pray it works."

"You try working anything on me, pretty boy, and I'll knock you unconscious and tat and pierce your body as I see fit."

Randy smiled that demon-possessed, Cheshire cat smile.

"She's workable. At first I thought she was kinda slow, but with a bad attitude and weapons. But now..." He waggled his eyebrows.

At least Sabrina had the distance of a whole floor and locked doors to protect her from Randy's mothering. With Bride staying in his home, things could turn tragic.

Sabrina shifted her gaze to Zeus when he mumbled something while focusing on eviscerating a second burrito down the middle. His gaze glinted at Bride as he lifted the knife from the abdomen of the crammed-together ingredients. "I can make him disappear," he told Bride. "Permanently."

Sabrina felt a spike of fear and protectiveness for her best friend.

"Day I can't handle some normal, you got permission to disappear *me*. Permanently."

Zeus nodded, his gaze taking on a faraway look as if he imagined that in Bride's words he'd been gifted with a double-sided blade that allowed him to stab Bride with the right side and Randy with the left, and never the two blood flows would meet.

"No disappearing anybody," Sabrina said. As if she had any influence over him. "No killing."

"There's always killing. Thou shall not be the one being killed. That's a commandment I live by."

After about twenty minutes of them eating in near silence, Zeus took the remains of the meal from the table and walked toward the kitchen. Sabrina and Randy settled back on the futon in their usual spots and quietly debated over which DVD they would watch.

Zeus returned and waved a hand at Randy and Bride. "Get out."

Bride stood while Randy crossed his arms over his chest and pulled his legs into lotus position, looking up at Zeus like a defiant mystic.

Zeus's face became blanker. His fingers tapped a quick rhythm against his thigh.

"Uhm, Randy, it has been a long day for us. Let's let Zeus get some rest, and I'll see you in the morning," Sabrina said.

"He's ruining movie night," Randy said as he unfolded his body and stood, following Bride to the front door. He paused to kiss Sabrina on the forehead and whisper, "Don't give him none, Bree. We'll never get rid of him then, and I can't have him hanging around messing up our groove."

"Don't worry. I'm not giving up anything but a space on my futon."

"Good girl," he praised as he left the apartment.

After locking the door, Sabrina turned to see Zeus standing behind her. His hand wasn't empty anymore. His fingers were engaged in a rapid dance with a blade she was coming to recognize as one of his favorites. "You promised me a kiss."

"Calm down. You'll get your kiss." The pace of his fingers slowed. "I was just trying to get through the night without bloodshed."

He gripped the blade and stared at her for over a minute before he blinked and re-sheathed it behind him.

"Go take a shower. I'll get the futon ready."

"You should come with me."

She squelched the image of them soaping each other's bodies in the shower. "Don't think so," she mumbled, turning to the basket next to the arm of the futon. She pulled out the bed linen, regretting that she only had the limited space of a studio. "Towels are in the upper closet," she said as she avoided looking at him.

Her heart was beating rapidly in her chest at the idea of sleeping with him. As she let out the futon, she realized Zeus's body was possibly longer than her mattress. He'd either have to sleep with his feet dangling over the bottom, or he'd have to draw his legs up.

The image of him spooned behind her, large hand reaching over to her front, stroking her breasts, abdomen...lower. She groaned in frustration as she snapped the sheet out over the mattress.

By the time she was finished, he walked into the room wearing only a pair of white boxers. She quickly averted her gaze from his body and slipped silently past him as she went to take her shower, hoping she could wash away all the indecent thoughts and images of him playing through her mind.

The warm spray of water only intensified the responsiveness of her body. She hung around the bathroom well beyond the time it took to shower, groom herself, and put on her nightshirt. She had to achieve a sense of calm before she dealt with Zeus; otherwise there was no hope.

Walking back into the living room, she realized what a fool she'd been to waste time fretting over how she would deal with the sexual energy between them. Zeus was propped up on all three pillows with an arm behind his head watching a rugby match. While she had been in the bathroom agonizing over what could happen between them during the night, he had assembled the flat-screen television, placed it on her wall, hooked up the illegal cable box, and forgot she existed.

I am an idiot, she thought as she turned out the hallway light and crawled onto the mattress, snatching one of the pillows from behind Zeus's fat head. She settled on her side with her back to him and closed her eyes, refusing to acknowledge her disappointment.

Not sure if it was Zeus's calm silence, the drone of the television, the weight of the day's events, or a combination of the three, she found herself lazily sinking into the world of sleep. It wasn't until she felt her body being pulled from her side to her back that she realized how deeply she had fallen asleep. She opened her eyes to find all the lights turned off and only the faint light from the side window filtering into the room, creating shadowed spaces in the dark.

Zeus's body shifted on top of hers, his forearms planted near each shoulder as he held his face only inches from hers. His warm, mint-tinged breath fanned across her right cheek as he inhaled and exhaled rhythmically. Sabrina reached up and stroked her thumb from his jawline to the fierce cut of his cheekbone. His gray eyes gleamed freakishly, almost iridescently, in the dark of the room.

"I want my kiss," he said.

She lifted her head and pressed her lips to his once, twice, three times in precious touch and retreat. The gentleness of the encounter ended quickly as Zeus lowered his head and pressed hers deep into the pillow as his kiss devoured her. He shifted against her, forcing her legs wide and sinking his lower body into the space between. He molded her trembling inner thighs against his outer thighs. It was both the wrong spot for him to be in and the perfect spot for him to be in, as the length of his hard flesh, separated from her only by her thin cotton panties, stroked against her clit. Sabrina groaned and spread her legs wider. They ground into each other with a desperate need that couldn't be satisfied with anything less than him burying himself deep inside her over and over again.

Zeus grabbed her nightshirt and pulled it up and off her body in a single motion. Cool air caressed the heat between her legs as his lower body retreated from hers. Her panties were pulled from her body so roughly she feared she'd have friction burns running down her legs in the morning. Zeus shifted his weight and lowered himself back down, the length and width of his thick penis hot against the wetness pooling between her legs.

Zeus's mouth tasted hers, then moved to the hollow beneath her ear and down the side of her neck in a mixture of kisses, licks, and bites until he found the bud of her nipple. He sucked at her nipple, hand squeezing it so hard it was nearly painful. Sabrina cried out from the intense pleasure running from her breast to her core. She pressed him more deeply against her folds as he sucked harder. Zeus grunted as he fed from her in desperation. Need spasmed through her womb when his mouth found her other nipple as his thumb played in the wetness he'd created on the other one. Her body convulsed in mini orgasms.

Zeus's head dipped lower down her body, creating a hailstorm of anticipation. *Please God, let him do it. Pleeease God.* Zeus paused at the crescent-shaped rod of metal in her navel. She thought she would scream in frustration, but then his tongue played with the belly ring. His lapping and tugging placated some of yearning, lulled her senses, accustomed her body to the feel of his mouth. The tip of his tongue burrowed deep into her belly button, as if this were a way to reach the cradle of liquid pooling in her womb, catching it before it trickled down the swollen passage of her vagina.

Sabrina undulated her hips, skimmed her hands over his head. She couldn't believe any part of this man could be so soft, but his hair was like down.

Zeus's hands gripped her hips, controlling them to stillness. His shoulders spread her legs wider, and he went still again, his face only inches away from the place where she was weeping for attention. She tried to guide his head into her center, but his neck was strong; his head wouldn't move. The bastard chuckled, and she knew for sure he was a demon sent to torment her.

Sabrina tried to take what control she could and arched her pussy toward his waiting mouth, only to have him force her hips back into the mattress.

Zeus blew a cool stream of air against her clit, and her eyes teared.

"Please," she whispered, pathetic and weak in the grip of demanding need. "Please, Zeus."

His tongue lightly stroked the tip of her protruding clit, and her hips bucked within his grip. Breaking free from his own chains of restraint, Zeus growled, spread her legs wider, and pushed his tongue into her trembling flesh over and over, fucking her with tongue and fingers as ferociously as he had latched on to her nipple.

She arched her head back, her ragged screams filling the room as he took control of her body and fucked her with his mouth as effectively as any man had fucked her with his dick.

Sabrina felt hot tears trickle into her ears. Zeus did just enough to get her to the edge but not enough to send her over. He chuckled again, and she groaned in frustration. He was playing with her. He knew she wanted release more than she wanted her next breath. She was on the verge of wrapping her legs around his head and putting him in the most intimate form of a headlock when he lowered his head and gave her exactly what she needed but was too far gone to verbalize. God, his fucking mouth was amazing. He fed and sucked and licked and filled her with fingers pressed deep into her with no gentleness, only domination.

She lost what little sense she had as she came in waves of wetness that rushed from her body, bathing her ass and thighs. His mouth and fingers played in her essence until all she could do was buck and shake as her vaginal walls convulsed with the longest and most intense orgasm she had ever experienced. Just as the spasms dissipated, Zeus pumped another finger into her tightness, stretching her almost beyond reason, and just that quickly the sensations grew more, not less intense, and again her body was flung against the hard truth of another orgasm.

Eventually her back and hips made their way back down to the mattress, and when she finally had the strength to open her eyes, she found Zeus looking down at her, his arm cocked up and resting on his hand. For long quiet moments he just looked at her, his face so expressionless she had no clue what was going on behind those silvery eyes. A wave of self-consciousness and mortification spread within her.

"What?" she asked, her voice raw and defensive.

His head tilted, and his mouth cocked up on one side. Why that was becoming sexy to her, she didn't even want to contemplate.

"You didn't see what just happened. I did. Saw it, felt it, tasted it." His hand gripped and squeezed her thigh as if determining its strength. "You came so hard you nearly crushed my skull between your legs. If I wasn't so hardheaded, I'd be dead."

She couldn't help it. She broke out in a fit of laughter as she tried to push his hand away. He only gripped harder, kneading her thigh muscles.

"Go ahead, say it, Sabrina. It's easy. Just say, 'Zeus, you are the best fuck I have ever, or will ever, have.'" He shifted a little closer. "And I haven't even fucked you proper yet."

"I'm not saying that."

"Oh, you will say it."

"Only in your delusional mind."

"You'll say it in both my minds, sane, delusional. Either way, I'll hear it."

He shifted his body on top of her, his face suspended above hers as he exhaled air that smelled enticingly of her. She wanted to taste herself on him. She wanted to share in every indecent act imaginable with him. It was terrifying.

Zeus shifted again so the thick length of his shaft was no longer pulsing against her thigh but the mushroom tip pressed a fraction of an inch into her opening.

"You'll say it," he gritted out. It almost sounded as if he were mad, but his lips pressed against hers as gentle as a sigh.

She reached up and pressed his mouth more firmly against hers, sending her tongue in search of his control. She wanted to consume him until he felt powerless to do anything but devour her just to free his soul from the temptation of her mouth.

Zeus groaned, low and raw. She knew she'd broken something loose inside him. He reached over to her end table, and moments later, she heard the ripping of foil. Once sheathed, he lowered his body on top of hers, the hardness and weight of his chest pressing her breasts flat, pressing her back more firmly into the mattress. He sucked her tongue into his mouth while using one arm to lift her knee up and out, spreading one thigh wide. He was going to take her, but she wanted to have him trembling and insensate, *more* insane, and locked in her control before he could.

She angled his head and bit a trail down his neck, pausing in one spot when he gripped the pillow beneath her head and groaned.

She smiled. She'd discovered one of his erogenous zones. She reached down and slid her fingers over the clenched muscles at his back, working down his spine until her fingers reached the seam of his ass. She stroked and kneaded a well-muscled cheek, her pleasure growing as she allowed her sensuality to guide her in pleasuring Zeus.

In this moment he was her hard man to soften. She glided her hand over, then firmly stroked and gripped his sac. A strangled roar filled the room, and she wondered if she'd pushed him too far. Zeus froze above her, muscles in near rigor. In a breath his hips cocked back, surged forward, rammed into her hard and without apology.

Sabrina screamed as her body was lifted off the mattress. She dug her fingers into the bed, struggling to find purchase while her lungs constricted, afraid to take in air for the fear of him surging forward again, pushing all the air from her respiratory system and causing her to asphyxiate.

They were frozen this way for an eternity of heartbeats. Unmoving except for the throb of his penis inside her, the weight of his silver gaze bearing down on her, the contraction of her inner walls trying to ease around the thickness and length of him expanding her so extremely she was riding the edge of pain. It was too much. He was too much. If he moved, she was terrified he would break something essential inside of her and she'd never be able to have sex with another man again.

Sabrina forced air in and out of her lungs, forced her body to relax as she placed her hands on the sides of Zeus's hips, slowly pushing them back incrementally. His length pulled halfway out of her, and cool air licked the heated places that were no longer pressed against him.

Slowly, ever so slowly, she pushed farther back, fighting not to groan as her pussy released one ridge of him after another. Just keep going, her mind whispered. He'd be out and she'd roll away before he could slip back in, and she could calmly explain why this would never work with him being as big as he was and her being as tight and out of practice as she was.

With only about two inches of him remaining inside her, she dared to look up. He watched her with intense speculation and then slowly one side of his mouth hitched up. Her eyes widened at the impossible. Instinctively she gripped his hips firmly and attempted to push them back, but it was too late. He plunged into her. Hard.

"Uhhhhh," she cried out, her back arching from the shock-pleasure-pain of him rooting so forcefully back into her. He pulled both arms over her head, one hand holding her wrists immobile as the other worked its way back down her body. He spread her thighs wider, further exposing her vulnerability. Zeus's strong fingers found her clit and began to strum.

"You're not in control here, Sabrina," he said, his breath hot against her ear. "This is me fucking you."

He pinned her arms tighter above her head and surged into her again and again, wild, animalistic, making her scream her throat raw for this savage, glorious ride.

She heard herself begging, sobbing, "Please don't...don't stop. Please..."

She couldn't...she needed...she...

She arched, hips moving to his relentless pace. His mouth found her nipple again, and the world fell into darkness, sparkles of light, like embers raining down and detonating in a barrage of orgasms so powerful they nearly separated her consciousness from her body.

She was trying to stay sane when she felt Zeus's rhythm increase, felt him stiffen and shout, felt his hot seed sear her inner flesh.

Losing all muscle control, Sabrina drifted. Sated. Warm. Peaceful. Zeus cradled her head in his hands as he licked tears from her face.

"Say it," he demanded.

She smiled. He was relentless, this unstable demigod who almost felt like he was hers. At least in this moment. She would give herself that. This moment. Sighing, she drifted further into it until she found sleep.

CHAPTER NINE

"Say it," Zeus found himself ordering her again, jarring her from sleep. He wasn't sure why he wanted to hear the words, but it was important.

"Please let me sleep," she mumbled.

"Say it, or there's no telling what I'll be forced to do."

Her arms came around his shoulders as she stroked the back of his head. "Best fuck I ever had."

"Will ever have," he said, reminding her of the rest.

"Best I will ever have." The words were slightly slurred, but he'd take them. Sabrina's body went completely lax beneath his.

He closed his eyes, taking in the scent of her. Of them. He was still semierect inside of her, gliding his hand over her breast as he decided one time with her hadn't been enough to extinguish the need to have her. No, it only made the need worse. He took her nipple in his mouth and sucked. She moaned in her sleep. He continued to suck until she whimpered.

He sighed, letting the nipple pop free of his mouth. He continued to lap at it gently until she settled again. He kissed it once, twice. He loved breasts. Her breasts. But he'd let her rest.

He pulled out of her and settled on his side, molding her against him. He looked down at her, his head cradled against his palm. He'd probably have to take her two or three more times before the need went away. Four at the most. He rarely had the same woman more than once. Never more than twice. They tended to think they mattered after the second time, but they never did.

He pressed Sabrina more firmly against him, securing her with his forearm so she couldn't drift away in her sleep. Like him, she didn't connect to a lot of people. She had Randy, and until Zeus decided otherwise, she would have him. Sometimes that was all the choice people had in life. Accept what was. He wanted her, and that's just the way it was.

He traced the stubborn set of her jaw.

He knew she'd try and run from him in the morning. Distance herself, pretend like she'd never lost her ever-loving mind as he fucked her senseless. His dick twitched at the memory of being gripped so tightly inside of her. Obviously she hadn't been with another man in a while, which was good. The thought of her with...

He rose off the lumpy futon, reaching for one of the blades on the table. He paced around the bed, blade twirling in his hand as he looked at her brown skin, which still held a sheen from their joining. Her nipples were pebbled and peaked out, begging him to come back and play.

An image of her riding some dark-skinned man flashed through Zeus's mind. The blade faltered, broke rhythm, then became a metallic blur as rage consumed him like hellfire. In the blink of an eye he gripped the blade's hilt and used another unnamed, consuming emotion to propel it across the room, where it lodged into the wall. He grabbed the used condom from the mattress, tried to breathe some control back into his mind and body, but the room was too small, like a fucking coffin.

His heart beat in his chest like a beast slamming into the bars of its cage, fighting to be set free. What was this? Was he dying? Should she die for making him feel this way?

He walked out of the living room, afraid of what he would do if he continued to look at her and see... He growled as he stomped into the bathroom, disposed of the condom, and turned the sink's faucet on cold. Dunking his head beneath the single stream of water, he worked it over his hair and face, trying to remove any thoughts of Sabrina with another man. He had to calm down, or he would hurt something, someone.

He braced his hands on either side of the basin, looking down into it as water dripped from his nose and chin. He closed his eyes, remembered her fingers lightly caressing his face, remembered it was *his* scent on her body, and breathed easier, relaxing.

Zeus opened his eyes and straightened as he looked into the mirror above the sink. His face was hardened against the emotions from a moment ago, but his eyes, cold enough to make the dead pray for warmth, hinted at something inside that was still weak and needy. And it was there because of her.

He retreated a step, wanting to be free of the fucking constriction of this place. How could she stand to live where he could barely move, barely breathe. He needed to be outside in air that wasn't poisoned with her scent just so he could *think* straight. He walked back to the living room and pulled on his pants, preparing to go out to the tiny courtyard garden and allow his blades to dance in the darkness. He didn't make it to the narrow hallway before stopping at the wall where one of his blades was embedded halfway through.

His blade had faltered in his hand. That hadn't happened since he was a kid, not since blade and man had joined as one spirit united.

She'd disrupted the rhythm of that union.

He turned around, watched her sleep soundly, unaware of the destructive energy gathering inside him. He couldn't allow her to disrupt his blades' rhythm. Walking to the foot of the bed, he pulled down the thin sheet until it was pooled below her feet.

If she disrupted his rhythm, she weakened his bond with the spirits of the blade. If his bond was weakened, he would be vulnerable. The day he'd devoted himself to the blade, he'd pledged to never again be vulnerable. He liked being inside of her, liked the heat of her pussy as it gripped him and drew him deeper, but he wouldn't die for her. Wouldn't die for anyone.

He had to cut out the vulnerability, get her out of his system.

Using his blade-free hand, he grabbed another condom packet, bit into it, and sheathed the thin protection over his thickness. Reaching down, he grabbed Sabrina's ankles, turning her until she lay on her stomach. The roundness of her ass caused blood to pound through his shaft as it pointed in the direction it needed to go.

Sabrina stirred. "Zeus?" she called, her voice still thick with sleep as she rose up on her elbows and turned to look behind her. He saw her eyes widen as she took in his erection, the blade in his hand, and the wild destruction he knew was reflected in his eyes.

"Oh shit," she said as she tried to roll off the side of the bed.

Quicker than thought, he surged onto the futon and pressed his palm against her back, pinning her to the mattress from behind. Zeus tossed his blade to the table and used his free hand to spread her legs on the outside of his. He smiled, feeling no humor, only lust and this damn need to work her out of his system. He wanted no part of craving or being compelled by her. No one and no thing would interfere with his bond to the blade.

He gripped her hips, pulling them up and toward the tip of his dick.

"Zeus, wait," she said, sounding panicked.

It's okay, he thought as he stroked her ass. He wasn't going to hurt her. He leaned over her prone body, rubbing his cheek against her coiled hair. So soft. He reached down and around to stroke her clit as he pressed slowly into her hot wetness from behind. He closed his eyes against the sensation, stroking her, pumping in and out of her. He had to go slow, make sure that when he was done, she no longer whispered in his mind. With this slow fuck he'd turn her into just another warm body he'd come inside and walk away from. No regrets.

He pushed in and out even more slowly. He was in no rush. He'd stay right here all night long if he had to.

Sabrina broke his rhythm when she moaned, arching her back to take him deeper. He could feel her arousal building. He could feel it in the way she breathed, the way her skin heated, becoming slick with perspiration, in the way her clit grew more engorged as he worked it with the fingers of one hand, while the other slid between the mattress to grip her breast, her nipple a defiant pebble against his palm. He squeezed and dragged his thumbnail over her nipple.

Go slow, he admonished himself as his hips jerked rapidly three times. But so gooood.

Sabrina moaned again and bucked back against him, demanding he pick up his pace without using words.

Go slow.

He dragged his hand from her breast and up the back of her neck, weaving his fingers through the soft coils of hair, and gripped, angling her head so her neck was exposed. He licked and sucked that tender area where his blade loved to cut. Her pulse was wild and rapid, blood pumping through the artery with a force that let him know she was fully awake. He bit her, and she let out a grunt of surprise. He tightened his grip on her hair, his hips surging harder than intended, causing her to cry out louder. Zeus shifted his weight and pressed her head against the mattress as his hips continued to pump steadily, not urgent but no longer languid either. Sabrina tried to position her hands against the mattress and push her torso up off the bed, but he drove his cock into her harder, unwilling to set her free from her current position. He rode her like this at his leisure; her moans and wiggling ass wouldn't compel him out of his rhythm. He was going to succeed.

"Zeus, please," she begged. She wanted him to rock into her harder, faster, but he wouldn't. He liked it this way, just like this, where she could only moan, groan, and whimper.

He surged hard and fast once. He liked that all she could do was take it. That was the only option he would give her.

"Zeus," she said with each thrust. It became a chant. "Zeus, Zeus, Zeus, damn, baby, uhn, Zeus."

He ground on steadily, sweat dripping from his face, unwilling to give her what she begged for. More of him. He wouldn't give her any more, only take.

Her back arched. Her hands clawed the mattress as her pussy rippled, pulled, contracted around him as she shook with orgasm.

He ground his teeth and grimaced out a smile. It was so easy to make her come. He released her head. She was too limp to challenge him. He gripped her hips, pulling them into the exact position he needed them to be in, and he drove forward. Hard. His hands clenched her hips, holding her in place during the impact.

So good. She felt so damn good. He could fuck her forever.

He growled. *Not forever. No more after this.* He surged into her again. And again, jackhammering into her with so much force he could barely maintain his hold.

When she came this time, the gripping suction of her pussy was his undoing. He ended it hard and fast. Without the condom he imagined he would have pushed his seed so deep he would've decorated her vaginal walls in brilliant bursts of white.

She passed out in a sloppy sprawl across the bed. Zeus lowered himself on the bed and gathered her tightly against him while still nestled inside of her. He closed his eyes as he pressed his head into the back of her shoulder. His fingers dancing rhythmically against her thigh. The feeling he'd wanted to extinguish was still there. Expanding even. He would rest, then go at her again. He was positive the third time would be the surgical blade that cut the ethereal cord of need connecting them.

SABRINA SNEAKED OUT of her own apartment, half-naked and afraid of making even the smallest whisper of sound for fear Zeus would wake up and his dick would somehow land straight inside her woman's hidey-hole again. After four rounds with him, her body couldn't take any more. Well, it probably could with the way her nipples tightened just thinking about how thoroughly he had fucked her.

She froze when she closed the front door and it snicked shut. She pressed her ear to the wood, waiting to hear him stir, but when no movement or footsteps sounded, she tiptoed down the hall and up the stairs toward Randy's apartment, groaning as she got a whiff of herself. The scents of Zeus and sex dogged her every step. Maybe it was a mistake to put on his shirt, but it had been the closest and easiest option.

At Randy's door she tapped lightly, certain he was already up. It was nearly eleven in the morning, and unlike her, he was an early riser. True to form, Randy opened the door bare-chested, with black silk pajama bottoms and a half-smoked joint dangling from his mouth.

He inhaled as he squinted and cataloged every shameful detail of her appearance. Finally he nodded and allowed her to slip into the apartment. She scuttled over to the built-in bench crafted beneath the bay window overlooking the street. Sitting with her back against the wall, she pulled her knees up and stretched the hem of the shirt down, tucking it beneath her feet.

Along the same wall that accommodated the front door was Randy's plush gray couch. Bride sat slumped down on it, legs slightly parted, wearing a cream linen slip that was scrunched midway up her thighs. Her thick black hair was pulled back into a sloppy ponytail, yet she had the nerve to watch Sabrina as if weighing her worth. The woman had tattoos all over her body – arms, chest, legs – and already she was dangling a tumbler filled with amber liquid between her thumb and forefinger. Who was Bride to make judgments?

In its makeup-free state, Bride's face glowed with the radiant unblemished health of a child. In Sabrina's experience, white people who drank as much as Bride seemed to wear the aftermath on their faces. If you took away Bride's tattoos, piercings, and the blankness of her gaze, she would resemble some delicate pixie chick.

Turning her gaze away from Bride, Sabrina watched Randy as he paced back and forth in front of her. He finally came to sit next to her on the bench and pointed what remained of his blunt in her direction. "You nasty bitch," Randy said, smothering the end with his fingertips. "Thank God, or Zeus, as the case may be. I swear, if you didn't get laid with a hot – even if he's mental – man in your home, I would have written you off."

"That's not what you were saying last night."

He shrugged and slumped back against the narrow column of space where the window ended and the wall began. "Why are you sneaking into my apartment like some runaway slave?"

"Because I'm sore and I need a break, and if he woke up and rolled over, his dick would have found a way inside of me again and again until I wouldn't be able to walk...and there's no guarantee he would have stopped even if I hung a CLOSED FOR RENOVATIONS sign around my hips." She sighed. "I left for the well-being of my pud."

Bride downed the remainder of the liquid and cocked her eyebrow.

"This white broad is sending me," Randy said in that deadpan voice he used when he was irritated. "Had me smokin' since seven this morning with all that sitting-and-watching shit she does. She doesn't talk, doesn't acknowledge she's even heard you. That little nod was the most she's communicated since she's been here, Bree. What kind of special-ed muthafuckas do you have us associating with?"

Because his back was to Bride, Randy didn't glimpse the tilt of Bride's lips. That's when Sabrina knew the other woman was enjoying herself. Enjoyed the off-putting reactions she engendered. Maybe *enjoy* was too strong a word to define Bride's minimal emotion, but the other woman wasn't actively hating her assignment. That much Sabrina knew.

"We could always swap. I take Bride, and you take Zeus," Sabrina said, feeling more at ease. Interactions with Randy always helped her feel balanced. With him she didn't have to hold herself back for fear of how he would react. She'd had to do it with Ernesto. Hell, she'd even had to do it with her sister, because Sam had always been more fragile than anyone Sabrina had ever known. For most of their lives it had been Sabrina's unspoken job to protect Sam from breaking. In the end she was forced to admit she was unable to fulfill that responsibility.

"Just what kind of fool would I look like telling Zeus he couldn't stay with the woman he'd screwed himself unconscious with because I needed to take a break from Helen Keller's doppelgänger?"

"Yeah, put like that, it might not go over well."

"Doesn't matter how I put it. He'll either break my neck or eviscerate me, but he won't be leaving your side."

"Four times may have been too much," she mumbled. What they'd done might not have had any effect on someone like Zeus, but she found herself wanting....

Maybe that was just the natural outcome of good sex. It made you want more. Of everything. "Best sex I ever had," she told Randy. "He even made me say it."

Bride snorted. "He would."

Randy cringed and shifted around to look at Bride. "Lord and heaven above, it speaks."

Bride rolled her eyes and stood. Sabrina and Randy watched as the other woman left the living room and walked a steady line to the kitchen.

CHAPTER TEN

Zeus woke up instantly, yet kept his eyes closed. What registered first was that he was hard and Sabrina was no longer sprawled over him. He sensed she wasn't even in the room, and doubted she was in the apartment. Without her warmth, despite the blanket, he was cold.

He opened his eyes and sat up, swinging his legs over the side of the low-lying bed. No, not bed, hard-assed futon. He'd have to get her a better mattress. Continuous sleeping and fucking on this thing would leave abrasions all over his body. It was worse than sleeping on dry earth.

Zeus stood and saw the items Sabrina had worn to bed the night before littered across the floor, but his T-shirt was gone. He flexed his fingers, picked up the knives on the side table, and twirled the blades, allowing them to complete their morning ritual. As the pace of the blades increased, the compulsive need to bury himself in Sabrina's body diminished, and he was able to clear his mind and allow instinct to point him in her direction. No doubt the direction would lead him to Randy's apartment. Before all was said and done, Zeus would likely have to stab Randy just to show Randy and Sabrina that her visiting without him could be bad for Randy's health as well as the longevity of his life.

He tossed his blades into the mattress to loosen his wrists. Sabrina would be pissed when she saw what he'd done, but she'd understand once he let her know he was going to get her a new one. He pulled on a pair of jeans and walked to the kitchen.

She didn't have any food. She didn't have any coffee; she didn't have beer; she didn't have shit, not even canned food. She had a half carton of milk, but the stamp said it had expired three weeks ago. Why the hell was she keeping it?

He poured the clumpy remains down the sink and turned on the faucet to wash away the evidence of her less than stellar home-keeping skills. More than food or drink or cleanliness, he still craved her. Didn't make sense. A lot of things about him didn't make sense to other people, but he always understood himself. Except where she was concerned. Four times wasn't a charm. He still wanted her, more than yesterday. The compulsion had rebounded, and she wasn't here. Unacceptable.

He went back to the living room and pulled another T-shirt from his duffel bag, grabbed his phone, tapped in the code to unlock it, and dialed.

"What's up?" Big Country answered. "I see your girl sunning in the window upstairs. We laid money on whether you two would even make it out of her bed today. You lost me a wad of money, son. With all the fucking I heard during my rounds, I just knew I had a sure thing."

Zeus peeked through the heavy brown and gold curtains that looked out on the side of the building and could just see the end of Big Country's van parked on the street.

"Where's the tail?"

"Let's just say us good ol' boys got a little restless last night and decided to have some fun."

"Dead?"

"Fun and killing ain't synonyms to regular folks, Zeus."

"I would have killed them."

"Sorry to break it to you, cousin, but you ain't real regular."

160

Zeus hung up, pocketed the phone and Sabrina's keys, and headed down the hallway to the back interior stairs toward Randy's apartment. On the second floor, a white guy holding a white cat cradled in his arms stopped in front of him. Zeus looked from the man blocking his path to Randy's door and felt his fingers twitch.

"Are you lost?" the smaller man asked like he owned the world as well as the universe it rotated in.

Zeus shot his hand out and grabbed the cat, dangling it in the air before letting it drop to the floor. "I like cats." He didn't. Quicker than thought his Bowie knife was fisted against his palm. Stupid cat was circling and bumping against Zeus's leg. For some reason, domestic animals liked him.

"If you don't move, I'll cut through you to get to where I'm going."

The man paled as if Zeus's words had dropped the hallway temperature by fifty degrees.

Zeus curled his lip in disgust and pushed past the man, who smartly kept his back hugged against the wall as Zeus walked up to Randy's apartment and pounded on the door twice. Randy opened the door, his eyes automatically going to the blade in Zeus's hand. Zeus motioned down the hall, and Randy leaned out the door to see the man pressed against the wall, clutching his cat.

Randy opened the door wide and motioned Zeus inside. Zeus immediately took in Sabrina on the window seat, just where Big Country had said. She was wearing his shirt and nothing else. He felt a vibration in his chest as his balls tightened painfully with the need to take her again.

"Stop growling," Sabrina said casually, and the rumbling quieted, though the pain in his balls didn't.

"You left."

"I did."

"I wasn't done with you."

"You were asleep, Zeus. That's about as done as done gets."

Sabrina slid off the padded bench with a cup of something steamy clutched between her palms. Before she could move away, Zeus closed the distance between them and took possession of the cup.

"You leave me with lumpy milk and sit up here sipping on hot chocolate?" It even had marshmallows melted on top.

"Hey, don't give me shit about the lumpy milk in my fridge. You could have had a kitchen filled with food, but instead you chose a living room filled with electronics. Deal with it."

He drank what remained of her hot chocolate and handed the cup back to her before turning toward Randy. "I need food."

Randy slanted a confused glance at Sabrina, and she shrugged.

Zeus felt the vibration in his chest again. He was hungry and horny and still felt *something* inside of him calling out for Sabrina, yet they thought they would silently communicate about him when...

"Damn," Randy muttered.

Zeus realized Randy was focusing on the blade spinning through Zeus's fingers.

Sabrina's hand touched the center of his chest, and the blade slowed. Her hand was warm. He looked out the window but mentally followed her hand as it trailed down his abdomen to his hips, fingertips hiding just beneath the waistband of his jeans. He leaned his head toward hers, breathing in and liking her new scent. It was a mixture of him and her and sex. He pulled her fully against him, his dick straining to find a way back inside her.

"I'm hungry," he ground out.

He felt her smile against his chest. "I thought you wanted Randy to take care of that for you."

Zeus pulled away from Sabrina and glared at Randy, who shrugged. "You did ask me to feed you. I've got enough for a few mouthfuls."

Zeus grimaced while Sabrina tried to smother her laughter.

"There are leftovers in the kitchen," Sabrina told him as she pulled away.

He reached out to grab her again but was distracted by the sight of Bride walking into the room with a piece of link sausage dangling from her mouth like a limp dick. Images of times he'd been threatened by some pervert trying to force that reality on him as a child filtered through his mind. The memories triggered a primal rage, and just like that, the need to hurt something, to kill, had his fingers dancing.

"YOU WANT SAUSAGE? Home-fried potatoes? Food's on the stove. Big Country cooks like his mama at least tried to raise him right," Sabrina said.

Her words were pressured, and she tried to laugh, only to have it come out as a pathetic titter. What she'd said was true enough; Big Country had cooked up a storm in Randy's kitchen, but she'd been rambling, attempting to distract Zeus from whatever darkness had descended upon him.

Too quick to comprehend, the dangerously sexual, socially intolerant, slightly crazy, and highly irritating man had reverted back to the vacant-eyed demon that had saturated her in other men's blood while she was on the warehouse floor.

"Gotta hunt. Appease this hunger." Zeus's mouth cocked to the side as if he'd made a joke. A joke that came from a world where suffering and humor were indistinguishable.

She looked over at Bride, who watched Zeus in an under-eyed way that reminded Sabrina of an animal determining if it was going to fight or flee. Randy simply looked confused by the sudden tension in room, but she saw his body react unconsciously, adjusting to a combat stance.

Sabrina grabbed Zeus's wrist, the one not brandishing a weapon, and pulled him toward the door. "Hey, Randy. We need to take care of a few things. See you later."

She pulled Zeus down the hall and stairs and back into her apartment, closing the door and locking it behind her, as if *that* would be the thing that kept him from going out and killing somebody.

He watched her silently, and she watched him, her gaze drawn to the blade playing through his fingers. His body wasn't tense, actually seemed loose, but the intensity of his gaze cut through her. Sabrina felt both terrified and euphoric as she realized Zeus's blades helped him harness and guide the violence built up inside of him. If the blades danced through his fingers, they weren't dancing over someone's – namely her – flesh.

Sabrina took a step closer to him and placed her hand on his chest, over his heart, giving him something to feel besides the need that drove him to kill. She felt his heartbeat, his heat beneath the cool T-shirt. She also felt him flinch from the contact, as if her hand burned. She smiled when he chuffed out a breath, like a beast confused about what to do with its suicidal prey.

Sabrina knew she wasn't suicidal. As bad as life had been, it was her life, and she would stand toe-to-toe with the devil himself to keep it. For the hundredth time she wished Sam had held on to the same determination, but her sister hadn't.

"I can't die today, you know. You promised you'd teach me how to use a blade to defend myself."

He frowned. He hadn't actually promised her that, but she wasn't above lying if it kept her alive a little longer. "I'm hungry, Bree," he said, stepping closer, close enough for her to feel the hard ridge of muscle press against her abdomen.

The wetness pooling between her legs was her body's initial response to his declaration. It was a shame, but her body had been conditioned to him faster than Pavlov's dogs had been to the bell. She wouldn't give him her life, but she would gladly give him her body again.

Randy was right. She was a nasty, slutty bitch. It wasn't a title she usually wore, but she'd wear it with a crown when it came to Zeus.

She rubbed against the hardness of his shaft and heard Zeus draw in air as if he was a man tortured.

"Am I making things hard for you, big man?" she asked as she slipped her hand down his chest and molded it against his straining penis. She allowed her head to fall forward, and rested it where her hand had been near his heart. "I'm sorry, Zeus. I don't mean to make things hard for you, but people have always told me how difficult I can make things." She tweaked the head of his penis, bound beneath the taut material of his jeans. He groaned, and she smiled, rubbing her cheek against his chest.

She so meant to make things hard for him.

His fingers fisted in her hair, pulling her head back and exposing her neck. He held her head immobile as his mercurial eyes consumed every pore, every angle, every emotion that had ever left an imprint on her face.

Sabrina inhaled, dragging his scent deep into her, imagining she imprinted her essence onto his DNA as she exhaled. Zeus's mouth brushed over hers more gently than she'd imagined his need would ever allow. She groaned, tweaking his tip again, and cried out as the beast rose up and tried to devour her.

Zeus bent her backward with the force of his kiss, his forearm a steel band of support at her lower back. He lifted her as he straightened, and she wrapped her legs around his hips. The rub of his jean-clad erection against her clit caused another guttural moan to escape as she rode the length of him. He pressed her back against the front door and ground into her, lifting one of her legs and draping it over his shoulder. If not for the higher powers of yoga, he probably would have snapped every bone in her body with the way he flung her limbs around.

Hands tugged at her shirt. She felt her breasts exposed to the cool air only for an instant before hands and lips fastened on them. She cried out as she bucked against him, begging him to free himself and fill her.

Not until Zeus loosed her nipple and growled did she realize the jarring vibration at her back was someone knocking, *banging*, on her door. Zeus hit the door one time. Hard. She had to turn to make sure he didn't leave a hole.

Sabrina scrambled to pull the T-shirt back down while Zeus continued to grind against her.

She slid her leg down so it hung in the crook of Zeus's elbow and unwound her other leg from around his hip and let it dangle toward the floor. Zeus's fist tightened against the back of her head, angling it to the side so he could suck her neck. Her vagina fought to take what Zeus had to offer, but her mind forced her to reach up and spread her hands across each side of Zeus's face as she pushed his head away. She rained kisses over his eyes, his cheeks, forehead, then his mouth, coaxing him into a languid kiss. She pulled away and stroked her thumbs over his eyebrows and cheekbones.

Zeus relaxed into her touch, though she could see he hadn't fully released the reins of his need.

Another round of knocking had him cursing and reaching for the doorknob.

"Wait. Zeus, wait. Go to the kitchen. I promise. Let me handle this, and I'll come in there and feed every craving you need fed." She kissed him in the spot of his third eye, and he eased back.

"Two minutes. You got two minutes, Bree. If you're not on the counter straddling me as you place food in my mouth, someone's going to get hurt. And it won't be me...or you."

That meant Randy or Bride or whichever Brood member was at her door owed her their life. She watched Zeus walk to the back of the apartment before she unlocked and opened the door.

Her intention of teasing the person in the hall vanished as she looked into the vibrant blue eyes of an expensively dressed stranger. Her first thought was that one of Randy's new boy toys had gotten lost. But why did he look familiar? Maybe it was an intensity in his eyes, which rivaled Zeus's. She took a step back.

"Sabrina." The stranger smiled at her with so much sincerity and kindness she couldn't decide if she should return it or run. When she noticed the two large, well-dressed men behind the man standing in front of her, instinct urged her to run. She couldn't move.

"You are more beautiful than I remember. It feels like I've been searching for you half my lifetime."

A wrongness settled over her. Not just with the situation, but with him. He felt familiar, and he felt...*wrong*, despite the pretty packaging. She took a step back, confused about why she was being so passive. There were killers after her, and for some reason she couldn't find her voice, couldn't react to the man who appeared to be so captivated by her.

Then it clicked.

"Kragen," she said.

Rapist, torturer, killer of over a dozen women who all looked disturbingly like her. The man who'd had her beaten and kidnapped, possibly with every intention of raping, torturing, and killing her also.

She took another step back, and they followed her into her apartment. She wanted to call out to Zeus, but she knew with every fiber of her being the two men behind Kragen were strapped with guns. She didn't want to be taken, but more importantly, she didn't want Zeus shot or hurt if he charged in and tried to protect her. Taking a deep breath, she regrouped and did what she had learned to do all her life – talk until she could find the best opportunity to escape.

"You remember me." Kragen's smile was all things pleased.

"You look familiar, but no, I don't remember you. I lost some of my memory a while ago, but I remember the men who abducted me saying the name Kragen. They described you as the man who'd hired them. A pretty boy playing with daddy's money, they said. You're here, obviously a wealthy man, obviously attractive. It stands to reason you're the man that paid them to kidnap me."

She watched the play of emotions on his face as she spoke. In the end his mouth settled in an indulgent smile.

"You were always my smart girl, weren't you, Sabrina? It was one of the qualities that kept you burning through my blood all these years."

He took a step toward her, and she took another step back, racking her brain for some sign that she had any history with this man. Sometimes she didn't remember things, but that was singularly related to the details of some physical altercation she had with Ernesto.

"If we have such a wonderful history, why have me kidnapped? Why have me beaten nearly to death?"

She didn't think the sadness and grief he displayed was fake or contrived, but what she did know was he was the closest thing to evil she had ever come into contact with. But it didn't matter that his expression seemed to beg her forgiveness.

"I made an error in judgment. I gave men I didn't know or trust the job of securing you until I arrived. They weren't supposed to hurt you. I promise. If they weren't dead already, I would take pleasure in allowing you to watch them die."

Yeah, well, she'd already watched, and it hadn't been a pleasure at all.

"So, um, the cops were telling the truth when they said my abductors were dead? I hadn't seen anything on the news."

"They were alive when you last saw them?"

She nodded, sticking to the story she'd told the cops.

"The only way I was able to get away was because they left me by myself. When I came to, I escaped from a window. I never looked back."

"I'm glad you made it out alive. I never would have forgiven myself if I had lost you to their incompetence."

"Lucky for all involved – "

A pan clattered in the kitchen. Sabrina flinched.

"Ah, the bodyguard, I presume?" The man, Kragen, looked over to the bigger of the two men, who reached inside his coat as he trod softly down the hall in the direction of the kitchen.

Zeus! she screamed in her head. When her mouth tried to follow suit, Kragen's hand covered it as his other arm fastened around her like a manacle.

"No. I don't want you to see any more violence," he said.

Then stop bringing violence into my life, she thought. Her heartbeat was an erratic staccato, a silent rhythm that called out for Zeus to protect himself.

She heard a struggle. Waited. The silence that descended was almost as deafening as the gunshot that followed.

"Come, Sabrina. It's time I take you where you belong."

She fought for her life then. She didn't want to go. She wanted to run, not away but down the hall, to the kitchen. She'd always been about self-preservation, but she needed to get to Zeus.

Behind her, behind Kragen, there was a metallic *click, click*. Sabrina craned her head around to see a gun barrel pressed against Kragen's temple. Bride reached inside the coat of the other burly guy as Kragen released Sabrina.

Bride palmed the other man's gun and motioned for him to get down on his knees. Good ol' silent Bride.

"And I thought we'd taken care of your guard detail," Kragen said.

"Actually she's not my guard. She's my neighbor."

He smiled. "How unfortunate for me, huh?" He turned to look at Bride. "Hello, neighbor. As charming as I'm sure you are, I'd rather have not made your acquaintance."

Bride kicked in the knee of the man who was over twice her size, sending him to the floor a little more rapidly, because apparently he wasn't getting to his knees fast enough.

A shadow filled Sabrina's hall and silently moved closer to them. When she saw it was Zeus, she took a step in his direction when she should have run from him. Fast.

She prayed there wasn't a dead man in her kitchen, but as Zeus moved through the shadowed hallway, her heart sank. Something bad had been unleashed in him, and he was stalking through her home.

Sabrina moved away from Kragen, and he had the good sense to let her. He must have sensed the man advancing was beyond being reasoned with. Zeus's eyes, gray orbs in the shadows, were locked on to Kragen, who appeared unfazed by the almost certain death stalking him. That man had his own demons, Sabrina determined. And strangely, they didn't appear intimidated by Zeus in the least.

"So, the rescuing bodyguard survives," Kragen said. He was aware of Zeus, but his eyes were focused on Sabrina as if he didn't comprehend the level of danger he was in. Maybe the sight of her was the last thing he wanted to see before he died. Though she didn't think he believed he was going to die.

Sabrina didn't believe he was going to live. Not the way Zeus's energy was filling the air with dark jags of electricity. Flashes of silver appeared from the shadows to Zeus's left, then more flashes to his right. In the moment between Zeus striding from shadows and arriving in the muted light of the living room, she almost believed he was a god made flesh. Pale, golden-bronze beauty, power, death. Hell, he was making her as delusional as she was. Those weren't flashes of electricity bursting from his hands but light reflecting off rapidly revolving metal blades different than any she had seen him use before. There was no hilt on these blades; they were flat, oblong pieces of double-edged metal with needlepoint tips. No place for a normal person to safely hold without having their fingers cut to shreds.

He was a man possessed. God, demon, it didn't matter. Whatever humanity he'd displayed when he touched her, held her against his warmth, was devoured by this metal-eyed killer.

The blades in his hands moved so rapidly they blurred. Silver streaked through the air. Bride shifted, moving into the hall and out of sight. When Zeus's blade sank high into the right side of Kragen's torso, he was propelled backward into the hall, sliding down the wall across from her door.

The bodyguard kneeling on the ground reached for something at his ankle, and another flash of silver catapulted into him. He fell face-first. Sabrina didn't scream, didn't make a sound when she saw that the tip of the blade had pierced through to the back of his neck. He was dead in a matter of seconds.

Kragen wasn't so lucky. He was like a fish on the hook, waiting for death to come.

"I could shoot you," a voice offered Kragen from the hall. Bride. Was she being humane, or did she simply want the kill?

"A knife *and* a gunshot wound? I don't think Dolce or Gabbana would forgive the insult."

There was a moment of silence. Sabrina imagined Bride shrugging her acceptance on the other side of the wall.

Movement inside her apartment forced her to turn back to Zeus. There was another blade in his right hand when he stopped alongside her. She'd never seen this one either. It was like a small machete. Where the hell he was pulling them from, she had no idea.

"Go upstairs," he commanded, his voice surprisingly normal.

"No."

"Then go to the kitchen." He shook his head as if to clear it. "No, the bathroom."

"I'm not leaving," she said. Something in the region of her heart rooted her where she stood, because she believed Zeus would need her to pull him from the depths of nothingness once Kragen was dead. "You'll need me to be your witness."

"You'd let him hack me to pieces like yesterday's mackerel, my love?" Kragen asked, smiling as if this whole situation was humorous.

"Look at my face. I've been kidnapped and beaten because of you. If not for him, it would have been a lot worse, so, yes, I will bear witness to whatever punishment he decides."

Kragen positioned himself a little straighter against the wall. "I always said you needed to develop a harder shell, Sabrina. You were always such a timid thing. I don't know if I should be proud you took my advice and became a bit bloodthirsty during our separation."

Zeus twirled the machete slowly as he advanced. "He's damaged. Need to put him down, Bree."

Kragen's gaze followed Zeus's advance. There was no fear in the injured man. No conflict, only acceptance. She knew it wasn't death Kragen accepted, but the belief that no matter what was said or done Zeus didn't have the power to destroy him.

Sabrina agreed with Zeus. Kragen *was* damaged. He was a sadist who supposedly enjoyed hurting women before he threw them away, as if they had less value than his designer suit. But she wasn't quite willing to see him murdered before her.

Kragen slumped farther down the wall. "You're breaking my heart. I know you say you don't remember, but what we shared was more powerful than anything you could have had with this crude mercenary. When we're together again, you'll see. I'll forgive your affairs of desperation, but when we're together, there will be no one but me. Just you and me."

"Insane," Zeus muttered as he leaned forward and pulled the smaller blade from Kragen's shoulder. Kragen yelled out as if he'd been stabbed again.

A buzzer sounded down the hall, indicating someone was being let in the front door. Sabrina stuck her head over her door's threshold to see Detectives Cassidy and Sedgewick enter the building with guns drawn.

"Drop the weapon," Cassidy ordered, pointing the gun at Zeus. A killing would be easy to justify with Zeus holding the machete close to Kragen's head.

"Detective," Sabrina said, ready to defend Zeus against the detectives' trigger fingers.

Cassidy didn't acknowledge her as he leveled the gun at Zeus's head. "Drop it."

Zeus released the blade.

Kragen cried out as the tip lodged in his leg.

Rapid footsteps stomped overhead, and in moments, Randy was descending the stairs, only to come to an abrupt stop as he took in the sight of the cops pointing guns in her direction and Zeus standing over a bleeding Kragen with a mini machete sticking out of his thigh.

Randy held up his hands. "Officers, I'm the one that called you. Me and my roommate here." He pointed to Bride, who was still leaning against the wall near Sabrina's door with an unlit cigarette dangling from her mouth. "Heard a loud crash, then a shot, and thought someone was breaking into Sabrina's place again. I just knew she and Zeus were dead. You okay, Bree?"

"Yeah, I'm okay. Zeus protected me." She didn't want to say *again* because the cops didn't know about what really happened at the warehouse.

Zeus pointed toward her apartment. "Dead men inside. This is their boss. Guess his name?"

"Kragen?" Cassidy said as he lowered his gun. His partner was slower to follow. Cassidy approached and looked Kragen up and down.

"EMTs are on the way," Sedgewick said. His fingers played with a chain around his neck as he eyed Zeus.

"What happened here?" Cassidy asked.

"Purely a misunderstanding," Kragen said. His skin had grown paler; maybe due to blood loss, maybe because he was about to be arrested, especially with all the bodies he had hidden in his closet.

"There wasn't a misunderstanding," Sabrina countered. "I answered the door, and he was there with two of his men. He sent one to the kitchen to 'take care' of Zeus. The guy in the living room was reaching for what I believed was a weapon, and Zeus must have agreed because he buried one of his blades in the other man's throat. This guy," she said, waving toward Kragen, "said his name was Kragen and tried to get me to go with him. What are the chances he has the same name as the guy the kidnappers were working for? He tried to force me to come with him. Zeus stopped them from taking me."

Cassidy looked at Kragen, who shrugged. "Like I said, a misunderstanding."

"They didn't come here to welcome me back home, Detective."

For the first time since he'd entered the building, Cassidy looked at Kragen as if he were something other than an attempted-murder victim.

Kragen leaned his head against the wall and closed his eyes. "Like I said, it was all a misunderstanding. My men are loyal to me to a fault, and sometimes they behave in ways I do not condone to protect my interest. Will the ambulance be here soon?"

Cassidy nodded. "It's gonna hurt like hell when they pull that knife from your thigh."

"Not a knife. It's a kukri, custom-made," Zeus corrected.

"Sabrina, my fiancé, went missing a number of years ago." Kragen informed them. "When I finally found her, men who were not as loyal as the ones who died today, chose to kidnap her, knowing I would pay any amount they requested for her release. I am a very rich man. Today my men may have acted prematurely when they learned another male was in the apartment posing a possible threat to my Sabrina. I couldn't know the lethality of the man's response." He gritted his teeth and closed his eyes before continuing. "I came to San Francisco last night for business, as well as to verify if the Sabrina I'd been engaged to was the same woman before me. She is."

"I've never met this man in my life," Sabrina told Cassidy. "He's delusional."

"She likes using that word," Zeus said to no one in particular.

"It's not that I like it. It's that these last couple of days have put me in direct contact with people who could be certified as such."

The piercing wail of sirens grew louder and more irritating the closer they came.

Detective Sedgewick came out of Sabrina's apartment and nodded to Cassidy. "Two men dead inside, both armed with some deadly hardware."

"Armed but not dangerous," Zeus said, his eyes glinting with what she recognized as humor. Sabrina didn't think the cop, Sedgewick, was conscious of gripping his chain.

More cops arrived and processed the scene and asked a million more questions. Kragen was taken to the hospital when she secretly wished he would go straight to hell via the morgue. With all the traffic and the dead men awaiting the coroner, her apartment no longer felt like hers.

"Are you going to be okay?" Detective Cassidy asked. Maybe because she'd been staring at the same spot on the wall above Zeus's new television since she'd sat down. It had to be blood.

"I'll be okay, Detective. I've survived worse."

"Well, I'm sorry you had to. If we hadn't been pulled away, we could have stopped this from coming to your door."

"But you didn't," Zeus said, coming up behind Detective Cassidy.

"Keep pushing it. I may still arrest you."

Zeus shrugged. "And cause your already strapped department time and money? Go ahead. I'll be out in enough time to make the five o'clock news. Bodyguard arrested for stopping a second kidnapping in almost as many days. Won't be a good look for you, Cop."

Wow. Forget the fact that he'd strung more than two sentences together. Zeus had just shown he was capable of solid reasoning.

Cassidy looked embarrassed. "We had a unit sitting on her place, but there was a report of a domestic situation where the perp was threatening to shoot himself and his wife and kid – "

"And Kragen just happened to show up when the detail was sent away."

"You think he had someone watching the place as well?" Cassidy said.

"Don't you?" Zeus challenged.

"We'll look into it. Ms. Samora, do you have someplace safe to stay tonight?"

"We'll manage," Zeus told the detective.

"Well, could you manage without cutting or stabbing someone?"

"Probably not."

Detective Cassidy closed his eyes and rubbed a hand over his forehead. "Didn't think so. I'll be in touch soon."

"Thanks, Detective."

Zeus frowned. "Why thank him?"

"I'm thanking him because I appreciate how he's handled this situation and because it's polite, Zeus."

Detective Cassidy nodded toward her and left the apartment with his partner.

Bride walked farther into the apartment and plopped down next to Sabrina. "I need a drink."

"Me too," Sabrina said, leaning her head back and shutting her eyes.

CHAPTER ELEVEN

The crowded interior of Randy's living room felt like barbed wire wrapping around Zeus's neck, cutting through skin, preventing blood and air flow to his brain. He was light-headed from the need to destroy everything around him just so he could fucking breathe. He looked at his supposed Brood mates: Price, Big Country, Bride, Lynx. He needed distance from all these fucking people, with their words and needs and noise.

Sabrina reached out and placed her hand on the small of his back, rubbing gently. The blade dancing through his fingers lost some of its momentum and quieted against his palm.

He needed to protect Sabrina, keep her safe, and he couldn't do that here with all these bodies pressing him in. He couldn't do it in a building where his shoulders nearly touched walls every time he moved.

He wanted, he needed her again, but the space was crowded with Brood members. And Randy. Zeus didn't want to keep thinking about Sabrina. Nothing but his consciousness and the spirit of the blade should command his attention this much. The blade began to move through his fingers again.

He cut his eyes to the side and looked down at Sabrina. "You need to move away," he told her.

His voice was rough, but talking was hard. He needed silence and separation. When she pulled away, the wildness inside of him grew instead of lessening. This fucking assignment was causing him a disturbance. And Sabrina looked at him with the same wary speculation she'd had back in the warehouse. He closed his eyes and let the blade dance.

He didn't like the idea of her not trusting him completely. He really didn't like Coen sitting on the couch next to her, ready to take his place.

The blade picked up speed.

In this tight space he could kill every Brood member in under sixty seconds. There was no one in their organization better than him at the up-close kill. Cizan was gruesome with his hands, but Zeus had the blade. The other Brood members might get a few shots off, but he could walk away with a few bullets lodged in his flesh. He nodded. They could all be dead in under a minute, and he'd be able to leave with Sabrina, in peace.

"It was still a bold fucking move for him to come here in person, knowing she had some kind of protection." Lynx said.

"Yeah. How y'all think Kragen found out about Sabrina being back home so quick?" Big Country asked.

"You thinking – "

"I'm knowing. Them boys ain't have a clue where we were, but they knew Zeus was inside and knew he had backup somewhere. He had his men prowl around the building this morning, drawing us away to track them. They pull the detectives off the place with that report of a domestic dispute; then Kragen and his other goons walk right up to the goddamn door pretty as you please. Only a rat in OPD working for Kragen could help clear the ballroom so quickly. The cops are the only ones who knew Sabrina was back home. Only stands to reason a cop told Kragen that Sabrina had professional assistance."

"The detectives?" Zeus asked, half hoping it was true. Then he could give Sabrina a good excuse when they found Detective Cassidy with that damn pen shoved through his covetous eye. And I know covetous,

Zeus thought. The nuns had tried to teach him not to covet for years. Outside of blades, and now Sabrina, the lesson had stuck.

"Don't reckon I know if it's the detectives, but I'll find out," Big Country said.

"You know you can't stay here," Price said to Sabrina. Zeus knew this. He hadn't planned on keeping her here anyway, but it was better for Price to say it instead of him. Seemed like it was her job to fight against any suggestion he made. "We tried it your way. It's time we took you back to Mama's House, where...."

Zeus wasn't taking her back to the Brood's haven. Sabrina shook her head no, as if she agreed with his unspoken thought. Zeus held his tongue, waiting for Price to conjure some of that diplomatic bullshit. It would make it easier when he gave his suggestion.

"I can't stay here tonight, I know that, but I'm not going to Mama's," Sabrina said.

"You can always come and stay with me, Bree," Randy offered.

She shook her head. "Any other time you know I would, but I can't accept the idea of you being more caught up in this. I'm thinking between the cops and the Brood, even if Kragen's released, it would be insane for him to try anything else, but..."

"He seemed sane to you?" Price asked. "When he had you kidnapped, or when he was talking as if you were his long-lost love, or when you saw what he did in those photos, did any of it seem sane?"

"But all that happened when he thought he was in control. He's exposed himself. It would be idiocy for him to do anything else knowing you guys are protecting me. And if he does, the cops will *have* to act."

"There's something you're failing to understand," Price said, frustration coating every word. "He knew about Zeus. He knew about the detectives. He didn't know about Bride, but he was smart enough to plan for the likelihood that Zeus brought backup to help keep watch. The point of all of this is that he came *anyway*. Men like him don't give a shit about who they're facing off with because they think they're smart and powerful enough to come out on top. So trust when I say he will keep trying."

"And if you go missing anytime soon, he has the perfect alibi if he's locked up in the big house," Big Country added.

"All I'm saying is give me a couple of days," Sabrina said. "If you don't want to stay with me, don't. Call Mama and tell her I've waived my right to protection."

Zeus clocked the exact moment Price's patience snapped. Saw the tick in his left eye, the clenching of his jaw. The other man took a step toward Sabrina, physically crowding her. "The day you dictate what my team will or will not do is over. You'll –"

Zeus threw his blade close to Price's right shoulder, causing the other man to lunge to his left or risk being impaled like Juarez had been. Unlike Juarez, Price found his footing instantly and came up with a nine millimeter aimed at Zeus's head.

"Mothafucka, you let loose one more blade in my direction, and I'll fill you with so many holes everyone will think your nationality is Swiss."

Zeus nearly smiled, satisfied with the other man's reaction. He was quick. And unlike Juarez and Coen, he wasn't a pussy.

"Don't threaten what's mine. Don't get in her face. Then we'll see how everything goes."

Price's aim held. Zeus could tell he wanted to shoot, wanted Zeus to give him a reason, and Zeus didn't blame him. He was an unpredictable threat, and Price already had his hands full with Sabrina and managing the rest of the people on his team. It would be easier for Price to shoot and deal with the consequences later. Unfortunately, the consequence for Price would be his own death. The spirit of the blade sang that truth out clear and strong.

"I get this is your job, Price, but it's also my life, and I refuse to allow another man to control how I live it, even if he believes it's for my own good." Sabrina didn't blink as she spoke to the man still pointing a weapon at Zeus.

He liked that. Liked how his woman didn't back down. He folded his arms over his chest and watched her, her chin in the air, eyes steady on the threat, forehead creased in a slight frown.

He felt...something. An emotion. Proud. He felt proud of Sabrina. When was the last time he'd felt the emotion for anyone? Once he taught her how to work a blade, she would be the closest thing to perfection a woman could ever hope to be.

He inhaled. Swore he could smell the scent of her just there, between her legs. He remembered being there, the taste, the feel. Blood pumped low and strong as his dick remembered too.

"We'll hole up someplace close," Zeus said, though all he could see was Sabrina's breasts as his mouth sucked her nipples. He heard the echo of her guttural moans as he tried to hammer through her. "No surveillance or security detail to bring attention. Just her and me. We'll go to ground and surface only if we have to. If Kragen gets out of jail – "

"With his money and connections, he'll be out," Big Country said.

"Then he'll be looking for another opportunity to take her," Lynx added.

Price lowered the gun, holstering it behind him. The man seemed almost sullen over the fact that he didn't get to shoot. Something was off about Price. With all the Brood.

"All right. Take her to ground, and we'll lock it down here," Price said. "London's left England and is headed our way. He'll be the inside track into Kragen's world of privilege. Between us and London, we should have Kragen facing serious charges and prison time, or dead, within the next couple of weeks."

"Who's London?" Sabrina asked.

"Pretty boy with prettified words," Big Country said.

"He's a cousin to the Brood from across the pond," Price told Sabrina easily. "He got some high class ways us average folk don't seem to know nothing about."

Zeus didn't understand why most of the team was smiling. He'd never met London. He'd only heard about him in bits and pieces, but the fact that he was pretty with pretty words made him want to keep Sabrina far away from the man.

"Do you think they'll let me break the yellow tape to get a few things?"

"If they don't, we'll wait till they're gone and act like we got permission." Lynx grinned.

Zeus knew she wouldn't need anything more than a toothbrush, and they could get one of those on the road. He planned on keeping her naked and in bed for the next two days, more if he had his way.

"What about Randy? Will he be kept safe too?" Sabrina asked.

"Swap out one of these men with the mute, and I'll be right as rain," Randy said from his spot near the kitchen entrance.

"Thought we were besties," Bride mumbled into the shot of rum she'd pilfered from Randy's cabinet.

"Have you people ever considered an intervention?" Randy asked Price.

"Why? She's got one of the steadiest, most reliable gun hands in the Western hemisphere."

"She's not staying with me," Randy said.

Price tossed Zeus a satellite phone. "If there's a problem, hit number one."

As the Brood discussed weapons and surveillance issues, Sabrina closed her eyes and leaned her head back against the couch. Zeus reached for her hand and placed it against the small of his back. He saw her smile faintly, stroking again. Her touch relaxed him, allowed him to tolerate the Brood for another thirty minutes, but five seconds after the thirty minutes, he walked to the door and opened it. The Brood members all looked his way, then gathered their shit and exited the apartment.

Price – the last to leave except for Bride, who remained tucked up on the bench seat – paused beside Zeus. "Don't let her out of your sight, and don't let her sweet talk you away from your duties. The desperation in Kragen's actions makes him even less predictable. He's seen her, knows she's within his reach; he's more dangerous to her than he's ever been, Zeus. Sabrina, this sat phone is for you. Hit this button, and we'll be able to locate you no matter where in the world you are."

"Thanks, Price," Sabrina said, reaching for the phone.

"Thank Mama," Price said as he left the apartment.

Zeus pulled Sabrina up from the couch. "Let's go. Remember to pack light."

"Where are you taking me?"

He didn't answer immediately because he was watching her breasts as she stretched.

"Zeus?"

"Not far."

"In Oakland?"

"No."

When they had packed the car and were heading down I-880 South, Sabrina turned toward him, skin glowing in the afternoon sunlight.

"You going to tell me where we're headed?"

"To one of my getaway spots."

His place was enclosed by nature and made him feel like the last hunter-gatherer in the world. She would like it. It was bigger and more comfortable than her inner-city shack, and they would be allowed to do the things he liked to do in all the ways he liked to do them...but together.

Once they were at his cabin, she would want to do everything she could to show her gratitude.

MAXIM LAY IN the hospital bed, contemplating the last few hours.

His lawyer and Reed had already spoken with the police and DA, and they'd negotiated a way for him to go back to his hotel suite before the evening was over. Once there, he would devise a way to be with Sabrina again.

Sabrina. She was magnificent. Worth every moment of time he'd spent searching for her. Their time away from each other had allowed her to mature like a fine wine. Her body was tighter, more athletic, and the loss of weight made her appear slightly taller than he had remembered her. Her hair no longer hung like inky black silk just past her shoulders but was a riot of multihued twists that seemed to match her new confidence.

A part of him grieved over the memory of who she had been, over her lost innocence and vulnerability, of who they had been together. He felt shame because he hadn't protected what they had more vigilantly, but he'd been younger, less experienced in successfully fighting his parents for what he wanted. Like a simpleton, he'd sought their acceptance of her and, in doing so, had betrayed her, betrayed their love, their connection, and justly so, she'd left him. It wasn't until she was gone that he'd truly embraced his strength and capabilities. He'd been weak and had yielded to the pressure of his family instead of being the man of conviction she'd needed him to be. She was angry and unwilling to open her heart to him. She didn't know that, like her, he had changed. Become stronger. More powerful than even his father.

She didn't know.

He had to get her to their home. Make her see. Make her believe in him again. The incident at her apartment had set him back. He'd lost two men who, in truth, deserved to die with the poor showing they'd made. They had left him facing his competition without protection. And that was what this Zeus person was, competition for Sabrina's affection. It galled that his reunion with her had been marred. He'd given her the impression he was still weak. Still incapable of protecting her. And Zeus had shone like some avenging force, blocking him from what was his.

Reed walked back into the hospital room and sat down. He avoided looking at Maxim. Reed hadn't agreed with the plan, hadn't wanted Maxim to go to Sabrina's apartment even with two members of his team accompanying him.

"If anything happens to her, you're already at the top of the suspect list and will go straight to jail."

"We'll just have to make sure nothing happens to her, then, won't we?"

"If they ever get any substantial evidence, they will arrest you, sir. Elias had to talk hard and fast even after dropping a hailstorm of powerful names indebted to you and your family."

"And that's why we have him on retainer."

"Needless to say, you are prohibited from leaving town in the event they need to question you further. Elias is certain they will."

Maxim shrugged. The amount of narcotics in his system stopped him from feeling any pain from the motion. "I wouldn't leave without her, anyway."

Reed ran his hand over his jaw, showing a rare display of frustration.

It was true; Maxim had made a poor decision. Anticipation had impaired his judgment, and Reed had been forced to witness it. Perhaps he shouldn't have approached her so boldly. He'd underestimated his opponent, and it had resulted in the loss of his woman and disappointment from his loyal assistant.

"It was badly done, Reed. I promise you I won't behave so impulsively again. I should have heeded your counsel, my friend, and this outcome is my punishment. Don't make it worse by losing faith in me."

"Never, sir."

"So, where do we stand?"

"There are no charges either from the initial kidnapping or the visit that was made to Ms. Samora's apartment. The crime scene investigative unit is done processing the apartment, but I'm sorry to say, sir, your butterfly is again in the wind."

"With him."

"Most likely. Our man in OPD heard that her protection has absconded with her. For her safety, of course."

Maxim took a deep breath and rested his head on the pillows propped up behind him. "It's okay. I have her scent. She'll eventually attempt to reestablish her life. Make contact with her friends, go home, go to work. She'll come back. She won't be able to stay away from me too long knowing I'm here. Her memory will return once the trauma of the warehouse incident wears off."

"Sometimes memories don't return, sir. Sometimes inside, people don't heal."

"She's strong. The good times we had won't escape her forever, and if I'm there, willing to beg forgiveness, she will return to me."

Reed remained quiet a few moments.

"Might I suggest you return to the hotel? Going back to the oceanside house may be a bad idea given the circumstances."

Maxim closed his eyes. "To the latter, I agree. Do you think it would be best to find an appropriate hotel in the East Bay? The Claremont, perhaps?"

"No, sir. It's best to be closer to the San Francisco airport. Just in case."

"Your honest opinion. What do you think of my Sabrina?"

Maxim heard his assistant shift in his chair and opened his eyes to see the other man leaning with his elbows on his knees and his hands clutched between them. Reed stared at his interlocked fingers.

"I think she's everything you said she'd be. Beautiful, intelligent, strong. None of the women I've seen you with have truly done her justice."

Maxim couldn't suppress the pride he felt in Sabrina and in himself for choosing her.

"All that said, I fear what she can do to you. I fear she'll use your love, your history against you."

Maxim waved a dismissive hand. "Don't fear for me. Once Sabrina and I have spent time in our oceanside home, once we eventually come up for air, the last thing she'll want to do is cause me harm. That's what my room is for. Working out differences so love can flourish."

"I can only hope what you say is true," Reed said, standing. "I'll go and see what's happening with your discharge papers."

Maxim watched Reed leave the room, knowing his assistant was displeased. Reed was protective of him, but Reed didn't know Sabrina. A little time in her presence would lead Reed to care for her almost as much as Maxim did.

CHAPTER TWELVE

"Where in the hell are we?" Sabrina asked, refusing to get out of the car. She was cranky and hungry and wanted the comfort of being in a familiar place. He'd said they would stay close to Oakland, but after an hour on the road she'd fallen asleep knowing their definitions of "close" were miles apart. She rolled down the passenger-side window, unbuckled her seat belt, and stuck her head out the window to get a better view of her surroundings.

Oh hell no. She wasn't getting out of the car and staying in the run-down cabin in front of them.

"What is it with you and your friends buying these creepy-ass, dilapidated buildings? And wasn't there this movie called *Cabin in the Woods?* Was this place the movie's inspiration?"

Zeus remained silent.

"I'm not going in there, Zeus, so you might as well back the car up, turn us around, and take me back to someplace with people...and buildings. And graffiti. Someplace where I can fall asleep to the sound of sirens wailing through the streets." She looked around the area – trees upon trees for as far as the eye could see. "I already miss the homeless couple who get into fights in front of my building every Saturday night."

189

Zeus reached for his door, and she reached for him, grabbing his biceps to stall him. "I'm serious. I'm not staying in that place tonight. I want to go home. I...."

He opened the door and stepped out of the car, pulling free from her hands. He walked to the trunk, taking out her battered, hastily packed suitcase and two duffel bags he apparently kept in the trunk for himself, and walked toward the creaky-looking porch.

She folded her arms over the top of the open window and rested her head on the back of her hands as she watched him fish out another set of keys from his duffel bag. He opened the front door to shadow and darkness. She couldn't see what awaited her on the inside, but Zeus, the big idiot, picked up the bags, walked over the threshold, and slammed the door shut with his booted foot.

"Asshole," she muttered, sitting back in her seat and facing forward to look into the trees.

He isn't going to just leave me sitting out here, she thought. A much more rational and accurate thought followed. He's Zeus; of course he'd leave her out here. As a matter of fact, he just had.

She looked back over at the cabin. A dim light glowed behind thick curtains. Thinking of how badly she'd misjudged K.C. and Dominic's house, she acknowledged that maybe Zeus's hideout would be cozy, modern, and warm inside. Maybe it was as comfortable as her home.

Something skittered through the fallen leaves on the ground, and it didn't sound like the small squirrel-like somethings she was used to in her neighborhood, either. She didn't see anything when she looked out the window, and it freaked her out. She wasn't the scared type, but she bit back a shout as the sound moved closer to the car. Flinging her door open, she sprinted toward the cabin and up the stairs, barreling through the front door only to freeze when it shut behind her.

"I'm damned," she muttered, looking around the room. Cobwebs hung from the ceilings like translucent harem veils. Dust coated the floor and furniture coverings. The cabin had high ceilings, which made the room feel cavernous, especially furnished with only two pieces of furniture. The sheets covering both items might have once been the pure white of clouds, but they were a dark grimy gray that made the sidewalks in downtown Oakland seem pristine. One item sat against the wall opposite her, in the shape of a sofa, and the other was to her right, in front of the curtained window.

"Zeus?" she whispered, only to have her voice swallowed by the gloominess of the place.

He didn't respond.

Sabrina reached for the gray-stoned blade sheathed at her back. Maybe she didn't know how to use it like a professional, definitely nowhere near the level of skill Zeus displayed, but if someone – or something – came at her, she would start slicing. And if she had to fight Zeus to get the keys to his car and get the hell out of here, she would. Hell, he could be a real life Leatherface for all she knew, and like a fool she'd willingly accompanied him to his killing fields.

Attempting to rein in her paranoia, she closed her eyes and took a deep breath. When she opened her eyes again, Zeus was standing in front of her with a bucket in each hand – one held supplies and the other steaming hot water.

She flinched and took a step back.

Zeus held the items out to her. "Place needs cleaning."

She snorted. "Then hop to it."

He stared, continuing to extend the items out to her.

"You can look at me all you want, but I do not work for Merry Maids. You want your cabin cleaned, I may *help* you, but I won't be the only one doing all the cleaning."

He shrugged and dropped the buckets, water sloshing over the side of one. "You clean this room, and I'll take care of the rest."

If she was an ungrateful person, it wouldn't matter that he had helped her clean her place without being asked, without complaint. The truth was, she was grateful to him for it, and if doing this one task helped him out, she should welcome the opportunity.

And *after* it was done, she was leaving.

"Fine. I'll help, but you better have some real food around for me when I done. Or else."

"Threats. Cute," he said, nodding at the blade dangling limply against her thigh. He shook his head and offered a shadow of a smile before turning and walking down a wide hallway that appeared to connect to the kitchen.

Sabrina resheathed the blade and looked around the room again. Stepping to the window, she pulled the mustard-yellow curtain back and frowned as she peeked out. She wasn't afraid of what crept around out there. Darkness had descended over the forest at a faster pace than it seemed to in the rest of the world. She'd left the car door open, and the interior light illuminated her brown leather backpack sitting right there on the passenger-side floor. Opening the front door, she walked onto the porch. Except for the occasional crunch of leaves from forest creatures skittering around unseen, this place was cocooned in silence. When she took a step in the direction of the car, things called out to each other from the high tree branches. They didn't sound like the small, lively sounding birds inhabiting the spindly limbed trees in her neighborhood.

Sabrina gauged the distance between the porch and the car.

About fifteen, maybe twenty feet.

The noise in the trees had quieted. She reached for her blade again, ignoring how automatic the motion was becoming. No more than forty steps and she could make her way to the car and back.

Just forty steps, Bree. You've survived two of the most insane days of your life; you can't let an overactive imagination defeat you.

She bounced on the balls of her feet, knife clutched in hand, and sprinted forward. Reaching the car, she grabbed her bag and felt something brush against her leg. She screamed – she did; she was woman enough to admit it – as she leaped up and balanced on the edge of the open doorway of Zeus's car. Zeus would probably kill her if he saw how she was misusing his stupid car. She'd almost impaled herself in the throat as she tried to hold on to the blade and the roof of the car.

The things in the trees screeched, and the things on the ground were stalking her; she *knew* they were. If they were scared or intimidated, they would have remained silent and still. But the forest was a cacophony of sound. She was being hunted, and the loud creatures were the audience of cheering fans waiting for her to be taken down.

Sabrina steeled herself. After the life she had lived, she would not go down easily. She would fight Bambi and Sasquatch too if it meant she lived to see another day. She strapped her backpack around her shoulders and jumped away from the car, twisting around and landing in what she decided was her battle stance, waiting for the first challenger to appear. The sounds of the creatures continued to taunt her, but none came.

"That's what I thought," she said, closing the car door and sauntering back to the house. Something big and black flew at her, its soft wings grazing her forehead, and she hollered again and sprinted the last few steps to the front door, yelling even louder when she saw the black figure standing just outside the door. Of its own volition, her hand swung the blade in a wide arc. She felt a blow to the wrist that sent the blade skittering across the wooden porch floor.

"What are you doing?" Zeus's voice rolled over her, low and flat.

"I was attacked," she gritted out, looking back at the forest. "Bastards," she yelled as the noise only grew more exuberant. They were laughing at her.

She growled and stomped into the living room. She would have slammed the door, but Zeus was there to gently close it behind them. She heard a *click*, and a low-wattage bulb came on overhead. When she looked at Zeus, his face was expressionless, but she knew that glint in his steel-colored eyes. The bastard was laughing at her *on the inside*.

He'd probably witnessed the whole thing and chosen to watch instead of help her.

"Bastard," she said, wanting to punch him in the stomach but opting not to, because in the end, it would hurt her more than it hurt him.

"You have a great ass. I loved how it bounced when you hopped on the car after the rabbit brushed up against your leg." She heard both lust and humor in his voice and shivered. She chalked the reaction up to the adrenaline rush.

"Did you plan to hot-wire my car and escape back to Oakland?"

"I needed my bag. I wanted my iPod, so I could listen to my music as I cleaned *your* house."

Zeus shook his head and rolled his eyes as he walked to the object in front of the window. He pulled the dirty cover off, causing a plume of dust to rise in the air. She covered her mouth and nose with the sleeve of her jacket and stood, dumbfounded, when she saw the tricked-out entertainment center. Wide-screen TV, surround sound stereo system, a gaming system with DVDs and games stacked to the side.

"In the middle of nowhere, Zeus? Really?"

He nodded. "You can put your music in the docking station and play whatever you want. I'll be in the back." He paused as he turned to leave, dangling her blade between his fingers. "And, Sabrina, remember lesson one. Hold on to your weapon, or you might find yourself being stabbed with it."

He left the room, and she was alone. The sounds outside were barely muted by the walls and closed windows. It was like being the hated contestant at the Thunderdome out here. Fucking animals.

Placing her music in the docking station, she opened the "oldies #2" folder that had a compilation of Sam & Dave, Otis Redding, Bobby Blue Bland, and other R&B singers.

She sang and cleaned as her skin and clothes became more soiled than the room she was cleaning. When the water in the bucket was as black as muck, she lifted it and made her way to the back of the cabin.

The kitchen on the other end of the hall was tidy, stark, and spacious. She walked to the right and peeked into a spotless bathroom. Farther down there was a medium-size bedroom. Walking in the other direction, she found Zeus in a much larger bedroom, reclining on a California-king-size bed, watching a rugby game. There was no sound because a pair of headphones was plugged into the TV on one end and straddled Zeus's rock head on the other.

His mouth cocked up on the side when he noticed her standing in the doorway.

She almost threw the bucket of water on him. "You bastard," she muttered when he slid the headphones forward, resting them in his lap.

"Don't know why you're constantly bringing up the facts of my birth."

She dropped the bucket and took a step forward. He continued to grin, far from being intimidated.

"I have been working like a slave in there, and you're in here watching TV?"

"There was nothing to do back here. Cleaned it on my last visit."

"So why didn't you come help me up front?"

He waved toward the television. "Because the match is on. My team's playing in the quarter finals."

She just stared at him because, one, she was at a loss over what to say, what to do. Of course in Zeus's world it made perfect sense to let a guest clean his filthy-assed living room while he lay on his butt and watched his team play a rugby tournament.

By the way he kept watching the bucket at her feet, he must have sensed she was about to snap, and he was trying to figure out in which direction she would do it.

"I got steaks and potatoes on the grill out back. That's got to be worth something."

For a moment all Sabrina could do was stare at him. She took a few deep breaths and left the room before she did something that would force him to pull his blades. Even though he was likely the most qualified to do so, she would *not* let a crazy man drive her bat-shit crazy.

She walked to the bathroom and stripped, too upset to appreciate the clean simplicity of the space – claw-foot tub, a wide, shell-shaped pedestal sink, and cold stone floors. She bathed with his soap and used his lotion to moisturize her body. She wrapped a large blue towel around her because her clothes were in the small suitcase in his room.

Opening the bathroom door, she jumped, suppressing a shriek when she saw Zeus standing inches from the doorway. He stared at her in that intense, gray-eyed way of his. Without meaning to, her gaze strayed over him, taking in the hard length of flesh pressing against the crotch of his pants. She wondered how long he'd been standing there but couldn't find enough saliva in her mouth to ask.

She clutched the towel tighter and took a step back, which caused Zeus to take a step forward. Her heart beat faster than the black hearts of any of those demon-possessed rabbits lurking in the dark woods. The area between her legs had grown damp with heated moisture that had nothing to do with the tub of water she had just stepped out of.

Zeus took another step toward her, and she retreated another step back. They repeated the steps to that particular dance two more times until she felt the press of the sink against her butt. He took one last step and pressed the length of his hard body against hers. His arm snaked around her, and she felt its heat through the thick material of the towel. She closed her eyes, fighting the need to spread her legs for him. Her pussy clenched as his hand palmed her ass and squeezed. He ground his heated length against her abdomen. She groaned, her hips rotating to both ease the ache and seek out the erection that caused it.

Zeus lifted her onto the edge of the sink, his hips filling the space between her trembling thighs. The sink was cold against her bare ass. She wanted this. She wanted him, but she wouldn't reward him for using her to clean. Reaching back to steady herself, her hand encountered the bar of soap close to the faucet. She gripped it like it was a blade and struck

Zeus on the side of the head with it as his lips played along the side of her neck. The corner of the soap came back dented. Zeus pulled back, frowning down at her with confusion and lust.

"Back off before I shove this bar of soap up your ass."

"You would sodomize me with my own soap? Is that how you like it, Bree?" he asked, tilting his head to the side in reflection.

She dropped the soap in the sink and pushed against his chest, scrambling back to steady ground tightening the towel around her again.

"What I'd like is to on put my bedclothes, eat, and go to bed."

"Don't you want to...finish? I'll make it quick."

"You're an idiot," she said, walking around him. "I'm not letting you screw me. Go jack off to your rugby game."

She walked to his room, snatched up her suitcase, and walked past him again on her way to the smaller bedroom. Slamming the door shut, she locked it, though she knew if Zeus wanted to get in, he would. She put the overlong, spaghetti-strapped nightshirt on and slid into a pair of pajama bottoms so old they looked dingy even though they were clean. There was no TV, radio, or any other form of entertainment in this room. The bed was pushed up against the corner of the far wall. There was a squat, tired-looking wooden dresser, an older end table near the head of the bed, and a junkyard reject of a shadeless lamp placed on top of it. The naked bulb was covered with a layer of dust.

Sabrina's stomach made a sound so fierce it reminded her of the wild animals outside. She put her hand against it, but it continued to grumble. She heard a screen door open and close. A few moments later it grumbled again as Zeus came stomping back into the kitchen. She moved to the locked door. The promise of charbroiled meat compelled her to open it and walk toward the large square table in the center of the kitchen and sit down, daring Zeus not to serve her.

"There are no sheets on the bed in that room," Zeus informed her as he placed two sturdy terra-cotta plates on the table.

She ignored him, though he had her stomach's full attention as he forked a slab of juicy meat onto her plate. String beans were doled out after he placed a foil-wrapped potato next to the steak.

"Where'd you get all this stuff?"

"Meat and beans were in the deep freezer. Potatoes in the yard," he said, sitting down with the bottle of ale he'd pulled from the refrigerator. There was a lukewarm glass of tap water for her.

"Thank you," she uttered, somewhat shamed. Okay, so he hadn't helped her clean, but he'd cooked for her. It meant something.

"You really want to thank me, come over here, pull out my dick, straddle my lap and – "

"Stop."

"Just saying. You really want to thank me..."

"You've gotten all the thanks you're going to get, Zeus."

As she cut into the steak and put the first bite into her mouth, she rethought her last statement. She wanted to climb on him and thank him from the deepest recesses of her inner sex. The meat was seasoned to perfection and as tender as love's first kiss. She moaned, her eyes rolling back in ecstasy.

"And that's how I fuck you without ever laying a finger on you."

She ignored him. Smug bastard. But he was right. All her five senses hummed with satisfaction. She took a bite of her string beans and scowled at him. She did not get horny over food. At least not before Zeus had cooked for her. The man was nearly a stranger. A strange stranger, at that, but every time he touched her with his body or by proxy via food, she descended into a fit of arousal. She wasn't shy about sex or her sexuality, but she'd had no idea how powerfully her body could respond until Zeus had shared his own brand of thunder.

Eventually she stopped inhaling her food long enough to notice he had not touched his. He watched her with that immovable gaze. Waiting.

She sighed and leaned back in her chair. Her attraction to him was illogical. Even when he was pissing her off, or ignoring the fact that she was a woman capable of making the best decisions for herself, she wanted him.

"You want to know what's really silly?" he asked, leaning forward.

"A grown man choosing to make me believe he was helping with the cleaning when he was really hiding away in a room watching some stupid game?"

"First, I wasn't hiding. Second, rugby is *not* stupid."

"So say all men about stupid games."

"Only real men play rugby," he said, dismissing her as he dug into his food.

"Do you play?"

"When I have the time. Learned when I was a kid living in Marseille with the nuns."

"I can't imagine you playing team sports." She smiled.

"Liked hitting people when I was a kid, and I could take a hit. Also liked how the game is organized."

"So why not football? American football, that is."

"Wasn't born here. They had rugby back home, so I learned rugby. Plus, there's stuff touching you in American football. Don't really like to be touched."

"For someone who doesn't like to be touched, you sure do a lot of touching," she said as she reached for her glass.

"I like touching *you*," he said, waving the steak knife in her direction. "When something feels as good as you, makes sense to touch. Got the blades; also got you."

She had to admit there was something intensely addictive about his touch. She had never felt the same intensity with any other man, and after the abuse she had experienced with Ernesto, she shouldn't feel this way about a man who was so obviously violent.

"So, if you don't like being touched, why would you play rugby? They touch a lot in that game too."

He shook his head and looked at her as if she were denser than petrified oak. He stood abruptly and pulled her toward his bedroom, navigating her to the foot of the bed and forcing her to sit. He disconnected the headphones, and the sounds of the rugby match filled the room.

"Look at the players there. What do you see?"

"They're dressed in all black?"

"Exactly. Not so hard to understand, is it?"

Hell no she didn't understand, but him treating her like she was developmentally delayed didn't prompt her to want to ask questions.

"I'm sure this all makes sense in the world of Zeus – "

"Zeus's world. Mount Olympus. That's what I should call this place."

"Whatever. The point is, me recognizing one of the teams is wearing all black doesn't help me know what you're trying to have me understand."

"I don't like to be touched," he said, then left. She heard him in the kitchen, finishing his meal, and not ten minutes later he was back in the bedroom.

"I don't like things pressing on me, weighing me down. American football has too much equipment. Rugby, you got your uniform and your cleats and your cup. Everything else is optional."

"I used to want to be a dancer." The words exited her mouth before she'd realized they wanted to come out.

Shut it, Sabrina. You don't share your life with anybody. Shut the hell up. She'd made the mistake of opening up a little with Ernesto, and he'd used every bit of knowledge about her to exploit, play on, or prey on her so seamlessly she hadn't even realized that she was being manipulated.

"Break up? Break up for what, Brina? I was wrong, baby. It won't ever happen again. You know I love you, would do anything for you. It's you and me, Brina. I'll take care of you and make sure you're never lonely or alone. I'll never abandon you like your mother and sister did, not even when the times are hard. I love you just that much, baby, and I never want to see you hurt again."

Sabrina knew Zeus was waiting for her to say more, but she watched the television, watched the hard-bodied men running down the field in a formation she didn't understand.

"I like that one dance move where they twirl down from the pole while hanging upside down. Did you ever learn to do that?"

It took her a moment to realize what he was talking about. When she did, she snatched a pillow from behind her and swung at him, connecting with nothing, he was so fast.

"I said dancer, not *stripper*, you idiot."

"I prefer the lap dance, but Big Country swears the – "

"That is not dancing," she gritted out, trying to regain her composure. "Jesus, men are such idiots. I said I wanted to be a dancer. For sane, somewhat well-adjusted people, that means a trained dancer – modern, jazz, ballet, West African, take your pick. A stripper takes her clothes off to music, and though some of them are good, even trained, stripping is not dancing."

"You say toh-may-toe, I say toh-mah-toe. Who knew you'd be such a dance snob?" He leaned back on the bed. "You ever strip before?"

"No."

"Not even for your man?"

"No, not even."

"You ever want to? Strip for your man, that is?"

She shrugged. The only man she'd ever wanted to please so desperately had been Ernesto, and he hadn't liked her taking too much control in the bedroom. To him, a little striptease would have been proof she'd been cheating on him. He would've said the only place she could have learned such behavior was in another man's bedroom. He liked to believe she was some naive thing that needed to be kept away from the ugly desires of other men. A striptease for Ernesto would have ended in violence. Him accusing her and lashing out, and Sabrina, never one to be cowed, always defending herself. Toward the end there had been too many bloody nights sparked by his insecurity over her fidelity. The irony was that, for as long as they'd been together, there had been only him.

"Would you strip for me?"

She felt the familiar heat churn low in her belly. He was watching her in a cool, contemplative way, but his eyes, polished silver, gave proof of the desire burning inside of him.

If she extended her foot, slipped it between his legs, she knew she would find him hard and ready; she knew this.

"Possibly," she dared. "If you asked me in the right way."

"Strip for me," he gritted out as if she were causing him physical pain.

She smiled and straddled the bed on her knees. She rolled her hips in a dirty wind, inching her nightdress up her thighs as she did. Then she cocked an eyebrow and plopped down on the bed, propping the pillows against the headboard and leaning back against them to continue watching the match, cutting the cord on whatever degenerate fantasy he was having.

"No, I won't strip for you, because first you have to learn to ask."

His jaw clenched and unclenched many times as she smiled over at him. He eventually broke eye contact and rubbed a frustrated hand over his face.

"Well, will you at least *dance* for me?" The way he said dance made it clear he thought little of the art form.

She snorted. "Oh no, poor man. That'll require even more good behavior than a striptease."

"Tease. That describes you perfectly."

She continued to smile. It was nice seeing him disgruntled. And he hadn't reached for a single blade during the entire discussion.

"What's so special about dancing, anyway?"

She rolled to her side and hugged the pillow against her head as she spoke to him. "Lots of things. Like when you dance, you feel strong, but you also feel fluid. You flow. But mostly, most importantly, when I danced, I never felt alone. It was like being connected to everything by rhythm and movement."

"That's what it's like with my blades."

"Blade dancer," she teased.

He pulled her knee over his thigh. "I like that. Blade dancer. Me and my blades dancing to the tune of the blade's spirit."

It was probably a bad call on her part to indulge his delusions, but she had to admit there was a certain divineness to how he could work his blades.

"So are you going to train me on how to use them tomorrow?"

"Yeah. Tomorrow we'll dance together. With the blades."

"You better not cut me, Zeus. I'm serious."

"Woman, I'm not some green boy. I cut only when I intend to."

The stadium went into an uproar, and Zeus sat up and surged toward the television.

"What happened?"

"Try."

"Try what?"

Again, he looked at her as if her name was Idiot. "Big fucking hit. Turnover. Try."

"Is that good?"

"For the All Blacks it is. That Wallaby half-conscious on the ground, he's done in. He won't think it's so good."

"So why are they holding the guy up by his shorts like that?" she asked later as one guy's teammates lifted him in the air by the shorts to catch the ball.

"Not a good time for questions."

She huffed and leaned back into the pillows. She intermittently watched the game and watched Zeus watching the game. He wasn't one of those animated fans. He sat on the edge of the bed silent, still, and engrossed.

Sabrina closed her eyes after a while. The game was interesting and fast moving, but she didn't know enough about it for it to keep her from resisting the pull of sleep. Maybe my exhaustion also comes from the fact that my body is still healing, she thought.

"Hey."

The word drifted to her from across an ocean of darkness, but the utterance might as well have been the anchor dragging her to the deepest fathoms of sleep.

CHAPTER THIRTEEN

Zeus leaned on his side as he watched Sabrina sleep. He'd turned the television off, and her features were submerged in shadow. She was curled in fetal position on top of the bedcovers, a section of the comforter folded over her legs. Zeus reached down, flipped the comforter off her, and dragged his hand from the knobby part of her ankle all the way up to her hip. Her skin was melted chocolate beneath his fingertips. When would the need, the pleasure, from touching her skin cease?

He brushed a twist of hair away from her face, only to watch it spring back to its original position. He played in the soft mass just because he liked the feel of it against his rough palm. When playing in her hair wasn't enough, he rose from the bed and stripped. Naked, he paused, experiencing another rush of pleasure. She was sleeping in his bed. His. He got hard, his dick straining to claim her. She was in his bed, was his to satisfy. Confident with that knowledge, he left the room and took a quick shower. As the water ran over his skin, he felt as powerful as the god his mother had named him after. He was rich with possessions that he could use to tempt Sabrina to remain with him. She wasn't used to having much, so she'd be grateful. He would share what he had to get what he wanted, which was her body, available for his use for as long as he wanted to use it. And if being the benevolent god didn't work, he had no problem embodying the demons the priests had accused him of being possessed by.

Returning to his bedroom, he saw Sabrina hadn't moved from where he had left her. In his shower fantasy he'd imagined her awake and naked on her back, legs bent and spread wide, liquid ready for him to climb up and push into her. He watched, mesmerized by the rise of her breasts as she breathed. She was deeply asleep, beyond this world, but he was talented enough to bring her back and send them both to a place they would inhabit together. And like Adam and Eve, they would be the human inhabitants, and the only snake the one dangling between his thighs. Leaning over, Zeus slowly turned Sabrina onto her back.

She made a sound somewhere between a moan and sigh, and he froze in the process of angling his knife toward her shoulder. He remained still, not wanting her to wake up. He hadn't gotten to play yet, and he suddenly wanted to play.

Once she'd settled, he resumed cutting the strap of her nightshirt. He spread her arms and cut the sides, from beneath her armpits to the hem. He removed the top piece, humming with pleasure. Her breasts were ripe and waiting to be squeezed and sucked, but he tuned them out, diligently cutting the ugly drawstring pajama bottoms from hip to ankle. When he made his way to the inseam between her thighs, he closed his eyes and rested his head against her pelvic bone, shaking with the level of restraint needed to go slow. All he wanted to do was bury his face in her crotch and suck her essence straight into him.

Soon. I will wake her soon, he thought as he finished cutting away her clothing. Perfection. He reached out and squeezed her breast, playing with it before lowering his head to the puckered nipple, sucking. "Wake up," he commanded.

Sabrina writhed, her body undulating beneath him as her gaze locked on to his, silently pleading for more. He sucked so hard on her nipple he wouldn't have been surprised if he'd drawn milk. Trailing kisses from her solar plexus down to her navel, he moved toward the springy curls that veiled his heaven.

He massaged the flesh covering her pelvic bone with his thumbs before stroking his hand over the roundness of her ass. He inhaled the moist scent of her arousal mixed with his soap, branding her head to toe as his. Before their time together was done, he would have marked her so deeply, any thought of sex would always resurrect his image, his taste, his touch, him.

He pushed a finger deep inside of her. Her breathing stuttered. So fucking wet. He pushed another finger inside and worked her with both hand and mouth, lingering because this gave him so much pleasure his dick was on the verge of exploding without even being inside of her. He was losing himself in her, and he didn't lose himself with women. He may suck, he always fucked, he came, and he left. He didn't want anything more, and he didn't give anything more.

He was so attuned to Sabrina he felt the moment her breathing changed and she began her descent. She came in an explosive wave of orgasmic energy that flowed into him.

Once her body calmed, softened, her hands stroked his hair, fingers both light and soothing. He stilled and closed his eyes, savoring the gentleness of her touch. He would never forget this one moment. He would engrave it in his memory, in his sensory structure. No one had ever touched him this way before. No one had ever played in his hair. He'd had it grabbed from the back once as his attacker used it to slam his face into a grimy stone wall back when he was young. He'd had it raked with impatient, manicured fingernails, even had it chopped off by nuns who hadn't the patience to deal with its unruliness. No one had ever played in it. He likely wouldn't have tolerated it if any woman other than Sabrina had tried.

His body grew lethargic as he enjoyed a sensation so compelling that it overrode his need to come. He rested his head on her hip and pulled his fingers out of her warmth, reaching around to hold on to her thigh. He sighed. Sex in a minute. Soon, he promised as he his body grew heavy and his mind slowed.

⸻ ◆◦◆ ⸻

THOUGH ZEUS WAS asleep, Sabrina continued to stroke hair soft as sheared silk. It should be a sin for a man so hard and unmanageable to have such soft hair. A part of her believed it wouldn't matter if his hair was coarse, locked, thin, permed – well, maybe not permed – she would find pleasure in gliding her fingers over it.

She liked this intimacy, liked that he allowed it, seemed to take pleasure in it. She smiled. He'd liked it so much he'd been distracted from finding his own release.

Feeling his stubbled cheek against her naked skin, Sabrina frowned. Didn't she have pajamas on when she went to sleep? Looking down, saw she was naked and Zeus had cut the clothing from her body. Lord, she thought as she resisted the urge to grab his oh-so-fucking-soft strands and toss him off her. She definitely did not have enough clothes to have him cutting them off her when the mood hit him.

Instead of abusing his hair, she soothed herself by continuing to stroke it. I'll just tell him, she thought. No more cutting up clothes. He had the capacity to be practical sometimes. Maybe he thought it was romantic to cut the clothes off his bed partners. Her snort of laughter filled the room, causing Zeus to growl in his sleep. He's just like a big jungle cat that doesn't like being disturbed, she thought, smiling. Zeus settled, gripping her hip as if she were his custom-made pillow.

She closed her eyes, relaxing into the moment. It was a terribly bad idea to indulge in feelings of fondness, intimacy, and connection when it came to Zeus. He was a killer, and she was in hiding, hunted long before this Kragen guy came into the picture.

She'd promised herself she wouldn't have anything to do with disturbed, violent men once she'd left Ernesto. Zeus was as disturbed and violent as any man she'd ever known, and she was lying in bed with him, still wanting him inside of her, embedded so deeply they both forgot what it meant to be apart. That's how deep her damage went. She hoped this wasn't yet another Samora curse – attracting and being attracted to killers. She should get up, go to the smaller room, and in due time walk away from a bad choice before a choice had to be made. Five minutes, she promised herself as she relaxed into the pillow, not fully ready to let go of his warmth or the steadiness of him pressing her into the bed. In five minutes, she would leave.

In two minutes, she was asleep.

———————•••••———————

MAXIM WAS BACK at his hotel suite before the clock struck midnight. With the witching hour upon him, he felt compelled to do something dark and dangerous. Unleash the rage he'd held in check for the better part of the day as he lay in the hospital.

He couldn't go back to his house on the coast because he believed the police or the people protecting Sabrina would follow him and find out about the location. He didn't have Sabrina. No, not only did he not have her, the oversize ape who'd killed two of his men and almost had him arrested had her. Maxim didn't want to contemplate what Zeus was doing to her. No one, not even the police, knew where he had taken her. If the police knew, Maxim's informant would have reported the information to him.

To top off this hellacious day, he was back in the overcast gloom of San Francisco. He was really beginning to hate this city. A phone, his phone, rang somewhere in the suite, but he ignored it. He hobbled to the bathroom to examine the damage the flat-eyed killer had done to his shoulder. Eight bloody stitches. And if it hadn't been for the ruthless negotiation of one of the best lawyers money could buy, he and his eight stitches would be secured in housing generously provided by California's correctional system.

Maxim shifted his gaze in the mirror and saw Reed's reflection in the doorway, holding a phone out to him.

"No calls, Reed."

"It's your father, sir. He won't be put off by some 'brainless flunky.' He said he would talk to you by phone or in person, your choice."

Maxim didn't hold back his sneer. Reed was more intelligent than any person on his father's staff, and unlike them, Reed was pleasant to be around.

He stepped forward and grabbed the phone, taking it off mute. "Father."

"Maxim, imagine my disappointment when I received a call from Elias stating you were under investigation for kidnapping."

"Must I?" Maxim said, stepping back to the mirror and re-taping the bandage covering his shoulder wound.

Silence stretched out on the other end. Maxim could picture the angry flush spreading across his father's face. It was there every time Maxim said something "impertinent."

Gin and tonic, Maxim mouthed to his assistant. After the day he'd had, it was more than acceptable for him to drink straight from the bottle and chase it with a handful of pain pills if he chose.

"Why are you doing this? You should have moved on from that indiscretion years ago, but no, you take this woman who was nothing – no family, no status – and you pretended she was more than she could ever hope to be. How many times have I told you, boy, you let nothings go. You never hold on to them. But you. No, you track them down and play out some parody of love. I will *not* let you put your mother through the humiliations of having to deal with your twisted infatuations again. You end this."

The *or else* hovered, unspoken, but Maxim heard it loud and clear.

"Threaten me, old man, and I may be forced to react." The bastard knew Maxim did not react well to threats. He always had a habit of retaliating in very unseemly ways. "So, I trust the gathering in the UK is going as you planned?" he asked, stepping out of the bathroom and flicking the light switch off.

"GODDAMN IT," ZEUS shouted as he shot up in the empty bed. What had happened? Had she drugged him? She was conniving. He wouldn't put it past her. One minute he'd been in her, readying her for a deeper invasion, and then...nothing. She'd drugged him or knocked him unconscious or....

Where the hell was she?

He pushed off the bed, naked save for the crumpled pieces of her clothing stuck to his skin. Frustration urged him to shred them into confetti-like bits.

"Sabrina," he yelled, something he normally didn't do. He felt a slight unease when there was no response. He grabbed his kukri and his Bowie and stepped out of the bedroom into the empty kitchen, only to be greeted by more silence.

The Bowie began to tap against his thigh as he imagined Maxim's men coming to his cabin, disarming...disarming... *Hell*. He hadn't done a perimeter check, set the alarm, or cuffed Sabrina to the bed frame before he'd lost consciousness. She could be long gone. She could have taken his keys, fought off her killer rabbits, and left him.

"Sabrina!"

Silence.

He stalked toward the front of the cabin and froze at the opening to the living room. The room was spotless and gleaming, but it was the sight of Sabrina sitting on the sofa wearing a tank top and boy shorts, his earphones on as she played *Insidious Realm* – one of the best role-playing games ever – that had him cocking his head in confusion.

"Thought you didn't play video games."

She didn't respond. He walked over to her, and she barely spared him a glance as she battled a troll. And quickly died.

She snatched the headphones off her head and glared at him as if it was his fault. "This game sucks. It's too damned hard."

"No, it isn't."

"Yes, the fuck, it is."

Like he was gonna argue. The game did not suck. She just sucked at it. "How long you been playing?"

"Three hours. Three freaking hours of my life I'll never be able to get back."

"You like it."

Her head fell forward in defeat. "I do."

He stood her up, sat down, and resettled her on his lap. Her body was tense, not languid and malleable like it had been the night before.

"You're naked," she muttered.

"I'm also as hard as a fucking pike, but I don't hear you saying anything about that."

She tried to stand, but he held her around her waist with one arm while maneuvering the controller with his free hand. She relaxed a little when he hit the menu button and brought his hands together, resting the controller on her stomach. She leaned back against his chest, watching the screen as he went through the weapons, magical items, and tools she'd accumulated thus far. He shook his head in disgust and proceeded to delete her saved game.

"Hey." She reared up, reaching for the controller, trying to pry it from his grasp. "That was *my* game."

"We have to start at the beginning so you can learn what to do. You're not going to beat the troll because you don't have enough knowledge, skills, or the right weapons to beat him."

She looked over her shoulder and scowled at him. He could tell she wanted to yell at him, but she also wanted to know how to defeat the creature. He waited as she worked it out. Eventually she squinted, giving him the evil eye. He made sure his gaze was stony, though he felt like grinning at her intimidation tactic. She turned and leaned back into him, crossing her arms over her chest to indicate she was still pissed. As if he gave a shit.

When she wiggled her ass, impatient for him to continue, he was caught in a dilemma. His dick urged him to throw the controller across the room so he could play his own game with her body.

"Show me already," Sabrina demanded as she flicked her hand out toward the television screen.

His eyes darted between the controller and her breasts. Show her. What should he show her? How to play a game he'd mastered ten times over, or how to navigate the crown of his penis into her mouth? Handless. With her eyes closed. His grip loosened on the controller. *Show her.*

She reached down and took the controller away from him. "To hell with it. I'll work it out myself. I was doing fine before you interrupted me, anyway."

"You'd died."

"I would've figured it out. That's what I did before you barged in." She adjusted herself on his lap again, and he groaned. "And I'm not having sex with you, so you can tell your little friend to stand down, go back to sleep, or whatever it is they do when they're not needed."

"Hang around," he said, taking back the controller and inputting her name.

"What?"

"They just hang around until they're needed."

He scrolled to the character she had chosen for herself before and selected it again. He went to the main weapons window and scrolled through the choices, pausing when he noticed her back vibrating against his chest. When he looked over at her, she was laughing silently.

He frowned. "What?"

She smiled, and his thumb twitched spastically over the bud of the controller. He wanted to suck her smile straight into him, store it away inside, unearthing it only when he was trapped in the dark, ugly place that sometimes descended over him.

His eyes flicked back to the TV. "Why did you choose the mallet? It's too big for your character."

She laid the back of her head on his shoulder. "I chose it because I wanted to beat my enemies into a bloody pulp."

He flicked the cursor to the Genesis Sword. It didn't look like much, but it would evolve into a powerful weapon of pure killing beauty. He clicked on it.

"Why that one?" she asked.

Was she aware her foot was stoking up and down his shin?

"It's light and sharp. The best choice for this character. You can move easily with it, and it gives you distance – not too much but enough. Always go with something that's strong, dependable, and cuts clean."

"Reminds me of you."

"Exactly like me. The best choice for you."

She snorted and snatched the controller when he chose garments which left her character almost nude beneath the black cloak. Rude.

The final area of selection was her magical abilities. Here they had a problem. Big problem. He'd helped her to see reason with the first two items, but she wasn't budging on the last two. When he tried to wrestle the controller away from him, she bit him. To stop himself from pinning her beneath him and biting her back while sticking his dick into her hard and fast, he closed his eyes, pinched the bridge of his nose, and breathed, because it was pointless to try and reason with a woman who obviously had something against the state.

When he opened his eyes, she was sitting straight up in his lap, her legs bent with her feet steepled together between his knees. She had chosen healing as her third magical selection, switching it to her primary magic.

Ridiculous.

At least he'd talked her into Medusa Magic, which allowed her character to temporarily freeze opponents, and Ethereal Magic, the ability to move about unseen.

"Sabrina, this character needs more offensive magic. She's physically weaker. To win, you – "

"Black Thorn is my character. I've given you your say, but I'm keeping healing and choosing..."

She scrolled to the glittery pouch and selected it. "Glamour."

By the gods and devils of torment, she was killing him.

"Oh hush," she said when the metal of his blade rapidly tapped against the wooden part of the seat frame. His hand stilled. "Black Thorn will need this when she's talking to those tight-lipped villagers, or when she has to be seen as someone or something that will help her in her quest."

Her quest would end quickly with these bullshit choices. He tried reason one more time. "Sabrina, there's a creature on the tenth level that won't – "

"Look," she snapped, turning back to him. "I let you dress Black Thorn in straps of skimpy material and didn't say shit. I'm choosing healing and glamour, so follow my earlier lead and don't say shit else about it."

She turned back to the screen and pressed the button to begin the opening narration and animation.

He settled back and relaxed against the sofa. "You're not going to win."

"Oh, I'll win," she said, standing up and walking over to the television.

He liked watching the sway of her hips encased in the hugging underwear she wore. His friend twitched. When she crouched down and pulled the headphones from the console, allowing the ethereal music to permeate the front room, his breath quickened as he remembered her kneeling on her futon as he slammed into her over and over without restraint.

"I'll win just so I can rub it in your face."

She turned and paused, her gaze automatically moving to the part of him silently trying to make her see it was the joystick she should be playing with. She moistened her lips, her chest rising and falling a little more shallowly. Was she remembering the feel of him thrusting inside her? Remembering how her satin vagina pulled like a tourniquet around him, squeezing him until he burst open inside her, drenching her fruit in his cream.

He didn't utter a word. He wanted her to be compelled by her own need. When her gaze slid up his chest to his face, and came to rest at a point behind his head on the wall, his chest deflated, though his dick continued to hold out hope.

"Either put it away or get out of my seat."

His eyebrow rose as he contemplated her long and hard, waiting for her to realize she didn't own anything in over a hundred-mile radius except for the few contents packed in her bags. The rest was his, including her. He had handcuffs in his duffel bag. He could strip her naked, secure her to the headboard of his bed, and let his friend do the rest.

With the hand holding the Bowie, he waved her over to him.

She tried to suppress a triumphant smile but failed spectacularly. She scrambled back to him and adjusted herself around his erection again. He watched as she went on her adventure across Moreland. His blade, tapping against the wood at a steady clip, drew his focus away from the piece of flesh straining between her open legs.

She paused the game and looked back at him in exasperation.

"Just play the fucking game and don't say shit else about it," he said flatly, mirroring her earlier words.

She shrugged and turned, lying fully back against him, doing exactly as he commanded. A short time later he wanted to drag his blade across his throat.

She had to be the most aggravating, nonsensical player in the history of people across the world that had played any game ever. She did what she wanted to do and rarely took his well-thought-out advice. It was divine intervention that made him throw his blade across the room when she bought another cloak instead of the magically created shield in the Elven store.

Twenty minutes later she wanted to free a supposedly magical squirrel for fifty silver pieces from a swindling peddler he'd encountered in his own play simply because she wanted a partner to share in her adventure.

She made absolutely no sense.

"I bought the squirrel, Zeus. Drop it."

"Fucking squirrels aplenty on the other side of the door, but I don't see you inviting them in here to 'share your adventure'."

"You got one more time to throw my words back up at me."

"What, not two?" He smirked, grunting in surprise as her puny elbow jackknifed against his ribs. If she showed the same kind of assaultive skill in the game, she might have a raindrop's chance in hell of beating the level.

Zeus tensed in confusion as he watched her move to the village nursery and buy seeds to donate to the village garden. Why would she do that?

She looked over her shoulder, eyes wide. "What? It's a poor village and the kids need food."

———❖———

"ENOUGH," ZEUS SNAPPED. He stood and sent her tumbling to the floor in an undignified heap. If not for the ache in her hip and her strong survival instinct, she would have laughed.

That said, she still had to pretend to search for the controller to hide her humor. The bronzed psycho godling didn't stand a chance against a vindictive Samora female with a point to prove. Maybe he'd think twice before trying to make decisions about what she should and should not do. Even in a fantasy realm.

"Hey," she said, pausing the game. Zeus stopped before disappearing down the hall, apparently too disgusted to turn around and look back at her. Which was fine. It allowed her to openly ogle his tight ass, wide back, and strong legs. His skin, the palest butterscotch, made her want to lick him from foot to head. Again. "You're still going to teach me how to protect myself with a knife, aren't you?"

"If she fights with a knife the way her character fights with a sword, I'm going to have to buy her a gun and call it a fucking day."

She didn't know if he was talking to himself, some unseen entity, or to her.

She got up, saved her game, and turned off the television. "You know, I was thinking. Maybe it would be better if you trained me to use a sword instead of knives. Maybe it would help me be as dangerous as Black Thorn."

He walked away.

No sense of humor. She smiled, opening the curtains. The window she looked out of was crystal clear from the cleaning she'd given it the night before. Last night the forest had felt like the entryway into an alternative universe, where flying demons swooped down from the tops of primordial volcano craters. Today it looked like a forest. A simple forest.

Turning, she smothered a scream when she saw Zeus standing inches away from her. She thought she saw a shadow of a smile floating around his mouth, but then it was gone.

"I'm hungry," he said.

"What, am I supposed to do go hunt squirrel for you or something?"

"It's your turn to cook."

"I think we pretty much established last night that I clean and *you* cook."

"One hunger or the other, Sabrina. You decide."

He turned and walked to the back of the house. Demanding, self-centered prick, she thought walking to the kitchen to inspect his refrigerator and cabinets.

She took sausage from the freezer, pulled a box of blueberry muffin mix from the cabinet, had Zeus bring in three potatoes, and in under an hour, the table was filled with home-fried potatoes, sausage, muffins, sliced apples, and cranberry juice. Sometime during her meal prep, Zeus had dressed and settled against the kitchen wall next to his bedroom door, silently sharpening and oiling over two dozen blades of various shapes and sizes.

"Go wash your hands and come to the table before it gets cold."

He sheathed some blades against his body and rolled others in a long suede and leather piece of material which had slots for every blade. He stored the roll in his bedroom, walked to the bathroom, and quickly returned to the kitchen, drying his hands on a large towel. Sitting, he looked at her with expectation.

She snorted and sat in the seat across from him. She served herself, thinking his food would go stale and moldy before she did the same for him.

Sabrina felt at ease as they ate in near silence.

"Food's good," Zeus eventually said. "Too bad you can't play like you cook."

She switched a mouthful of muffin to the right of her mouth. "Do you really want to go there?"

"It's true. You can't play worth a damn, and you cook better than you let on."

"So what if it's true. I've been cooking most of my life; I've only been playing the game half the morning. If you said I played the game better than I cooked, then I'd have to wrestle you into submission until you changed your mind."

He stilled and pinned her with a lust-filled gaze. "You play the game better than you cook."

She prayed for deliverance from men who exploited every opportunity to pacify their dicks. No divine intervention came.

"Maybe if we can just have sex again, I'll finally stop wanting you."

Why did it feel like he'd just punched her in her chest? Because he didn't want to want her?

She drank the remainder of her juice, hoping to flush the irrational hurt from her system. It would be beyond insanity to share anything with this man besides her body. Instead of feeling hurt, she should thank him for the reality check. When this situation with Kragen was resolved, they would move on and that would be that. Until then, though, he wasn't going to be the one in charge of when or how often she shared her body with him.

"Maybe I've already stopped wanting *you*," she said, then resumed eating.

"Right. If I slipped my fingers inside your underwear, you'd be wet and ready for me just like every time before. You'll never stop wanting me."

"Have you ever been stabbed in the eye with a fork?"

"No."

"Do you want to be?"

"Hell no."

"Then I suggest you don't say another word about me, you, and sex today."

He sat back in his chair and folded his arms across his thick chest. "What if I don't bring up sex until after lunch?"

So he was going to negotiate with her about her body? She guessed it was a step up on the evolutionary timeline. He could've dragged her by her hair, kicking and screaming, to his room, tossed her on his bed, and taken her caveman-style. I am demented, she thought as she pressed her thighs together, stilling the ripples of pleasure rolling through her womb.

"We're here to hide out so you can keep me safe, Zeus. That's the only reason we're here, remember?"

"We're hiding out. I'm keeping you safe. I'll even teach you how to use a blade, and we'll still have plenty of time left for fucking."

"I'll consider it," she said, trying to reestablish a sense of self-control. "But you have to be very good to me."

"I've been good. Was going to handcuff you to the bed, but I didn't. That was being good."

"Not good enough."

He shrugged.

"You teach me to fight with a sword. I'll be able to take out bad guys in the game *and* in real life. Do you have a sword here?" she asked. She didn't miss the desperate look in his eyes.

"NO."

HE STOOD and took his dishes to the sink. He'd lied more in the two days of knowing her than he had since he was a kid – and that had been under the threat of torture and death.

He had swords here, even a katana small enough for her to handle. She wasn't using his swords.

He cleared the table, ignoring her protests about still eating, and walked to the bedroom to retrieve the knives he would use for her lessons. He passed her still sitting at the table and stopped at the back door. Waiting.

"You said you'd be nice to me," she said.

He hadn't said shit about being nice to her. He'd alluded that he would be good. He'd cleaned the dishes off the table and placed them in the sink for her to wash later. He was going to take her out back and teach her how to work a blade. That was being good. Not fucking her because she was conflicted about her desire, that was being good.

"Get dressed, Sabrina. Meet me out back in five."

Her breasts bounced rhythmically as she stood, the motion testing his restraint.

"Jesus." She glared, waving at his growing erection. "When will you learn to control that thing?"

Why the fuck should he want to?

Zeus left the kitchen and walked across the clearing to the aluminum shed just beyond the tree line. Unlocking the deadbolt, he slid the double doors open and stepped into the shadowed interior, reaching up to pull the cord on the battery-operated lantern hanging from the roof. A number of blades hung from fixtures on the back and side wall to his left. To his right, his Suzuki V-Storm motorcycle stood beside other items he used for training.

He picked up the circular piece of wood supported by three legs and propped it against the wall. It was the first bull's-eye he'd bought in the States, its black and red circles of paint barely adhered to the wood's surface. Grabbing it, he walked out of the shed and closed the doors so Sabrina couldn't see what he hid inside. If she saw the array of swords, he definitely wouldn't be having sex tonight.

Zeus set the bull's-eye up near an old oak tree with a trunk wide enough to hold on to any stray blades that might miss the smaller plank of wood in front of it.

Sabrina stepped outside in a pair of jeans and a torso-hugging purple T-shirt that read *F*#@ Barney*, with a T. rex dripping purple goo from its clenched teeth.

Liked the T-shirt. Liked the sweet, chocolate-skinned woman with wild, multihued hair more. Waving her over, he watched as she stepped forward, her gaze scanning the treetops nervously. Probably looking for rabid squirrels and rabbits. A shadow of a smile drifted across his mouth as he met her near the bull's-eye.

"We start here," he said, pointing to the bull's-eye.

She frowned at the pockmarked wood. "I thought you were going to show me how to protect myself, not play some childhood game."

"You know how to throw a knife?"

"Of course."

"Okay," he said and pulled her back about twenty-five feet. "Show me."

She threw the blade, and it landed at least ten feet short of the target. Pathetic.

He shook his head and went to retrieve the blade from what he considered the funeral pyre of leaves beneath it. He asked the blade's spirit for forgiveness as he walked back to Sabrina. To go wide of a target was one thing, but to fail to even get your blade past the halfway point... well, that was just embarrassing.

He reluctantly handed her the knife again. "This is a knife, not a baseball. Stop acting like your wrist is broken and throw harder."

She did. The blade landed about a foot in front and to the right of the last throw.

"This is the reason you die in *Insidious Realm*. You throw your blade like that at a real enemy, and you're dead. Life bar completely red. Dead."

"What's the point of this little rant, Zeus?"

"Point is, you don't stand off against a target and think you've got the ability to take it down when you have no fucking clue about how to use your weapon. Never pretend you have a skill when it can easily be proven otherwise."

"So, you gonna talk me to death or show me how to hit the damn target?"

He dusted off the blade, feeling perplexed. When was the last time he'd been accused of talking someone to death?

Not ever.

Drawing back his arm, he flicked his wrist and the knife flew, striking dead center with a *thump*. He lined Sabrina up in front of him, lifted her wrist and arm, and played out the correct motions dozens of times, displaying wrist motion, elbow placement, arm positioning. Once he was satisfied with her technique, he stepped back and gave her the blade again.

"Throw."

She let the blade fly free and whooped when it struck wood. It didn't seem to matter to her she'd just penetrated a tree to the left of the target.

Her smile was radiant. "It went a *lot* farther this time."

Maybe he wasn't cut out to be an instructor.

Zeus rubbed a hand back and forth over his head, holding back words that would have crushed her joy. Yes, she had the distance, but she'd be just as dead if it was a live target. He suddenly felt as if he had agreed to do the impossible. How was he going to teach her how to use a blade without being rude, offensive, and truthful? By remembering if she was mad at him, he wasn't going to get laid.

"Good," he lied. "This time think 'hit the target'."

"How hard can it fucking be?" he mumbled as he went to retrieve the blade for a second time. Playing a golden retriever was going to get old. Quick.

CHAPTER FOURTEEN

"Hey, Briana, I got some mail for you," Mrs. Aria called out.

Seven-year-old Briana jumped off the couch and sprinted to the kitchen. The only time she got snail mail was when her mother wrote her. For almost the last three years no letters, cards, or gifts.

Mrs. Aria had told her that her birth mother had died in a fire down in New Orleans. That was where Briana had been born, where her mother had lived. That was where Mrs. Aria Jace and her husband, Mr. Leman Jace, had met Briana's mother days after giving birth to her and promised to raise Brianna, keep her safe until her mother came for her. Her mother would never come. At first Briana told herself she didn't care; she'd never even known the woman, anyway. But she did care. She still had all her mother's presents and letters, with envelopes, folded in a box she'd decorated in glittering letters. It was named the "Your Mama Loves You" box because that was how her mother had ended all her letters. Each letter Briana had ever gotten was pressed one against the other in the order they had been received. None of the gifts had ever been used because she was saving them.

"Who's it from?" she asked as she crashed into the wood-and-granite-topped island Mrs. Aria was putting groceries on.

"Well, you'll just have to open it and see, won't you?" Mrs. Aria smiled. But it was a sad smile that crossed the elderly woman's wrinkled brown face. She hadn't been the same since Mr. Leman's stroke six months ago. And it scared Briana.

This package couldn't be from her mother, but that didn't stop Briana from hoping. Maybe there had been a big mix-up and her mother had survived the fire but was too injured to tell anyone before, and once she'd healed enough, she would be desperate to see Briana, come for her, and never let her go again.

Briana reached for the large stuffed package. The writing looked identical to her mother's writing. It was the one thing she knew intimately about her mother. She knew every loop and slant of her mother's writing. She'd learned to tell when her mother was sad or excited or rushed by how she wrote. This was her mother's writing, and she'd been sad when she wrote it.

Briana stared at the package, afraid to open it.

"I can open it for you, tell you what's inside," Mrs. Aria said, using the gentle I'm-always-going-to-love-and-care-for-you voice that helped soothe Briana.

"Can I take it to my room?" she asked.

"Course you can, Bree. I'll be up to check on you as soon as I can put the groceries away."

Briana grabbed the package and ran up the stairs, closing the door with enough force that the loud *bang* shook her even more. Walking across her room, she squeezed into the small space between the nightstand and headboard, leaning her back against the wall and drawing up her knees. Her heart was beating fast-fast, as if she'd been running from monsters. If monsters were real. But she knew they weren't.

She held the package in front of her face and turned it around, stopping when it came full circle. Why did she get this today? She shook the package, but nothing rattled around inside. Maybe it was a whole stack of letters, all the ones her mother had written but never sent because maybe she didn't want Briana to get more attached.

She continued to suspend it before her, reluctant to open it. She didn't want to lose the dream that her mother was alive and coming to get her. She didn't want to let go of her mother's promise that one day, when things were safe, she would come and bring Briana home to her. She'd made the promise every time she wrote to Briana.

When she was old enough, Briana had wondered who, or what, was so bad her mother would give her baby to strangers to raise. Lucky for her, the Jaces were the best people in the world, but they were older than most of her friend's grandparents even. After the stroke that left Mr. Leman bedbound and Mrs. Aria sad and tired all the time, Briana was always afraid they would die soon, leaving her alone in the world.

She stroked the seams of the package, her fingers gliding over the ink.

Then she cried, because somehow she knew this would be the last time her mother ever spoke to her.

———◆◄◘►◆———

AFTER FIVE DAYS of cohabitating with Zeus in his cabin, Sabrina was finding it difficult to imagine life without him. They just seemed to fit, in both temperament and outlook. They were both no-nonsense people with strong personalities. They were both minimalists – Zeus because he couldn't tolerate clutter and Sabrina because she was accustomed to not settling in one place for very long. They both had strong passions they shared with each other. Repeatedly. Their biggest difference came from the fact that she *really* wasn't good with a blade. It didn't make sense. She picked up most new things pretty quickly. It was a survival skill. Adapt, keep a low profile, move on.

It was late afternoon, days after she'd first started practicing, and she still hadn't mastered any aspect of this crap training. Her arms felt like lead, and it seemed each day Zeus added some new element that kept her from adjusting to anything he had shown her before.

Why the hell he was focused on knife throwing instead of blade wielding was a mystery he refused to explain. It was senseless.

"I'm done," she declared, sheathing her blades against her sides and back.

"You haven't hit the target once today. You're not done," he said, tossing her another blade, which she caught with ease. "I don't even need you to hit the rings on the bull's-eye anymore. Just hit the fucking wood it's drawn on."

"I. Am. Done."

Zeus proceeded to curse her nonexistent skills and hit his head against a tree hard enough to shake a few leaves loose. To his credit, he'd used his body and hands over and over again to help her understand what the motions should feel like. He'd brought the target closer and still she couldn't hit it. She was useless at throwing a knife, but hell, she wasn't training for a circus act, so why was this so fucking important? She hadn't felt this incompetent since trying and failing at saving her sister.

And Zeus's constant criticisms hadn't helped.

He could stay out here all night breathing in tree spores and squirrel shit for all she cared, but she was going back in the house, taking a bath, and laying down for a long nap. She was walking away when something hard struck her on the ass.

"Son of a..."

When she turned and looked down, there was a golf-ball-size rock that rolled to a standstill inches away from her foot.

"That's how you hit a target. Learn first. Rest later."

Sabrina knew in some little, corroded chamber of his heart he was trying to help her. On some level she knew this, but when fatigue, anger, and a longstanding negative reaction to being pushed collided, Sabrina grabbed the closest thing at hand and threw it.

The blade sailed through the air, perfectly on track to embed itself squarely in Zeus's chest.

She was horrified as she realized what she'd done. Zeus smiled at her and twisted around, plucking the blade out of the air by its hilt. He used his own continuous motion, fluidly redirecting the blade and letting it fly straight to the center of the bull's-eye. She hadn't thought of this before, but she clearly saw it. Zeus was a show-off. A cocky, arrogant, I-am-a-god-with-a-blade show-off.

Retrieving her blade, Zeus walked back toward her with slow strides, her blade dancing excitedly through his fingers.

"*Now* you know what it feels like. No thought, only intent and motion. Your big woman's head with stupid woman's brain chatter got in your way. Sometimes you just need to stop thinking and let the blade do what it wants to do."

Sabrina looked down at his large hand offering the blade back to her. Despite his knowledge of battling with sharp objects, the idiot lacked good sense if he thought it was safe to give a woman he'd just insulted a weapon. Especially after she'd just thrown said weapon at him.

Grabbing Zeus's wrist with one hand, she used her other hand to extract her knife and sheath it. Trailing her fingers over the vein in his wrist, she smiled up at him before turning her focus to his hand. She traced the faint lines on his palm, stroking her finger gently over each of his fingers. She couldn't pretend she didn't like the roughness there, the strength, but still...

"Zeus?" She looked up at him. His gaze was glued to their hands. He was mesmerized. But of course he would be, she thought. His hands, not his heart or his head, seemed to be the seat of his soul. She spiraled her finger around to the center of his palm. Bull's-eye. He was breathing a little rougher, his nostrils flared. His eyes, gleaming and intense, never left the motion of her fingers.

Sabrina knew if she let her eyes drift south, he would be hard. Her heart rate quickened with lust and anticipation. She was playing with fire, but the power she held made her feel giddy, daring. Why shouldn't she provoke him? Hadn't he rode her hard all morning, thrown a rock at her? Maybe he was too skilled to let her pierce his seemingly immortal hide with her blade, but she had other skills.

"Did you just call me bigheaded?"

"Yeah," he muttered lowly as if hypnotized by the sensual spell she was weaving into his palm.

"It's rude to call someone bigheaded," she said as she lifted her finger away from his palm. The only contact they maintained was her other hand gripping the back of his wrist. He looked up at her then, muted desperation lurking around the edges of his metallic gaze.

"You have a near perfect-size head," he said as he guided her fingers back to his palm. "Just meant you think too much. I found a way to shut those thoughts down."

She stroked his palm again. "By throwing a rock at me and causing me pain."

"Yeah. Worked."

She coaxed his fingers into a fist and wrapped both of her hands around it, gripping firmly as she looked him squarely in the eyes.

"Zeus, you throw a rock at me again, and I am going to kick. Your. Ass."

It was an empty threat, but it gave her a sense of power. Until he threw his head back and laughed. She smiled at the sound. It felt as precious as a child's trust. More so, because she'd never heard him laugh.

Sabrina tossed Zeus's hand away in mock disgust when his laughter settled into a smile. "Not that funny."

"Exceedingly funny," he contradicted.

She rolled her eyes and turned to walk back to the house. He grabbed her around the waist and hauled her back against him.

Yep. He was definitely hard.

Zeus wrapped his other arm around her shoulders, right beneath her collarbone. She felt like she was wearing a human straitjacket.

Struggling halfheartedly, she attempted to free herself. Using his head, Zeus tilted hers to the side, and sucked the corded tendon running down the length of her neck.

The feeling of his mouth and tongue leached all resistance from her body. The arm against her collarbone loosened just enough for him to reach his right hand over to cup and massage her breast, while the arm wrapped around her abdomen pulled her tighter against him.

"Zeus...."

She intended to tell him to stop, to put her down and let her go, but his fingers burrowed beneath her T-shirt and bra, and plucked and squeezed her nipple. She felt liquid heat slip from inside of her body and pool in her panties. She needed them off, needed them replaced by his large hand.

"Sabrina," Zeus groaned. "Haven't I been good enough today?"

Laughter spilled straight from her soul. "You threw a rock at me and called me bigheaded. That's far from being – " She sucked in a startled breath as his fingers deftly slipped beneath her panties and stroked her, bathing her clit with her own moisture. "Shit!"

"But this is good, isn't it? Good enough to make you forget all the bad?"

She braced her foot against his shin and pushed her ass harder against his groin.

"Yeah," he gritted out. She could feel him smiling against her neck. "That's good, isn't it? So good."

He pushed three fingers into her again and again while his thumb stroked her clit.

The forest grew silent at the sound of her cries as orgasm shuddered through her.

Sabrina closed her eyes and went limp, her body trembling in aftershock. She moaned as Zeus slipped his fingers free from her underwear and walked with her collapsed against him.

Zeus set her on her feet and maneuvered her around so that her back pressed against the trunk of a large tree. Sabrina opened her eyes when he pulled off her pants, leaving her lower body bare. Before she could speak, he shoved his jeans down around his thighs, lifted her up against the tree, and pushed deep inside of her. He didn't pause to let her adjust, but thrust into her wilder than any animal around them. The thickness and force of him pumping into her threatened to overwhelm the integrity of her vaginal walls. She tried to catch his rhythm, but his hands gripped her ass tighter as he shifted her thighs higher and wider, giving him full access as he grunted toward his completion. The sound of flesh slapping against flesh overlaid their groans and her sharp cries. With two final pumps, Zeus became rigid as he shot hot semen deep into her womb. The feeling of his seed jetting into her pushed Sabrina into another orgasm, more intense than the last.

She sighed, spent. Her head lolled against Zeus's shoulder, and she closed her eyes. If Zeus let her go, she would fall to the ground like an oversize brown leaf and remain there until she'd regained her strength.

Zeus, who hadn't stirred since his violent ejaculation, lifted her head and stared down at her. The remoteness in his gaze disturbed her. She remained silent, unsure whether he would pull away or reach behind him, pull one of his beloved blades, and slit her throat.

"It won't work," he eventually said.

"Maybe not, but it worked just fine a minute ago," she joked weakly.

"It won't go *away*," he gritted out, striking the tree.

She flinched as if he'd struck her, and in a sense he had. He was unprotected and buried deep inside her, yet he continued to act as if the only value she had was satisfying him until he no longer needed her in his life. She was so over people rejecting her and treating her like she wasn't worth the breath God breathed into her at birth.

Gathering her coldness, she tried to push away, but Zeus wouldn't budge. He just stood there, looking down at her.

"Look, Zeus. You're making this more than it is. Remember, I can be off your hands with a phone call."

He rolled his eyes as if she were being unreasonable. "You can't leave. Didn't you hear me just say I still want you?"

"Get the fuck off me," she snapped. She hadn't intended to show anger, but it was better than acknowledging the pain.

"You leave when *I'm* done, not a damn second before."

She blinked. Attempted to speak, but no words came out. Dumbfounded. She was completely dumbfounded. Did he really believe his wants and needs were the only ones that mattered?

A sound descended from above, and she jerked her head back just as a pinecone struck Zeus on the crown of his head and tumbled toward the ground.

Zeus frowned at her. "A pinecone just fell on my head."

Sabrina looked up into the far reaches of the treetops. The sky above barely peeked through. Grateful at least Mother Nature had her back, she turned back to Zeus. "If I had a vote, one of those big fucking branches would have fallen and split your thick skull open."

"Lucky for me you didn't have a vote."

<hr/>

ZEUS TUCKED HIMSELF back into his pants as he watched Sabrina pull her pants up and brush away leaves and dirt. She tried to walk past him, but he grabbed her arm, stopping her in her tracks.

"You're mad at me. Why?"

She looked down at his hand, then back up at him. He knew there was little she could do to cause him physical harm, but the look she threw him was evil enough to make him wonder if she could.

"I'm not mad at you," she said calmly. "I'm mad at myself."

He snorted. Like hell she wasn't mad with him. If she had the skill, she'd bury her knife in his throat and stand over him as he bled out slowly.

She tried to shake free of his hold, and he released her, wary as she walked toward the back door of the cabin. He followed her silently because he didn't know what else to do. He would have to watch her. People usually broadcast their thoughts with their actions and weren't even aware of it.

After watching her for two hours, he assumed he no longer existed in her world, that he was a nonentity. She stepped over and around him, looked past or through him. When he went to her room and lay on the bed beside her, she didn't say anything, not even when he reached out and placed his hand on her hip. Her breathing was so soft and even he'd thought she had fallen asleep. When he moved closer, molding himself along the length of her back, she leisurely rose from the bed and walked out of the room. The television came on in his bedroom a few seconds later. He turned to lay on his back in the too-small bed. Watching her was not giving him the results he wanted. She was ignoring him. People didn't ignore him. They avoided him, stayed out of his way, attacked and were killed by him, reluctantly accepted him, like Mama's Brood, but no-fucking-body ignored him. Zeus rubbed his hands over his face. Hopping out of bed, he walked over to his room. He was done trailing her all over the cabin like some attention-starved mutt too beaten down to understand being pitiful didn't get you what you wanted.

Sabrina was lying on his bed, propped up on all four of his pillows, attention focused on some travel show. He closed and locked the door, but she didn't even look in his direction. He growled in frustration, and she fucking ignored that too.

He was done with this shit. Climbing on the bed, he pulled two of the pillows from behind her pile, placed them against the headboard, and leaned into them, bending his knees as he too watched the television.

Zeus frowned. He'd already seen this show. It was one about Trinidad and a few other Caribbean islands. His experience hadn't been anything like the host's tame tourist bullshit. He had a place in the Caribbean; he didn't want to hear about it on his fucking television. He reached over, took the remote from her, and turned the channel.

She didn't react.

He ground his teeth together, vaguely aware of the twitch that had started on the outer edge of his right eye. He turned to a nature and science channel just in time to see a computer-generated enactment of a star going supernova, exploding into trillions of sparks of light. It was exactly what he felt like, exploding, destroying himself, and everything around him just to see if she would notice enough to be affected.

"Turn back," she said with quiet menace. As if he gave a –

In a blink, her boy-brief-covered ass was straddling his groin and she had her knife – the knife *he* had gotten for her – pressed against his throat. Even if it was in the wrong place to sever an artery, his heart swelled at her accomplishment.

"Turn back," she demanded again.

He couldn't help it; he didn't want to help it: he got hard.

Zeus leaned back into the headboard, allowing the blade she had pressed at his throat to slide against his flesh, drawing blood.

"Jesus, Zeus," Sabrina hissed, breaking rule number one and dropping the blade so she could rip off her pillowcase and hold the material against his neck.

"Just blood, Sabrina. If you want to work with knives, you need to get used to it."

"I cut you," she said in disbelief.

"Yeah," he said, smiling. Even though it was his movement that had caused the cut, he didn't think he'd ever felt this proud of another person. She'd moved damned fast with her blade. She was the only woman who made him want to fuck like a god of procreation. Sowing his oats in her again and again.

He lifted his hips, rocking into her cradling warmth. She closed her eyes and rubbed weary fingers over her brow while her other hand pressed the bundled material against his neck. Scratch had probably stopped bleeding the moment she'd applied the first bit of pressure.

He rocked again, closing his eyes on the pleasure spike that burned through his blood. He was addicted to this feeling. She could ride him into the night on this feeling, and he'd never lag. He would be a sexual endurance athlete, getting higher and higher on endorphins the longer they did this one thing they did so well together.

He opened his eyes when the cloth fell away from his neck. Sabrina leaned forward, placing her hands on the headboard, trapping his head between. He groaned in protest as she lifted her hips off his dick, but rejoiced again when he realized that her breasts were suspended just below his mouth.

"I shouldn't have sex with you again after what you said to me," Sabrina said.

What the hell had he said? He couldn't remember ever needing a woman to talk to him about what was bothering her, but in this instance, he needed her to tell him because he didn't have a clue.

He palmed her breast, squeezed a nipple. A low, need-filled curse made him smile against her neck. Feeling encouraged, he urged her hips back down onto his erection.

Maybe this will be the one last time, he thought to himself. Or at least he thought he had. When she tensed above him, he knew that he had spoken the words out loud, said something wrong. Again. Fuck. Fuck!

He acted quickly, rolling her over so she was on her back and trapped beneath his weight.

"Let me go," she said.

"Can't," he muttered as he stroked his nose against her temple. He liked whatever coconut-blended scent lingered in her hair.

"If not now, when, Zeus?"

Never. "Soon," he lied. "Just tell me what I keep saying to piss you off."

She turned her head away, tuning him out again.

He savored the contour of her jawline, her cheekbones, the steel in those molten-brown eyes, though one was still faintly discolored from the violence she'd endured during her abduction.

He ground into her, and her eyes fluttered closed, her hand tentative against his hip, as if uncertain whether she would pull him closer or push him away.

"I'm just the self-centered sociopath, remember?" he said, quoting her prior words. "It's your job to make me understand."

That last part wasn't just a manipulation. He wanted to understand; he wanted her to be there to bust his ass over something he wouldn't have considered.

"It doesn't matter anymore. You can be as self-centered and crazy as you want to be. Just let me go."

Her words incited the primal part of him that wanted to feed death and pain to anything and anyone who tried to keep her from him. That part of him wouldn't let him let her go. It accepted that she was his the moment he'd touched her on the warehouse floor. It had claimed her and hadn't let her get far from its reach since she'd first gazed up at him in all his bloody glory. Zeus didn't comprehend relationships. He'd thought his attachment to Sabrina was purely physical because that was all it had ever been with women. When faced with the idea of losing her, he knew that there would never be one last fuck. Not until one of them was dead and buried. He knew this. She was as tangled up inside of him as the spirits existing in his blades. Maybe more. Sabrina was bound to both of them, Zeus and his spirits, and just as those spirits had claimed him as a boy, he would claim her completely.

Lifting his weight off her, he reached over and pulled a blade from beneath his mattress. He gripped the material covering her body and proceeded to cut away at more of her clothing. Sabrina was so still he wondered if she thought she'd be disemboweled. Zeus hadn't believed he could put someone else's safety and protection above his own, his worldview hadn't accommodated that kind of thinking, but for Sabrina he always would. It was his duty as her man.

Lowering himself back down, he slowly pushed into her until there was no place left for him to go. Sabrina moaned, arching into him, her breathing shallow, her warm wetness binding them together as efficiently as any vow or metal band ever could.

He retreated slowly from her body, feeling her muscles relax, then swiftly plunged back into her. This union they shared was simple. It didn't need to be complicated. It burned away every pretense and left only their flesh and spirit.

Zeus allowed himself to succumb to their union, to let it overwhelm his senses. Sabrina pulled him into her. Her mouth consumed him until all that remained were grunts, screams, breath, heat, satisfaction, fulfillment, peace, darkness.

CHAPTER FIFTEEN

Briana sat on the bed beside Mr. Leman, caressing his wrinkled hand as he stared at her, still unable to talk the way he had before the stroke. She wiped the tears away from the corners of his eyes before they pooled in his ears. She hated when tears got inside her ears. Mrs. Aria sat beside Briana and wiped the wetness from her own face. Briana couldn't cry. Tears wouldn't come anymore. All she felt was scared.

Soon she would have to leave the Jace's home. Mrs. Aria couldn't continue to take care of both Briana and Mr. Leman, even with all the nurses and therapists coming to the house to try and help Mr. Leman get better. Briana had let Mrs. Aria know she could take care of herself. She could even help take care of Mrs. Aria and Mr. Leman if she needed to. She knew how to clean and even how to cook a little bit. Mrs. Aria was old-school and felt like all women needed to know how to take care of their household. Briana had been making her bed since she was three.

Briana had tried to convince Mrs. Aria she could take care of them. She was smarter and stronger than her classmate Carrie Riley, and Carrie was in charge of helping take care of her younger sister and brother. Mrs. Aria had sucked her teeth and muttered something about Carrie's trifling mother before she had turned to Briana and let her know it was *her* job to make sure Briana stayed a child as long as she could. She'd said it was only grown folk's place to take care of grown folk's business.

"Don't cry, Mr. Leman," Briana said. "Mrs. Aria promises I can come back home and visit whenever I can. We'll still be a family, and you'll get better, and maybe when you do, you guys can come and visit me at my new home."

Mr. Leman nodded once.

Mrs. Aria stood up. "Come on, Bree. Let's go finish dinner so Mr. Leman can get some food in him that will make him stronger."

Briana smoothed her hand over Mr. Leman's once more before standing and walking to the door.

"La ooo ba,' girl," Mr. Leman said from the bed.

Tears miraculously gathered in her eyes once again. "I love you too, Mr. Leman," she said before fleeing the room.

Downstairs, in the kitchen, Mrs. Aria continued to let the greens simmer while the chicken baked in the stove and the potato salad cooled in the 'frigerator. Briana sat at the countertop, mixing the ingredients Mrs. Aria had prepared for the chocolate cake, her hand *accidentally* getting cake mix on it, forcing her to lick it away.

"You think my aunt cooks like you?" she asked Mrs. Aria.

Mrs. Aria snorted. "Child, don't nobody cook like me, but I'm sure she's good in the kitchen. If not, she'll have you there to direct her."

Ms. Maywether, Briana's teacher, had said she was too good at directing others. Sometimes she also said "dictating to others."

"You think she got the packet yet? You think she's coming to get me soon?"

"What have I told you about being patient?"

"I know, but what happens if she doesn't want me? Where am I going to go then?"

"You're going exactly where your mother wanted you to go if the time came me and Mr. Leman couldn't care for you the way she wanted you to be cared for." Mrs. Aria stopped stirring the greens. "Do you know how blessed you are?"

She didn't feel blessed. She felt scared and angry because she was losing everything she knew.

"Your mama loved you enough to take care of you from the day you were born and is still doing it even after the day she died. That's how blessed you are. She loved you enough to make sure you were protected and loved well beyond the time even we were able to. If she says your aunt will come for you, well, you have no cause to doubt her."

Briana knew she could get popped in the mouth if she reminded Mrs. Aria that her mother had also promised she would come for her when she was able – now she never would – so she stayed silent.

Her mother had set up a safe deposit box if the time ever came the Jaces could no longer care for her. Mrs. Aria had emptied the box the day she'd come home with the final packet for Briana. The next day they'd sent a same-day delivery to an address in New Orleans where her aunt had lived, but she didn't live there anymore. Briana had gone on the Internet and searched for Sabrina Samora, only to come across the reports of a kidnapping of a Sabrina Samora out in California. The photos of that Ms. Samora resembled the ones left in the packet her mother had left for Briana. Though Ms. Samora was shades darker, she looked just like both Briana and her mother, Samantha.

From the news reports, Briana had located Ms. Samora's new address in California and had given it to Mrs. Aria, letting her know she had found her aunt online. She didn't tell Mrs. Aria about the kidnapping because the last report stated Ms. Samora was back home safe. Neither Mrs. Aria nor Mr. Leman used the computer often, so she doubted they'd learn about it. Maybe the people who had kidnapped her aunt were the ones that had kept her mother away from her.

Maybe because they were dead, it was safe for her to be with her family.

———————◆•••◆———————

SABRINA WOKE UP driven by the need to get away, but she was squished between Zeus and the mattress. He lay half on top of her, half curled around her body, as if she were a well-used, malleable, spineless teddy bear...or he the bear and she the honeycomb he'd glutted himself on. Either way, before he woke up and she succumbed to her unfortunate tendency to welcome him into her honeyed recesses, she had to get away. She had to leave, to run, in order to protect herself. Protect her heart. It wouldn't take another loss. Yes, she'd miss him. Yes, it would hurt once she'd gone, but it would hurt a lot less than whenever he arbitrarily decided he was done with her.

Sabrina tried to wiggle free of Zeus, but he grunted and held on to her tighter.

"Zeus, wake up," she whispered.

He didn't. It was as if sex was a drug he continuously overdosed on.

You just worry about kicking your own habit, she warned herself. She couldn't believe it was possible to come so hard, or so often, in so few days. Sex with Ernesto had always satisfied him. And to be fair, he had given her pleasure sometimes, even though she had never had the primal orgasms Zeus ripped from her body.

Zeus's breath rumbled in his chest, the vibration of his snores making her sensitive places more sensitized. She was doomed if she stayed here.

As she stroked his forearm, she plotted, resolving to simply give him what he wanted. If he didn't want to be attracted to her anymore, she would help him not be. Any woman worthy of her gender knew how to push a man away. Once she was gone, she'd still have the protection of the Brood until Kragen was dead or in prison. It will work out, she promised herself. Everything would work out.

The next time Sabrina opened her eyes, the bedroom was empty. Zeus had woken her two more times to work off his lust, but he was no longer beside her. Maybe he had finally succeeded in fucking her from his system. Rising from the bed, she felt lethargic. She walked to the door and opened it.

The kitchen was full with the smell of Zeus's cooking. Her stomach rumbled. Zeus stood at the stove, sprinkling something green into a pan. His densely muscled back was bare and his jeans hung low on his hips.

He looked at her over his shoulder, then turned back to the stove. "Go wash up."

She obediently walked to the bathroom, primarily because she was sticky and smelled to high heaven. She stepped into the shower feeling exhausted and heavy. She diligently washed him from her body. Washed him from her hair, her breasts, her face, her vagina. She didn't need to walk back into the kitchen with any of those places resonating with his touch.

Stepping out of the shower, she dried off, walked to the mirror, and looked at the last vestiges of her kidnapping ordeal. Slowly but surely, she was returning to her pre-kidnapping state. I will always return to myself, she thought. Sometimes with pieces missing or lost, sometimes with new pieces that gave her a new understanding of the world or her place in it, but she always came back to herself.

Banging at the door made her jump and turn, snatching it open. "What the hell is your problem?"

"You're taking too long. Food's ready and I'm hungry."

"So eat," she hissed. It wasn't like he'd cooked for her, anyway.

Zeus took a step forward, reached his hand under her towel, and touched the part of her that responded to him despite her willing it to stop. He stroked twice before pulling his hand away and lifting his fingers up for examination. He looked back at her.

"Thought you'd got your period," he said, dropping his hand to his side, rubbing her slippery wetness over his fingers. "You're acting like a b – "

"If you say what I think you're about to say, I promise you I will make your big ass understand what it means to fuck with a force you don't want to reckon with."

Flat gray eyes took her measure...and disregarded it. "You're acting like a bitch. I'm hungry. Let's go eat."

She blinked. Watched him walk back to the table.

If she'd had just *one* of her blades as she walked to the table, she would have cut his dick off, diced it into bite-size pieces, and fed it to whatever demon-possessed wildlife was outside.

She retreated to her room after eating and cleaning the dishes. She changed into a T-shirt and a pair of worn jeans. She threw on a pair of ankle socks and walked to his room, climbing on top of the bed beside him as he watched another nature show, his back propped on pillows, one folded back and cradling his big head.

He didn't even glance at her as she settled beside him.

Sabrina reached for the remote and turned the television off, plunging the room into shadows.

"Payback?"

"Call it whatever you want. You kept me up almost all night. I'm tired."

She flopped onto her side, facing the door, and gave him her back. She tried to breathe evenly, tried to relax, but she was aware of him, so still beside her despite her provocation. She knew her anger, her attempts to irritate and punish Zeus, were more about failing to find that piece that was *hers*. Again. For some reason the tiny spark of hope, the enduring belief that if she opened herself *just one more time*, she would win the reward. Instead she got rejected. She sighed. It wasn't Zeus's fault or responsibility if she cared for, was possibly even coming to love him. It was hers. And she would deal with it. Like she always had.

Soon fatigue and the weight of too many emotions refusing to be repressed sent her into a restless sleep. She dreamed she was alone in dark nothingness, floating untethered until lightning split the sky, blinding her, burning her up in its electric heat. She woke to Zeus's hand between her legs and his mouth sucking on her neck. He slowly worked his way down her body until his mouth replaced his hand. She grunted, moaned as he turned voracious in his hunger. Hips bucking wildly, Sabrina hollered as a searing orgasm ripped through her.

But Zeus wasn't done. His large hands anchored her waist as his mouth continued to work against her core, forcing her to come again. She was a shaking, twitching mess by the time Zeus rolled onto his back, breathing slow and even.

He had just flung her soul out of her body and scattered her essence over the heavens as if it were stardust, yet he lay beside her as if the experience were no more eventful than watching leaves fall.

Sabrina attempted to get up, but Zeus's large hand reached over and pressed against her stomach.

"Reciprocate the favor," Zeus said, his voice guttural as he pulled her hand to his throbbing erection. "It would be rude not to."

She just barely contained the snort of laughter as he pretended the social graces mattered to him. "I can be nice."

"Show me," he demanded. "Show me how nice you can be."

Sabrina watched him steadily, challengingly, before lowering her gaze to his denim-encased erection.

"Get naked," she ordered, stripping away her bra and tank top.

Zeus swiftly shucked out of his pants and sprawled over the bed, legs and arms spread wide like Leonardo da Vinci's Vitruvian Man. His penis was thick and long, and she could literally see it pulsating before her.

She knelt between his thighs and shifted back, sitting on her heels as she massaged the area around his groin – rock-hard lower abs, thighs, hips.

"You ready for this, big man?" she asked, hands transferring to her breasts, squeezing them together, massaging them, kneading them as she waited for his response. He made a guttural sound that was indecipherable in any language other than the language of desperation.

Leaning over, she used his dick as a breast massager...or her breast as a dick massager. "Zeus," she said, breath hitching as her nipple collided with the slit in his penis that bathed her areola in his precum.

"Now," he gritted out as he reached for her head.

She reared back, escaping his grasp, and, lightning-fast, reached and fisted the base of his dick so tightly he bucked, yelling out. She used her thumb to press against the flesh in the center of the mighty structure.

"Sabrina, please," he growled.

She smiled with only one side of her mouth and pumped him balls to head, her grip mercilessly firm and barely able to encircle his thickness. "That's it, Zeus baby. I want to hear you beg."

"I won't – "

She bent over and took him as far down her throat as she could, pumping him with her hands and mouth, massaging his sac, lapping at the base of the head. He muttered insensibly. When she increased her pace and let her tongue dance over his heated flesh, he gripped her head and begged for her.

He held her head firmly, and she felt his shaft swell just as he roared and released, gushing bursts of semen down her throat. She lapped at him until all traces of his seed were gone, leaving him breathless and trembling beneath her long after he'd come.

He pulled her up and on top of him, holding her securely.

"What did you do to me?" His voice was a hoarse whisper.

Parting gift, she thought as she closed her eyes and stroked his collarbone. She rested there until she felt him slip into a deep sleep.

"Sweet dreams, Zeus," she said as she carefully slipped out of his hold and rose off the bed.

She opened and closed drawers until she found what she was looking for, then tiptoed to her bedroom. She grabbed her blades and sheathed them as she dressed, sticking two ornamental chopsticks through the bun she twisted on top of her head. She put on her shoes, and, slinging her bag over her shoulder, crept down the hall and out the front door, locking it behind her.

She walked out into the wild darkness and took a steadying breath.

"I've just taken out the baddest thing around here," she whispered to the things waiting in the darkness. "Any of you furry-assed bastards want to fuck with me, I will gut you," she said, her heart pounding. She prayed she didn't have another encounter, mostly because it would eat into her escape time.

The forest remained silent, and she turned on the flashlight. As quietly as possible, she made her way to the driver's side of Zeus's Charger and pressed the remote. Quickly she climbed in and softly shut the door behind her. She secured her seat belt and turned the key in the ignition, nervously looking to the front door, half expecting Zeus to burst through at any moment.

Squashing a wave of grief, she wheeled the car down the path. She couldn't waste time mourning Zeus. Not now. Once she was far enough from the cabin, she turned on the headlights. When she heard something that sounded like an enraged grizzly's roar, she sped up, more afraid of what was coming after her than the dangers of the road that lay ahead.

ZEUS JERKED TO wakefulness the moment he heard the roar of his engine coming to life.

Sabrina.

He leaped out of the bed and stomped bare-assed through the house. He reached the front door and pulled it open just as the red taillights blinked out of view.

Rage was a whirlwind whipping around him, beating away all emotion except the betrayal and violence that fed it. She'd left him. Sneaked away when he'd decided she was meant to stay. He'd expected her to be there when he'd never wanted or needed another person to be there for him.

He gritted his teeth and walked back to his room; cold determination settled over him with each step. Never again, he thought as he pulled on and fastened a pair of jeans. Reaching for his gray suede boots, he laced them to his feet and slung on a T-shirt before strapping down with metal and walking out the back door toward his shed.

Just like a woman, he thought. She'd abandoned him as quickly as his Algerian mother had abandoned the pale, gray-eyed infant boy he'd once been. But unlike his mother, Sabrina was bound to him in this lifetime and the next. He'd teach her what it meant, along with some other much-needed lessons about loyalty and fucking boundaries. He couldn't believe she had taken his car. *No one* drove his car but him.

Zeus went still after opening his shed, sensing danger. He pulled his blade, the compulsion to kill rebounding after all the days of being dormant. He scanned the darkness. Had it been Sabrina's presence that had calmed the need?

Blade in hand and thumping against his thigh, he stalked the periphery of the shed. He inhaled deeply, scenting something wild and big. Probably bear, he dismissed. He went back in the shed and got two more small weapons, securing them, as he'd already done with his favorite blade, inside what looked like wounds and damaged flesh on his body. Only Dominic and the man who made the silicone prostheses for Zeus knew the damaged flesh wasn't real.

After pushing his Suzuki outside, he locked the shed and got on the bike. When it roared to life, he peeled off through the woods. He accelerated, imagining that he was balanced on the edge of a blade aimed straight in Sabrina's direction. There were only two routes she could take once she hit the main road. He headed down the mountain in the direction they had come, hitting over a hundred miles per hour, until he saw the faded illumination of red taillights. He cut his headlamps and sped on in the dark until there was about seventy feet between him and his car.

He followed her to a run-down motel on the outskirts of Big Sur.

Cutting his engine, he watched from a distance as she walked to the motel's office. He could make out the long-whiskered guy with stringy, shoulder-length, dirty-gray hair. She gave him a credit card, and he gave her a key card. Zeus waited in the dark as she drove his car to the back of the motel, only to see her come back to the front and slide the key card into the corner door farthest from the front office.

He drove his bike forward, following the direction she had driven his car, and parked next to the Charger. He paused when his phone vibrated, and leaned against his bike as he reached for his mobile with no intention of answering it. He looked at the display, and Sabrina's name was illuminated. She'd betrayed and abandoned him, and she was calling to say what, you're a sociopathic rude fuck and I couldn't stand being around you any longer?

He wanted to crush the phone, but instead he stared at it as he tried to rein in his rage. The phone stopped vibrating and went black. He looked up to the starless sky. He didn't know the best way to deal with this situation, and for the first time, the spirits in his blades were unnaturally silent.

The phone vibrated once, indicating Sabrina had left a message.

There was no real point in listening since he would be in her room soon. Yeah, he wanted to yell at her for taking his car, for leaving his protection, leaving him. He wanted to fuck her into submission. He wanted her to tell him what he needed to do to make her to stay, but he had a feeling none of it would happen if he went in and handled things the way he normally handled them. Sitting sidesaddle, with his legs crossed at the ankle, he retrieved Sabrina's voice mail.

There was a long moment of silence, followed by her voice.

"Hey. I know it'll be a while before you get this message, but...um... thanks for the blades. I hope you don't mind that I kept them." Another

pause. He fought the urge to walk to the door and... *"You're a good man."* He frowned and looked at the phone as if it had morphed into Jesus on the cross. *"My mama would've described you as a man with a few issues but nothing a little loving couldn't take care of. I can't be like that."* What the hell kind of sense did she make? If you care for someone, you're not supposed to leave, are you? *"I can't afford to see if her advice will work out this time. It's never worked before. As much as I call you crazy, I know your biggest problem is thinking you can do, say, and have anything you want. You really need to work on that."* He could hear the dry smile in her voice. Pleasure rumbled through his chest. *"I've called the Brood and told them where to pick me up so you don't have to worry about my safety. Your job is done. I do care, my blade-wielding sociopath. Oh, don't be mad about your car. I'll call again and let you know where to pick it up. Bye, Zeus."*

He listened to the message four more times, and when her voice went silent the last time, he'd convinced himself the idea of keeping a woman in his life only a few hours at a time was genius. The moment he was compelled to keep one forever, look what happened. Chasing her down in his own car because she didn't want to be like her mother. She has to learn to butch up, he thought as he walked toward the front of the motel. He wasn't letting her go.

Zeus stood beneath the shadow of a tree and watched until the lights in her room went dark. He waited another forty-five minutes, walked to the door, and illegally let himself in. Moving through the dark, he stopped where she lay faceup on top of the bedcovers wearing her T-shirt and jeans. Her bra and shoes sat neatly on the worn wooden chair next to the window.

"A part of me believed you would let me go, you'd finally be through with me, but another part, that instinctual part, knew you would find me." She spoke through the shadows separating them.

Zeus pulled out a blade and whirled it through his fingers as he looked down at her. He recalled the first time he saw her on the warehouse floor, remembering the unholy lust that had compelled him to touch her even then. There was no longer a part of her that he hadn't touched.

Ignoring her attempt at conversation, he cut a thin strip off the bed's blanket, and he tied her hands to the rickety wooden headboard. Sabrina remained silent, angling her head to the side as she watched him. He pulled off his jacket and boots. The rest of his clothes soon followed. Kneeling on the bed, he lifted the bottom of her T-shirt and sliced it up the middle, laying her breasts and taut abdomen bare.

She thought she could take the sight of her luscious form away from him and he would just let her? He undid her pants, gently pulling them down her legs. "Mine," he proclaimed. Her body was his. And he kept what was his.

He eased himself over her, covering her chest to chest, groin to groin. "Open for me," he said, resting his temple against her forehead and settling his lower body firmly between her parted legs.

"Zeus?"

"Huh?" he uttered before capturing her mouth with his. He felt wrenched wide open when she kissed him fiercely, holding nothing back, taking him, making them inseparable again. He lost himself in her, felt her jerk her arms against the headboard they were bound to.

"You don't leave."

"Zeus..."

"Never again, Sabrina," he warned before crushing his mouth to hers, not willing to listen to anything that wasn't a confirmation of the words he had just uttered. "Say it."

She moaned but didn't say the words he needed to hear. He continued to pleasure her, stretching her tight inner muscles until her sobs became the sweetest penance. "I won't leave. I won't. Never again."

He came so unnaturally long and hard inside her he knew the blade spirits had to be binding them together in this life and the next. "You're mine," he said as he shifted and unbound her wrists, knowing nothing made in this material world could link them as completely as the spirits had just done. He collapsed onto the bed, exhaustion a hundred-pound cement block pulling him into the deepest fathoms of sleep.

"And you're mine. Forever. God and your spirits protect us," she muttered.

He hugged her to him as he fell into the depths, feeling a sense of utter completion.

CHAPTER SIXTEEN

Maxim woke to repetitive banging. The vibration resonated as if his head were submerged under sand. He peeled back eyelids that felt gritty against his eyeballs and looked around the room to see the latest Sabrina replica sleeping in a tight ball at the foot of the hotel bed. He briefly wondered if she was dead but recalled the restraint he was forced to wield due to circumstance and injury.

Pushing the cover back, he stood up and walked over to the bedroom door, opening it. Reed stood in the dark hallway fully dressed and groomed despite the earliness of the morning. Maxim's internal clock told him it was somewhere close to four a.m.

"Reed."

"Sorry to wake you, but our man in OPD called with a hit on one of Ms. Samora's credit cards. I called and confirmed it was a motel in Big Sur. The man who answered the phone stated a woman matching her description checked in alone a little after midnight and hasn't checked out. We have a window."

"So she's slipped her guard. No doubt she's trying to find her way back to me." Maxim looked behind him at the woman stirring on the bed. "I'll meet you back at the cabin. Bring my woman to me there." He paused. "Try to ensure she's not harmed, Reed. I will be very disappointed if any more injury comes to her because of my men's incompetence."

"Yes, sir."

"And, Reed..."

"Sir?"

"If the mutt happens to be there, leash him and put him in a cage so Eddie can tame him. Might as well extract as much pleasure from the dawning day as possible."

"Yes, sir."

Maxim shut the door and turned to see the woman sit up on the bed. He watched her tie a blue wrap dress around her body. How could he have ever used her? She lacked the radiant earthiness of the woman he truly wanted.

The escort donned a black trench coat, which fell to just below her knees. Maxim was impatient to get to his cabin without notice, but first he had to deal with the matter at hand.

The woman looked at him and waited in surly silence before pulling out her phone and running her fingers over the keyboard in rapid clips before sliding it back into her pocket. "It's been real, sweetness, but I've got to get going."

He waited for her to leave and raised his brow when she continued to stand there expectantly.

"It's extra if I stay past midnight."

Of course.

Maxim walked to his bedstand, picked up his wallet, and pulled out a few bills totaling a thousand dollars. He held on to the money as she grabbed for it. "Do you have a card?" he asked. He knew he wanted to feature her in one of the discipline rooms during Basir's unauthorized Consortium gathering.

She smiled. "That's cute. Like I've got Fortune 500 pussy. Just have your man call the service again, and Darwin will handle the rest."

Once she'd left, Maxim hastened to the bathroom to wash off the last traces of her vulgarity. She had been a desperate man's diversion. Being cooped up in the hotel room these last few days, recovering from the wounds the bodyguard had inflicted, had left him with little choice. He couldn't go out and hunt down someone of Sabrina's caliber. Plus, the San Francisco police were keeping a watchful eye on him. No doubt he had the Oakland PD to thank for that bit of extra care.

Eddie was the only person in the living room when Maxim entered. Both he and Eddie wore shabby jeans, scruffy sneakers, and SF Giants hoodies. Urban disguise. He grinned.

"Looking good, sir. How are you feeling?"

"In sore need of retribution."

He would see the mutt who had mauled him dead and dismembered before the day was done. First would come the lesson where Zeus would know pain, the punishment for stealing Sabrina away. Then, but only after he was broken and begging Maxim for forgiveness, death would follow.

"I've had our men set a false trail for the cops and anyone else who has you under surveillance. We'll let the team create a little space for us, then head out."

Maxim nodded. "And let's have me back in town in enough time for Sabrina and I to put in an appearance at Basir's *secret* gathering."

"Of course, Mr. Kragen. I'll see you downstairs in thirty. Remember, I'll be in a brown 1992 Honda Civic."

Maxim smiled. "Charming."

Once he was alone in the suite, Maxim retrieved the small bag he was unwilling to let anyone else touch. Inside were items he had bought for Sabrina – designer clothing, accessories, diamonds, and other precious jewels, all infinitely more expensive than the common canvas bag that bound them. He wanted to spoil her with all the finer things she'd gone without since leaving his care.

Making his way out of the suite, hood concealing his identity, he took the elevator down to the garage. He waited in the shadows until he spied Eddie in the ragged Honda. Eddie pulled up to him and popped the trunk, coming around to help Maxim fold himself inside of it.

"Only for love, Eddie."

The densely muscled black man grimaced. "If this is what comes from lovin' a woman, I pray love never finds me."

"Trust me; you'll thank God and the devil when it does."

"Yet another reason to stay an atheist," Eddie mumbled.

"You say that," Maxim said knowingly. "But when the right...er, person, comes around, you will be absolutely powerless."

Eddie shut the trunk on Maxim's declaration.

Eddie would see. Just the sight and smell of Sabrina had ignited an awareness, a compelling connection that would always identify her as his. Though the day in her apartment had ended in his shame, shame was sometimes a necessary evil. It helped to reorient one to his own humility, his own humanity. This was a truth his father and his father's cronies couldn't seem to understand. From shame came resolution, a call to be more, be better. He had to be better for Sabrina. She would soon see he was stronger and wiser. She was intelligent enough to conclude the talking ape watching over her was little more than an idiot. A man with limited future options, Zeus could never be wise, but once he was caged, Maxim would grant him the gift of a slow and painful death.

———◆◆◦◆●◦●———

"STOP TOUCHING IT!"

"It's mine. I'll touch it when I want."

"You sound like a child."

"I sound like a man speaking the truth."

She rolled her eyes. "Whatever. Let me see it."

"No."

"Zeus..."

"No."

"Okay, keep it, but when you rub it bald, don't say I didn't warn you."

"I won't."

She angled her head, peering up at him with patience he knew was false. He couldn't care less. He wasn't handing it over to her. He had given her his lifelong protection, his body. He'd given her a free pass for stealing his car, and he'd extended the bond of the blade to her. He wasn't offering up any more pieces of his eroded soul just for her to poke around in.

"Why'd you pull it out if you didn't want me to touch it?"

"Because."

She waved for him to continue, but he remained silent. The truth was he didn't know why he'd pulled it out.

She jumped up and straddled his legs, pressing a hand against his chest as she tried to pry the ring from his fist. She was so weak.

If she were smarter, she'd take her blade, cut the flesh and tendons that allowed him to make a fist, and pick the ring right from his palm. Instead she sat on top of him, stirring his body to readiness.

She grabbed his head, splaying her fingers over his ears as she pulled his face closer to hers.

Zeus leaned up and kissed her. Just a little taste.

Sabrina groaned in defeat and slid down to lay beside his chest.

"I just want to see it for a minute," she whined, sounding like the child she'd accused him of being.

He shook the gold band in his hand. Maybe he could stand to be a little benevolent if it ended in her expressing her gratitude. "There's a cost to everything, Sabrina. You willing to pay?"

"Yes."

He shook his head. "Bad bargaining. Always know the price before you commit."

"Whatever. Just tell me what you want, Zeus, and I'll give it to you."

It's been over an hour, his dick reminded him. More than an hour was too long. Too long, too long, his dick chanted.

He opened his palm, and the delicate gold band gleamed.

Sabrina picked it up reverently and stroked it as if enraptured. He would've only been half surprised if she began to salivate and call it *my precious.*

"It's beautiful," she said, sliding it onto the ring finger of her right hand. It only went halfway down before stopping.

"She must have been a tiny thing," Sabrina reflected.

"Sisters said she was. Sister Agnes said it was a miracle she was even able to deliver me."

"How big were you?"

"I don't know. Average, I guess."

"What does your birth certificate say?"

"Eleven pounds, four ounces...twenty inches long."

Her eyes bugged, and she blinked at him like a sleepy owl. He reached out and twisted the ring around her finger. "What?"

"Condoms," she whispered. *"Jesus Christ,* we really should have used condoms more than we did." She struggled to pull away from him, but he pinned her thighs against his.

"I'm clean, Sabrina. No worries."

"No worries?"

Why did she sound so panicked? He had enough money to take care of her, his kid, and ten others if they had them. "Jesus Christ, I could be pregnant with God-fucking-zuki. My goodness, what she must have gone through to give birth to a fully formed toddler."

Zeus turned his head, blindly looking at the motel room's wall.

"Think that's why she left?" He'd wondered about the answer to that question for the first few years of his life, but then he'd decided the why wasn't important. He had to live with her decision no matter what the answer was.

The panic Sabrina had shown a few moments before quickly transformed into something much more serious. She pulled the ring from her finger and held it in front of his face. "She left you with the only valuable possession she likely had. Look at the inscription inside."

"It's her name."

"Zahira Sauvageau. Did you ever search for her?"

"*She* left me."

Sabrina stroked the left side of his chest as if attempting to soothe a heart that had long ago forgotten how to ache. The languid caress eased the rage that surfaced when he thought about the woman who hadn't believed he was worth keeping.

"She could have searched for you."

"I know she didn't find me."

"Doesn't mean she didn't try. How old was she when she had you?"

"Sixteen."

"Shit, she was a *child*. Likely with very few options. She could have been pressured by her family. She could have been... We don't know what she went through, but I imagine, as a young girl, she believed she had little choice about what happened to you, or hell, what happened to herself. She gave you this and left you with people she thought were bound by God to watch over you and care for you.

"It's painful to be left behind, to be abandoned. Trust me; my mother did it often enough when she was using, but she came back. And sometimes I believed I hated her when she did. When she was gone forever, I knew I'd never hated her; I was just angry. I was just a child, and despite everything she put us through, I loved her. She was my mom, and she was an addict. Don't think because your mother made the choice she made, that she didn't love you. This ring tells me she loved you without question. That she wanted you to carry a piece of her with you."

She plucked him on the forehead. "Despite the pain your big head may have caused during birth."

There had to be something wrong with him. He'd always believed that. His mother was French and Algerian, his father was Greek but unnamed on the birth certificate. Was it because he was a mutt? Was it something in his blood, something in his eyes, some deficiency, some evil in him that made her walk away? Maybe it had been what the nuns and priests called his "unholy taint." He'd always equated her abandonment with an act of hate, never an act of love, not until Sabrina's words hinted at the possibility.

He squeezed her hips. "I'm not using condoms. If it's meant for you to give birth to Godzuki, you'll give birth and thank me for him after."

"I never thought about bringing kids into this world."

"Don't think about it," he said as he stroked her ass.

"Zeus?"

"Sabrina."

"When all this is done, can we go on a search for her?" she asked, gripping the pendant around her neck that she never took off. "We have to hold our family close to us. Because when they're gone, we lose a part of who we are forever."

"Anything you want."

"Anything?" she said, tilting her hips, slowly sinking on top of him.

"Shit, woman, anything."

"Bad negotiating practice, big man."

"Whatever," he growled, pushing into her as the world literally exploded around them.

SABRINA SCREAMED WHEN the motel door imploded, sending shards of wood, glass, and sheetrock into the already shabby room.

In one fluid motion Zeus spun around her and grabbed his blades, advancing on the men spilling through the gaping hole. Before she could grab her blade, Zeus had fatally stabbed three men, and left one screaming and clutching an eye streaming blood. Sabrina sliced at the first hand that grabbed her arm and kicked the balls of one man so hard she cringed and rejoiced at his anguished cries. She fought her way toward Zeus when a shot rang out. She saw Zeus jerk back and fall to his knee, where he sliced open the thighs of two intruders before cutting their throats once they had fallen to the floor.

Another shot and Zeus tumbled to the floor face-first. Sabrina heard herself scream. She fought to reach him as more men came through the door and advanced, guns aimed at the back of his skull. Every fiber of her soul screamed she would protect him, protect Zeus. She fought hard, some part of her aware these men didn't seem to want to hurt her like the ones before them.

She would kill them. Resurrect Zeus in a river of their blood.

Save him, her heart cried, and she fought. She fought as if the spirits that possessed his blades possessed her body. She fought like a woman possessed by the power of a love she didn't believe existed. She fought with desperation bred from an unwillingness to lose another person she loved.

Reaching Zeus, she knelt over his exposed back and pressed her lips to his ear. "Don't leave me, crazy man. I need you. I need you to live..."

Something cold and metallic slammed against her temple. Her ears rang, a high-pitched tone that made her momentarily deaf. She slumped onto Zeus's back, her vision engulfed in blinding white light that ebbed into the unending black of unconsciousness.

Sabrina struggled to rise up through an eternity of nothingness. Her eyes were gritty, and her throat was dry and raw. Moaning from the pain lancing through her skull and the nausea in her stomach, she sat up and inhaled deeply.

"My beauty awakes." A voice reached out, anchoring her. She knew that voice. She opened her eyes and saw she was lying on a large bed too fine for the seedy little motel room she'd been in.

Kragen sat at the foot of the bed, watching her with a love and pride that were eerily disconcerting considering he was a complete stranger.

"Where's Zeus?"

Kragen waved a dismissive hand. "The bodyguard is no longer of importance to you."

"Is he alive?"

Impatience marred his blissful countenance. "For the moment."

"What do I have to do to make sure he stays that way?"

"Your behavior, his life – the two will never again be connected. Zeus will die, and you will live." He stood and walked over to the side of the bed where she lay. "You must live for me as I will live only for you, Sabrina."

"I want to see Zeus."

"You really don't. Your golden boy isn't nearly as attractive as you remember him being."

Sabrina's heart stuttered. Zeus probably had less than minutes. She'd seen what Kragen did to the women he deluded himself into believing he loved. It probably wasn't until the women failed to fulfill whatever fantasy he'd created that they died. Which meant that until Kragen played out his delusion to its conclusion, she had time. It could be days, weeks, months even. But Zeus...

Sabrina looked around the room. "Where am I? I don't remember this room," she said, playing the role of his long-lost love.

Kragen smiled. He looked so normal, so boyishly handsome. "I bought this place after I learned you were on the West Coast. I remembered you'd dreamed of what it would be like. Remember how we had fantasized about seeing the ocean together?"

He held his hand out toward her. "Come. Let me show you around your new home."

She shifted off the bed, feeling unsteady from the earlier blow to her head. On one side of the bed, she noticed the manacles bolted into the wall. She gripped her stomach as a wave of nausea threatened.

"You brought other women here," she accused, ignoring his outstretched hand and assessing her surroundings. There was a metal night lamp on an end table that could cave in half of Kragen's head if she swung it with enough force.

The room itself was sparse, but it didn't stop her from cataloging each object she could use to attack. The biggest problem was the manacles. Not only were they bolted to the wall, but there was a place on the bed's headboard that he could secure a pair of shackles to as well. If she was bound, she wouldn't be able to help herself or Zeus.

Kragen's face was flushed when she gazed back at him.

"As you know, I am a man with needs, Sabrina. For years I couldn't look at another woman because she wasn't you. After a period of searching and coming up with nothing, I succumbed to those needs. I never gave up hope of finding you, but I had to go on with my life with as much normalcy as I could. They were temporary. They simply filled a passing urge."

She wondered what was inside the ornate, dark wood armoire against the wall. A body? Bodies? Or a wardrobe of designer outfits, like the slate-gray one he wore?

"How many women have you had since we were together, Kragen?"

"Max. Please. You were the only one who ever cared enough to give me a nickname."

"How many women, Max?" she asked, strolling closer to him although instinct warned she keep as much distance between them as possible. "One? Five? Fifty?" She needed to know how many potential victims were out there. How many women he'd sacrificed to his madness.

He wouldn't look at her.

"How many, Max?"

"They meant nothing..."

"Is that supposed to make me feel better?"

"No, of course not. I..."

"Eight, a hundred?"

A muscle ticked in his jaw. So, he didn't like being questioned. Did he feel ashamed? Surely not because he was forced to admit his infidelities to the woman he claimed to want more than any other in the world.

Sabrina wandered closer to the armoire and reached for the metal handle. Kragen's hand fisted around her wrist, easing it away.

"Not yet," he mumbled, stroking the inside of her wrist with his thumb. "Not until everything has been worked out between us."

She swallowed back another wave of bile at the feel of his clammy hand wrapped around hers. "I don't see how anything could be worked out between us. You had me beaten and kidnapped. Twice."

"It wasn't my intention."

"You've slept with hundreds of other women – "

He smiled. "Hardly hundreds. No more than twenty-five in all the time since our separation."

She smothered a wave of sorrow. Twenty-five. That was so much more than the few the Brood knew about. "That many?" she said in a broken voice that was only half feigned. "I can't be with you. You say you've changed, but how can I believe you, Max? You've hurt me. You've had countless other women. I don't see how that makes you a better, more trustworthy man than the one I ran away from."

She had to get the hell out of this house. Away from the man who surpassed every level of insanity she'd ever experienced.

She needed Zeus. She needed to make sure he was alive. To make sure he was safe. She wanted his heat, his piercing gray eyes, his deadpan expressions that made her want to strangle him.

Because she didn't have him, she turned back to Max, allowing him to witness the tears gathering in her eyes. "How can I be with a man who only cares for his needs and callously disregards what I created for myself? That sounds like selfishness, Max, not love."

His hand shot out and gripped her around the throat, his face contorting in rage. Miscalculation, she thought as she tried to break his choke hold. She'd only intended for him to feel ashamed, but her words had obviously triggered the demon that drove him to do the sick things he did to women.

Suppressing the impulse to fight, she stopped struggling and stared him down as sparks of light burst around her, likely due to the lack of oxygen. "This is not love," she managed to get out.

Kragen blinked several times, released her, and turned away. "I'm sorry."

"How many times have you said those words to me, Max?" she said, trying to steady her breathing.

He scrubbed his hands over his face. "Too many. But I can't give you up again. You're the only one who's ever loved me. I'll make you love me again." He walked to the bedroom door. "I'm sorry for hurting you. It was never my intention."

"Max," she called as he opened the door. She moved toward him, still needing to help Zeus. "I'm willing to start over. I'm willing to give us a try, but it can't be with the blood of the man who protected me on your hands."

Kragen turned to face her, his expression unreadable.

"You may not like that he hurt you or he killed your men, but he did it to protect me."

"And touching you, sleeping with you, was that a part of his job?"

"No. That was him being a man and me being a woman. However, if you can forgive me one discretion, I will forgive you your many others. Let him go so we can enter this union better than who we were, Max. That's all I'm asking you, all I will ever ask on behalf of another man."

He stared at her intently, silently. She wondered if she'd made another miscalculation; then he nodded.

"There's no guarantee he'll live if I let him go."

"There's no guarantee any of us will survive from one moment to the next, but for our sake, I want to see you set him free. Whatever happens after that... Well, at least I'll know you loved me enough to give me this gift. To give us this chance."

It felt like an eternity, but eventually he held out his hand and led her down a wide hallway that, though short, reminded her of the one she'd seen in *The Shining*. After only a few steps, Kragen stopped her in front of another door on the opposite side of the hallway. He knocked twice, and the door swung open.

The iron-heavy smell of blood was the first scent to escape through the doorway. The scents of musk and sweat were soon to follow. Sabrina fought back tears, knowing Zeus had been in this room suffering, and those smells, ripe and nauseating, told her she didn't want to imagine what he had gone through while she lay unconscious on a mattress soft enough for fallen angels while he endured hell.

"Sir?"

The thickly built, brown-skinned man she had seen trailing her and Zeus at the electronic store filled the doorway, his chest bare, and his pants unbuttoned and only halfway zipped. He appeared to be sweating rivulets of blood

"Eddie, we're going to let Mr. Zeus fly free. Sabrina has requested it, and I've decided to grant her this request."

She saw Eddie look behind him uncertainly. "He's not really in the shape to crawl, let alone fly, sir."

"I want to see him," Sabrina said calmly, though everything inside of her felt desperate and terrified. The truth was she needed to see him. Needed to prove he was alive and able to get away from this place.

Eddie looked to Kragen for permission, and he nodded. Sabrina stood on her toes and kissed Kragen's cheek, hoping the action would give her more leverage in the future. She rushed into the room and came to a dead stop, her mind refusing to accept what her eyes were seeing.

Her man, Zeus, was naked and slumped against the wall, unconscious. There was a bullet hole in his upper chest and one in his right thigh, both still sluggishly leaking blood. She wondered if each wound was Kragen's version of an eye for an eye, because the wounds were similar in location to the wounds Zeus had inflicted on him.

Almost the entire length of Zeus's pale bronze abdomen was an assortment of black, blue, red, and yellow bruises. She knew his ribs had to be bruised, if not fractured, if not broken. There was a contusion at his temple, and the left side of his face was swollen.

Zeus.

Tears welled and fell from her eyes. She couldn't control the sob that rose in her throat, but she didn't let it spiral into a despair-filled wail. She swallowed several times. Zeus didn't need her tears. He needed her to help him get the hell out of here so he could come back and dismember each of these sadistic bastards.

The man wearing Zeus's blood walked across the room and stood beside him as if anticipating the next course of violence. Though most women might initially find the man's muscular good looks attractive, all Sabrina could discern was the stench of revolting brutality and an unnatural need to please his employer. A minion, she acknowledged. Years with Ernesto had taught her well how to recognize minions. Eddie was an empty man salivating at the feet of his powerful employer just so he could prove to himself and the world that he had worth and value. Both he and Kragen were so twisted they thought behavior like this was something to be proud of.

Zeus could have turned into a man like these two, but even with his killing ways, Zeus was not evil. He did what he did, and she wouldn't pretend otherwise. He was rude, antisocial, and deadly. Maybe the spirits in his blades really had saved him. Even if they hadn't given him much of a conscience, they allowed him to hunt down evil instead of perpetuating it.

Sabrina faced Kragen and wiped her tears away. He smiled as if in approval of her efforts at composure. Forcing herself to walk slowly, she knelt down next to Zeus. She didn't want to cause him more pain, but she had to touch his chest, make sure his heart still beat. She bent closer to him so his nose nearly touched her cheek. She felt a few coils of her hair tumble forward, as if reaching out to him.

One wrist was shackled to the wall, and though the thick chain was slack, she knew if he stood, it would be too taut for him to stand upright and defend himself effectively.

"Zeus," she whispered softly. The increase in his heart rate and the pace of his exhalations let her know on some level he knew she was there. Sabrina stood. "He's alive. I swear, I would never have survived the guilt if he'd died here. He protected me and deserves better."

"He touched what belongs to me and injured me with the intention of continuing to have what was mine. There had to be consequences for his behavior," Kragen said.

"Well, you've clearly had your revenge. He's taken his punishment, so let me clean him up and get him on his way...as best as he can."

Kragen smiled magnanimously and shrugged. "Sounds reasonable."

The idea of him being reasonable was absurd.

"Eddie, bring the first-aid kit. Tend to him as best you can within ten minutes, Sabrina, then I set him free to live or die as God sees fit."

Eddie walked out of the room and Kragen followed, pausing by the door. "I'll give you a moment to say your good-byes." Before closing it, he said, "Ten minutes, Sabrina, and after, you will give me your heart and soul."

Zeus grunted.

"For as long as you'll have me, I'm yours," Sabrina said.

He smiled. "Just as it once was."

"It's unfortunate I don't have any memory of our time."

"We will create much more pleasurable ones."

"I look forward to it," she said, imagining him dead at her feet.

"As you should," he replied, his gaze promising things she didn't have the time or the stomach to contemplate.

<hr/>

KRAGEN SECURED THE door, closing Sabrina inside with the soon-to-be dead man. He walked upstairs and saw Reed sitting at the table imputing information into his computer.

"What has our man in OPD reported?"

Reed looked up. "It's been all silent since the tag on your woman's hotel transaction."

"Why do you imagine that is? He's not off today."

"I could send one of our men out to check."

"No, I want them here. I'm going to grant Sabrina a wish. She wants us to let her charity case go, and I'm going to allow it. We'll send him out into the wild, and our boys will hunt him down." He considered for a moment. "The one who finally recaptures him will be rewarded with... I don't know. You think of something appropriate, Reed."

"Will do, sir."

"We'll bury him with the woman I had earlier so he won't be alone," Maxim said.

Eddie walked through the room carrying a bucket with water in one hand and the first-aid kit in the other.

"You did fine work in there by the way. Definitely worthy of its own reward."

Eddie smiled. "Thank you, sir. It was my pleasure," he said before closing the door behind him.

"What's next on his wish list?" Kragen asked Reed, who pulled up a spreadsheet on his external brain.

"Looks like a month off to indulge himself at the recreation lodge in Vancouver."

Maxim grimaced, recalling the particular focus of that holding. "Give him a month and a half. I guess I'll have to tolerate Mitchell while Eddie is away."

"I imagine you'll have little use for a personal bodyguard with Sabrina here to occupy your time."

Maxim felt indescribably light from this insight. No more searching, no more disappointing encounters with insufficient women. "I imagine you're right," he said as he stepped out onto the balcony to see clouds gathering fast over the roiling ocean. The strong winds whipped his hair about his face. He felt so free he could almost take flight over the turbulent waters.

He breathed the crisp ocean air. This time everything would work out. He would take her to Basir's gathering and introduce his soon-to-be wife to some of the less prominent members of the Consortium.

It would probably kill his father...but that would only be an added benefit of their reunion.

⸻ ◆◆◆ ⸻

AFTER THE MINION left the medical supplies, Sabrina was again alone with Zeus. She fully believed ten minutes meant ten minutes – no more, no less.

Digging through the medium-size bag, she saw it was stocked well enough for a military field doctor. Before she'd left New Orleans, she'd bought a twenty-dollar black bag, filled it with first-aid supplies anyone could purchase at the neighborhood pharmacy, and supplemented it with some items she'd "borrowed" from her mobile emergency medical unit. As advanced as it was, her bag didn't compare to Kragen's.

She cleaned Zeus's wounds quickly and efficiently. Between her mother, Ernesto's men, and herself, she'd had lots of practice, even before she'd become an EMT in Louisiana.

"Zeus, baby, open your eyes. We don't have much time."

She cleaned the bullet wounds, injected him with a small dosage of oxycodone – just to keep the majority of pain at bay – reset his nose, taped gauze to his chest, and wrapped it around his leg. It wasn't right his body should be marred with more scars. He had gone through so much already.

Zeus opened his eyes. The whites had hemorrhaged, but the gray still gleamed metallic. The most beautiful eyes, she thought as she smiled at him and brushed a feather-light kiss over his jawbone, the only place on his face that wasn't bruised, busted, broken, or swollen.

She quickly but efficiently wrapped his ribs. "Have I ever told you how much I love your eyes?"

"Said...they were...freaky."

"But don't you know I love freaky?"

"Love my eyes?"

270

"Love your eyes."

"Me?"

She swallowed, unable to hold back the truth. She didn't want him to go out there and not have heard her say it. She wanted him to know someone loved him, that someone would grieve for the rest of her life if he was no longer in this world.

"I still don't like you very much," she said as she struggled to help him to his feet. "But I don't want to be with anyone but you, Zeus. Only you. I love you so much. I'll do whatever I can to protect you."

"No."

"Yes," she said emphatically. "Kragen promised to release you. I trust him to do it because I'll be watching. I'll be watching until I can't see you anymore; then you'll have to do what you've done since being an orphan on the streets of Marseille. You'll have to fight to survive."

"No," he said, struggling.

"Yes," she hissed. "I have time. You don't. I don't trust him any more than you do. I know he'll try to kill you the minute my back is turned, but at least you'll have a chance out there. You have none shackled to this wall."

"You love me."

She rolled her eyes. "Yes. Stay focused."

"No better reason to kill than for love, right?"

She snorted. "As if you need another reason." She rose on her tiptoes and brushed another kiss across his jaw before reaching into her hair and pulling out one of the Asian hair pieces he had given her. "Take this."

He shook his head, gritting his teeth. "Never lose your blade."

"You'll need something to fight with."

"I always have something to fight with." His silver eyes glinted with amusement. The man was buck naked! "Hey," he said in contemplation. Could be the drugs kicking in? "Think I love you?"

"You need to ask yourself that question?" she said, feeling a little petrified over the possibility that he didn't.

"How the fuck would I know?" he growled, frowning. "Who have I ever loved?"

"Okay, this is a conversation for another time...and you need to stop cussing at me."

"Well, think about it," he rasped out. "Let me know what you come up with."

She heard the door open behind her.

"It looks like my little healer has righted a lot of what you worked so hard to destroy, Eddie."

The minion snorted.

Sabrina turned to see the two men filling the doorway. She placed a supportive arm around Zeus's back, preparing to help him to the front door.

Kragen shook his head. "Eddie, assist our guest up the stairs. Sabrina, you and I will follow closely behind."

She held Zeus's gaze as Eddie approached. "Behave," she whispered. Zeus flexed his hands as if gripping invisible blades. She actually imagined the spectral outline of them.

Zeus nodded once at her; then his eyes tracked Eddie as he moved closer. Even with Zeus in this beaten state, without the chains, she would have approached with more caution. Eddie advanced with the overconfidence of a man who assumed his prey was powerless.

Handing Zeus off to the other man was one of the most tension-filled moments Sabrina had ever experienced. If Zeus snapped and attacked, it would be the last time she saw him alive. She knew this. Zeus remained silent, his gaze never leaving Eddie's face as his body weight shifted from Sabrina to the minion.

"Sorry to see you leave so prematurely," Kragen said to Zeus. "I had more fun planned for you."

Sabrina registered the moment Zeus's eyes turned flat as flint, emptying of all emotion. She'd seen that look before, cold, inhuman. It was no less terrifying outside of the warehouse walls. Following Eddie's physical cues, Zeus limped to the door.

Sabrina slowed her pace. Love him or not, if Zeus lost his shit, she wasn't going to risk being cut down once he flew into action. She didn't trust that whatever stared out of his eyes would recognize her in the heat of battle.

"Don't be frightened. Everything will work out," Kragen said, tapping her pendant. "I knew the moment I saw you wearing the gift I gave you on the night we first made love."

Sabrina stumbled, evading Kragen's hand as he reached out to catch her before she fell. Automatically her hand sought the moonstone pendant.

Ahead of them Zeus stopped at the stairs and turned.

"It's okay. I'm okay," she assured as she pulled away from Kragen's hot hands. "I just tripped. It's okay."

His gaze stayed locked on her as he refused to move at Eddie's urging.

"Really. Everything's fine. I'm fine."

The desperation in her tone must have penetrated, because he turned and allowed Eddie to help him navigate the stairs.

"He's very protective of you."

Sabrina clasped the necklace in her fist.

"I don't fault him for wanting to protect you. His punishment comes from abusing his position and taking advantage of a vulnerable woman. But in no way do I blame you. You've always had a trusting heart."

Tears burned behind Sabrina's eyes. Her sister, *she* had a trusting heart. The pendant had been hers. When Sabrina found it buried in Sam's drawer, Sam had begged her to take it, claiming it was a part of her past she didn't want to remember but couldn't forget. Sabrina had thought it was the heartache of lost love, but Sam had refused to talk about it.

Sabrina had hated the idea of her sister enduring something she couldn't protect her from, but she'd told herself to let it go, that Sam had to toughen up because heartache was a part of life. All you could do was survive it.

She looked at Kragen. Was he the reason her sister had taken her own life?

"New York. I met you in New York. It was about eight years ago. I extended my stay because I thought I was in love," she said, remembering the only vacation Sam had ever taken.

"I knew our time together would come back to you. I knew God wouldn't be cruel enough to allow you to completely forget me. Forget us."

Sabrina's ascent up the stairwell blurred as she recalled Sam's phone call the first night she'd landed in the New York.

"I'm not you, Bree. I cain't just...approach people and talk to them like I got a right to."

"Sure you can. That's the whole point of the trip, Sam. Be free, explore life. Hell, maybe you'll meet Prince Charming and he'll sweep you off your feet. And me, I'll just continue to collect the toads."

Sabrina smiled when she'd heard her sister's soft laughter. Sam was always so gentle and restrained, possibly a by-product of the strictness Sam's father incorporated to stop Sam from becoming anything like Sabrina or their mother.

"Maybe I'll just pretend I'm you," Sam said with a sardonic humor that actually sounded like Sabrina.

"Yeah, but be a nicer me, though. You're prettier, so use that too. Be a nicer, sexier Sabrina."

Sabrina hadn't ever been able to carry off sexy or nice for long, but she'd learned early to be good with people to get what she needed.

"You'll tell me about the necklace soon?" she asked, feeling as if she was losing her mind as she watched Eddie support Zeus to the front door.

Eddie walked Zeus out into the yard, then left him there, naked and alone, to find balance on his injured leg.

Zeus turned and looked at her. "Me?"

"You," she said. Absolutely him.

Zeus looked out over the misted forest. A storm threatened, yet he limped ahead as if unfazed.

She turned to Kragen. "You meant what you said? He gets to walk away."

"I meant it without reservation."

"Thank you," she said as she watched Zeus move forward until he was a shadow in the mist, then simply was no more.

He was gone.

Kragen took the opportunity to pull her into the circle of his arms, his breath fanning her cheek. "It's wonderful to have you back. I will do everything within my power to make sure you're happy."

"I trust you will, Max," she said.

He turned her back toward the door, and she looked behind her to see if she could catch one last glimpse of Zeus. Not one much for praying, she prayed to Zeus's namesake and all the spirits of steel Zeus trusted to protect him and see him to safety.

As she walked back into the house, she threw out an additional prayer that any being willing to listen protect her as well.

CHAPTER SEVENTEEN

Even injured, Zeus made less noise than the men hunting him.

Five. There were now five. He could hear them moving from different positions, tightening the noose...had he stayed within their perimeter. But with the first kill, he'd gotten behind it. When they realized they were one man down, the hunt would be underway in full force. But time was his enemy on this hunt. Sabrina was in the house with Kragen. The way he'd looked at her had made everything inside Zeus go quiet.

Sabrina loved him, and he was determined to learn what that meant. If Kragen had her too long, he could hurt her so badly she would lose the ability to love. Especially someone like him.

A branch snapped to his left, and he reacted, pushing his blade through the eye of one man, pulling it out only when the man's spirit stopped residing in his body.

Four.

Zeus was sweating from pain and exertion. His body was on fire even with the cold fog rolling off the ocean, even with the meds Sabrina had pumped into him. Zeus moved to an outcropping of boulders and rested, inhaling the briny air. This wasn't a good place to stop. Not a good place to rest. He was too exposed here, but he needed to take some pressure off his leg. After a few more breaths he moved forward, headed away from the sound of the ocean, away from the house and Sabrina. The men who hunted him would expect this, and he'd accommodate.

Disregarding the fire at his side, Zeus knelt down and listened. The world blurred, undulating as if it were as fluid as the ocean below. He couldn't close his eyes; that would only draw the darkness down, and someone was close.

Fisting his most treasured blade, the one he had secured in the faux wounded flesh against his thigh, he breathed out and inhaled as much as his ribs would allow. Tilting his head to the side, he was able to track the sounds of hesitant footfalls advancing in his direction. He could smell gun oil. Cologne, not cheap but nauseating as hell for a grown man. His blade itched to go to work. The coppery smell of blood would go a long way in making the cologne less offensive.

Zeus looked up when the man was no more than two feet away. He could see the automatic rifle butted securely against the man's left shoulder as he sighted ahead of him, scanning. When he got too close, Zeus cut through muscle and tendon. Blood sprayed, and Zeus smiled. He loved arterial flow. He didn't love the pain that caused his vision to go dark around the edges, but he loved the feel of his blade sinking into the man's kidney when he fell, then through the rib cage to his heart. Two rapid-fire gunshots rang out when the man's finger spasmed against the trigger, upstaging his pain-laden shrieks. Made sense that a man who wore cologne on a hunt would shriek when dying.

Zeus struggled to stand. Three more.

He moved away from the body as fast as his wound would allow before doubling back. He had to hunt. No more time for waiting. He wasn't a superhero; he was pragmatic. He knew he wouldn't stay conscious much longer. Eventually his system was going to shut down, and he needed Kragen's men dead before that happened or he'd be the one never to rise.

He put his back against a tree that wasn't as massive as the ones growing around his cabin. The salt in the air kept the area around Kragen's house more brittle than the vegetation on Zeus's land. The fog continued to roll around him like an army of ghostly spirits waiting for him to add to their ranks. He heard cursing. His chin slipped down to his chest as he chuckled.

He couldn't help it. He loved the moment when men discovered fear, realizing they weren't the baddest things walking the earth. Outside of being with Sabrina, there was no greater satisfaction than when the blade performed the ritual of separating spirit from flesh, allowing the dead to make their way into the world where Cizan's god ruled.

"We go back?" a voice muffled by the dense layers of fog asked.

"Go back to what? You think the boss'll be okay with us telling him we didn't get the man that's been fucking his woman?"

Ah, Eddie was out here. The man who had intended to rape him back in that room was still trying to stay on his tail.

"Boss ain't gotta know," the other man said.

"You're new to this crew, so I'll tell you once, that's not how we roll."

Zeus slipped around a tree and went to ground. Pain. It was everywhere. Almost unbearable, but he took it because he only had moments.

The three men arced around the last dead man – one at the head, one on the side, and one at the feet. Sweat slid into Zeus's eyes, aggravating his already unreliable vision as he crept forward. He gripped his blade tighter, squeezing out every ounce of power the blade was willing to give.

Zeus lay behind the man at the head, attempting to appear a misted-over shadow or some outgrowth of foliage. The minute the man farthest away, Eddie, bent down to check over the body, Zeus balanced on his good arm and leg, then flowed upright. The man near the head turned. Zeus's blade pierced the side of his neck. He yanked hard when it lodged, causing blood, flesh, cartilage, and bone to spew one way as the man's half-decapitated head lolled the other.

Two.

Zeus pushed the near headless body at the man standing to his left. The body caught a round of bullets before the gun went silent. The man who'd fired the gun was struggling to push his dead comrade off him as Eddie threw a punch that connected with Zeus's already bruised jaw. After the initial impact, his mind contained the pain. His returning punch knocked Eddie to the ground, and fast as he could, Zeus flew into the man with the gun, sinking his blade, in rapid succession, into the man's chest and abdomen, hitting heart, liver, and kidney.

Zeus fell to his knees, trying to shake off the impending darkness as the man bled out.

One.

The last of the huntsmen, Eddie, rose from where he'd landed at the dead man's feet. He was laughing, the sound crowish in the thick mist.

"Man, you come all this way only to find yourself right back where we started. Guess the saying 'you can't run from your destiny' is true." He tossed his gun behind him, rubbing a hand up and down his crotch. "Destiny. That's what it's called when I get a second chance to ram my dick down your throat and up your ass. I'll make you my bitch before I bag you and get a hefty bonus for my efforts."

Zeus felt the blood of all the other kills coating his skin. He knew he looked like something spit from hell, but Eddie wasn't afraid. He was aroused by the sight of Zeus. It meant something to defeat the killer of killers. What Eddie was feeling was the power play that existed between a sadist and his intended victim.

"Get off raping men?"

The man grinned as he unzipped his pants. "I'm not particular."

Zeus spit out a stream of blood. "Don't like men fucking me, Eddie."

"Guess I'll have to like it enough for both of us. And after, I'm gonna go back to the house, and when my boss gets done with your woman, I'm gonna do the same thing to her that I do to you. I will be the last thing you two share in this life."

Eddie approached slowly. Dude was huge. He could give Big Country a run for the most bulked-out muscle strapped on a human frame.

Zeus took a step, and his leg buckled. Eddie kicked out, knocking the knife from Zeus's hand before slamming his fist into Zeus's face. The darkness was falling fast. Zeus blinked back starbursts as he fell sideways, covering the dead man's head and part of his torso. Reaching beneath the body, Zeus found his hand lodged as Eddie kicked him onto his back.

"You ready to beg yet?" Eddie asked as he stood, straddling Zeus. His dick was erect and free of the pants and boxers that hung low on his hips.

Zeus squinted, trying to see Eddie's face beyond the man's erection. He snorted. He wasn't one to judge a man's dick, but Eddie's was pretty unimpressive.

"Won't feel a thing." Zeus laughed, nodding toward Eddie's dick.

Eddie retaliated by stomping his foot over the bullet wound in Zeus's leg. Zeus bit back the curse rattling around in his chest and throat. It was the closest he had ever come to screaming in pain.

When he opened his eyes, Eddie was shirtless, and his hand was stroking his bared erection. All else around them was darkness, and Zeus knew this darkness. Knew he was losing this battle, but he couldn't stop the descent.

"She likes...brown skin. Like yours. But loves..."

Precum dripped onto Zeus's chest. "I expected more fight from you, killer. Got you rambling, and I haven't even put you on your knees."

"I'll be better. After this."

"You'll be dead after this."

Zeus smiled through the pain. "Already dead. But it never stopped me."

Zeus pulled his hand from beneath the body. The backup blade he'd hidden beneath, after taking the man out, whispered as it sliced clean through flesh. Eddie's worthless appendage fell against Zeus's abdomen before tumbling onto the ground.

Screams. Ear-shattering screams. They would have shaken a feeling man to his very soul, but Zeus could only reflect on how much of a bitch it would be to go into the afterlife without your dick attached. Eddie crumpled to the ground next to Zeus, clutching between his legs. Zeus made it to his knees. Life-preserving instinct must have kicked in, because the other man, still holding on to the gaping wound, scooted on his side toward the gun he had tossed away, but it was too late. Zeus buried his blade into Eddie's thigh, then his abdomen, then his chest. But not in the heart. He had no heart.

"Eddie?"

The man attempted to struggle. To fight. His fist connected with Zeus's already busted nose, destroying the reset Sabrina had done earlier. The impact disoriented Zeus for a moment, but he was beyond feeling. He reacted by pounding the hilt of his blade against Eddie's temple twice, leaving the man dazed.

"Can you even be called a man?" he asked Eddie as he slit the muscles and tendons on each side of Eddie's shoulders, rendering him unable to lift his arms. He sliced through the corresponding places on Eddie's thighs, essentially making him a quadriplegic.

"This," Zeus said, sweeping the dripping blade over the length of Eddie's body. "This is how I chain a man. And this," he said, holding up his bloody fist, showcasing his blade. "This is the last thing you fuck with in this life."

Zeus straddled Eddie's body and placed the tip of his blade right below the hollow of Eddie's throat. Zeus closed his eyes, nearly losing consciousness. The image of Sabrina in the doorway of Kragen's house flashed through his mind. He shook his head slowly and opened his eyes. "My woman. She loves skin like yours."

He tried to wipe the blood away from Eddie's chest to give himself a clean palette, but the flow continued.

"Doesn't it sound something like love to want to give the woman who loves you anything she loves?"

He looked at his blade, and he looked at Eddie, feeling a little ashamed. It was always best to have the right tools for the right occasion. "It's not a filleting knife, but it'll have to do, Eddie."

Zeus dragged the blade's tip across the other man's clavicle and reset at the hollow of Eddie's throat, cutting down to his belly button. He tried to keep the blade steady and shallow despite the way Eddie bucked beneath him.

It was a testament to his skill and an honor to the blade that he could skin the man with so many of his own injuries, yet render skin from flesh he did.

"Stop screaming, Eddie. It'll be over soon."

Eddie didn't stop. Zeus closed his eyes. Eddie's wails were causing the pain in his head to expand, almost fracturing his mind. Zeus lifted the blade and let it fall with finality. Gurgling sounds, then silence. Zeus sighed.

The sound of the ocean waves battering against immovable stone met him in the silence. He cocked his head. Was that thunder he heard in the distance? He had no time to wonder. The darkness wouldn't be stopped. He slid off the partially skinned body and fell to the ground, looking up into a mist-cloaked world that held no answers about how he could save Sabrina before he died.

"IS HE DEAD?"

"God, I hope so."

Silence. Then laughter.

"Hell, son, didn't know you had the hater gene in you."

Fingers touched Zeus's neck. He gripped the blade that had been loose in his fingers and moved to ram it into whoever hovered over him.

"Hold on, Humpty Dumpty," a voice said as a foot slammed down on his wrist, pinning it to the ground. "You kill Lynx, ain't nobody else got the skill to put you back together again."

Zeus opened his eyes, one nearly swollen shut, and looked up at the group standing around him. The Brood.

"Sabrina."

"Gone. House was empty when we got here."

"Basement," he said as he struggled to sit up. Bride assisted him. "Hidden."

"Big Country here is good at finding hidden spots. It's empty."

Zeus remembered the thunder. "Car?" he asked, trying to remember the brand of car they had shoved him into. "Lincoln."

Big Country rubbed a slow hand over his jaw. "Passed one on the road not ten minutes back."

"Kragen," Zeus grunted.

A flurry of curses and recriminations rang out in the darkness.

"Help me up."

Zeus's request silenced the Brood.

"Did the half-crazy man just ask for help?" Price asked.

"Half?" Lynx said. "He ripped through the poor bastard's throat."

"Gives another meaning to the term deep throatin' it," Big Country said.

Zeus was lifted off the ground by Big Country and Bride. He balanced on one leg, not trusting that the other would support him.

"Chief's got eyes on all Consortium and Kragen-related locations within a hundred-mile radius. He'll show up at one, I'm sure," Coen said, rubbing his head as he eyed one of the bodies. "Think I would have wanted to be this one," he said, toeing the first of the four men Zeus had killed in this spot.

"Yeah, definitely wouldn't want to be him," Lynx said, pointing to the man lacking the eyeball.

"Tell y'all what, I'd rather be any one of these poor fucks if I can keep my skin and dick attached," Big Country drawled.

"Jesus Zeus," Price said, rubbing his head.

He didn't understand what the big deal was. Every one of the dead men had tried to kill him. He just refused to let them. With Bride's help, he limped his naked ass toward the Suburban, its headlights illuminating the bodies on the ground.

"Take me to the cabin," Zeus said once he'd settled on the blanket Price had covered the middle seat with. The others piled into the vehicle.

"What fucking cabin?" Price asked.

He gave them directions as Lynx draped a blanket over his lower body and worked on the new injuries he'd accumulated as well as the ones Sabrina had doctored earlier. He didn't reject the second dosing of pain medications. He needed to find Sabrina. Kill again. He would kill until the fear of losing her disappeared or his body gave out.

"How'd you find me?"

"We went to extract Sabrina only to find her motel room busted up to high hell. The guy at the front desk gave descriptions we reasoned were Kragen's goons. Big Country deep scanned the properties nearby. We figured Kragen had to be close to get there before we did, and oh my lucky charms, what did we find? This place deeded to a Mr. Reed Miller. Kragen's assistant."

"Unfortunately we also happened to find you bare-assed and half-dead," Coen muttered.

"Sabrina loves me and my ass." Zeus smiled, once again feeling smug.

Price frowned at him in the rearview mirror. "Was that a smile on your lips?" He looked over at Lynx. "Did that creepy-ass mothafucka just smile?"

"Coulda been gas," Big Country said. "Ya know, like babies."

Zeus tuned out the chatter about how delusional he was, and laid his head back and half closed his eyes. Not a couple of weeks ago the constant banter between the Brood could have driven him to homicide.

Now it eased him, distracted him from the fear he felt over the situation his woman was in. I am becoming more normal, he thought as he mentally cataloged which weapons he could use to quickly slaughter with only one arm at full strength. The image of the short-handled, dual-sided ax filtered through his drug-induced peace, further calming his mind. The original ax blade had taken down hundred-year-old tree trunks, which meant it could hack through the human body with little effort on his part.

"But what if?" Lynx said in a reflective silence. Zeus opened his eyes. "What would it mean if Zeus was able to find someone to love him, yet none of us have?"

"Who the hell would want something as merciless and deceitful as a woman's love?" Price said. "Might as well strip naked, cover yourself in blood, and walk into a cage full of starved lions."

"Looks like Zeus already did." Coen snorted, eyeing Zeus from the passenger seat.

"Okay, this foolishness ends," Big Country said decisively. "We're all capitalistic-minded men, and I tell ya it's bad business to waste time on entanglements with women. You put a couple hundred on the table, and that'll pay for the best kinda lovin' a man can hope to have...the temporary kind. Of a sexual nature, mind you."

"Pathetic," Bride said behind him. Zeus heard the flick of her lighter, the sound and smell of paper and tobacco turning to ash.

"Turn up here," Zeus said as they approached the road to his cabin.

A few minutes later they were parked in the clearing outside his front door.

"It looks scary as hell out there," Lynx said, looking out all the windows to get a panoramic view of Zeus's forest.

Zeus and Price stepped out of the Suburban and looked around.

Lynx was an idiot. His forest was serene.

With Price's assistance, Zeus made his way to the door, his limp less pronounced because he could hardly feel any pain. Zeus didn't have his keys, so Price picked the lock and entered the cabin behind him.

———◆◆×◆◆———

"THANKS," HE SAID to Price as he closed the front door. Sabrina had been saying he needed to show gratitude. "I appreciate it." He didn't, but he could at least tell Sabrina he'd said it.

The other man looked at Zeus as if he'd sprouted three more heads. "Well, fuck me," Price muttered.

Zeus snorted. "Won't ever be that appreciative."

Back in Price's truck, Zeus noticed a tension among the Brood members who'd remained inside. All four held weapons in their hands.

"This forest is haunted," Lynx said as he scanned the area outside his window.

The ever-tedious Coen took a deep breath, secured his gun, and asked, "So where we headed?"

"To Sabrina," Price said, starting up the Suburban. "Zeus placed tracking devices in some of the weapons he gave her. She only has one left on her. Zeus's device will lead us to wherever she is."

CHAPTER EIGHTEEN

Sabrina sat in the ornately upholstered wing-backed chair as she observed Kragen and his assistant speak with the older Middle Eastern man.

"Well, I must say, Maxim, she is quite beautiful. In an untamed sort of way. I can understand your need to see her safe and protected, but I can't quite determine why you would bring her to my home. Unless..."

The older man eyed Sabrina with a disturbing heat in his gaze. Kragen had built an elaborate delusion about her, about them, that had yet to advance beyond non-threatening displays of affection. This other man looked at her as if she was purely a sexual instrument. He was not someone she could seek help from. He was another Consortium member, which probably meant he'd given up his soul so long ago there was only something hideous housed in its place.

"Your name, girl."

"Sabrina."

"Ah. The infamous Sabrina. Your father had much to say about her at one time. That was many years ago, I know, but I believe he would have no greater esteem for this woman with the passage of time."

He walked toward Sabrina and stood beside her chair. She cringed when his thumb slid down the unbruised side of her face.

"Soft," he muttered. He turned to Kragen, who was currently two shades of crimson. "I can almost understand your obsession with this one."

"A night here would be a favor returned to you tenfold, Basir," Kragen said. Though his voice was respectful, Sabrina heard the steel within. "Erani informed me your family left town yesterday, so I'm sure my companion and I will bring little disruption to your household."

"But you misunderstand. As I couldn't join the others at the Consortium's gathering, I have created my own celebration here."

"When have diverging desires ever stopped our members from getting their needs met?"

"Please forgive my bluntness, but I don't particularly like or trust you, and I have no desire to have you roaming about my home."

Kragen grinned. "Lucky for us both, neither like nor trust are qualities that bind our group. And as for roaming, I have no desire to leave whatever room you assign me to until we depart in the morning. I'm sure I'll be busy with far more important things," he said, gazing at Sabrina before turning his gaze back to the other man. "So I'll ask again, before walking out of your home never to return, ensuring nothing linked to me and mine is ever extended to you and yours, will you allow us the generosity of your home for the night?"

Sabrina watched as the silent animosity between the two men swelled, but then the older man capitulated, nodding to Kragen. "Very soon there will be a vote on who will succeed Answorth on the procurement and care of the women. I want you to not only back my bid for this position but to lobby for me to win."

Kragen leveled the other man with a calculating gaze before nodding. "One of the specialty suites will be at my disposal?"

"None of my guests have yet to be assigned rooms. Which one would you prefer?"

Both men turned to look at Sabrina. She couldn't run. Not yet. Not with at least three of Basir's guards dressed as servants and three of the men accompanying Kragen just beyond the door. The white minion,

Kragen's assistant, more sleekly dressed than Kragen himself, had a hardness beyond his wiry body and lifeless eyes. His constant regard promised he wouldn't hesitate to intervene physically before she could take two wrong steps.

"Might I suggest the Black Room?" Basir said.

Sabrina frowned at him. "The Black... You racist son of a – "

"The Black Room is fitted for those whose spirits need to be broken by the subjugation of the flesh," Kragen explained to her before turning back to Basir. "And it's altogether inappropriate for the woman who will be my wife. Let me make this clear. Sabrina is not to be harmed in any way. If she is, there is only one consequence. Death to the offender."

"Ah, young love. It will soon pass." Basir turned to Reed. "And you, little viper, what room would you prefer?"

"I won't need a room," the white minion said without looking up from his tablet.

"We'll take the Gold Room. Sabrina has always had a love for gold."

She hated gold. It was Sam who had liked the flashy metal.

"Decadence is the order of the evening for you," Basir said. He motioned for the thin servant hovering near the room's entrance. "Salim, have everything made ready for our guests. Until then perhaps you will join me for tea."

She hated tea, but Kragen nodded.

Across the room, Kragen's minion glared at Sabrina. She rubbed her temple with her middle finger, smirking when his face flushed. He could fuck himself six ways to Sunday and she wouldn't give a shit. Thinking about it, she doubted this man could do anything to her. Kragen wouldn't allow it.

She prayed Zeus was free and alive, that someone had found him like he and the rest of the Brood had once found her, that someone had saved him. She needed him to live even if she didn't. She had no illusions. If Kragen succeeded in getting her on his plane in the morning, taking her away with no money, no ID, no means of communication, she'd probably never be found again. Not until she was dead like the others.

Sabrina listened as Maxim and Basir spoke of nothing of interest. She wished she were surrounded by Zeus's silence. He wouldn't feel compelled to waste energy on false politeness or veiled threats the way these men did.

It was almost nine thirty in the evening, a little over an hour since they'd spirited her away from Kragen's cliff house. She didn't know why, but she knew their departure had been a reaction to some unforeseen event. As they approached Basir's home, she'd seen that the land was expansive and the home itself was huge. Those factors could work in her favor or against her. On one hand there was a lot of space to run and hide. On the other, she didn't know the layout. During the drive she'd heard Kragen and Reed discuss the cameras in the rooms they took the women to. Kragen had ordered Reed to sweep and electronically clean the room they would use, possibly override Basir's surveillance system.

Kragen stood and extended his hand toward her. "Our room awaits," he informed her.

Charming. He could be absolutely charming. Which was probably the reason so many women had died by his hand. Sabrina stood and allowed Kragen to lead her through the house behind Basir and his servant. Reed followed in their wake.

They stopped at a set of polished cherry-wood doors that opened to an elevator.

"Enjoy your stay," Basir said, motioning them inside before walking away.

The room they were escorted to wasn't ornate or gaudy as she had suspected it would be. Yes, there was gold – gold patterns in the drapery and on the bedding, gold lamps and mirror frames, golden threads in the rich cream throw rug. It was the cream that balanced the room, giving it sleek sophistication.

How is it people who deal in so much ugliness live in such splendor, she wondered.

"How do you like it?" Kragen asked.

"It's beautiful," she answered truthfully, then quickly followed it with a manipulation. "You honestly do know my likes and dislikes. I see how we could have fallen in love with each other."

"I'm sure you'll remember it all. You'll love me again soon."

She smiled. "Maybe even more than I did before. Do you know why I love gold so much?"

Kragen asked Reed to leave the room. Reed nodded once, barely looking up as he ran his hand over the surface of the tablet. She wondered what held his interest so intensely.

Sabrina smiled at Kragen with appreciation when Reed left the room. Her smile faltered when Kragen reached for her hand and brought her fingers to his lips. "Your mother had a gold chain with a pendant. Your grandmother gave it to her when she was pregnant with you. Your mother told you the pendant was the only thing of value she'd ever been given before she was blessed with you. You said the pendant and its history were the greatest gifts your mother had ever given you."

His words, his knowledge lay into Sabrina like a whip that's pain didn't stop with the severing of flesh. It lashed through the vulnerability in her very soul. If she hadn't been sure before, she was sure now. This was the man who had destroyed her sister's will to live.

When they were younger, Sam had made up all kinds of fantasies about the gold pendant, but the truth was it had been a gift passed from mother to oldest daughter for four generations. Not even when her mother's addiction was at its worst had she tried to sell it. It represented the strength in their lineage. Even when the individual beneficiary was at her weakest, she always possessed an inherited strength.

As a child, Sabrina had hated that pendant. She knew her mother had loved Sam's father, yet she couldn't stand Sabrina's sperm donor. It hadn't seemed fair that Sam should get the pendant and the father their mother couldn't get over losing. It hadn't been fair Sam could go to that father before their mother had died, while Sabrina was moved from foster home to foster home, living in houses with men who wanted her to call them daddy yet looked her up and down as if she were a grown woman.

"I'm sorry, Sabrina," Kragen said, wrapping her in his arms. She stiffened. "I'm sorry to bring up bittersweet memories."

It took Sabrina a moment to realize tears wet her face. The memories she had about the history of the pendant weren't bittersweet; they were just bitter. She stepped out of Kragen's arms and wiped her face.

"I shouldn't be such a baby. I just... It surprised me that you knew. I wouldn't have shared that story with someone I didn't care about." And it was true. Sam wouldn't have shared that part of her life with someone she didn't care about or trust. The bastard had lulled her sister into a false sense of safety; then he'd hurt her.

Kragen pulled Sabrina back into his arms. She didn't resist his embrace, but she did resist the desire to rip his throat out.

He pressed a kiss to the side of her head. "There are so many stories I can tell you of our time together. I had you for almost a month, and in the short time, you owned every part of me. I had no choice but to find you again. It was the only way we could be whole again."

"After I returned home, I learned I was pregnant," she said. "There was an accident, and I lost a part of my memory and the baby."

She'd been out of town and had been devastated when she'd returned to New Orleans to learn Sam's baby girl had been stillborn. She'd wanted to be an aunt even if Sam had been too depressed to want to be a mother. Sabrina had believed in her heart that once Sam gave birth, there would be nothing more she'd want than to be a mother to her child.

"I could barely function after, could barely survive the loss," she told Kragen, verbalizing her perception of her sister's experience. "It felt like all my life, all I ever really knew was loss."

Her words were an amalgamation of her truth and Sam's truth. Her sister had been pregnant. Her sister *had* had an "accident," which in reality was her first suicide attempt. The second, years later, also classified as an accident, had been successful. Kragen had taken Sam from Sabrina when her sister had been the only thing she'd had left of her family. She knew loss.

When she pulled away from Kragen and looked up, she felt a feral sense of satisfaction at the pain etched over his face. In his own twisted way he'd cared for Sam. It only seemed fair he should suffer over their encounter. Her sister surely had.

"Our baby would have been a beautiful little boy," she lied, knowing how much men wanted sons. "A merging of the best parts of each of us."

Her hands went to her abdomen. What if she herself was pregnant with Zeus's child? The times they'd had unprotected sex far outnumbered the times they'd used protection.

"I'll make it up to you. We'll make another baby."

Shit. So not the response she wanted to hear.

Kragen grabbed her by the back of the neck and pulled her against him. His mouth descended as his free hand pressed her hips toward his groin. The already rigid length of flesh pressing into her abdomen made her want to throw up. She closed her eyes and groaned as he pressed kisses along her cheek, jaw, and down the side of her throat. As his mouth took hers, she tried to pretend he was Zeus, but his scent was wrong, his taste was sour, his body was too small.

She jerked out of his embrace.

"I can't, Max. It's too soon. I need time. I need to get to know you again. Your mind, your heart. I can't make love to you for the first time in a stranger's house," she added desperately. "When we come together, I'd like it to be in the safety of our home. In our bed. No matter how beautiful this one is," she ended jokingly.

She climbed onto the bed. It was too soft. She preferred sleeping splayed over the warmth of Zeus's hard body.

"Come on," she said, propping the pillows up so they could stretch out side by side. "Come and lie beside me. Tell me stories of us, so when we're on the plane tomorrow, I'll know I'm truly headed home."

Kragen undressed, stripping down to a pair of white silk boxers, his erection tenting the material. His body was fit, but he didn't carry the height, the density of muscle, or the tree-trunk thighs Zeus had.

She prayed for the hundredth time that he was okay.

———◆◆◆◆———

"BASIR AHADI'S ESTATE," Price said, pulling the Suburban to a stop.

"Fucking Basir's estate," Big Country mumbled in disbelief.

"Didn't I say that New Prophet-Messiah bullshit sounded like some serious Jim Jones crazy for the twenty-first century?" Lynx asked as he leaned forward in his seat.

Zeus looked at the expanse of manicured lawns and hedges illuminated by track lighting. A multileveled mansion was the crown jewel of all the splendor.

"You sure she's in there?" Coen asked Zeus.

Zeus stared at Coen. If he wasn't conserving energy, he would have been inclined to stab the other man in the throat. He was feeling just that provoked.

"Body language translation: hell yes, dipshit," Lynx said.

Zeus pointed to the house, refusing to acknowledge what the trembling in his hand meant.

"Lots of bodies in there, people. Well over thirty," Big Country said, looking down at the infrared image of the house's structure on his laptop screen. "Smallest number on the third floor, largest on the first and second floors. There's a basement level, but I'm only showing one reading there. We got patrols around the perimeter of the house and lands. Waiting on Terry to upload the floor plan."

Zeus laid his head back and closed his eyes. The clicks of Big Country typing rapidly was the only sound to fill the silence.

"Got it. Merging the specs with the live imaging." After a few more clicks on the keyboard, Big Country grunted. "Looks like we got a party going on. My guess, Sabrina ain't the one in the basement. Kragen wouldn't leave her alone."

"Maybe he's got her chained or caged or something," Lynx said.

"No. He'll keep her close," Zeus said, opening his eyes as he reached for the door.

"Hold up," Big Country cautioned. "Look at this." He extended the laptop forward so Price and Coen in the front seats could see as Lynx and Bride leaned in from the back.

"This is the patrol's pattern. Based on their route and the amount of time it'll take to get to the house, that point right there," he said, pointing at the screen, "is the best point of entry. Won't have more than three men close if we time it right."

"That's the fucking front door, man," Lynx said.

"Hey, I didn't hire the idiots doing security. That spot right there is the point of least resistance."

"Stealth mode or *Set It Off* mode?" Lynx asked as he opened his door. Battle adrenaline energized the already excitable man's voice.

"Why would we go on a rescue mission in *Set It Off* mode, Lynx?" Coen asked.

"To honor one of my favorite movies ever?"

"Only one person in their crew survived."

"As long as the one person who survives in real life is me, I don't give a shit." Lynx smiled as he stepped out of the truck.

Zeus opened his door.

"He stays here," Coen said to Price. "He's beat up to hell and back, and he'll only slow us down."

Zeus reached for his blade, and they all readied to take him down. He couldn't afford the delay a fight with the other Brood members would cause. He settled back in his seat, laid his blade across his lap, and closed his eyes. "Bring her back safe or there will be hell on earth."

"Like his forest," Lynx whispered.

"To hell with the forest, son. You see what I saw up at Kragen's place?" Big Country asked.

"Trying to forget. Desperately trying to forget."

Zeus heard the trunk open, heard the team suit up. He knew there was enough firepower between these five people to level Basir's home.

"Zeus, bring Bertha around if we call for pickup," Price ordered.

He didn't open his eyes, nodded.

"And, Zeus, one dent, one scratch on my ride...me and you gonna go round and round."

"Not healthy to have that kind of attachment to an object," Zeus said, paraphrasing words Sabrina had once said to him about his blades.

Price muttered more threats before slamming the trunk. Not long after he and the rest of the Brood had melted into the darkness, Zeus sat silently inside the trucks interior. After a few minutes he opened his eyes and unzipped the bag he'd brought with him. He grabbed his ax and secured a few more blades to his body before exiting Price's Big Bertha. It would have taken Kragen about an hour to reach Basir's residential compound from his craggy cliff house, yet the night air was warmer here, the sky clearer. Stalking toward Basir's home, Zeus accepted the possibility that if the spirit of his blades demanded it, with the exception of Sabrina, very few people inside the house would make it out alive. And, if they tried to interfere, Mama's Brood included.

CHAPTER NINETEEN

Sabrina fought, pushing against Kragen's shoulders and chest, turning her head to the side in an attempt to avoid his mouth locking on to hers. He licked the area between her shoulder and neck before grabbing her wrists and securing them over her head as he forced his hips between her thighs. He ground his erection against her, and she cried out when he savagely bit down on the flesh he'd just licked.

She had been delusional to believe he had truly cared for her sister, that she could use his supposed love to bide her some time and avoid this moment.

Kragen lifted his head away from her shoulder and gazed down at her. His mouth peeled back in a savage smile. His free hand pushed beneath the waistband of her yoga pants and stroked her over her panties. She cried out in rage, bucking and twisting so violently she was able to free one hand and rake her short nails over the side of his face, drawing blood. Kragen hissed, but her actions only seemed to fuel his pleasure, because he grinned down and stroked her faster.

"I always loved how you resisted. Always, the harder you fought, the harder I took you, the harder we came." He groaned against her ear.

"Oh, how I've missed you, Sabrina." He attempted to work her pants down her hips from the inside.

"Get off!" She bucked and tried to roll to the side.

"Soon. I promise."

Sabrina fought yet got nowhere. Panic and fear mounted as she lost the battle against both Kragen and her emotions. Kragen slid one finger inside of her, and she screamed with disgust and helplessness.

"Stop!" she cried out, but her words were ignored.

Stop, Sabrina. Just stop, she said to herself. She had to control her reactions, because all efforts to affect Kragen led nowhere.

Kragen struggled, one-handed, pushing the barrier of her clothing down her thighs while his mouth rutted, almost in a frenzy, against her bra-covered breast. Her eyes focused on the ceiling, traveling the length of the burnished-gold crown molding. She imagined Zeus, pale golden-bronze skin, unsmiling, mercurial eyes locked on her as a blade danced in his finger.

Stretching her free hand overhead, she freed the only part of him she carried outside of her heart. She pressed the top of the ornate chopstick and saw a cylindrical sliver of metal push out the narrowest end. She would have laughed at her man's ingenuity, but Kragen had gotten her pants and panties to her knees and was attempting to work his underwear down around his ass. Fueled by vengeance, she tried to ram the weapon into his carotid artery, but it landed in the trapezius muscle close to his throat. He howled and rolled out of her reach, falling ass first on the other side of the bed.

The door slammed open, and Reed loomed, his tablet in one hand and a gun pointed in her direction in the other. His gaze flickered to Kragen on the floor, bleeding from the wound she'd inflicted. She slipped the chopstick back into her hair and righted her clothing. She slowly moved off the bed and stood near the window, believing Reed wouldn't shoot unless Kragen ordered him to.

"Sabrina. Sabrina Samora. Age thirty-seven years. Daughter of Teresa Samora and Henry Danielson. Younger half sister to Samantha Redding. You were orphaned to foster care at age eleven." Reed walked to Kragen. "Are you all right, sir?"

Kragen grimaced. "If it was up to my beloved, I think I'd be dead. She stabbed me with something."

Reed sat the tablet on the bed and checked out his boss, gun still pointed at Sabrina.

"Puncture wound. Bleeding, but not too bad. Should I have Basir bring in medical supplies?"

Kragen lifted his gaze from the screen and frowned at her. "No," he said, looking at the tablet again before he tapped the screen. "Seems I'm always getting stabbed when I'm around you, Sabrina."

"You can thank Zeus for that."

"Well, no I can't. Being he's dead."

He handed the tablet back to Reed. With assistance, he stood tall when all Sabrina wanted to do was sink to the floor and curl up. She placed her hand against the wall to steady herself. She was an idiot to believe Zeus could survive when she knew he could barely walk, let alone defend himself. She had sent him out there to die and...

Oh, God. Zeus is dead, she thought, sobbing.

"You promised you would let him go," she said. She'd never see Zeus alive again. She could no longer pretend all her prayers had made a difference.

"I held my promise. But you, Ms. Samora. I thought you could fulfill my dream of regaining the love of my life. Regaining my soul. But I find you can't possibly fulfill that dream because you're not the woman responsible for creating it."

"You don't talk to me about love, you sick son of a bitch. You killed my sister just as surely as you killed all those other women. You're not capable of love, and no sane person is capable of or *willing* to love you.

You are just some sick demented *thing* that rapes and kills women who looked like Sam for your pleasure."

Kragen looked at Reed. "So she knows about the other women. How is that, I wonder."

"Give me a little time. I'll take her to one of Basir's specialty rooms and happily find out for you, sir."

"That won't be necessary just yet, Reed. First I want to know how you uncovered the truth."

"She didn't fit," Reed said, looking at her as if she was the disgusting one. "From all your stories, I couldn't see this woman as the woman you talked about. Time doesn't change someone so fundamentally, sir. I knew you wouldn't believe just my intuition without evidence to back it up. So I dug deeper."

Kragen dragged a weary hand over his face. "Yet again, I'm humbled by your dedication and commitment to me."

"The woman you remember was good. She was worthy of your love. From reports I gathered once I searched using her true name, she was kind and humble. This one is some piece of trash relation who probably dreamed of having her sister's life. She's been conditioned to bounce from one place to the next, never establishing roots. She's been in relationships with men who are also insignificant, dead, or in jail. Not very different from her mother, actually. There is a man, though. Ernesto Diaz. He's been looking for her a long time and is eager to have her back. I don't imagine it'll be a happy reunion if you choose to return her."

"How did you know about the other women, Sabrina?" Kragen asked, standing at the foot of the bed.

She backed up into the corner near the bed's headboard, needing the support of the wall to stay upright. "Detective Cassidy," she lied. "When Zeus and I went to the station, he showed me pictures of a number of women who had gone missing. And they looked like me. Or, should I say, they looked like my sister. After you came to my apartment, I knew it had to be you. You killed them, and you killed my sister. I know the monster you are."

He flinched when she slapped him with that knowledge.

"Your sister died in a fire," Reed said. "Mr. Kragen wasn't even in the country at the time of her death."

"Sam killed herself. It was her second attempt. They ruled it an accident, but I knew better." She wanted to fight the tears but let them flow. She let them honor her love for her sister. "When she came back from New York, she was broken, and I never knew why... I couldn't understand why. Until you recognized this," she said, holding up the pendant. "Even going to the grave, she couldn't tell me what had happened to her. I kept this close at all times. She never realized...never realized how strong she was. She escaped you. She was strong enough to escape you and live all those years later, but she didn't see it."

Although Sam hadn't been able to talk to Sabrina about what had happened to her, in her own way she'd left Sabrina a piece of the puzzle. "I'm so glad he never found you, Sam. I'm so glad he can't hurt you anymore."

"All my sins and secrets laid bare before you," Kragen said to Sabrina. "Reed, can you retrieve something to patch up my wound? Any more stabbing and I'll think everyone sees me as a human pincushion."

"Sir..."

"Don't worry, Reed. She won't take me unaware again." Kragen nodded toward the door.

"Yes, sir."

"Samantha." Kragen said her sister's name almost experimentally. "A beautiful name. She was a beautiful woman, and we shared a wonderful fantasy, but in the end maybe it was just that, a fantasy. Nothing your sister and I shared was real. Not even her name. What exists between you and I is hard truth. Perhaps all these years of searching for a dream were fated to bring me to the one I was truly destined for. The one woman who sees me and refuses to cower or beg as all those others. Even at this very moment, you stand there, staring me down, daring me to be my best. For you, Sabrina, I will be. For you I will be what I am incapable of being for any other woman."

It was amazing to witness just how fluid his reality could be.

"You raped her," Sabrina said. "You held her captive and raped and beat and tortured my sister. If you think I'm going to lie down and let you do the same to me... Let's just say it's not going to play out the way you think."

His smile turned cruel. "They all think that way in the beginning, but in the end they all give me exactly what I wanted. You will give me what I need over and over again. You won't want to exist unless my dick is pumping somewhere deep inside of you."

Sabrina felt some of the wildness that had overcome her when she was a child left with no options but to claw her way out of a bad situation. "Kragen, you try to touch me and I'll give you more than you want or can handle."

"So brave. So foolish. I'm going to enjoy digging my way through your body from the root all the way up to that vicious mouth of yours. I will possess every inch of you."

"Just try it, asshole."

Kragen stalked forward as she pushed off the wall and settled in a defensive stance Zeus had taught her. He grabbed for her, but she knocked his hand away, slamming her other fist into his jaw. She tried to put her foot through his dick and invert the son of a bitch, but he shifted and her foot grazed off the outside of his thigh. When she tried to correct her balance, he backhanded her, spinning her into the wall. She grimaced as he fisted her hair and slung her onto the bed. She tried to scramble to the other side, but he caught her ankle, flipping her onto her back. She kicked out her feet, rapidly hitting him in his wounded chest, his gut, and the side of the neck.

"Bitch!" he said, securing one leg he pulled her closer and punched her twice in the face. She continued to fight, but she was dazed, her movements less effective.

Tasting the coppery blood pooling in her mouth, she spit it toward his face and reached for her chopstick again. Instead of stabbing him, she scraped the metal tip down his face from temple to cheek.

He cried out, his hands going to his face as he flung himself away from her. Instead of running for the door, she leaped in his direction, her weapon poised to pierce his eye. Kragen shifted again, grabbed her wrist, and slammed it over and over against the corner of the end table.

"Never lose your blade," Zeus had instructed. She feared Kragen had fractured her wrist, but she never released her weapon. Kragen flipped her onto her stomach. Her wrist throbbed, but she wouldn't let go. She couldn't. Kragen pressed her face and throat into the carpeted floor. She could feel the heat of his erection pressing over her ass. Being held down, feeling him press his length against her, terrified her like nothing else could, and she struggled harder. Kragen chuckled as he thrust against her, grunting. Her struggles only seemed to arouse him more.

Sabrina had believed she was strong enough to withstand whatever he was capable of dishing out, but in this moment, she knew she had lied to herself. He pulled her clothing down her thighs, his erection bouncing against her bare ass as she tried to buck him off. She was losing touch with time, space, and matter in her seemingly useless struggle.

He had no right. She closed her eyes. Only Zeus had permission. She screamed in rage. She would *kill* Kragen for this. Kill him.

There was a thump, and Kragen's hand went lax against the back of her neck as he cursed softly. His weight shifted, and she exploited the opportunity, scooting from beneath him and crawling forward in the direction of the bedroom door. She felt moisture spray over her body. It was raining blood. So much blood. Where did it all come from? It was in her hair, on the floor, on the bedcovers....

"You all right?" a cool, disembodied voiced asked behind her.

She jerked at the sound and looked back to see what could only be described as something not fully of this earth. Zeus was saturated in blood and human bits. The whites of both eyes were red. His soft golden hair was bloody. His thin white T-shirt and jeans were saturated, as was the double-sided ax he held. Kragen's headless body lay at his feet.

"Zeus," she whispered, clumsy in her attempt to stand. She took a step toward him but slipped on the blood-soaked carpet.

Zeus lunged and caught her before she fell on the body.

"He told me you were dead," she said, wrapping her arms around his neck. "I thought you were dead, that Eddie had killed you and thrown your body in the ocean."

"Overactive imagination," he said, lightly running a finger over her face. "He beat you up pretty bad."

"I got in my licks."

"If I could, I would resurrect him. Kill him for each cut, each bruise, all the pain."

"He would have raped me."

"We would have handled it. I'd have helped you get back right."

She snorted, laying her head against his chest. "You don't even know the definition of right."

"It means the opposite of wrong and left."

She laughed through the hurt as her body trembled uncontrollably. He pulled her tighter against him, resting his chin on the crown of her head.

"I can get used to this, you always being there when I need you."

"You love me?"

"Um hum."

"Say it so they can hear it."

She turned around to see Big Country, Price, and Bride at the bedroom's door. Each Brood member held a black balaclava in their hand.

Lynx pushed through the group and came to a standstill after tripping over Kragen's head. "You have *got* to stop with the severed body parts," he shouted as he righted himself. "This is the twenty-first century, man. You don't have to do this barbaric shit. Buy a gun, put a bullet in them. Pop, pop, bad man goes down. Done."

"Lynx, you don't get to yell at the hero because he makes a mess. He saved my life, and I love him and all those blade spirits that possess him," Sabrina said.

Zeus smirked, cocking up a brow at the crowd. Smug, she thought. He was being smug.

"So it's true? Oh hell no," Lynx said, pushing back through the group as Big Country tipped an imaginary cowboy hat at them. Bride rolled her eyes and followed Lynx down the hall.

"Thought I told you to stay with Bertha," Price said.

"Did. Then she kicked me out."

Price rubbed the back of his neck as he continued to address Zeus. "Basir's guests are secured on the first floor. Coen is downstairs dealing with the victims. We took all the video feed, but we'll need to clear out of here before the cops arrive."

As they walked into the hall, Sabrina saw two more bodies. One was Reed. "Did you kill all of Kragen's men?"

"Only the ones that got in my way," Zeus said.

"All," Price muttered. "A few of Basir's security too."

"What about Basir?"

"Haven't found hide nor hair of him or the lone individual that was in the basement. We'll hunt Basir down in time," Big Country assured her.

Sabrina and the Brood left the house masked, with no survivors able to identify the group that had caused so much destruction. Big Country contacted Terry, who had spoken with the guy named London. London was already orchestrating the dispersal of information. Apparently, the English guy she had heard on the phone at Mama's House had a smooth tongue when it came to manipulating events, spinning them in whichever direction Mama and her coconspirators wanted him to.

Sometime in the wee hours of the morning, they arrived at Mama's House, washed up, and got medical care before briefing Mama and Terry. Eventually each Brood member made their way to their beds.

High on painkillers and adrenaline, Sabrina lay on Zeus's bed and closed her eyes. She heard the door to the bathroom open and moments later felt Zeus lie down beside her. He pulled her against him, his hold on her the only thing from keeping her floating off in the pitch-black oblivion of his room.

"You know we have to get married," Zeus declared.

"You *know* we've known each other less than a month."

"You really think anyone else would put up with you?"

"Yep."

"Do you want to see more men die?"

"How 'bout we get married in France? We could save up, go find your mother, and don't say no, because I want to tie up loose ends before starting a new life with you. We need to hold family close, remember. We've lost too much," she said, wishing Sam and her mom could have lived to see her become something more than a person who needed to guard herself from the world. Wished Sam could have lived to experience her as a better sister.

"Just so long as you know we're getting married."

"Well, Zeus, now I know."

He grunted, and soon they both fell into drug-induced sleep.

The next morning Sabrina woke alone. She dressed slowly, careful of the injuries she'd sustained, and went up to the second level to find Zeus. She found him in Mama's living room. He was dressed and seemingly on his way out the door.

"Where are you going? You can barely walk."

"Be back tomorrow. Loose ends. Lynx will take you back to my cabin. "

"Man, I'm not going back to that fucking place. I'll give her cab fare," Lynx said.

"I'm going back to *my* place. I need to deal with my job, the cops, my apartment. I doubt I'll get my security deposit back at this point."

"Bride and I will go back with her," Mama told Zeus. "Help her straighten things out."

He shrugged and limped out the room, Big Country and Lynx tight on his heels.

"Where are they going?" Sabrina asked.

Mama's smile was cold and slightly terrifying. "Like Zeus said, they have to tie up loose ends."

<hr/>

THE MIAMI NIGHT was thick with humidity. Even inside the ranch-style house, Zeus's T-shirt felt like a layer of skin he would soon have to shed.

He hovered over the man's body, watching dispassionately as he slept.

In sleep, Ernesto Diaz looked too vibrant for a dead man. His skin was a much lighter shade of brown than Sabrina's, but still darker than Zeus's. Diaz's skin resembled the olive tones of the people from Cizan's culture. He had closely cropped black hair and angular features that made him look suitable for a boardroom or a magazine cover. But he was a thug. Higher up in the food chain than most with his drugs and laundering, but a thug nonetheless.

Zeus tapped the hilt of his blade against the space between the sleeping man's brows. The moment Ernesto's eyes opened, he reached for the semiautomatic that had been hidden beneath his pillow.

"Lookin' for this here?" Big Country asked as he held the gun up.

Ernesto froze, then looked from Big Country to Zeus to Lynx. "Money's in the safe, hombre. Behind the painting."

"Oh, I think you know we ain't here 'bout no money," Big Country said.

"We're here because our Brood mate found a woman crazy enough to love and marry him. Your ex has been lying low a long time trying to avoid getting on your radar," Lynx said.

"Our Brood mate here has issue with how you treated her. He won't allow his woman to be afraid of what could happen if you were to ever find her. None of us will," Big Country said.

"Means you gotta go, hombre," Zeus said. "Can't have my woman worrying."

"You got it all wrong, friend. Sabrina, she is *mine*. When I find her – "

The blade struck.

"You won't find her," Zeus reassured the man clutching his throat.

"Well," Lynx said once the man was dead. "That was...uneventful."

"You're as fickle as an old woman," Zeus told Lynx. "One minute too much carnage, the next not enough."

"Whatever, man."

"Let's go to the titty bar on Barrington Street and get a beer. Haven't had a good brew in days," Big Country said as he walked toward the bedroom door scratching his crotch.

Lynx looked back at the body. "We should probably call London."

"Why call?" Big Country asked. "He'll be stateside in a few hours. Plus, ain't no need for a spin. This cocksucker could've been done in by any number of folks 'round here. He wasn't well liked."

Back out on a street made dark when they had killed the lights earlier, they got into the rental car, a sedate black sedan. After a few minutes of the car sitting idly, Big Country turned to the man in the driver's seat. "Problem, Zeus?"

"Sabrina loves me."

Lynx rolled his eyes. "Yeah, we know already. Get over it."

"Not ever."

EPILOGUE

Sabrina waited three steps from the bottom of the stairwell as Randy trotted down in jeans and a green T-shirt, carrying a handful of mail. "This was all that came while you were gone," he said, kissing her on the forehead before turning to walk down to her apartment. "Gotta get back in there before Helen Keller and the mama bear from hell totally destroy my organizational efforts. I mean, really, Bree. Who ever heard of linen and shoes going in the same box? Please."

Sabrina smiled as she sat gingerly on the third stair, feeling like an old, arthritic woman as she flicked through the envelopes. She saw mostly bills and junk mail. Her splinted hand froze when she saw the envelope with a return address identifying both Mrs. and Mr. Jace and Samantha Redding as the senders. It was an Illinois address. Her heart stopped, then sped up as she placed the rest of the mail beside her and carefully opened the bulging manila envelope.

Hey Bree,

So I'm gone, and I know you have a lot of feelings about that. I arranged to have this letter sent out if certain events came to pass, and they have. First, though, I've been asking you this most all my life. I'm gonna ask it one last time. Please forgive me.

311

I know what I did was wrong. I tried to fight against this outcome only because of you, not for Daddy or none of that side of my family. Just for you. I tried all those years to get back right. I know I worried you something terrible. I know what it cost you to bury Ma, and I'm sorry for making you bury the only other family you've ever known.

You have to know, if not for you, I wouldn't have tried to stay as long as I did. I thought that once I escaped hell, I'd be free. But it stays with me, Bree. No matter where I went and what I did, even in my own home, hell never let me go.

I know you don't want to hear this again, but I'm so sorry for abandoning you when we were young. I was never able to be as strong as you needed me to be. I know, if the situation were reversed, you would have fought for me. You always did. I should have pitched a fit until my daddy pulled you from foster care and brought you to me. I tried too hard to be the good one, and it always cost you. I don't want you to pay for my weakness anymore. I am asking you to nurture my strength. The part of me that fought to live when I wished it away. This part of me I had to let go, and I need you to retrieve her.

I lied to you about her birth. My baby girl lived, but I had to let her go. I couldn't chance her father ever finding me and getting hold of her. I'll only say he was the man who hurt me in New York, and I won't say nothing else, except that, more than death, I fear his evil ever touching Briana. Your niece's name is Briana Samora. Though they love her, her guardians, Mr. and Mrs. Jace, are getting older, and they're tired. She needs your love, strength, and protection. She's smart and beautiful, Bree. Just like you in a lot of ways...but don't let that scare you. I'm smiling when I write that. I know it might seem strange, but I haven't felt this kind of peace in a long time.

Along with this letter, I've also put some legal papers, which include her birth certificate and adoption papers. All that's needed is your signature on the last. I put some pictures of Briana I've gotten over the years, as well as a few letters the Jaces wrote me about her. The Jaces and Briana both have received their own letters. They'll know you're coming. I'm praying a lot of things are right in your life. Lord knows I shouldn't, but I'm praying Ernesto is dead or in prison and don't ever threaten you or my child. I'm praying her father never finds out about her. I'm praying both of you are happy. I love you, Bree. Don't ever forget that one truth. I've never loved anybody more than I've loved you and my little girl.

Until I see you again in the afterlife. Good-bye, Sister.

Sabrina did all she could to protect the photos and papers from the tears rolling down her face. Lowering her head to her knees, she sobbed. It hurt so much. She'd loved her sister so much, and she was gone, and for some reason it felt like she'd lost Sam all over again in this moment.

"You all right?" Bride asked beside her.

She nodded into her lap, unwilling to expose her pain to the other woman. She heard the beeping of a cell phone, and moments later, Bride's, "Here."

Sabrina wiped away her tears and looked up. Bride was extending her cell phone toward her.

"Hello," she said into the phone, her voice barely audible to her own ears.

"Hey."

Fresh tears spilled down her face. "Hey," she said as she smiled and sobbed.

There was silence on the other end as grief worked its way through her.

"I'm on my way," Zeus said as she quieted.

She nodded. "Zeus?"

"Humh?"

"You remember what I said about needing to hold our family close?"

His silence made her wonder if he had, if he would be willing to make family, her family, a priority in his life.

"There a Godzuki inside you?"

Doing what would have been impossible just moments ago, she laughed, pushing a stray loc from her already tear-blurred vision. "I don't know about a Godzuki just yet, but I have a niece, Zeus, and she's alive, and she needs us to come get her."

"Like I said, on my way. And Sabrina... What's a part of you is a part of me, and I hold on to what's mine to the death. Thought I'd already proven that."

"You've proven it, big man," Sabrina assured him. "But you know me and my big woman's head with stupid woman's brain chatter. Sometimes it gets in the way of what my gut and my heart have already made clear. You always come through when I need you most, Zeus, and it's just another reason I love and trust you."

"You love and trust me."

"Always."

"Look here, cousin," Big Country drawled in the background. "This here's a car. We just got off a plane, and no matter how fast you push this bitch, she ain't gon' fly, so believe me when I say, I refuse to die over some foolishness you call love, not today."

Sabrina smiled. "Stop torturing your Brood mates and get back to me safe."

"Always," he said before disconnecting the call.

THANK YOU SO MUCH FOR TAKING
THIS JOURNEY WITH ME.

On The Edge of Love is the first book in the *Mama's Brood* series, but if all goes as planned, there will be many more stories in this series to come. If all goes as *envisioned*, there will be stories of romance, of dark fantasy, and yes even of horror, as I love to read and write in all these genres.

My perfect life: The Sacred Trio, good health, loved ones, reading, writing, travel, adventure, and simply sitting down with someone and sharing who we are.

Please feel free to reach out:

Facebook: Shay Rucker, Author
Twitter: @shayruckerbooks
Website: shayrucker.com

Made in the USA
Monee, IL
03 April 2022

94049620R00184